WELL BEHAVED WOMEN

CAROLINE LAMOND

One More Chapter
a division of HarperCollins*Publishers*
1 London Bridge Street
London SE1 9GF
www.harpercollins.co.uk
HarperCollins*Publishers*
Macken House, 39/40 Mayor Street Upper,
Dublin 1, D01 C9W8

This paperback edition 2023
1
First published in Great Britain in ebook format
by HarperCollins*Publishers* 2023

A catalogue record of this book
is available from the British Library

ISBN: 978-0-00-852766-2

This novel is entirely a work of fiction. The names, characters and incidents
portrayed in it are the work of the author's imagination. Any resemblance to
actual persons, living or dead, events or localities is fictionalised.

Printed and bound in the UK using 100% Renewable Electricity
by CPI Group (UK) Ltd

This book is produced from independently certified FSC™ paper
to ensure responsible forest management.

For more information visit: www.harpercollins.co.uk/green

For Ross, Leo & Jessica

Caroline is c ____ ing in Paris before reading PPE at Oxford University. She trained as ____ fell into a career in finance, going on to write various commercial fiction novels under various pseudonyms. She's also written comedy for the BBC and Comedy Central.

Caroline now lives in London with her husband and two young children. When not writing, she's mostly reading, travelling and aspiring to have a life as interesting as the women she writes about.

 twitter.com/carolinelamond
 instagram.com/caroline.lamond

Chapter One

MAYBELLE

Los Angeles, USA, 1919

I t was her clothing that first drew my attention. Shallow, perhaps, but you can't blame a girl for noticing.

She wore a richly-hued silk dress, gossamer-light and exquisitely detailed, that danced around her figure as she walked. Fluted hem waltzing with shapely ankles. The rings on her fingers dazzled and shone; a knotted headscarf taming her thick russet bob.

I watched as she placed her order with the girl behind the counter, saying something in low, throaty tones that made the waitress smile.

On reflection, perhaps it wasn't merely the clothes that sparked my interest. Rather the stylish comportment, the evident self-assurance, the elegance and sophistication and myriad desirable traits she possessed that I, nineteen years old and fresh off the train from Jonas Springs, Kentucky, most certainly did not.

She turned unexpectedly and caught me staring, saw me hastily look away as the heat flamed in my cheeks. I pretended to be absorbed in the view from the window, the dusty motor cars rumbling along La Jolla and onto West Third to join the herd of vehicles that seemed to grow in number every day. A woman strolled by, past the palm trees and electric lights, dressed like a duchess but yelling insults at someone only she could see, as a man stepped out of the way to avoid her, head bowed, shoulders rounded, dirt and world-weariness clinging to his skin. I wondered who all these people were, where they were going, what was their story? The insurance salesman, the construction worker, the pot washer, the attorney, heading to the office, to lunch, to rendezvous with a secret lover, the whole gamut of human life going about their daily business beneath the sultry Californian sunshine. This city of angels – half a million of them and counting – could not have been more different from Jonas Springs, KY, pop. 371 where I knew everyone and everyone knew me, from Pastor Abbott, to Miss Wilkerson the schoolmistress, to old Emmett Fisher who owned the general store and made the best lemonade in three counties. Los Angeles was, in contrast, a daily assault on the senses, a nerve-wracking, exhilarating existence where the night never drew truly dark and—

'Is this seat taken?'

There was a certain inevitability to the question. Despite there being half a dozen unoccupied tables, I wasn't surprised that the woman had chosen to sit opposite me.

'No, ma'am.'

She smiled, and I winced inwardly at my own gaucheness. The woman sat down and I studied her details: shapely brows,

2

a little thicker than the fashion; lucid amber eyes, like a tiger once seen in a book; a pronounced Cupid's bow, emphasised by the dark red lipstick she wore. She sipped her coffee, then removed a slim cigarette from a silver case.

'Would you like one?'

For the briefest of moments, I considered accepting the invitation, longing to appear as worldly and cosmopolitan and the kind of person so at ease with themselves that they knew just what to do or say in any situation. Afraid to make a fool of myself, I shook my head. 'No, thank you, ma'am.'

The case snapped shut. I watched, fascinated, as the cigarette was lit with the strike of a match, the established ritual as the woman leaned back and took her first inhalation, ruby lips forming a soft O, shoulders relaxing on the outward breath. The smell was sharp and musky and not altogether unpleasant. I realised I was staring again.

'My apologies, ma'am, please don't think me ill-mannered. It's just… well, I ain't seen many ladies that… uh…' I trailed off, gesturing awkwardly.

'Smoke? Men don't have the monopoly on such pleasures, you know.' The woman laughed and her eyes sparkled. 'Where are you from? No – wait. Let me guess.'

Now it was my turn to be scrutinised and I immediately grew self-conscious: hair a tumble of long, fair ringlets, not at all in the modern style; simple cotton dress equally outdated. I wasn't wearing a scrap of make-up and a handful of freckles, that had arrived during my seventh summer and never departed, were scattered across the bridge of my nose.

'Tennessee?' The woman frowned. 'Let's try… Nashville? Knoxville?'

3

My smile was generous, pleased by her fallibility. 'Kentucky.'

'Ah. Close.' She shrugged, tapping the embers into an ashtray. 'I'm Josephine.'

'It's a pleasure to meet you. I'm Maybelle. Maybelle Crabtree.'

'Of course you are.' My reply seemed to amuse Josephine. 'Well, Maybelle Crabtree from Kentucky, how'd you like to taste your first cigarette?' She extended a hand, grey smoke streaming from her fingertips like a witch performing a spell. 'It's easy. Inhale, like you're taking a breath – not too deeply or you'll choke. Then purse your lips, as though you're kissing a lover, and blow all your troubles away...'

Her tone was soothing, her words alluring. I sensed an unspoken challenge, understanding that the decision I made now would determine how I was perceived by this stranger. Without knowing why, I wanted to please her. I reached out and took the cigarette. The devilish pairing of paper and tobacco had burned a quarter of the way down, a fiery orange heat glowing at the tip. The end was stained berry, moist as I touched it to my lips, and I followed Josephine's directions to the letter – a cautious inhalation, no spluttering or stinging eyes, a pleasant surge of chemicals through my body – before handing it back with something akin to relief.

I drained my coffee, eager to get rid of the unpleasant taste, and Josephine waved to the waitress to bring another.

'No, thank you,' I shook my head. 'I'm afraid I—'

'My treat.' Her manner suggested she didn't expect to be refused. 'So, *ma belle* Maybelle, tell me about yourself.'

'I... There isn't anything to tell.'

'Oh, I'm sure there is. How did you end up in Los Angeles, all the way from Kentucky? That's quite a journey.'

Josephine extinguished her cigarette, and I warily eyed the remains. In truth, I was somewhat discomfited by her interest. Since arriving in the city, mere weeks ago, this was possibly the most meaningful interaction I'd had; the first exchange that went beyond *good morning* to the streetcar operator, or *good day* to the newsboy, or *wasn't the price of brisket a scandal?* from a disgruntled customer in line at the butcher. Of course, there were the people I encountered when I went about my work: the lost, the angry, the dispossessed were always eager to engage and argue. And then there were the men, sometimes twice, three times my age, with their looks of appraisal as though I were a prize-winning cow on Cartwright's farm, following me along the street to suggest dinner, a drink, a hotel room right around the corner, only to spit and curse when I shook my head and politely declined. But there was no one who'd been interested in *me.* No one whose playful eyes and teasing questions reminded me of my best friend, Sarah Beth, back home.

'My Aunt Ida and Uncle Henry live out here, over in Atwater. I was sent to stay with them.'

'Sent?'

Something about Josephine invited confidences.

'Last year, my daddy took sick with pneumonia and he...' I swallowed thickly.

'You poor thing. I'm so sorry.' Josephine reached across, her hand covering mine. Our eyes found one another, the warmth and reassurance in hers encouraging me to continue.

'It was real hard after he... We got behind on the rent for

5

the farm, and I was another mouth to feed and… Well, my momma wrote her sister and here I am.'

That would suffice.

Our hands were still touching and, embarrassed, I withdrew mine, making a show of wiping my cheeks.

'Do you like it here?'

'It's… different.'

'Good different or bad different?'

I screwed up my face. 'I reckon I'm still deciding. I miss home. I miss my momma, and Walter and Frank, my brothers. Here it's… it's so big, it's almost too much. I've never seen so many people in one place before, not even at the county fair. But it's exciting too.' Josephine nodded slowly and, though she made no reply, I sensed that she understood – was empathetic at least. Feeling brave, I took a fortifying gulp of coffee and asked, 'What about you? Were you born here, or…?'

Josephine chuckled, a raw, throaty laugh that was laced with sadness. 'Oh, honey, we'd be here until the small hours if I told you *my* life story.'

I forced a laugh, feeling duped somehow; foolish for almost revealing my secrets whilst Josephine remained a mystery.

The coffee shop had grown busy without my noticing. All the tables were full, the room animated with a low hum of chatter, the clatter of cutlery, the rumble of the percolator. The day's menu was chalked up on the wall, the unfamiliar names mocking my alien status in the neighbourhood. Might I enjoy Shrimp Louie? Did Dungeness crab have the earthy sweetness of line-caught catfish, fresh from the creek? Could a Waldorf salad offer the ambrosial comfort of my momma's celebrated biscuits and gravy? Truth be told, I'd spent several minutes outside passing back and forth beneath the smart green awning, summoning the nerve to come inside and take a seat.

'Do you like movies?' Josephine asked.

'Well, ma'am, I've only ever seen one my whole life, but it was the most magical thing. It was called *The Poor Little Rich Girl*, with Mary Pickford, and the story was so charming, and Miss Mary was downright adorable.'

'That was a great movie,' Josephine agreed. She stretched languidly, heavy gold rings shimmering in the sunlight that stole through the window. 'Say, how'd you like to go to a party?'

'A party?'

'Sure. Do you know many folks here? Then you should come, see and be seen, meet new people. How old are you, Maybelle?'

'Nineteen, ma'am.'

'Then you oughta be a regular social butterfly, not hiding out in old backwater Atwater with Aunt Ida and Uncle Henry. Such a waste of a pretty face.'

I coloured. 'Oh no, I don't think—'

But Josephine had already taken a notebook from her purse and was scribbling in a looping, cursive hand, tearing out the page and passing it across the table.

'Can you read my messy writing? Hayvenhurst, 8080 Sunset Boulevard, Hollywood. Swing by this evening. Mention my name.'

Chapter Two

ALLA

Yalta, Crimea, 1878

S team rose from the bathtub in dense white clouds, the fogged mirror on the wall rendering Sonya little more than a ghostly silhouette in the candlelight. She returned to the kitchen, heaving the metal pan from the stove before lugging it across the corridor and depositing its bubbling contents in the tub. Was it hot enough yet? She dipped a hand in the water and quickly retracted it, her fingers reddening and swelling.

The house was quiet, with only the distant sound of conversation on the street outside that peaked and fell away as the passers-by walked on. Impulsively, Sonya opened the door to the children's bedroom. The curtains were hanging at an angle, letting in a sliver of moonlight; enough to distinguish the outlines of their sleeping forms. A gentle snuffling came from Volodya's bed. He was five years old now and growing so quickly, his unruly dark hair – so like her own – in stark contrast to the white pillow. He'd kicked off his blankets and Sonya silently gathered them up, conscious of the chill in the room as she tucked them snugly round his sprawling limbs.

In the opposite bed lay his three-year-old sister, Nina, curled up like a kitten. Her long blonde plait followed the curve of her small back; her teddy bear, Misha, was clutched tightly to her chest.

Sonya retreated to the doorway, pausing for a moment to savour the stillness. Her breathing slowed in time with her babies', their quiet slumber bringing her a momentary sense of peace.

'Sweet dreams, my darlings,' she whispered, touching her fingers to her lips and casting a kiss into the darkness.

Sonya loved her children desperately. But she didn't want this one.

Beside the bathtub she undressed quickly, folding her clothes and placing them on the chair. She looked down at her body, at the heavy, veined breasts that had grown fuller these past few weeks, noticing that her hands automatically cupped the small protrusion of her stomach. Already it had hardened and rounded where before it had been soft and fleshy. Neither Yakov, her husband, nor Mikhail, her lover, had noticed the changes. If all went to plan, they never would.

Sonya dipped one foot in the near-scalding water of the bathtub. For a second she felt nothing, but then the pain registered, the burning, blistering sensation as every instinct cried out that she should stop. She refused to listen, stepping in with both feet, gritting her teeth against the angry heat, willing herself not to cry out as she lowered herself fully, the sensitive flesh on her thighs, buttocks, back, shoulders seared like a piece of meat.

She reached for the bottle she'd placed beside the tub. Made of amber glass, its contents had cost her an extortionate five silver rubles, bought from a *babushka* with sharp eyes and filthy fingernails. Sonya uncorked it and retched, the sour, pungent smell turning her stomach. She took a sip and gagged, almost bringing it straight back up again. It tasted foul; astringent and bitter.

She thought of her husband, of the irony of him being a pharmacist (and her lover, his assistant) yet for this remedy she'd had to visit an old woman who lived in a shack halfway up the mountain. Yakov wouldn't be back until the early hours, she felt certain. After supper, he'd gone to the barn they rented on the outskirts of town that served as his laboratory, where he worked on the preposterous inventions he was convinced would one day make them rich: food pills, artificial ice, medicated soap. Sonya shook her head at the ridiculousness of it all. Yakov laboured for hours, presenting his ideas to businessmen and university professors, trying to get meetings with government officials, yet no one ever took him seriously. Perhaps that explained why he was always so angry.

She tipped her head back and drained the bottle, heaving and spluttering, liquid trickling from her mouth in her haste to do the deed. It dribbled down her chin, pooling in the hollow of her throat before finding its way between her breasts in dirty brown rivulets. It looked like the dregs in the bucket after the maid had scrubbed the floor. It tasted like it too.

Afterwards, Sonya lay there for a long time, the mist clearing, the air cooling. She wondered how long it would take to work. She wondered if it would hurt. She wondered how much blood there would be, and whether she could clean it all up before Yakov came home.

She was still sitting there, shivering, long after the water had gone cold.

There was snow on the mountains. The distant peak of Ai-Petri – St Peter – was blinding white on this glorious winter's day where the temperature was barely above freezing yet the sky was blue and cloudless. Sonya stood on the first-floor balcony overlooking the street below. She wore no coat or hat or gloves and her fingers had long since gone numb.

Her gaze followed the jumble of rooftops down the hill to the sweeping expanse of the Black Sea. The name seemed wholly inappropriate today; Sonya had never seen a more perfect shade of cerulean. Near the horizon the waves were choppier, the flat colour broken up with crests of white, fishing boats tossed on the salty swell.

She remembered how she'd felt when she first arrived in Yalta: leaving her hometown of Berdichev was bittersweet, but she was buoyed by the prospect of a new life with her husband and two young children in this mimosa-scented city on the water. Sonya had hoped that, away from her wealthy, domineering family, Yakov might feel like less of a failure and revert to the shyly romantic, charmingly awkward man she'd fallen in love with. Two years later, and that hope seemed pitifully naïve, the fresh start now seeming more like a prison sentence. Sonya had no confidantes, no social life of which to speak, her beautiful ballgowns from Paris and Vienna mothballed and boxed in her closet, awaiting a time when she might be invited to dinners and dances with the aristocrats and politicians who inhabited the enormous gated villas set back from the promenade. Ennui had driven her to take a lover; a dearth of candidates meant she plumped for her husband's assistant.

The first time she had run away, she fled to her family in Berdichev, who refused to countenance a divorce and sent her straight back to Crimea. The second time, a few weeks later, she escaped to relatives in Odessa, but Yakov followed and brought her home. Back in Yalta, in their pretty wooden house with the view of the bay, he'd beaten her so savagely she'd feared she might never walk again.

Perhaps she should go up to the roof terrace and throw herself off, Sonya thought idly. She was running out of options. It had been three weeks since her first attempt to get rid of it, and still the unwanted baby in her belly refused to budge, defiant in the face of steam baths and herbal draughts and running up and down the stairs in an effort to dislodge it. It was clearly a stubborn little thing; Sonya almost admired its tenacity.

'Sonya!'

Through the miasma she heard someone call her name.

'Sonya, it's me!'

The voice was coming from the street below. Looking

down, she saw Mikhail outside the pharmacy. Full of nervous energy, he glanced left and right to ensure no one was watching, but the passers-by – busy with their errands and their chatter, momentarily distracted by a group of excitable children who were chasing a yapping terrier – paid no heed.

'Come down! I need to speak to you.' He beckoned hastily and darted back inside.

Sonya did as she was bid, closing the double doors and descending the staircase that separated the family's living quarters from her husband's business on the ground floor.

She'd always rather liked the pharmacy. There was something both fascinating and mysterious in the tall shelves of dark wood, the highest of which could only be accessed by ladder, housing myriad coloured bottles containing tonics and lotions and potions and powders and poison. There were locked glass cabinets to which only Yakov held the key; the air thickly scented with camphor oil and carbolic soap, herbs and spices, lavender and liquorice; the countertops home to apothecary scales, a well-used pestle and mortar, and all the other accoutrements of the profession. Yakov was particularly proud of the newly installed soda machine, an American innovation he'd read about in a journal, where carbonated water could be mixed with syrup to create fizzy drinks. He was convinced that these sweet, sparkling sodas were the future; Sonya preferred her traditional cup of tea.

'Darling, you're freezing!' Mikhail dashed across the shop to meet her, his face brimming with concern as he clutched her hands in his. 'How long were you standing out there?'

Her lips were ringed with blue. 'I'm not sure…'

'Sonya, my sweet, I've done it! I have it all planned!' His dark eyes were feverish as he interrupted her, his news too important to wait. 'Our escape!'

Sonya stared back, bewildered by his youthful enthusiasm. Mikhail wasn't the best-looking man – his forehead too large, his eyes too close together, his stature a little too short for her tastes – but unlike her husband he was kind and amusing and provided some much-needed excitement in her dreary life.

'We'll go to Constantinople! I have an uncle there and he can find me work – hopefully as a pharmacist, but if not, then I'll do whatever it takes to—'

'Mikhail—'

'Wait, hear me out. We'll go on Christmas Eve. Make an excuse and slip away as you're leaving church. I'll be waiting with a carriage. We'll head for Sevastopol then take a boat and then we'll be free! Free to be together for the rest of our lives my darling.'

He looked so eager, and it made what Sonya was about to say even harder.

'I'm sorry,' she said softly. 'I can't.'

'What is it, my love? Are you scared of Yakov finding us? Because I promise you, my precious one, that I'll do everything in my power to protect you and keep you safe. You don't have to be afraid of him anymore! I'll make sure he—'

'I'm pregnant.'

Mikhail blanched. He ran a shaky hand through his copper-coloured curls, blowing the air from his cheeks like a punctured bicycle tyre. 'Is it mine?'

'I don't think so. I've worked out the dates and…' The

colour rose in her cheeks. 'So you see, we can't continue... I have to stay with my husband.'

Mikhail inadvertently took a step backwards. 'So that's it? It's over? Even though he's a monster who beats you and Volodya and—'

The shop door opened, the bell letting out its familiar clang as Yakov walked in carrying a large box wrapped in brown parcel paper and tied with string. Tall and wiry, he cut a deliberately distinctive figure with his florid suit and waxed moustache, his fair colouring belying his Jewish roots.

'Mr Leventon!' Mikhail stammered, guilt writ large on his face. 'I didn't expect you back so soon! I've been holding the fort here. Sales have been brisk, although it's slowed up a little now, but I've been selling bottles of rose water like they're going out of fashion. Oh, and we're almost out of castor oil, but I've added it to the list...'

Yakov ignored Mikhail and looked across at his wife, his voice thick with sarcasm as he remarked, 'Playing shop are we, darling?'

Sonya kept her composure. 'I was wishing Mr Ivashko a happy Christmas.'

'How thoughtful.' Yakov swept past, and Sonya followed him upstairs without looking back.

Their bedroom was at the rear of the property, elegantly dressed and dominated by a large bed of carved walnut topped with a yellow damask counterpane. Festoon curtains hung at the sash windows, and below sat the leatherbound ottoman that had housed Sonya's trousseau, on top of which Yakov carefully placed the box.

'Do you know what this is, *babochka*?'

Sonya shook her head.

'It's your Christmas present. I went to the post office to collect it. It came all the way from Paris.'

'I… Thank you.'

'You're welcome.' Yakov kissed her. 'Open it now.'

'But it's not Christmas yet.'

'I know, but I'm too excited to wait. I want to see your face.'

Sonya's smile was hesitant as she reached for the package, fumbling over the knots whilst Yakov watched intently.

'I'm sorry it's not better presented. I wanted to cover it with ribbons and bows, but I was too impatient to give it to you.'

'Don't worry, my dearest. That doesn't matter to me.'

Once unwrapped, the box bore a French name, embossed in gold, and an address on the rue du Faubourg Saint-Honoré. Sonya removed the lid to reveal an exquisite evening gown of rose-pink silk, its puffed sleeves decorated with red chrysanthemum tufts and a red satin bow encircling the waist.

'Oh,' she breathed, clearly delighted. 'It's beautiful.'

'I knew you'd love it. Do you want to try it on?'

'Of course!' Sonya lifted the dress reverentially from its nest of tissue paper, feeling the softness of the material, already imagining how perfect it would look with the garnet earrings she'd been given by her mother on her 17th birthday. There might even be an opportunity to wear it in the coming weeks – Yakov's cousin had invited them to a festive gala at the Botanical Gardens – although the waist would need letting out, and she might have to—

The blow came out of nowhere. The back of Yakov's hand full force against Sonya's cheek. It left her reeling and she fell against the bedpost, stumbling to stay upright.

'Whore,' Yakov swore. The glob of spittle that followed landed wetly on her cheek. Sonya reached up to wipe it away and saw that there was blood on her fingers. Already the room seemed darker, her vision blurring as the tender skin around her eye socket bloomed like a crocus in the snow. The pain was nauseating, and she could only hope he hadn't broken her cheekbone.

'Wishing Mr Ivashko a happy Christmas were you? Lying bitch.' He snatched the dress from her hands, the fabric tearing with a sickening sound. 'You don't deserve this, *shlyukha*.' The insult was punctuated with another rip, the delicate material shredded and spoiled. Yakov threw it at his wife. 'You've always been a flirt, haven't you? You've never thought I was good enough. An embarrassment to you and your rich family.'

This time he grabbed a fistful of her hair, throwing her to the floor. Sonya cried out, scrambling to stand, instinct and experience warning that beneath her husband's boot was a dangerous place to be. But he was faster and the kick was brutal, the strength of his rage behind it as his foot made contact with the small of her back. It knocked the air out of her and she struggled to speak.

'Please, Yakov, please!' She wasn't too proud to beg. 'I'm—'

'Shut up!' he hissed. 'Shut your stupid, lying, ugly mouth, you little—'

'I'm pregnant,' Sonya managed.

Yakov stopped instantly, looking stunned.

'I'm having another baby,' she repeated, her breath coming in ragged gasps. 'Isn't that good news? You're going to be a father again, darling.'

Sonya smiled up at him from the floor, her left eye bloody

18

and purple like a cut of beef. Yakov's face was blank as he held out a hand and helped her to her feet.

Five months later, on the third of June 1879, Mariam Edez Adelaida Leventon – known as Alla – was born, and Sonya instantly fell in love.

Chapter Three

MAYBELLE

Los Angeles, USA, 1919

'Heavenly Father, we thank you for the food you have provided us this day. For giving us a roof over our heads and a bed to sleep in at night. We ask for your blessings upon this house, and everyone who resides within it, that you keep us safe from harm and steer us along the path of righteousness, so we might resist the wicked devil and his sinful ways. Temptation is all around us, and we must stay vigilant. We thank you for bringing everyone to their place around this table, that you might offer them redemption through your divine forgiveness, as they dedicate themselves to you, our Lord and Saviour. We give thanks for the blessing of family and are 'specially grateful to you for bringing Maybelle into our lives. Give her strength and watch over her, that she might continue to do your holy work and spread the joyous word of our Lord Jesus Christ. Amen.'

'Amen,' said Aunt Ida.

'Amen,' I murmured, and my sentiments were echoed along the length of the table. The gathered dozen began to eat, tucking into the hearty meal prepared by Aunt Ida of stewed rabbit with vegetables, a hunk of cornbread on the side.

'So, Maybelle, how was your day?' Uncle Henry asked jovially. The Reverend Henry J. Walker – to give him his full appellation – was a solid, country type, with boyish blond hair sitting thickly on top of a moon-like face, friendly and open and devoted to his religion, determined to spread the Good News in a state where he, his wife and his niece were the only regular practitioners.

I nodded, swallowing a mouthful of potato, as the others turned expectantly. 'Today went real good. I gave out all my pamphlets, spoke to some new faces—' here I flushed, recalling my meeting with Josephine '—and people seemed interested.'

'Do you reckon we'll have any newcomers on Sunday?'

'I sure hope so. Aunt Ida, this cornbread is delicious.'

'Thank you, Maybelle, you're most welcome.' Aunt Ida was short and round and, despite her marriage not being blessed with children, maternal in a way that had never come naturally to my own mother. Ida's softness was in contrast to her sister's hard angularity, her natural warmth the antithesis of Dorothy Crabtree's cold disappointment. 'Billy helped me make it, didn't you, Billy?'

A young man around my age, with dark hair and a port-wine birthmark across his eye that gave him the appearance of wearing a patch, nodded shyly. He was always helpful and solicitous; nothing was too much trouble for Billy.

'An' I shot an' skinned the jackrabbit,' chimed in Herb, another new recruit. Herb's expression was an unsettling mix of stupid and sly; he had a habit of looking sideways at a person, and when he smiled there were half a dozen gaps where his teeth should have been. He was fond of telling the tales of how he'd lost every one of them, each yarn a variation on a theme involving bar brawl heroics and hard liquor *an' you shoulda seen the other fella!*

I tried to hide my dislike, reminding myself that Herb had repented of his sins (of which there had been many, if you believed his stories) and joined the Southern Baptists of California – a name that sounded paradoxical, but was absolutely necessary for the expansion of the Church, according to Uncle Henry. Some years ago, Henry had petitioned the state convention for a small stipend so that he and his wife could move west and establish what would become the First Baptist Church of Atwater; there'd been a similar undertaking in Santa Clara in the 1850s, but the Civil War put a stop to that attempt, depleting money and personnel until the pioneers were forced to retreat to home territory. It was perhaps a testament to Uncle Henry's persuasive skills that the convention agreed, and thus he and Aunt Ida became missionaries – albeit domestic ones, their target misguided Methodists rather than African tribes. I remembered the collections organised by the local congregation back home, poor farm folk giving what little they could spare for our brave brother spreading the Holy Word in a godless land.

Uncle Henry and Aunt Ida leased a farmstead, settling some way out of the main city where the rents were much cheaper, comprising forty acres with barns and outbuildings, citrus trees and assorted livestock. Every weekday morning, Uncle Henry took the streetcar into Los Angeles to preach to the heathen commuters or visited construction workers in Glendale to distribute pamphlets and spread the Word. Everyone was welcome in this new congregation – Henry and Ida made no judgements, for that was for God to decide – and the poor were offered a place to sleep and a hot meal once a day in exchange for work on the farm and consent to baptism by immersion.

Now the red barn was home to almost a dozen people, a ragtag bunch of misfits and proselytes and reformed felons; mostly men, although there was one married couple, and a Hispanic woman, Marisol, who spoke little English but was clearly devoted to her newfound religion. In addition to those who lived permanently on the farm, more came each Sunday to the service led by Uncle Henry, and our little flock was steadily growing. I was tasked with imitating my uncle's role – declaiming in the streets, converting the unbelievers – but while the Reverend was undoubtedly a natural evangelist, secure in his vocation and a gifted orator, I found such public displays uncomfortable, feeling exposed and embarrassed. Yet I knew I was lucky that my aunt and uncle had taken me in, grateful to them for offering me a home after everything that had happened last summer in Jonas Springs.

'Thank you, Herb. They're delicious too,' I replied evenly, as he gave me that side-eyed look and a leering grin that exposed the toothless void.

I suppressed a shudder, casting my gaze downwards and finding my food suddenly unappetising.

After the meal, and after Billy had helped me wash the dishes whilst the others sidled back to the barn, I feigned a long, indulgent yawn and announced, 'I think it's time for me to turn in. Goodnight y'all.'

'Goodnight, Maybelle. May He watch over you until morning,' said Aunt Ida, putting her needlework to one side and rising from the rocking chair to kiss me on the forehead.

'Don't forget to say your prayers, child. Think on your momma and brothers back home.'

'I sure will, Uncle Henry. Goodnight.'

I strove to keep my face neutral, to keep my pace measured as I walked down the corridor to my room at the back of the single-storey house, but I was longing to be alone with my thoughts, to try and steady the pounding in my breast that came every time I thought of what this evening might bring.

Breathlessly, I pushed open the door to my room. It was simple but homely, with a small wooden bed and a desk-come-dressing table, the patchwork quilt I'd brought from home neatly folded and draped across my chair. A cross-stitched quotation (*'Blessed are the pure in heart, for they shall see God'* – *Matthew 5:8*) hung above my bed, a gift from Aunt Ida, and my childhood comforter, a sock toy of indeterminate species – perhaps rabbit or cat, possibly bear or mouse – sat propped up against my pillow, one of its button eyes long since disappeared.

Once inside, I turned the handle firmly, double-checking to ensure the door was properly closed, listening a moment to be certain no one had come after me – Aunt Ida reminding me to collect the eggs in the morning, or Uncle Henry with a fresh batch of pamphlets he'd forgotten to hand over – before hurrying across the threadbare rug to the satchel by my nightstand, pulling out the note that was hidden at the bottom.

Holding it in my hands, my pulse began to race – here was evidence of the encounter, irrefutable proof that Josephine existed and had invited me to a party on Sunset Boulevard tonight! I stared at the elegant penmanship, letting my fingers trace the curves of the letters, my lips mouthing the exotic-sounding words – *"Hayvenhurst"*, *"Hollywood"* – like an incantation.

I raised the note to my face, inhaling the faint scent of Josephine's perfume, a blush rising in my cheeks despite there being no witnesses to this intimate act. Traces of musk and jasmine infused the air and all at once the details came rushing back – the way Josephine's blunt, auburn bob brushed the nape of her neck as she tossed her head; the way her pale eyelashes curled enticingly at the ends; how full and lush her lips had seemed encircling the cigarette – with an intensity that left me giddy.

I washed my face at the bowl on the washstand, the cool water refreshing against my hot skin. I brushed my hair, impulsively adding a green ribbon, then changed out of the dusty, rather ugly dress I'd been wearing all day into a clean, white smock with lace at the bodice and hem. It was simple, but I didn't have anything else. Then I lay down on my bed and waited.

There was no question that I wouldn't go. I liked to think I was more rebellious than Josephine might give me credit for, imagining the look on her face when she saw that shy, softly-spoken Maybelle from Kentucky had been so bold as to attend the party where she didn't know a soul, journeying all the way across the Franklin Hills to Hollywood. Or perhaps Josephine had never intended that I would show up at all; and now my fantasy tilted, seeing her expression filled with shock and distaste and pity, and my stomach rolled sickeningly at the thought. The mere possibility shamed me, and I wondered once again why I placed such value on the opinion of this stranger.

The light was fading as I heard the familiar sounds of the farm winding down for the evening, the yielding creak of the floorboards as my aunt and uncle headed for bed. I had retired earlier than usual and, in my impatience, it seemed to take an age for Henry and Ida to follow suit. They rose with the sun, but some nights Henry would stay awake until the small hours, labouring over his weekly sermon beneath the old kerosene lamp, or debating a matter of scripture with one of the converts. Fortunately, tonight was not one of those nights.

When all grew quiet, I slipped off the bed and pulled on my boots, breath quickening in anticipation as I crept over to the window. It was past eight o'clock and darkness had fallen. On clear nights I could see the distant lights of the city; I'd often looked out at the shimmering horizon, wondering about the people out there, what revelry kept those lights burning so late. Now I was about to find out.

I unfastened the catch on the window. The squeak sounded louder than a gunshot to my guilty ears and I froze, every sense alert. But the house remained as still and unresponsive as ever and I slid open the window, savouring the rush of cool evening air before hitching up my skirts and swinging my legs over the frame. It felt thrillingly familiar; I remembered the way I would sneak out late at night back home, running through the corn fields beneath a strawberry moon, following the path down to the creek to meet Sarah Beth and Tucker and half a dozen of my peers from the neighbouring farms that I'd known for a lifetime.

But I wouldn't think about that now. Noiselessly, I dropped from the sill to land softly on the ground, sliding the frame almost back into place, save for a fingertip's gap at the bottom. For a second I hesitated, glancing in the direction of the barn, suddenly overcome by the unnerving sensation of being watched. I shook it off, telling myself not to be so foolish, then turned towards the track that led to the streetcar stop and began to run.

I heard the party before I saw it. The house was a veritable mansion at the end of a curving driveway half-hidden by tall trees, and as I drew closer I heard shrieks of laughter above the jazz music, and what sounded like the splash from a swimming pool followed by cheers and applause. I approached like a ghost in the darkness, my long white dress caught by the breeze. My heart was hammering, and I knew that what I was doing was madness: travelling across the city at night, all alone, with no idea of how I would get home; risking the wrath of my kind-hearted aunt and uncle; risking making a complete and utter fool of myself… and all because of a brief encounter with an intriguing woman.

Yet, despite the risks, I felt somehow compelled to accept the invitation, driven by a desire to glimpse another world and discover whether I might possibly be someone other than plain old Maybelle Crabtree, destined to marry a nice country boy and spend the rest of my life as the wife of a farmer or a clergyman, eventually departing this earth leaving barely a mark upon it. Even if it was just for one night, I wanted to taste the forbidden fruit.

A cherry-red Cadillac sped past and I jumped, flattening myself against a bush as the headlights skirted over me. Up ahead, the motorcar pulled to a stop, and through the foliage I got my first proper look at Hayvenhurst. It was a two-storey, Spanish-style affair, with white walls and terracotta roof tiles and a balustrade balcony that ran the full length of the western façade. Every window was ablaze, the house a beacon of gaiety lighting the shadowy landscape.

I watched as two giggling women climbed out of the Cadillac, dressed in daringly short drop-waisted gowns, strings of oversized pearls jangling at their wrists and necks. The blonde's hair was swept into an elegant chignon, the brunette's close crop styled in waves. Cheeks were rouged and lips painted. I felt my own inadequacies forcefully: the modest dress, the childish ribbon in my hair, the dearth of make-up – I didn't own so much as a pot of powder. I suddenly longed to flee, to catch a streetcar back to Atwater and be asleep in my bed before anyone missed me. But the moment passed. I took a breath and steadied myself, and followed the women through the open front door.

Inside there were people everywhere – laughing, dancing, drinking, crowding the hallway, sitting in small groups or twosomes all the way up the sweeping staircase. A minstrels' gallery ran above the entrance hall and a young woman dashed across it, arms waving, whooping with excitement. The scene was like nothing I'd ever witnessed before, but I found it thrilling, trying not to gawp at the wooden panelling and the marble statues, the purple velvet furniture and the crystal chandeliers, everything grander and more lavish than even Bobby DeCourcy's house, and his folks were the richest in Jonas County. Then I remembered the reason I was there and realised I couldn't see Josephine anywhere. Boldly, I made my way deeper into the house, passing through to a grand open parlour where the walls were covered with canvases and exquisitely hand-painted with scenes from the Greek myths. Here were multiple armchairs and sofas that the guests lounged upon, whilst in the corner a handsome man played a grand piano, a woman in a glittering gown draped across it, huskily singing a song whose lyrics caused me to blush.

Someone grabbed my arm and I turned in relief, expecting to see Josephine. But this woman had white-blonde tresses and a curvaceous figure and I'd never laid eyes on her until now. She spun me around then grasped me by the waist, encouraging me to dance. I froze, shocked at being touched so intimately by this stranger. And not merely a stranger, but a woman.

My family were not tactile by nature; momma was rarely loving or affectionate or free with her caresses as some mothers were and, beyond a goodnight kiss from Aunt Ida, I could hardly remember the last time I'd been embraced. The sensation awakened suppressed memories, stirring conflicting emotions: surprise, excitement, fear. My barriers had been rudely breached, but amidst the outrage it was somehow thrilling, undeniable proof that I was entering a world so completely at odds with the one in which I'd been raised.

Yet I wasn't ignorant of the consequences of giving into desire, however brief the moment or however delicious the feeling, and I knew the repercussions could last far longer than any momentary pleasure.

'I haven't seen you here before,' the woman said, raising her voice to be heard above the hubbub. She leaned in close, and her breath was unpleasantly warm against my neck. 'What's your name?'

'Maybelle. I'm… I'm looking for someone.'

'You're what, honey?'

A man and a woman whirled past, shrieking outrageously, and my words were lost.

'I'm looking for someone,' I tried again, more loudly, realising I didn't even have a surname to offer. 'Josephine. Do you know her?'

But the woman had stopped listening, scanning the room to see whose eyes were upon her as she danced provocatively, paying no attention as I disentangled myself and pulled away. I supposed I must have looked lost and overwrought as another guest took pity on me.

'Are you all right?' The woman was wearing cropped trousers, like a schoolboy, and she peered at me from behind round, horn-rimmed spectacles.

'I'm looking for Josephine,' I repeated, beginning to wonder whether I'd imagined the whole encounter. Had my fears come true and this was all a cruel trick, Josephine never imagining that I would take the casual invitation so seriously? 'I met her this afternoon and she invited me here tonight. She's got bobbed hair, to here, and she… she invited me…' I finished helplessly, wondering if I should have brought the note as proof.

'Ah!' The woman's eyes lit up. 'I might know who you mean. The elusive Mademoiselle Colbert, *n'est-ce pas?*'

I stared at her blankly, uncomprehending, wondering what I'd said to elicit such a bewildering response.

'Follow me.' The woman smiled enigmatically and set off through the crowd, greetings and kisses handed out liberally as she went. I tried to keep up, bug-eyed, whilst drinking in the detail. There were women smoking cigars, women dressed in trousers, women wearing monocles and cravats. A short, moustachioed man was deep in discussion with an exceptionally tall, impossibly slim Black woman. The man was gesticulating wildly with his champagne coupe; every time he waved his arms, he spilled a little more champagne on the Turkish rug and now the glass was almost empty.

Outside, a five-piece band were playing on a terrace beside the swimming pool, and I couldn't help but stare at a man in a lounge suit, drinking a cocktail and completely soaked from head to toe, a puddle of water pooling around his feet – clearly the reason for the cheering I'd heard earlier. As I turned back to my Good Samaritan, I saw that she was tapping a gentleman on the shoulder, saying, 'Joe, someone's looking for you.'

Then the gentleman turned round and it took me a moment to realise that it wasn't a man at all but rather Josephine, resplendent in a tailored evening suit, looking for all the world like a swell in a crisp, white shirt and formal black bow tie. Her hair was slicked back with oil, and she stood with a kind of swagger I would never have expected from the sophisticated woman I'd met earlier that day.

'You came!' Josephine swooped down, kissing me on both cheeks. I caught a trace of the cologne I remembered from earlier, felt the soft press of her body beneath the starched shirt. For a moment I felt light-headed.

'I'm so happy to see you. You look…' Josephine paused, stepping back to admire me, a wistful note in her voice as she said softly, 'you look simply marvellous. Do you have a drink, marvellous Maybelle? Let's get you one.' She stole two coupes from the tray of a passing waiter, thrusting one into my hand.

'Thank you,' I breathed, not knowing whether I was referring to the drink or the compliment or simply the fact that Josephine seemed so delighted to see me. I took a sip of champagne to steady myself; the bubbles were dizzying and delicious. I'd only drunk alcohol once before, when Sarah Beth had stolen a bottle of her daddy's moonshine, spiriting it down to the creek for us all to share when—

I realised Josephine was staring at me, expectation in those sloping amber eyes, and I knew I needed to say something.

'Your house is beautiful,' I managed finally. 'I've never seen anything like it before. Do you really know all these people?'

Josephine laughed, showing pearly teeth in pink, fleshy gums. 'Oh, no, it's not my house. It belongs to a very good friend of mine called Alla. In fact, we call this place "The Garden of Alla".' Josephine laughed again, although I wasn't sure what the joke was. 'Come on, I'll introduce you.'

Josephine reached for my hand to pull me through the throng, the gesture so casual yet so unexpected that I caught my breath, stomach fluttering uncontrollably, assailed by memories of our first meeting mere hours ago when Josephine had taken my hand to comfort me. It was as though my body recalled every sensation: soft, warm flesh; slim fingers bound by solid gold rings; the insistent press of Josephine's palm making my skin tingle.

'By the way,' Josephine turned around, pushed closer by the crush. 'Call me Joe. All my good friends do.'

I'd barely had time to digest this revelation before Josephine – Joe – had stopped in front of a remarkable-looking woman, holding forth at the centre of an eclectic group. She was diminutive, dressed all in black, with a mass of uncontrollable dark hair that sprang wildly from her head at all angles. Her eyes were expressive and thickly kohled, her nose rather large, her lips pursed and coloured with a claret so dark it was almost black. Whilst she couldn't be called beautiful, there was undoubtedly something striking about her, and she looked up as Joe approached.

'Alla, this is Maybelle – the girl I was telling you about,' Joe said, and I felt a shiver of pleasure to learn that Joe had spoken of me.

Alla looked me up and down, her manner slow and deliberate, as I smiled nervously, hoping she approved of what she saw. I couldn't have known that in the crepuscular light, dozens of flickering candles dotted around the grounds, I looked luminous – fresh-faced and wholesome and the epitome of innocence.

'Well, well, well.' Alla's accent was unusual – perhaps European, I guessed – and she glanced briefly at Joe, one eyebrow raised, lips curving into a smile as her gaze slid back to me. 'And aren't you a sight for sore eyes?'

Chapter Four

ALLA

Zurich, Switzerland, 1886

Outside the landscape was verdant and mountainous, the sky slate-grey and ominous. Alla swallowed, clearing her throat, then looked across at her father.

'Papa, where are we going?'

Yakov didn't reply, staring straight ahead and giving no indication that he'd heard. The train rumbled on through valleys flanked by steeply sloping pine forests, past pretty little villages and lakeside churches and grazing cows – the familiar sights of Alla's childhood.

'Where are we going?' she tried again, adding bravely, 'Are we going to visit Mama?'

The muscle at the corner of Yakov's left eye began to spasm, his knuckles whitening as he balled his fingers into a fist. Alla didn't dare to repeat the question, afraid of receiving a cuff for her impertinence. They *must* be going to see her mother, she decided. Why else would Yakov have collected her from

Yedintsy, where she'd been living with her uncle, bringing her hundreds of miles from southern Russia back to Switzerland?

Alla hugged herself inside, overjoyed that she would soon be reunited with her beloved *mamochka*. She missed her so much that at times she could hardly bear it, her love for Sonya only equalled by her hatred of her father, with his stupid moustache and his showy clothes and his readiness to dole out a whipping.

It had been Christmas time, Alla remembered. She'd been living in Bern, with Sonya, but Yakov had come to take them back to Zurich where a terrible row had ensued, her mother screaming, her father making free with his fists. Later, she recalled sitting on her mama's knee, curled into the comforting scent of eau de toilette and powdered skin, while Yakov shouted and her mother cried quietly. He'd presented Sonya with a sheaf of papers, and she had protested but eventually signed. When Alla awoke the next morning, Sonya was gone. How long ago had that been? Months? Years, perhaps? To seven-year-old Alla, time was elastic. She only knew that she hadn't seen her mother since that night, and with every day that passed the ball of sadness that she carried inside her heart grew blacker and more noxious, lodging itself so deep that it could never be purged.

Alla took an apple from her satchel, shining it on her sleeve then biting into it, milk teeth piercing the waxy skin. She wished she were wearing a prettier dress to meet her mama again – the blue checkered wool with the lace collar perhaps. Or the emerald velvet with the pearlescent buttons. She took another bite of her apple, the tartness making her mouth water. Oh, but how much she had to tell when they were reunited! Of school, and of her cousins, and of Polina, the tabby cat that had slept on her bed at Uncle Ilya's house, and of how she longed for a straw bonnet decorated with yellow flowers but Yakov refused to buy her one. Perhaps Volodya and Nina would be with their mother too – although she didn't really care either way, Alla reflected.

The last thing her father had told her was that her siblings were staying with his sister, their Aunt Lysenka, in Geneva where she worked as a surgeon. It felt like a long time since Alla had last seen her brother and sister, and she certainly didn't feel close to them; the tight familial bond that she'd read about in books, or witnessed between her cousins at Uncle Ilya's house, was an enigma to her. Amongst the Leventon progeny there was competition, rather than camaraderie, although it was clear that Nina was their father's favourite; with her blonde hair and slender figure, she resembled Yakov physically, and seeing himself reflected in miniature appealed to his vanity. In contrast, when Yakov looked at his youngest daughter, with her long, dark hair, moon-like face, and intense expression, all he saw was his ex-wife, and for that he hated Alla. He'd told her enough times, she reflected bitterly, crunching down loudly on her apple as she recalled how—

'Quiet!' Yakov snapped, lashing out, knocking the fruit from her hand in his fury. Alla cried out as it flew through the air and her fellow passengers turned to stare, wondering at the commotion as the apple bounced twice, three times on the carriage floor before coming to rest, the white flesh soiled and spoiled.

Alla fell back against her seat, lips pursed in a mutinous line, shaking with anger as she turned her head away from her father and stared blankly at the tranquil scenery flashing past the window.

~

The distinctive skyline of the Swiss city hove into view, the bells of Grossmünster church ringing out to mark the hour as a burst of steam blew the train into the Hauptbahnhof. Yakov held Alla's hand tightly – almost painfully – as he led her to a waiting carriage, which drove out of Zurich and began to climb the winding mountain road to the west.

This is where my mother lives!

Alla was beside herself with excitement, her hands gripping the side of the carriage, her head whipping from side to side, expecting at any moment to round a corner and see Sonya waiting in welcome, arms outstretched.

The vehicle climbed higher, the spires and roofs of the city growing small as a child's toy set, the vast lake insignificant at this distance. Alla began to grow impatient – and somewhat apprehensive. She couldn't imagine what her mother – her lively, sociable mama – would be doing up here, so far from civilisation with only the mountain goats for company. Reluctantly, Alla reached for her old travelling cloak, pulling it tightly around her; she'd wanted to look nice for her mother but the air had grown cooler, the leaden skies threatening rain and leaving her with no choice but to sit huddled and swaddled as the horses plodded onwards.

Before long, the carriage turned from the main road, bumping over the uneven ground. Alla sat bolt upright as she spotted a lone farmhouse in the distance, made of stone with a sloping timbered roof and a smoking chimney rising from the centre of the somewhat lopsided building. In the yard outside lay a watchful dog who jumped to his feet at their approach; beyond she glimpsed orchards and a pig pen, and Alla thought once again how odd it was for her mother to be living here.

She scrambled down as the driver unloaded her trunk, a sudden surge of nerves splintering through her that left her frozen, rooted to the spot. She stared at the ramshackle house, overcome by the unsettling feeling that she was being watched from the windows, but the reflection made it impossible to see.

'Come on, child.' Yakov was almost at the cottage. 'Don't dawdle.' He rapped sharply on the door, and it was opened by a stout woman with pendulous breasts and a thatch of grey hair. It was a long time since Alla had seen her mother, but she was almost certain that this wasn't Sonya.

She looked up at her father in confusion. 'Where is my mama?'

Yakov's expression was one of barely concealed irritation. 'This is Frau Groelich. You're going to live here now. Forget about your mother. No – more – mama. *Ever.*'

Alla let out a cry of horror, then collapsed to the ground.

She awoke from her faint to find herself lying on a narrow bed, two curious faces peering down at her: the woman – Frau Groelich – and a girl, a little older than herself, with two long plaits and a fierce expression. Yakov was nowhere to be seen.

'Good. You're awake. I'll get you some water,' Frau Groelich said gruffly, leaving the room.

Alla looked around, her vision swimming in and out of focus. An identical bed stood beside the one she lay in, a narrow gap separating them. On the opposite wall were two cluttered shelves housing an assortment of childish paraphernalia: half a dozen dog-eared books, a prized collection of rocks and shells, a china elephant with a chipped trunk, a blunt pencil. Tattered curtains hung at the window, and the whole room had an air of shabbiness, unlit and gloomy on this overcast day. The girl was still staring at her.

'Where am I?' Alla asked.

'You're in *my* room.' Her voice was clipped and indignant. 'But I suppose it's your room now too, as Mutti says you're to stay here and we're to share. I'm Gretl. I'm eight. This is my doll, Heidi, and you mustn't touch her unless I give you permission because she's mine.'

'Where's my father?'

'He's gone. I don't think he wants you.'

'I don't want him either,' Alla shot back, defiance giving her strength. Then she remembered what had happened, and the impact was like a blow to the stomach all over again. 'Do you know where my mother is?'

'Um…' Gretl screwed up her face, sitting down beside Alla. 'She might be in Odessa. I don't know where that is, but I overheard Mutti talking before you arrived. She said your mother is a whore, which means she wears coloured feathers in her hair and has intercourse with lots of men. Do you know about intercourse?'

Alla shook her head.

'Don't worry, I'll tell you all about it,' Gretl said loftily.

'Here.' Frau Groelich appeared in the doorway, handing

40

Alla a cup of water. Gretl slid guiltily off the bed. 'Drink this, then I'll show you around. There's lots to do – you won't be idle here. My, but you've been allowed to grow so fat! Quite the little butterball. On Monday, you'll start at the kindergarten with Gretl – my sister is a teacher there – and your father wants you to take violin lessons.'

'I'd rather play the piano,' Alla retorted, stung by Frau Groelich's forthright opinions.

'And I'd rather not have to look after a cheeky little girl who's going to eat me out of house and home, but we rarely get what we want in this life.' She ruffled Alla's unruly hair with something approaching affection. 'Now, drink up, and we'll go meet the animals – and the rest of my children too.'

The days turned to weeks and life fell into a routine (school, music practice, chores). Alla enjoyed the novelty of stability, despite the family's eccentricities: Herr Groelich belonged to an anarchist group and spoke passionately of the coming revolution, where monarchies would fall and equality would reign; his mother, a wizened old woman who was forever conversing with God, lived in a downstairs room and terrified Alla; and there were four sons of varying shapes and sizes, who seemingly came second to the pigs in their mother's affections.

Alla was kept busy, expected to help with the housework, polish the men's shoes, fetch the water every morning and light the fire in the kitchen. Frau Groelich was teaching her to sew, so she might repair the men's shirts and patch the hand-me-downs she received from Gretl. But the most important lesson she'd learned was to stop asking for Sonya. Frau Groelich had brusquely suggested that Alla call her *die Mutter* instead, explaining: *'I'm everyone's mother here'*. Alla, experiencing a troubling combination of happiness and betrayal, had complied.

In secret, she'd begun to keep a diary chronicling all her experiences, so she wouldn't forget anything when she was finally reunited with Sonya. She'd begun violin lessons too, as instructed by Yakov and, to Alla's surprise, she derived immense satisfaction from the instrument. She was unexpectedly accomplished; whilst her classmates produced little more than ear-splitting rasps and scrapes, Alla's bow danced skilfully over the strings, bright and mellifluous.

She found that she enjoyed performing, revelling in the admiring glances of her peers, able to lose herself in the music and transport herself beyond the everyday tedium. And she enjoyed the praise that came her way when she did well; deprived of kind words for so many years, Alla slowly blossomed, like the edelweiss flowers on the rocky, mountain slopes. Unbeknownst to her, but observed by Frau Groelich, Alla was growing in confidence, emerging from the melancholy that had enveloped her since Sonya had left, becoming a bright, lively, imaginative now-eight-year-old.

It was a Sunday, and the heavy morning rain had given way to a dank drizzle that intoxicated the mountainside and made the trees lush as emeralds. Alla was feeding the pigs. She liked the way they came waddling over when she shook the food bucket, ears flapping, nuzzling into her hand like dogs. Her favourite was round as a barrel with a stumpy tail and a thick covering of coarse black hair – rather like Alla herself, Gretl had suggested unkindly. Alla chatted to them as they ate, scratching the lucky ones behind their ears, knowing she would return smelling of damp swine and shit.

'Why are you talking to the pigs?'

Otto, the second of the four sons, watched her as he leaned on the gate. He was fifteen years old, yet Alla firmly believed that she was better at arithmetic than he was, that she could write her letters more legibly and read more fluently. Physically, he was large and brawny, small dark eyes set deep in his doughy face like raisins in a bun, and he wore thick woollen trousers with a vest layered over a grubby shirt and a jacket that was too small.

'They're my friends,' Alla replied.

'I'll be your friend. I've got lots of friends. I'm in a gang.' He climbed the low fence and swung one leg over the top, straddling it like a horse. 'It's called *der Bund* and I'm the leader. I'll tell you a secret – we're going to kill the Tsar.'

'Why?'

'Pappi says he lives in a palace made of gold but keeps the workers oppressed. When he's dead, Pappi will be proud of me.'

'How are you going to kill him?'

'With a knife. I have a knife – do you want to see it?'

'All right.' A curious Alla didn't hesitate.

'I'm going into the woods. Come with me and I'll show you.'

Alla remembered Frau Groelich's stern face that morning, instructing her to clean and tidy her side of the room, to help bake the bread and run errands in the village before sweeping the grate and laying the fire in the pantry. She smiled up at Otto. 'Let's go.'

She followed him through the orchard, past the beehives and to the edge of Herr Groelich's land where an overgrown path led into the forest. Beneath the dense tree canopy the silence took on a different quality, thick and smothering and cocoon-like. Otto's gait was lumbering, his head bowed. Alla's boots were soon thick with mud, the recent rainfall rendering the trail like a quagmire.

'Who's in your gang?' Alla asked as they tramped.

'Xavier and Andreas.' Otto named his two younger brothers. 'And Albert.' The son of the neighbouring farmer.

A branch cracked somewhere in the distance and a flock of pigeons took flight, disturbing fat droplets of water that fell from the leaves.

'Are there bears in here?' Alla wondered. 'Or wolves?'

'Probably. But I'll protect you. If a bear attacked us, I'd kill it with my knife.'

They walked on for a mile, perhaps two, until the farm was left far behind and Alla realised she would never find her way back by herself; Otto had long since turned off the main path, making his way past fallen trees and bursts of heather seemingly at random until they reached a clearing that was surely his intended destination. Logs slick with lichen had been dragged into a circle around the remains of a fire, scattered stones piled into cairns. Otto turned proudly, arms extended wide to show off his domain.

'This is the meeting place of *der Bund*. It's top secret. You can't tell anyone.'

'I won't. Do you really have a knife?'

'I'm not lying.' Otto was indignant as he bent down and rolled up his trouser leg, pulling a six-inch blade with wooden handle from his sock.

'Can I hold it?'

Otto frowned. 'All right. But you have to be careful because you're not trained like I am.'

He held it out and Alla took it from him, eyes glittering as she examined it. Otto kept it scrupulously clean and the metal shone as she twisted it back and forth, catching the light that filtered through the beech trees. Experimentally, Alla pressed her finger to the tip, testing the sharpness; her skin yielded but didn't break.

'You're the Tsar and I'm going to kill you!' she roared, lunging at Otto, collapsing with laughter as he scrambled backwards so quickly that he fell over, leaf mulch coating the seat of his trousers. Embarrassed, he got to his feet, snatching the knife from Alla.

'That's mine! Give it back! You were only meant to hold it,' he admonished, checking to see that it hadn't been damaged.

'I was only playing. I didn't mean it.'

Alla stepped towards him and Otto eyed her warily. The light rain had slicked his mousy hair to his head, and he sniffed, wiping his nose on his sleeve. There was a pause before he asked, 'Do you want to join *der Bund*? You have to pass the initiation though,' he added quickly, seeing Alla's delight.

'What's the initiation?'

'You can't scream, or cry out, or even make a noise, no matter what happens. You have to stay completely silent.'

'All right,' Alla shrugged. 'Like what?'

A moment's hesitation then Otto sprang to life, his big body coiled as he began to circle her, the knife dancing wildly in his hand, thrusts and jabs intended to throw her off guard. Alla didn't move, didn't flinch. After a childhood with Yakov, she'd grown used to repressing her feelings, hiding her fear. The circle grew smaller and Otto drew closer. His pupils were large, his excitement palpable. The seconds ticked by, the space between them growing claustrophobic as the weapon searched for release. Finally Otto struck with a war cry, the blade slicing through the damp air, the serrated edge coming to rest against Alla's neck.

'I could cut your throat and leave your body here and no one would ever find it.'

Otto's face was barely an inch from hers, his wheezing breath stale and unpleasant. Nearby, something rustled through the undergrowth and Alla blinked. Otto jumped and the spell was broken. He stepped backwards, looking around him uncertainly. Alla remained immobile, her body held rigid. She wondered what would happen next; if the test was over or whether there was more to come.

Otto rolled up his sleeves, revealing brawny forearms thick with hair. He twisted his wrists, exposing the underside of his arms, the white skin traversed by a tangle of blue veins. Then he raised the knife once more. High above, a bird called a warning. Otto threw back his head and howled like an animal, the noise bouncing off the trees and filling the woods, growing louder and bigger until Alla wanted to clamp her hands over her ears and shut it out forever. Just when she thought she could take no more, Otto brought the knife to his skin and slashed, blood rushing to the surface and spilling out of his body. He did it again, and again, howling with each slash, until his arms were a mess of red rivers and Alla's ears were ringing, her heart racing with confusion and fear. Yet she overcame the instinct to run – whether towards him or away from him she couldn't have said – and remained stoic and rooted as the ancient woods around her, just as Otto had instructed.

He stood before her like a wounded colossus, arms outstretched, blood dripping onto the forest floor. Their eyes met once again, Alla uncertain yet defiant, Otto wild and feverish.

'Lie down.' His voice was thick, as though his throat needed clearing.

Alla did as she was bid. The ground was cold, dampness soaking through her clothes, mud clinging to her hair and oozing under her fingernails. She knew Frau Groelich would be furious about the state she was in and had no idea how she would explain herself.

'You can't make a noise,' Otto repeated as he moved closer. His pupils were so large his eyes seemed black, and he was breathing heavily. 'Not if you want to join *der Bund*. You can't cry out, and you can't make a sound, no matter what happens. This will be the ultimate test.'

Alla didn't reply, and Otto took her silence for consent. His bulky frame moving awkwardly, he lay down on top of her, the breath squeezed out of her by his weight, an agonising pressure on her lungs as her face was smothered by the press of his chest. Yet despite the rising panic, she remained perfectly still. She felt his hands fumbling at her ankles, the cool air on her bare legs as her skirt was pulled up above her waist, his warm blood covering her skin, staining her shirt. And she remained perfectly quiet. His fingers pushed at her thighs, forcing them apart, and then a pain more excruciating than anything she'd ever felt, as though he were stabbing her with the knife somewhere deep inside, the blade slicing between her legs over and over, faster and faster. She kept her eyes screwed shut, clamped her lips closed.

And still she didn't cry out.

Chapter Five

MAYBELLE

Los Angeles, USA, 1919

The California weather was as clement as ever on the day of Marisol's baptism: cloudless blue skies with no intimation of rain; enveloping heat – temperatures unseasonably high for late fall, Aunt Ida had commented – as ospreys circled above, drifting on the warm currents.

My face was flushed, my forehead perspiring, with circular, damp patches buried in the armpits of my dress as I dashed to and fro, fetching and carrying, lugging and greeting.

'I'll help you with those.' Herb loped over, flashing the toothless grin that made my stomach turn, as he laid claim to the stack of chairs I was carrying.

Despite the humidity, a chill settled over my skin. Wherever I turned recently, Herb seemed to be there: smiling, watching. There was nothing I could put my finger on, no troubling behaviour or inappropriate comments, but something about him put me on edge.

'Thank you.' My tone was curt as I walked back to the farmhouse.

Already people were beginning to arrive for this week's Sunday service, and every object that could conceivably be used for sitting upon was being ferried to the red barn to try and accommodate them. Aunt Ida was bustling round offering glasses of fresh orange juice and lemonade, whilst Uncle Henry was greeting the faithful, a steady stream of converts spilling across the grassy field from the streetcar stop. Children, dressed in their Sunday best, were noisily playing tag despite their parents' best efforts to enforce good behaviour, and the more sociable chickens had wandered across to see what all the fuss was about.

The house was cool, a welcome respite from the sun, and I gathered the remaining chairs from round the kitchen table. A noise in the next room made me jump – I'd thought the house was empty – and Billy emerged from the hallway, looking equally startled to see me.

'Billy, perfect timing! Would you give me a hand with these?'

'Sure. That's what I was looking for.' He jerked his thumb behind him before lifting the whole pile. 'More chairs.'

'And you didn't find any?'

'I didn't know if I should take them – Mrs Walker's rocking chair…'

I nodded, understanding. 'I'll get it. You take these – oh, be careful!' I cautioned as the stack leaned alarmingly, towering over his slender frame.

He manoeuvred awkwardly out of the doorway as I went through to the parlour, placing Aunt Ida's needlework on the side table and picking up her rocking chair, half-dragging it outside where I noticed Marisol, alone and anxious. She looked wonderful, in a plain white dress, her dark hair long and loose, and I told her so.

'Thank you,' she replied hesitantly, in accented English.

'There's no need to be nervous. Today is such a special day for you, and we're so happy to welcome you into the family of our King and Saviour, the Lord Jesus Christ. This is the beginning of your journey to salvation.' Uncle Henry would have been proud of me. I leaned across to embrace her, becoming aware as I did so that a car had turned up the track to the farm and was bumping towards us, its sole occupant a striking-looking woman who—

I forgot completely about Marisol and the dearth of chairs and half-ran towards the motorcar as it pulled to a stop. Joe stepped out, radiant in a demure eau-de-nil-coloured dress with a wide-brimmed hat; markedly different to the rakish attire she'd been sporting the last time I'd seen her.

'What are you doing here?' My pulse was racing, delight and bewilderment written plainly on my face.

'Aren't you pleased to see me?' The question was surely rhetorical. 'I thought I'd take a look at your Church. Besides, I need a little absolution in my life – forgive me, Father, for I have sinned…'

'That's Roman Catholics,' I muttered, as Joe roared with laughter. She was drawing quite a crowd; most of the congregation were manual workers, poor folk with patched clothes who struggled to put food on the table each week and, among them, Joe cut a glamorous figure. Uncle Henry hurried across to join us, introducing himself and pumping Joe's hand as though the King of England himself had arrived in our midst driving a gleaming Chevrolet.

'This is Joe – Josephine… Miss Colbert,' I corrected myself. 'We met earlier this week when I was distributing pamphlets in the city.'

'Maybelle was wonderfully persuasive. I was quite struck by her passion,' Joe said entirely straight-faced, and I frowned, wondering whether she was sincere, wondering at her motives for being here. It was no surprise that she knew where I lived – she'd insisted on driving me home after the party and, my lips loosened by illicit liquor, I'd told her all about Aunt Ida and Uncle Henry and their missionary zeal – but the last thing I'd expected was for her to appear at Sunday service. Had I left something behind at Hayvenhurst? Did she intend to expose my late-night escapade?

'Excellent, Maybelle,' Uncle Henry congratulated me. 'Well, Miss Colbert, you're most welcome to join us in the humble worship of our glorious Father and His only son, Jesus Christ, who died that we might be re-born, and you couldn't have picked a better day, for today we have a baptism. Our new sister Marisol is freely and openly choosing to publicly proclaim her faith in Christ – oh, happy day! Marisol! Marisol, come over here.'

More introductions were made and I could do nothing but stare dumbly whilst Joe, the very model of politeness, laughed at Uncle Henry's jokes and exchanged a few words in Spanish with Marisol and could probably have charmed the birds from the trees had she so desired.

'Do take a seat,' I became aware of Uncle Henry saying. 'We'll be starting shortly.'

'You're staying?' I burst out.

'Why else would she be here?' Uncle Henry chuckled, taking Joe's arm and steering her towards the barn.

Her presence wrong-footed me and, as the service began, I found myself stealing glances at her, trying to determine what she made of it all. It felt surreal to see her here, amongst the cows and affirmations.

'...and Marisol has professed Christ as her Saviour, and she will make that commitment in front of all of us – we are honoured to share that eternal joy with her today...'

Uncle Henry was in his element, revelling in the larger audience and the sound of his own voice, as the service continued interminably. He was undoubtedly an impassioned and knowledgeable speaker, but I was quite unable to concentrate.

'...for according to Scripture – the very words written in the Good Book and the only authority for faith – we are buried with Him through baptism into death in order that, just as Christ was raised from the dead through the glory of the Father, we too may live a new life...'

Some of the converts were called upon to give their own testimony – Billy spoke, quietly yet earnestly – and Joe appeared to be listening attentively, spine rigid, not flagging in the heat like so many of the worshippers. Even during the baptism itself, when the entire congregation filed outside to the enormous stone trough that the men had filled that morning, when Uncle Henry and Marisol climbed into the water and Henry said the words and Marisol was fully immersed, Joe remained alert and seemingly absorbed.

She made a generous donation to the collection plate and,

when it was all over, Uncle Henry made a beeline for her. I went to intervene, hearing my name as I approached:

'…And so I was wondering, Reverend Walker – it may seem an odd request, but I really was so impressed by Maybelle's… fervour when I spoke to her the other day – and I'm going to meet my sewing circle this afternoon. We're a small group of highly respectable, high-minded women—'

'—But of course,' interjected Henry.

'—Who gather once a week for needlework and Bible study, and I wondered whether I might possibly borrow Maybelle. I feel the ladies would be extremely interested in her, and in what she has to say.'

I looked from one to the other in astonishment, wondering how on earth Uncle Henry would react.

'My dear lady, that sounds like a wonderful proposition,' he beamed, eyes lighting up at the prospect of a dozen converts in the mould of the refined Miss Colbert. 'And would Maybelle suffice, or might you need my help? I flatter myself that my disposition – particularly with ladies – is sufficiently delicate that—'

'That's very kind of you, but it's really not necessary.' Joe turned to me and smiled. 'I'm sure Maybelle can handle us all.'

~

Ten minutes later we were cruising through Los Feliz in Joe's Chevy, my hair streaming out behind me like the American flag and growing messier by the mile. I found myself giggling uncontrollably.

'I can't believe you came. I can't believe you did that. I can't believe... I can't believe it!'

'For a woman of faith, you're sorely lacking,' Joe said archly, making me laugh all over again.

'So where are you taking me? Who are we going to meet?'

'I'm taking you back to Hayvenhurst, of course. The Garden of Alla. Some of the women you met at the party will be there, and some new faces too. It'll be fun. Most Sundays Alla has guests over, and everyone gathers around the pool. Would you like to borrow a bathing suit? Or you can go without, no one will mind.'

I wondered whether she was being serious, but her expression gave nothing away. I felt the heat flame in my cheeks, exasperated with myself for being embarrassed by a playful comment clearly made in jest, abashed by my own greenness. Yet I was unable to hide my blushes at the boldness of Joe's suggestion, the intimation of something so scandalous.

I watched her as she drove, not really understanding why she'd shown up today but thrilled that she had, flattered that a woman like this had apparently taken me under her wing. Her chin was raised, her profile strong, and I couldn't help noticing the soft curves of her body beneath her dress, her thighs mere inches from mine on the tan leather seats. Joe glanced across and smiled; I fought the instinct to look away and smiled back, a sudden moment of undiluted happiness as we sped through the hazy landscape beneath the blazing sun, passing fields and farms and the distant San Gabriel mountains.

'You're not angry with me, are you? For spiriting you away under false pretences? You'll have a good time, I promise you.'

'No, I'm not angry,' I said truthfully. 'Not at all.'

Not long afterwards we turned off the main road onto the rough track that led to Hayvenhurst. It was the first time I'd seen the property in daylight and the grounds were spectacular, lush with orange and avocado trees, mimosas and hibiscus and a magnificent rose garden stocked with more than a dozen different species. I felt nervous suddenly, amazed that I'd previously arrived alone and awed at my own courage. But then I'd had no idea of what lay in store, ignorant of the calibre of the other guests; Joe had since regaled me with tales of the actors and directors and producers who frequented Alla's parties and I saw how naïve I'd been.

I followed Joe through the house and out to the pool. The property felt more familiar to me now, but I could feel my habitual shyness returning as we drew closer to the shrieks and splashes.

'Joe!' Alla caught sight of us, calling out, 'And Maybelle. How wonderful to see you again.'

Joe strolled across, kissing her on both cheeks in a manner I found very sophisticated. I mumbled my hello and did the same, flustered by the unfamiliar gesture but overjoyed that she'd remembered me. She cut a dashing figure, reclining on a lounger, not in a bathing costume but shorts and a halter top, smoking a cigarette from a long black holder.

Once again I was struck by how, despite her diminutive stature, Alla dominated the proceedings. Every eye seemed to gravitate in her direction, unconsciously seeking her approval, and she had a real sense of presence.

'Sit down, darlings,' she encouraged us, in that unique accent which I now knew was the product of a childhood lived all over Europe. 'Joe, what a perfectly drab dress.'

'My dearest Alla, I've spent the morning at church, repenting my sins.'

'Church?' Alla couldn't have sounded more surprised if Joe had said she'd spent the morning on the moon. 'Truly, it's a miracle! Or perhaps you were visited by an angel...' she finished thoughtfully, her gaze settling on me.

Around the swimming pool, twenty or so women were lounging, swimming, frolicking. They were the height of glamour to my unworldly eyes, and some of their bathing suits were daringly risqué: shorts cut high on long, shapely legs; spaghetti straps displaying slender shoulders; necklines low enough to reveal décolletage. Hair was tied up prettily in patterned scarves, doe eyes peeking out from beneath floral sunhats.

I thought back to the bathing suit with matching cap I'd worn back home, the one that lay buried in the bottom drawer of my dresser and hadn't seen the light of day since last summer. I hadn't brought it with me when I moved to California, and now I was glad; it was baggy and black, with a high neck and knee-length bloomers, designed to camouflage and conceal the contours of the body. Here the women were flouting convention, pushing boundaries with costumes that fitted closely, showing shape and skin.

I'd recently read a newspaper article about women in Chicago who'd been arrested for wearing "abbreviated" bathing suits, the leg length measured by officious male police officers and found wanting. Beside Alla's inviting pool, the girls appeared to care little for the indecent exposure laws, and I was both shocked by their boldness and envious at their lack of self-consciousness. Once again, I felt out of place in my simple cotton dress, dirty and dishevelled from the ceremony preparation, hair unbrushed and skin flushed from the sun.

'You found her then?'

It was my Good Samaritan from the other night, looking completely different in a striped black-and-white bathing suit, but still with the same round spectacles.

'Yes,' I smiled. 'Or rather, she found me, this time.'

'Lucky her. I'm Gloria, by the way.'

'Maybelle.'

She pulled up a wicker chair and sat down beside me. 'So, Maybelle, what's your story?'

'My story, ma'am?'

'Yes. That delicious southern accent doesn't sound as though you were born and raised in California.'

She smiled at me, and I could sense that the others were watching us, my reply hesitant and self-conscious. 'That's correct. I grew up on a farm in Kentucky, with my momma and daddy and two older brothers.'

'I see.' Gloria didn't push any further, perhaps sensing my reticence. 'And do you work in pictures too? Let me guess – aspiring actress?'

'Oh no. Not at all!'

'Maybelle's only ever seen one movie her whole life,' Joe chimed in, as she lit a cigarette from the tip of Alla's. 'Isn't that right?'

'Yes, ma'am.'

'Well then you must see your second tonight,' said Alla. 'You're staying for the screening, yes?'

'Screening?'

'Alla's having an advance viewing of her latest picture,'

Gloria explained. 'It's called *Stronger than Death* and it's a romance, believe it or not, set in India.'

'We'll begin at seven,' Alla added. 'I have more friends coming, and I'd love you to stay, Maybelle.'

She had this way of looking at people, such intensity in those enormous dark eyes. I glanced across at Joe, who smiled and shrugged, intimating that it was my decision. 'It would be an honour, ma'am,' I heard myself saying. In truth, I had no idea how I would explain my coming home so late to Aunt Ida and Uncle Henry, but here, with the birds singing and the cicadas buzzing and the women cavorting, it was oh so easy to forget about real life.

'So if you're not an actress, how do you spend your days?' asked Gloria. The question was kindly meant, but I could see one or two of the other women glancing across, their stares scrutinising and not altogether friendly.

'I… Well, nothing as such. I live with my aunt and uncle in Atwater and help out on their farm. My uncle's a Southern Baptist pastor. He's trying to establish a congregation out here and… well, I guess you could say I help out with that too.'

'Ah, so you're a God-fearing woman.'

'I… I guess I am…'

'Southern Baptist…' Alla was looking thoughtful. 'What do they believe?'

'Well, ma'am, we believe that every person must profess the Lord Jesus Christ to be their saviour before they can be baptised, which means we don't hold with baptising babies. We believe in baptism by immersion, so—'

'Baptism by immersion? Like this?' A dark-haired girl who'd been sitting nearby, listening, ran over to the diving board, jumped once and executed a perfect dive before emerging from the depths, her short hair slicked back, water glistening on her skin. 'I'm baptised!' she cried out. 'Born again!'

A gaggle of the girls screamed with delight, and I couldn't tell whether their laughter was at my expense.

The woman swam to the edge of the pool and climbed out, well aware that everyone was watching her. Her body was lithe, with a flat bottom and small breasts, her skin tone and features hinting at Cherokee ancestry. She wrapped herself in a towel and came over to sit on Alla's lounger, plucking the cigarette holder from her mouth and inserting it between her own lips with a triumphant expression. Alla's hand instinctively moved to rest on the woman's thigh, stroking it softly, sending rivulets of water racing over her pale skin.

Joe stood up. 'I think I'll go and change. Maybelle, would you mind giving me a hand with my dress?'

I stood up hastily, pleased to be given an excuse to leave the poolside games.

'Don't mind Jean,' said Joe, as I followed her up the tiled staircase. 'She's just jealous.'

'Of what?'

'You, of course!'

'Whatever for?'

'Well, you're ten times prettier than her for a start. But all those women out there are competing for Alla's... attention. Jean's her latest favourite – Alla brought her back from her last trip to New York, like an unwanted souvenir. Jean wants to be an actress, and Alla's persuaded Metro Pictures to put her under contract for two hundred dollars a week.'

'Two hundred dollars!' I didn't think I'd ever *seen* two hundred dollars, let alone earned that much in a single week.

'I know, it's ludicrous. Women like her are ten a penny, there's nothing special about her.'

'There... there's a lot of women here today,' I ventured.

Joe blinked, pausing a beat longer than seemed necessary before replying, 'Yes, you're right. Alla enjoys female company, and we all feel more comfortable in our bathing suits without the male of the species present, wouldn't you agree? There'll be men coming later – probably Harold Lloyd, Rudolph Valentino... And Charles, of course.'

'Who's Charles?'

'Alla's husband.' Joe laughed wickedly at the look of surprise I was unable to hide. 'Did you want to stay for the screening? They're usually fabulous affairs with fascinating people.'

'I really should be home before then.'

'But do you *want* to stay?'

I swallowed. 'Yes.'

Joe smiled. She pushed open a door to one of the rooms and gestured for me to go ahead. 'This is one of the guest bedrooms. I often use it when I'm staying here,' she explained, opening the drawers of an armoire. 'I always keep a spare bathing suit or two. Are you sure you wouldn't like to borrow one?'

'Really, I'm fine. I wouldn't feel comfortable in front of everyone.'

'You should. You have a lovely figure. Here, which do you think I should wear?' She held up two costumes: one with blue and white stripes, the other a soft peach with a narrow white waistband.

'That one,' I murmured, pointing at the peach. I couldn't help but envision how she might look in it, with those strong, firm limbs and full, rounded—

'Good choice.' Joe turned around and began to unhook her dress.

'Oh, should I—?' I stepped towards the door.

'It's fine. We're all girls together.'

I didn't want to appear prudish so I stayed where I was; equally, not wanting to seem like a voyeur, I turned my back to Joe, distracting myself by looking around at the silken bedspread, the antique wardrobe, the gilt-edged mirror. A movement caught my eye and I realised I could see Joe in the reflection; nothing inappropriate, merely the curve of her bare shoulder as her dress slipped from it. She bent to retrieve it and her reflection disappeared. I looked away, feeling inexplicably guilty.

'Would you mind giving me a hand?'

I turned to see Joe wearing the peach costume. It fitted her every bit as well as I'd imagined, though it seemed rather shocking to see so much of her on display and I felt the heat flood my face. She was attempting to tuck her hair into a matching turban, twisting awkwardly to reach the back where the shorter tufts were coming loose.

My mouth felt dry. 'Of course.'

I approached hesitantly, my fingers catching the fine wisps of auburn hair at the nape of her neck, gently pushing them up beneath her headpiece and running a fingertip underneath to secure it. I wondered if she was cold as her skin had puckered into goosebumps. I realised I was holding my breath, lest an exhalation break the moment, and my eyelids fluttered, intoxicated by her proximity, the sensation drawing me back to a hot summer's night when—

'All done?' asked Joe, and her voice seemed to catch in her throat.

'All done,' I confirmed.

'Thank you.' Joe turned round without stepping back and then we were standing face to face, so close that you could barely slide a nickel between us. She was an inch or two taller than me and our eyes were almost level, breath merging with breath as I inhaled the faint, delicious scent of the gin and lime she'd been drinking by the pool. I felt a tightening in my stomach, my lips parting involuntarily.

'We'd better re-join the party,' Joe murmured. 'Alla will be wondering where we are.'

She moved away and I was left suddenly bereft, every sense denied its stimulation. I shook my head, gathering myself, and followed her from the room.

Chapter Six

ALLA

Yalta, Crimea, 1889

'Wait here.'

Yakov stalked off down the corridor, disappearing through a door and leaving Alla alone in the entrance hall. Her father's new house was certainly grand: there were carved stone pillars and ornate mouldings skirting the elaborate ceiling; thick Persian rugs and a life-sized oil painting of the owner whose cold, disapproving eyes looked down on his youngest daughter. Yakov had made his fortune in the three years since Alla had last seen him; he'd spent the journey from Zurich to Yalta telling her how he'd invented medicated soap, how he'd sold it to the government and they'd rewarded him with medals and wealth and made him an honorary citizen of Yalta.

On trains and in hotel rooms, right across Imperial Russia, Yakov had ranted and raved to his youngest daughter about how he hadn't been taken seriously for years, that he'd always known he would achieve greatness but had been consistently underestimated. He'd expounded his personal history whilst Alla had sat quietly and listened, telling her how he'd grown up in the Pale of Settlement, the western region of the Russian Empire where Jews were confined by Russian law.

Alla's paternal grandfather, Urish, had been an illiterate miller, and Yakov spoke in scathing terms about his impoverished upbringing and his father's lack of ambition. Urish, however, had had the foresight to send his five children to school, and Yakov had gone on to study chemistry at the University of Kiev. Despite his degree, Yakov was the least successful of his siblings in a family which now included two surgeons and a lawyer, and had had to content himself with a poorly paid job as a pharmacy assistant in Berdichev, dedicating himself to his "inventions" in his spare time.

As the years passed, Yakov grew increasingly miserable and bitter – and violent – about his lack of success. If Alla had expected that he might have mellowed now his ambitions had been realised, she was wrong. The journey from Switzerland had been as unpleasant as ever, her father flying into rages over the smallest misdemeanour, boxing her ears when she finally plucked up the courage to ask about her mother.

Yakov had said he was taking Alla "home", but she had no childhood memories of Yalta and didn't consider this pretty city on the Black Sea to be her home. He'd proudly declared that he owned one of the palatial houses on the edge of town, newly built and overlooking the harbour, his neighbours affluent and important people. But already Alla knew that the Groelichs' cramped, chaotic, ramshackle cottage had been more of a home to her than Yakov's mansion could ever be.

Footsteps echoed in the distance and Alla stiffened. The door re-opened and Yakov stood there, a tall, thin woman with a pinched face and a sour expression at his side. She wore an ugly, high-necked dress of brown silk, and she carried a bundle in her arms.

No one spoke, the long walk towards Alla conducted in silence. They stopped in front of her.

'This is my wife,' Yakov said.

'You may call me Aunt Dasha.' She bent down, offering her cheek to Alla who was too shocked to do anything except kiss it, as was expected of her. 'And this is Valentin. We call him Valya.'

Alla looked at the baby squirming in Dasha's arms. She wondered briefly how babies were made; Gretl had told her all kinds of wild stories and she had no idea whether or not they were true. She thought how different Dasha was from her own mama – or, at least, the hazy memories she retained of her mother. Dasha looked mean and peevish and joyless, words she'd never associate with Sonya.

Alla swallowed. 'Hello…' she began, but Yakov turned and walked away, Dasha beside him. Not knowing what else to do, Alla followed.

'This is the door to my pharmacy – it will remain locked at all times,' Yakov explained as they passed through the house. 'And you are forbidden to enter. Do not open the windows, the sea air is bad for Dasha's chest. Do not make a noise, my wife is not to be disturbed. Never enter our bedroom, never enter Valya's nursery, use the servant's entrance should you need access to the garden. And do not speak to the servants.'

'Where is my room?' Alla asked.

They had almost reached the end of another long hall, far from the blazing fires and plush furnishings of Yakov's quarters. Here it was cold and damp and musty, a moth-eaten curtain hanging limply from the wall. Yakov pulled it aside to reveal a small alcove with a child's cot bed pushed into the narrow space.

'You will sleep here. If you close the curtain and remain silent, you won't disturb anyone.'

Alla opened her mouth to speak, but Dasha interrupted: 'Can't she be quiet? She's giving me a migraine.'

'Get in,' Yakov barked. 'If you make a sound, I'll beat you.'

Alla climbed onto the cot and Yakov closed the curtains. She sat in the dark, listening to the sound of their footsteps fade away.

The mansion became Alla's prison. She was rarely allowed out; her father had decreed that the local schools were not of an acceptable standard for the daughter of such a prominent citizen, and instead engaged a series of tutors. He spent most of his time in the pharmacy, Dasha routinely afflicted by some ailment and resting in her room, so between lessons Alla would explore the house, pressing her face against the sea salt-encrusted windows, watching the world go by without her. She found Yalta charming and picturesque, but hated it at the same time, loathing all that it had come to represent – the loss of her freedom, oppression by her father.

Alla believed she would even have welcomed the presence of her siblings – if not as allies, at least to ward off the tedium –

but Nina was at boarding school, and Volodya had been sent to a military academy in Riga, all three of them at the mercy of Yakov's whims. Instead, Alla found solace in novels, reading curled up on her cot bed, curtains shut tight against reality. And she defied her father's rules to spend time with Melanya, the Russian-speaking maid, and the one person in the household who was kind to her.

At times, Alla found herself wondering why Yakov had brought her to Yalta. He didn't seem to like her, let alone love her, and treated her as little more than an inconvenience. Sparing no consideration for her feelings, he'd told her it was because no one else wanted her. Ten-year-old Alla reflected on his words and wondered if that were true and, if she were really so unlikeable and unlovable, what could she do to change that, to make people like her? Perhaps she'd need to transform into someone else entirely if she were to have any chance of happiness in the future.

From behind the closed windows, wrapped up in the heavy silk curtains, Alla watched the seasons pass by: the sea cresting and the crocuses blooming in spring; the long, hot summer when the tourists came to town and the boardwalks were overrun, before mellowing into the coolness of autumn as the streets grew quieter once again.

Alla had lived in the big house for over a year, approaching her second Christmas there. One evening, the family were eating dinner, the dining room silent save for the chink of cutlery on the china plates. Dasha no longer spoke to Alla, preferring to disregard her existence, and Alla spent her days mute, trying to avoid a whipping. Today, however, she had a question to ask. Alla picked at her food, unable to sit still, trying to judge her father's mood and choose the moment when he might be most amenable to her request.

'Sit up straight, child, you're turning into an ugly little hunchback. And stop shuffling or I'll beat you.'

Alla fought the instinct to fidget, obediently eating her boiled beef until she could hold it in no longer: 'Papa, Professor Savelson has invited me to play in his Christmas concert at the Hotel Russiya. He thinks I'm good enough. Do I have your permission?'

Yakov's fork halted in mid-air, speared French bean dangling like a flaccid moustache. Dasha's mouth hung open, masticated meat on display to the room. Slowly, Yakov put his fork back down, staring hard at Alla. She wondered if he was about to box her ears and instinctively recoiled.

'What did you say?'

'Professor Savelson – my violin tutor – would like to include me in the programme for his Christmas concert. But of course, you'd have to give your permission. May I? Please, Papa?'

She was trying not to beg, but her face gave away how badly she wanted to take part. Yakov glanced at his wife and Alla knew he was torn; his dream had always been for her to become a virtuoso and perform all over Europe, while he basked in the reflected glory. But he was loath to agree to anything that might bring his daughter pleasure or enjoyment.

'If I say yes,' he began slowly, 'then your performance must be perfect. I don't want you bringing shame upon the family.'

'Oh, it will be Papa, I promise. I'll practise every night!'

'More of that infernal racket,' muttered Dasha.

Yakov considered her response. 'I don't believe you. You'll

embarrass yourself and disgrace my good name. I'm a man of standing in this city – people respect me. Imagine if it became known that Yakov Leventon's dim-witted daughter had played badly in front of the dignitaries and governors, that she'd forgotten her notes and butchered a beautiful sonata. I could never show my face again. The answer is no. I absolutely forbid it.'

'Please, Papa!' Alla was distraught. 'It is a great honour to be invited, and Professor Savelson believes I'm ready. I won't make a single mistake, I swear to you.'

Yakov behaved as though she hadn't spoken. He continued to eat, the room lapsing back into silence, as Alla toyed miserably with her food but couldn't bring herself to eat another bite. She felt broken-hearted, sick to her stomach that the only thing she'd truly cared about in a very long time had been snatched away from her on a spiteful whim. It was bitterly unfair.

Yakov finished his dessert, wiping his mouth on his napkin, letting out a satisfied belch before sitting back in his chair. He stared thoughtfully at his daughter who refused to meet his gaze.

'I will allow you to take part, on one condition.'

Alla's demeanour changed in an instant and she sat bolt upright, prepared to agree to anything.

'You must change your name. You don't deserve to call yourself a Leventon. If and when you're good enough, then you may have the honour of using my name, but not before.'

'Of course. As you wish, Papa.' Alla's tone was contrite, but inside she was ecstatic. And she already knew exactly what name she would use.

Alla felt nauseous. The room was too small, the air filled with the rasping sound of violins being tuned and the overwhelming smell of rosin. Savelson's pupils were crammed into a drab antechamber beside the ballroom in the Hotel Russiya. There were fifteen of them in total, all older than Alla and all male, and their nerves were infectious, passed around the room quicker than scarlet fever.

Ephraim Savelson approached. He was pale, slim and tubercular, in his late twenties, an immensely talented musician whose career had been blighted by his ill health. 'How are you feeling?' he asked.

Alla's face was white, her stomach in knots, and she cradled her violin in her arms like a newborn. Outside she could hear the low hum of chatter and expectation as the audience filed into the auditorium. 'Petrified.'

'Don't be. You're a born performer.'

'They're all older than me.'

'I'll tell you a secret.' Savelson bent down, smiling, and whispered in her ear, 'You're better than all of them.'

'I don't believe you!'

'It's the truth. And to prove it, you will give the final performance. Your solo will be the climax of the concert.'

He smiled once again and moved on, leaving Alla more apprehensive than ever, her heart pounding, the room swimming in and out of focus as though she might faint.

Savelson was true to his word. One by one, the boys were called to the stage as Alla listened to their near-flawless performances, the hearty cheers and applause they each received before returning, relieved and triumphant. Alla's nerves mounted as the minutes ticked by, certain that she would be the one to disappoint Savelson. She could almost see the scorn in her father's eyes, imagining herself blinking dumbly in the lights like a frightened animal, arms hanging uselessly at her sides, her fingers refusing to function.

When "Adelaida Nazimova" was announced, Alla didn't move. She'd worked herself into such a state of anxiety that she'd completely forgotten her adopted name, and Savelson had to repeat himself three times before she finally realised, rushing onto the stage to a ripple of smothered laughter. Alla had recently read a Russian novel entitled *Children of the Streets* and the heroine was called Nadvezdha Nazimova; to Alla's ears the moniker sounded glamorous, sophisticated, magical, and so it was that Adelaida Nazimova was born.

She took up her position centre-stage, behind the music stand that Savelson had lowered especially for her, and looked out over the assembled crowd. The ballroom was large and only the stage was illuminated, but she picked out Yakov and Dasha a few rows from the front. They were purse-lipped and stony-faced, but their expectation of her failure only hardened her resolve to prove them wrong. She straightened her spine, tucked her instrument under her chin, and raised the bow.

Alla was only ten years old but she played like a dream, a vision in the festive green velvet dress that Yakov had bought for the occasion; he was determined that her appearance, at least, wouldn't be a source of humiliation. Alla performed two popular pieces – *Regrets* by Vieuxtemps and *Légende* by Wieniawski – and the watching crowd were spellbound. Alla herself was wholly absorbed in the music, dimly aware of the effect she was having but lost in the performance. She was note perfect, but it was so much more than that – she brought soul and emotion to the music, her whole body suffused with the spirit of the compositions.

As the last note rang out, the reaction surpassed anything Alla had envisaged. The audience rose to their feet with shouts of "Bravo" and "Encore", as she spontaneously took a bow, and then another, growing pink with pleasure. She stole a glance at her father and his wife; they, too, had given her a standing ovation and were clapping wildly – to do otherwise would have seemed peculiar, but could they possibly have enjoyed it? Might Yakov have been impressed by her performance and proud of his youngest daughter?

Professor Savelson stepped from the wings to stand beside Alla and the two of them took a final bow, before he held up a hand for quiet and began to say a few words. A movement at the back of the room caught Alla's attention: a woman wearing a red winter coat, with lustrous dark hair and a beautiful face. Alla reacted instinctively.

'Mama!' she cried out, cutting off her tutor mid-sentence. '*Mamochka!*'

Alla scrambled down from the stage, leaving her violin behind, as she ran down the aisle to the woman, everyone turning to look at the commotion. As Alla reached her, she realised it wasn't Sonya – the woman's face was too round, her eyes the wrong colour – and she stopped, cheeks flaming, but the woman laughed gaily and embraced her, congratulating Alla on her performance as the crowd clapped and murmured how sweet.

The stranger smelt of peppermint and cough drops – quite

different from Sonya – but the sensation of being held, of being loved and secure, was delightful, and Alla lingered in her arms. The moment was broken by a painful grip on her wrist that caused her to cry out, and Alla was sharply pulled away. She opened her eyes to see Yakov and Dasha looming over her.

'That's quite enough, Alla. Time to go now.'

Yakov yanked her hand once again, pulling her out of the ballroom, leaving the lights and the warmth and the applause far behind.

No one spoke during the carriage ride home. The winter night was bitterly cold, but the cloudless sky was littered with stars and the moon reflecting on the water was breathtaking.

When they reached the house, Dasha went straight to bed, alleging that the awful screeching had given her a migraine. Still Yakov said nothing.

'How did I do, Papa?' Alla ventured. She witnessed how the crowd had reacted, and she believed Professor Savelson's words when he'd whispered that she'd played superbly. 'Everyone clapped for me, did you see, Papa?'

He looked at her, his expression blank, then began to take off his belt.

Alla yelped in fright. 'No, Papa! What did I do? I was good, didn't you see? I was—' She broke off with a scream as the first lash struck the top of her arm, a searing pain as though she'd been burned.

'Please, Papa, please!'

The back of her legs this time, and the pain brought the tears.

'Just because a few provincial fools applaud you, don't imagine you're Paganini,' Yakov spat.

Now across her shoulder blades, then her buttocks, then the buckle to her face and then it all became a blur as Yakov gave his daughter the worst beating of her life, discarding the belt and using his fists, his feet, a lamp from the side table as she screamed for help but no one came to her aid.

'...Stupid... ugly... embarrassment... bringing shame on the family...'

The words were almost as painful as the blows.

'...You'll be sent away... The sight of you makes me sick...'

The accompanying blow was heavier than the rest but then, miraculously, the violence seemed to stop. Alla squinted, her vision blurry, and saw Yakov staggering backwards. His face looked peculiar, as though it were drooping on one side, and he was blinking repeatedly, seemingly confused. He clutched his head with a cry of pain and almost tripped over his own feet.

'Papa?' Alla's tone was tentative, fearful that this might be a trick.

Yakov's eyes met hers, his expression terrified, then he collapsed on the carpet with a thud.

Chapter Seven

MAYBELLE

Los Angeles, USA, 1919

I woke early on Christmas morning. Outside it was barely light, still and peaceful, and I lay warm beneath my blankets. And then I remembered.

I crept out of bed and stole over to my wardrobe, removing the small package I'd hidden beneath a pile of old fabric. It was beautifully wrapped in white tissue paper and tied with gold ribbon, and there was no label on it, but Joe had given it to me the last time I saw her and told me to save it for Christmas Day.

We'd fallen into a routine in recent weeks; Joe would attend the Sunday service and afterwards we'd leave together in her car, bound for the Garden of Alla. Uncle Henry and Aunt Ida were blissfully blind to the situation, believing I was meeting Josephine's sewing circle – a like-minded group of unassuming, virtuous women – for Bible study and needlework. Joe played her role perfectly for, despite my aunt and uncle professing their indifference to such worldly concerns, there was no doubt that her being well dressed and well spoken, monied and sophisticated appealed greatly to them, and she took care to dress modestly yet stylishly, to appear knowledgeable yet never to undermine Uncle Henry.

In truth, I felt as though I were living a double life. I lived for those Sunday afternoons, playing backgammon or chequers or card games around the swimming pool, watching movies in Alla's screening room, drinking cocktails and discussing theatre and literature and politics. It was an entirely new world for me, and my ignorance was undeniable, but I was slowly becoming brave enough to formulate and voice my own opinions, to believe that I had something worthwhile to offer the conversation. I discovered a love for sketching and for design, and my eyes were opened to new experiences – arts and culture and history and... other things.

Alla herself was endlessly fascinating. I loved to hear her speak about her career and her travels: she'd performed on stage in London, New York, Moscow and Berlin; spent a summer living in Paris; toured the US from north to south and coast to coast. She could be reticent at first, unwilling to open up about herself, but then the actress in her would take over and she would share the most wonderful stories, bringing them to life with impersonations and gestures.

And Joe was... indescribable. My feelings for her were a source of continual confusion because—

No, there was no confusion. I adored her. She was funny and charming and attentive and smart as a whip and... I could go on, indefinitely, listing those qualities that drew me to her like a moth to a candle. She possessed my every thought. At night I lay awake, thinking of her, longing for sleep to release me, only to dream of her. Sometimes, when I could resist no longer, I found my own release, afterwards drenched with sweat and racked with guilt, washing my hands repeatedly, terrified lest someone should detect my own scent on my fingers.

I gently stroked the stiff fabric of the ribbon, pulled the ends taut and it fell away. I unfolded the tissue paper, my excitement mounting, and there lay a small book with an exquisite marbled cover in shades of blue. There was no title and no author name, but it was clearly antique as the print had faded and the once-cream paper had been cut by hand. I flicked through the pages and saw it was a book of poetry, lingering over passages that caught my eye:

> As a wind in the mountains
> assaults an oak,
> Love shook my breast
>
> For even if she flees, soon she shall pursue.
> And if she refuses gifts, soon she shall give them.
> If she doesn't love you, soon she shall love
> even if she's unwilling.
>
> For when I look at you even for a short time,
> it is no longer possible for me to speak
> but my tongue is frozen in silence
> and immediately a subtle fire runs over my skin.

The last of these made me catch my breath. There couldn't

be a truer description of how I felt when I saw Joe – my words sticking in my throat, a hot flame of desire setting my body ablaze. Was it possible that she felt the same? That these unspoken, unacknowledged feelings that had consumed me of late might be understood – perhaps even reciprocated?

I thumbed through the book again, a beacon of hope newly ignited. I felt dazed, drunk on optimism, impatient to see Joe again. But then the niggling doubts crept in and I worried that I'd misinterpreted the situation, that she was nothing more than a generous friend giving a thoughtful gift of pretty poetry.

I knew I wouldn't see her today. We had a busy time ahead of us, with the Christmas Day service – likely to be a long one, as Uncle Henry had been working on his festive sermon for some weeks – and we were cooking for the congregation and for any poor folk who might stop by. I'd hoped Joe would drop in, but she'd already told me it was unlikely.

There was a knock at the door and panic swept over me. I hastily pulled up the blankets and hid the book beneath them.

'Good mornin', Maybelle.'

It was Herb's voice. My stomach clenched in revulsion as I wondered how long he'd been standing there, listening, waiting, whilst I was lost in my reveries of Joe. What on earth did he want? It felt highly inappropriate for him to be visiting my bedroom, surely crossing some unspoken boundary.

'Yes?' I replied snappishly, certain that I must sound queer and guilty.

'Your aunt sent me to hurry you along as she's real busy. Needs your help right away she said.'

I could hear the smile on his face as he spoke, could picture that lazy grin that made my flesh crawl. I composed myself before replying, 'Of course. I'll be right out.'

I froze for a moment, straining to hear his retreating footsteps, but I heard nothing and some instinct told me he was still there. Noiselessly, I swung my feet out of bed and stepped onto the rug, feeling vulnerable in my thin nightdress and undergarments.

'Merry Christmas, Maybelle.'

Herb's voice came once again and I jumped, my heart racing, instinctively folding my hands across my body as though for protection.

The words stuck in my throat as I replied, 'Merry Christmas.'

It was almost a week until I saw Joe, and the separation coupled with anticipation was a sweet torture. My days had been occupied with all the extra work on the farm, but my mind was free to roam and my thoughts inevitably came back to her. Last thing at night, I read and re-read the book of poetry, poring over lines, trying to detect hidden meanings in the words. One passage expressed my agony with a particular poignancy:

> Come to me now once again and release me
> from gruelling anxiety.
> All that my heart longs for,
> fulfil. And be yourself my ally in love's battle.

I was counting the days until we were reunited. Incredibly, Uncle Henry and Aunt Ida had granted me permission – albeit grudgingly – to attend a New Year's Eve party with Joe and the women of the sewing circle, the pretext being that we would have a quiet evening to welcome the new decade, and that Joe would drop me home shortly after the clock struck midnight. In reality, of course, we were spending the evening at Alla's. She'd promised the party to end all parties, and I trusted her to deliver.

I'd been giddy and distracted all day, working myself into a feverish state by the time eight o'clock rolled around and Joe's arrival was imminent. She was late and I worried that she wasn't coming at all as I took up residence beside the parlour window, skittish as a newly born colt until I spotted the headlamps in the distance. Joe knocked on the door and was invited in, conversing with Henry and Ida in her most reassuring tones. Yes, she would drive carefully. No, of course there wouldn't be alcohol, it was prohibited in the state of California. Yes, she would set off home as soon as the clock struck midnight. No, there wouldn't be any men present, just a small, sober gathering of Los Angeles' most upstanding female citizens.

'See you in 1920!' I couldn't resist yelling as we drove off, Uncle Henry and Aunt Ida waving from the porch and looking increasingly concerned.

Alone with Joe, I found myself tongue-tied, a peculiar tension between us.

'Thank you for my Christmas gift,' I managed.

'Thank you for mine.'

I'd given her a set of handkerchiefs, which I'd embroidered

with a "J" in each corner; I liked to think she'd see the humour in the present, in light of the alibi we'd presented. But it felt underwhelming after the gift she'd given me, and I told her so.

'I'm just happy you liked it.'

'I loved it.'

'Good.' Joe's hands gripped the steering wheel, encased in chic calfskin driving gloves. The roads were busy, the city on the move as everyone hurried to their parties and their loved ones. 'The poems were written by a Greek writer, Sappho. Have you heard of her?' I shook my head, and Joe looked amused. 'She was writing around six hundred years before the birth of Christ. You should find out more about her.'

'I will.' I wanted to say something more – something about how extraordinary it was that a woman writing over two and a half thousand years ago could produce words about human emotions that were every bit as relevant to me today. But I said nothing, and we lapsed into silence, and there was that tension once again.

'Damn,' Joe swore.

'What's the matter?'

'I bought a gift for Alla – a bottle of Ruinart. It's her favourite champagne, and almost impossible to get hold of right now, with the restrictions. I've forgotten to bring it.'

'Oh.'

'Would you mind terribly if we went back for it? I'd hate to turn up empty-handed.'

'No, of course not.'

'You're a sweetheart. Hold on.'

Joe swung the steering wheel to the left, making a sharp U-turn in the middle of the street as the traffic honked and I slid across the seat, almost ending up in her lap, the two of us laughing like fools.

Joe lived in a bungalow on North Gower Street in Hollywood. It was painted pale blue, with a white porch, and a small, neat front yard. I stayed in the car, thinking Joe would run in to pick up the bottle, but she said: 'Come on in! I can't leave you all alone in the street on New Year's Eve. Someone will steal you.'

I followed her up the flagstone path, realising I was more than a little intrigued to see where she lived, to discover the smallest details about this woman who'd unexpectedly become one of the most important people in my life.

Inside, Joe switched on a few lamps and I looked around. Where Alla's house was extravagant and Aunt Ida's taste was homely, Joe's style was minimal and modern. Her furniture was all dark wood and sleek lines, with an elegant cream couch and a wide desk piled high with books and papers, pride of place in the centre given to a handsome Underwood typewriter. There were framed Aubrey Beardsley prints on the walls, an overflowing bookshelf, and a stylish gramophone with a stack of 78s beside it.

'It's so nice, so elegant,' I murmured, taking everything in.

'I'm glad you like it.' Joe disappeared into the kitchenette and I browsed the pile of records. I'd never heard of any of them, but that wasn't surprising – I'd been raised in a small town where no one cared about what was fashionable or modern, and my knowledge of popular culture had been non-existent until I started spending time at Alla's. Some of the songs were in another language, words and names I didn't understand.

'Got it,' Joe called, as she came back through brandishing the bottle. She looked at the record I was holding, *La Coco* by Emma Liébel, declaring, 'Oh, that's one of my favourites!', before taking it from me and pulling it out of the sleeve. She wound up the gramophone, dropped the needle, and soon the scratchy sound of a brass overture filled the room. It was an upbeat tune, the singer's voice expressive and wistful. Joe lit a cigarette and let her hips sway to the music. I watched, mesmerised.

'Shall we have a drink before we leave?' Joe suggested. I hadn't even replied before she sashayed across to her drinks cabinet, preparing two gins with tonic water and plenty of lime. 'What shall we toast to?'

'The new decade,' I suggested.

'To the new decade – new friends and new beginnings.'

We held eye contact as we touched glasses and Joe began to dance once more, the beading on her dress reflected in the lights a hundred times over, a dazzling goddess spinning across the star-spangled night.

'I feel so plain next to you,' I laughed, indicating the pale floral dress I was wearing. Aunt Ida had made it as my Christmas gift and, whilst it was wonderful to have something new, the style she'd chosen was undoubtedly old-fashioned.

'You can borrow something of mine if you like. We're about the same size – although your hips are slimmer than mine, your bust a little larger.' Her gaze lingered and I flushed. 'Come with me.'

She stubbed out her cigarette and took my hand in that

commanding way she had, the way that made my stomach flip over.

Her bedroom was darker than the main room, the décor more sultry but just as tasteful, with black and gold the predominant colours. It was messier than the rest of the house too, as though in her private domain she could allow herself to relax more than her disciplined public persona might suggest. It felt strange to be in her bedroom, undeniably intimate, and I stood there awkwardly as she encouraged me to look through her belongings.

Her closet was a riot of colours and textures, tassels and feathers and ribbons. There was also, I noticed, a selection of trousers and men's shirts, waistcoats and jackets. Joe pulled out various dresses, holding them up against me, her fingers skimming lightly over my waist and shoulders. Between us we chose a selection, and Joe laid them out on her bed.

'Try these. Call me if you need help.'

She walked out and I was left standing alone in her room. Feeling self-conscious, I took a slug of my drink. The house had fallen silent, the record on the gramophone having finished and leaving the needle spinning in an infinite loop, but then Joe must have selected a new song and the low, emotive tones of a woman singing about love and loss rang out.

I unhooked my dress and stepped out of it, standing in just my undergarments, acutely aware of Joe's presence in the next room. I picked up one of her dresses, cream silk with lace and mother of pearl embellishment. It smelt freshly laundered and as I fastened it, I could tell it fitted like a dream. I glanced at her dressing table, at the brushes and pots strewn across the top, at the atomiser containing the scent that instantly made me think of Joe whenever I smelt it. I picked it up, sprayed a little on my wrists, closed my eyes as I inhaled.

'How's it looking?' Joe called.

I guiltily set the perfume back down as she entered the room, a blush colouring my cheeks.

'Oh, Maybelle,' she breathed, and her eyes were soft. 'You look incredible. Now I can never wear that dress again, it looks so much better on you.' She looked at me thoughtfully.

'What's wrong?'

'No, nothing. It's just…'

She came closer and I realised I was holding my breath. She took a lock of my hair, brushing it back from my face, grabbing a handful of bobby pins from her dresser and pinning it back. She did the same with the other side and stepped back to admire the effect. 'There. That's it.'

I glanced in the mirror and barely recognised the person looking back at me. 'I look so… so…' I tailed off, unable to find the right word.

'Beautiful,' Joe finished. She reached out to smooth a stray hair and I turned my head instinctively, almost nuzzling against her hand, as her fingers trailed gently across my cheek, the tip of my nose, coming to rest on my lips. I opened my mouth just wide enough to allow a fingertip and sucked gently, tasting her for the first time. I didn't stop to think about what I was doing; I just knew that it felt right, and realised I'd longed to do this since I'd first laid eyes on her in the coffee shop, more than three months ago.

Joe murmured my name ending in something like a sigh, her amber eyes half closed, and I knew that there was no turning back – that this was the start of something we both wanted. Her hands found my waist, drawing me closer until finally, deliriously, our lips met and it seemed we'd been waiting a lifetime for this moment. Our kisses were hesitant at first, her lips pillow-soft as I'd always imagined, but the urgency and the ferocity increased, bodies pressed together with mounting need. The dress which I'd slipped on only minutes before was soon slipped off again, my hair already coming loose from the pins, as I stood before her, panting and wanton, wearing only my corset and knickers.

'You're sure?' Joe asked.

I could barely speak, barely even nod in assent, so eager for us to continue what we'd started. I thought I might die if she stopped now, and I told her so.

We undressed one another slowly, sensually, until I was finally able to see her in all her glory, to see everything that I'd only been able to imagine until now: the small breasts with their pale pink nipples; the gentle curve of her stomach; the fullness of her buttocks and the inviting fuzz of dark hair between her legs. We fell back together onto the bed, a tangle of limbs and tongues and desire, and it felt incredible that I was finally allowed to touch her in the way I'd dreamed about, that she could caress *me* in the way that had occupied my nights since we'd first met.

Her hand stole between my legs and she found me, ready and waiting for her, slick with my own juice, and she used that to her advantage, sliding over the engorged little nub that brought such pleasure, such tingling and shuddering throughout my whole body. She was merciless, not giving me a moment's respite, fingers working busily, incessantly, as my hips moved in rhythm, rubbing against the flat of her palm as she kissed my neck, her breath hot on my skin until I could resist no longer and surrendered, an explosion of stars as I moaned and cried out. She held me close until my breathing slowed and I opened my eyes, overwhelmed and sated.

We kissed tenderly, more leisurely now that the initial fire had been quenched, searching one another's faces for reassurance. But my body was still ablaze and I wanted to do something for Joe. Acting instinctively, I worked my way down her body with butterfly kisses, my tongue finding those rounded breasts and sucking on her distended nipples in a way that I knew would produce the most exquisite kind of pain. And then I moved lower, over the taut skin of her stomach, onwards past her belly button, until I could smell the musky heat of her, burying my face at the very centre of her and – oh – if it wasn't the sweetest, most exquisite thing I'd ever tasted. I slipped a finger inside her, found her accommodating and added another, then a third, those tight muscles clenching and spasming as I worked her with my hands and mouth.

She called my name as she found her release and the angels couldn't have sung a sweeter song. We collapsed against one another, wondering at this new delight, giggling and shy and euphoric.

'Happy New Year,' I whispered.

'The very best way to welcome the new decade,' Joe smiled.

We never made it to Alla's party.

Chapter Eight

ALLA

Odessa, Russia, 1894

'A nd Madame Popova said to me, "Adelaida! It is forbidden to read subversive novels. You must destroy this book immediately!" And I said, "But Madame Popova, *Fathers and Sons* is one of the most celebrated works of Russian literature. Besides, censorship is foolish because it stifles free speech and places ultimate power in the hands of the censor – which is arguably more dangerous than the ideas it's trying to suppress".

'Then Madame Popova said—' Alla pinched her mouth tightly and stooped over, wagging her finger, as she adopted a thick Ural accent. '"—Adelaida, God disapproves of insolent little girls who are far too clever for their own good." And I drew myself up and said in my most innocent voice, 'Well *your* God might, but I'm not Roman Catholic so he has no jurisdiction over me!'

Natalia and Katerina smothered their laughter as their

mother, Yelena Savchenko, shook her head, trying to hide a smile. They were sitting in the parlour in front of a roaring fire, drinking tea from the samovar in their evening ritual. Alla was on her feet, the faded rug her very own stage, as she ran through the amusing, the frustrating and the entertaining incidents that had taken place during the school day.

'Oh Alla, you're so funny. And your impressions are quite uncanny – I can just picture Madame Popova, with her hunched back and her squint eye,' Natalia giggled. She was growing extremely fond of this hilarious, rebellious, little ball of energy that had recently arrived in their lives.

'You're becoming quite the entertainer,' agreed Katerina, and Alla beamed.

'But you must try to curb your tongue,' Yelena added a warning. 'I worry you'll be expelled, and then what will your father say?'

At the mention of Yakov, Alla's good mood dissipated, her expression turning sour. He'd made good on his promise to send her to boarding school – banishing her all the way to Odessa, to an institute run by a Greek princess – something which appealed greatly to Yakov's notions of grandeur. He was no longer a well man, having suffered a stroke on the night of Alla's violin concert which had brought about a complete change of personality. Now he was lethargic and easily confused, at times unduly affectionate, and it turned Alla's stomach as he tried to stroke her hair and kiss her face. In the end, she had been relieved to be sent away.

When she arrived at the Academy of the Holy Trinity, she discovered that the other girls were predominantly from aristocratic, noble backgrounds, all Roman Catholic, all slim and pretty and dignified. Alla was none of those. She was overweight, with bad skin and frizzy hair, vociferous and headstrong and Jewish. But by playing the clown she'd won the affection and admiration of her peers, who delighted in her outrageous remarks and fearless behaviour.

A few weeks ago, there'd been a fire at the Academy – an occurrence in which, Alla could honestly say, she had absolutely no involvement – and the pupils had been sent to board with local families until the dormitories could be rebuilt.

'Do you have any homework this evening?' asked Yelena. Tiny, grey-haired and forbearing, she reminded Alla of a kindly mouse come to life. She'd been widowed for almost twenty years and devoted herself to raising her two darling daughters.

'No,' Alla lied.

Yelena looked sceptical as Natalia rose to her feet. 'Come on, upstairs to your room. We need to rehearse.'

'I could help you. I'll read in for the other characters.'

'Thank you, but Mama will do that, won't you, Mama?'

'Of course. Come on, Alla. If you finish your schoolwork quickly you can join us later. I'll make you a cup of cocoa before bed.'

Reluctantly, Alla sloped upstairs, making sure to leave the parlour door wide open so she could hear all the goings on. She sat down at her desk, opening her schoolbooks and arranging her pen and ink. She was supposed to be doing a handwriting exercise, copying a passage from *Introduction to the Devout Life* in her neatest penmanship, but a peal of laughter drifted up from the makeshift rehearsal room and Alla's concentration was instantly broken. She could make out

Natalia's high, melodious voice, followed by Yelena's lower, measured tones as she voiced the other characters in the scene. Then Katerina chimed in – she was playing the governess of Natalia's character – and Alla could resist no longer, creeping along the corridor to eavesdrop at the top of the stairs.

The entire Savchenko family loved amateur dramatics, and both sisters were performing in a new play that coming weekend. It was a love story called *The Shoemaker of Kiev*, unoriginal and badly written by a local magistrate who considered himself a budding playwright, but the girls were throwing themselves into their roles with gusto. Natalia was playing Sasha, the daughter of a rich landowner and the object of the affections of the impoverished shoemaker. She wasn't conventionally beautiful, but there was certainly something appealing in her looks, with her honey-coloured hair and dimpled cheeks and shapely figure. Katerina, at 29, was five years older than her sister, with more severe features that leant themselves to character parts, meaning she was forever cast as the aunt, the cousin, the nurse or the housekeeper.

Alla found the women, and their hobby, fascinating. The acting profession had long intrigued her; she'd once voiced the possibility of becoming an actress but Yakov had reacted furiously. Actresses were whores, he told her. No daughter of his was going to enter that line of work! But the Savchenko family – gentle and kind-hearted and wholesome – were clearly not fallen women. Alla had great respect for Yelena, the mild-mannered matriarch, and had come to think of Natalia and Katerina as sisters. She certainly preferred them to her own sister, Nina, who'd moved in with Yakov and Dasha upon finishing her schooling and treated Alla abominably. Volodya was also back living in the big house in Yalta, being paid one ruble a week to work in the pharmacy. He'd rebelled against his military training, declaring himself a pacifist, and now dreamed of being a writer like his idol, Tolstoy – an ambition Yakov inevitably deplored.

The rehearsal downstairs continued, moving on to an impassioned scene where Grigori, the titular shoemaker, declared his love for Sasha. Alla mouthed the lines along with the actors; she'd heard the play so many times that she knew it word for word, had studied Natalia so intently that she could replicate her every gesture and reaction. She was so absorbed that she didn't notice Yelena had left the room and was now staring up at her from the bottom of the narrow staircase.

'Alla?'

Alla jumped, almost pitching headfirst down the stairs. 'I'm thirsty. I was going to get a glass of water.'

Yelena sighed. 'Why don't you come and watch? We've almost finished. Then you *have* to do your schoolwork.'

'And can I read the part of the shoemaker? Please?'

'Very well.' Yelena handed over the script and Alla took it gleefully, bouncing into the parlour and taking up her position across from Natalia. She cleared her throat and adopted her most agonised expression: 'I have long admired your beauty from afar…'

'I have long admired your beauty from afar…'

The young man playing Grigori was tall and slim and pale, with floppy hair and uneven teeth. Watching him act, Alla was convinced that she could have played the role better, certain that she'd delivered the lines with more passion and conviction when they were rehearsing earlier that week. Natalia, however, was a revelation.

Alla sat in the darkness of the draughty church hall, on an uncomfortable chair, behind a man whose enormous head partially obscured her view of the set. But she'd rarely been happier than she was right now, watching Natalia come to life beneath the lights, as though she were born to play Sasha. Natalia wore a wonderful costume of lavender silk, the heavy make-up accentuating her feline gaze, her hair pinned up to display her long, elegant neck. Her voice was bright and engaging, her movements graceful, her monologues delivered perfectly. Alla wasn't surprised that Grigori the poor shoemaker had fallen in love with her – she rather adored Natalia herself.

The more time that Alla spent with the Savchenko family, the less she could deny the shameful desire she kept hidden. How she longed to be an actress! She remembered the way she'd felt when she'd played the violin at Professor Savelson's concert – how satisfying it was to be admired, to be thought talented and clever and worthy of praise. She knew now that the bare boards of the stage held a magical, transformative power, one that would allow her to leave behind Adelaida Leventon and metamorphose into the celebrated actress Alla Nazimova. To forget her absent mother and her brutal father and all of her shortcomings, to step into another existence and become someone else – whether Ophelia or Nora Helmer or Tatyana Larina, or even a poorly written love interest in a provincial play such as this – seemed the most wonderful thing in the world. And now, thanks to Natalia, she believed it might be possible.

'You have made me the happiest woman alive!'

'And I the happiest man!'

The Shoemaker of Kiev reached its denouement as Sasha accepted Grigori's proposal, and the audience swooned and cheered as the curtain fell. Beside Alla, Yelena rose to her feet to proudly applaud her two daughters who returned to the stage to take their bows, and Alla clapped until her hands ached, hoping desperately that Natalia would see her and acknowledge her in some way. As though her prayers had been answered by a God she didn't believe in, Natalia scanned the spectators and found her mother and her friend who waved and cheered louder than ever. Natalia caught Alla's eye and laughed, putting a hand to her lips before blowing her a kiss, and Alla thought her heart would burst.

Then the house lights came up and she was rudely jolted back to reality, blinking dazedly as though waking from a dream. Nothing and everything had changed for Alla, but she was determined to hold onto this joyous, hopeful feeling, to wrap herself up in it as though it were a luxurious velvet cloak, one that would protect and shelter her on the arduous journey that lay ahead.

When they returned home later that evening, following refreshments and congratulations and greeting old acquaintances, Alla couldn't take her eyes off Natalia. It was as though she'd been sprinkled with stardust and shone brighter than ordinary mortals, yet Alla was the only one who could see it.

After the women had wished one another goodnight and climbed the stairs to begin their ablutions, Alla slipped out of her room and knocked softly on Natalia's door. She opened it wearing her nightgown and for a moment Alla could only stare, completely forgetting what she'd intended to say.

'Are you all right?' Natalia asked, looking concerned. 'Are you unwell?'

Alla shook her head. 'No, I am quite well. I only wanted to tell you how magnificent you were tonight.'

Natalia smiled, her eyes crinkling prettily at the corners. 'Thank you. You're very sweet.'

The response seemed insufficient, and Alla was frustrated that she hadn't fully conveyed her feelings. 'No, that's not all. I think... I think you're wonderful. You're so bold and beautiful and lovely, and I want to be just like you. I was so moved by your performance tonight, and now I know for certain that I want to be an actress. But I'll never be as good as you.'

'Oh, Adelaida!' Natalia clasped Alla's hands, genuinely touched as the tears sprang to her eyes. 'You are too good to me – I don't deserve such praise. But you must see how remarkable *you* are. You're ten times more accomplished than me, braver than I'll ever be, and I do so admire you.'

'*You*... admire *me*?'

'Of course. You have the rest of your life ahead of you and countless opportunities await. I have no doubt that you'll conquer the world if you set your mind to it – become a famous actress if that's what you desire – whilst I'll languish here performing in whichever amateur production will cast me. I'll always remember the astonishing young girl who captured my heart, and you'll have forgotten all about me.' Natalia kissed her on the top of her head, and Alla was momentarily engulfed in her warmth and her scent. 'Now, we must go to bed or we shall be exhausted for church in the morning. Good night, *lapochka*. May your dreams be as sweet as you.' Then the door closed and Natalia was gone, the house shadowy and silent as Alla tiptoed back to her own bedroom.

Her mind was racing and she knew she wouldn't sleep for hours. Instead, she placed her candle on her desk and propped up the small mirror, leaning in close and examining herself critically. Alla had never taken pleasure in her appearance; her father had always told her that she was ugly, and she had no reason not to believe him. At times she'd felt like a changeling child, dark-haired and swarthy-cheeked beside her petite, blonde sister.

Alla tried to study her face objectively. The candlelight was flattering, emphasising her cheekbones and smoothing out her skin. Her eyes were large and expressive, her lips a rather unique shape, her jawline passable. But so much was wrong; she looked nothing like Natalia, or the popular girls at school – the ones who were considered great beauties.

Her face was strewn with pimples, and she vowed to wash her face thoroughly with soap twice a day. There would be no more lazily rolling into bed at night, or rising so late in the morning that there simply wasn't time. And she needed to lose weight too, she thought, seeing the plumpness of her cheeks, the roll of fat beneath her chin. She would eat smaller portions, with no second helpings. And no puddings at all. If she were going to be a successful actress, she had to stop being such a glutton.

Her eyebrows were thick and bushy; she would borrow Natalia's tweezers in the morning to make them slimmer and more shapely. There wasn't much she could do about her nose, but she pinched her cheeks, admiring the blush effect, and nibbled her lips, bringing the blood to the surface as though she'd painted them.

Finally, she untied her hair and let it tumble down her back, black and coarse and untameable. The house was silent, its occupants sleeping soundly as Alla stared at her reflection, dark eyes glittering. Soundlessly, she crept from her room and padded downstairs to the parlour where Yelena Savchenko kept her sewing basket beside her armchair. Fumbling in the darkness, Alla located the scissors, her pulse racing as she ran back up to her room and grabbed a fistful of hair. She made the first cut before she could change her mind, black strands drifting to the floor and landing softly on her bare feet. Another snip, and then another, as the pile of hair grew and she was left with an uneven mop that finished just above her shoulders. Downstairs, the grandfather clock struck midnight as Alla twisted back and forth in front of the mirror, exhilarated by what she'd done. She thought of how the girls at school would praise her daring. She hoped Natalia would like it.

She blew out the candle and her reflection disappeared, but the image was etched indelibly on her mind. Tonight she'd taken a significant step away from being Adelaida Leventon, inching closer to becoming Alla Nazimova.

Now she had to find a way to make it happen.

Chapter Nine

MAYBELLE

Los Angeles, USA, 1920

'Maybelle, can you come here please?'

I was out on the back porch doing the laundry, a chore I hated with a passion. Two new men, riddled with lice, had moved into the red barn, and I'd been boil washing their clothes daily. I put down the washboard and dried my hands on my dress.

Uncle Henry and Aunt Ida were waiting for me in the kitchen, and when I saw their faces my stomach dropped into my boots. On the table in front of them was a small wooden box. I didn't need to look inside to know what it contained – the book of poetry that Joe had given me for Christmas, along with various other trinkets and souvenirs of our time together: the cork from the bottle of Ruinart, meant for Alla, that we'd drunk on New Year's Eve; a sprig of yellow acacia that I'd pressed between the pages of a book; a necklace Joe had bought for me when we attended the premiere of Alla's latest picture; and more than a dozen notes of love, hastily scribbled but with no mistaking their intention.

'Where did you get that?'

'It doesn't matter,' Henry said, as Aunt Ida chimed in with, 'It was found. You must have dropped it.'

I knew that was impossible; I'd hidden the box at the bottom of my wardrobe beneath a pile of old linen. There was no reason for anyone to go in there, and I realised with a sick feeling that someone had done this deliberately – someone had been snooping round my room, rifling through my private things.

'Who's "J"?' asked Henry. My mouth opened and closed but nothing came out. 'Tell us the truth, Maybelle. Have you been courting a boy?'

I almost burst out laughing at how wrong he was. 'No, I haven't. I swear to you, I haven't.'

'Wipe that smirk off your face and don't lie to us. You've been seen sneaking out at night.'

Aunt Ida choked back a sob and I realised the gravity of the situation. I'd been so wrapped up in the whirlwind of the last few months that I'd started to feel invincible, imagining, I think, that this arrangement could continue indefinitely. In addition to our Sunday routine, Joe and I now saw one another as often as possible. During the week she'd meet me in the city – I'd throw my pamphlets in the nearest trash can and jump in her car, heading wherever the mood took us. Other nights I'd sneak out and Joe would be waiting for me at the end of the farm track, car engine low, headlamps turned off. Sometimes we went to Alla's parties, but most times we went back to Joe's where we could be alone together and – oh! Those nights! Torrid and passionate and loving. I did things I'd never done before, experienced emotions I'd never felt. But we were never able to spend the night together, and it was the one thing we wished dearly – to be able to wake in one another's arms and languidly make love as the sun rose.

'It's not what you think,' I said feebly. That, at least, was the truth.

Uncle Henry stared hard at me, puffing furiously like a train. I noticed how grey his hair had become, his boyish looks erased by worry and wrinkles. 'From now on you're not allowed out by yourself. You'll be chaperoned at all times.'

'No!'

'You've brought disgrace on this family once, I won't allow you to do it again, not while you're living under my roof. Herb will accompany you while you continue the Lord's work.'

Herb! Suddenly it all made sense. I remembered him standing outside my door on Christmas morning, the slyness in his voice whenever he spoke. The thought of him in my bedroom, going through my personal belongings, dirty fingers raking through my undergarments left me livid. 'It was Herb, wasn't it? That damn weaselly snitch!'

'Don't you dare use that language,' Henry roared.

Aunt Ida had begun crying. 'I can't believe you'd repay us like this. We took you in. We gave you a home when even your own mother didn't want you.'

The blow stung and I felt my throat thicken, my eyes well up. But worse than Ida's words was the rising sense of panic at the prospect of never seeing Joe or Alla again. I'd discovered a new life more thrilling than anything I'd ever dreamed, with inspiring, unconventional people who accepted and understood me. I couldn't give it up now that I'd found it.

'It's not a boy,' I said softly. I don't know whether it was another denial, or whether I was trying to explain, but the words were out there now and I could tell from Aunt Ida's face that my mother had told her at least some of what had happened last summer in Jonas Springs.

'"J",' she whispered. 'That woman who comes here – Josephine.'

I coloured. My guilt was obvious.

'Get out,' Aunt Ida spat. Uncle Henry looked bemused by the turn events had taken; his wife had clearly never shared the extent of what she knew and kept her recent suspicions to herself. I took one final look at them – Henry disgruntled and disappointed, Ida openly weeping – and raced out of the door, tears streaming down my face.

On the path I ran into Billy. He tried to grab my arm, to ask me what was wrong, but there was something in his expression that instantly made me realise – it hadn't been Herb in my room at all, but Billy. I remembered how I'd caught him on the day of Marisol's baptism; sweet, shy, kind Billy, scarred by his birthmark, had been the one sneaking around the house, pawing through my possessions, out for what he could get.

I pushed him away and fled.

Joe answered the door to my frantic knocking. She was wearing wide linen trousers with a man's pinstriped shirt, her hair pulled up on top of her head and secured with an elastic band, a pencil tucked behind one ear. I'd never seen her dressed so casually.

'Oh honey, what's the matter?' she asked, the moment she saw my tear-streaked cheeks. I'd worried that I'd made a mistake by running to her, terrified that she'd reject me as everyone else had, but when she closed the door and took me in her arms, I knew I'd done the right thing. She led me through to the living room and sat me down, and I told her everything while she held my hand and listened without judgment.

'So you're looking for a place to stay, huh?'

'I don't have to stay here.' My tone was defensive. 'Well, maybe for a night or two until I find myself a job and a room to rent.'

'And what kind of job are you going to do?'

'I could be a waitress, perhaps. It looks easy enough. Or I could ask the girls at Alla's – one of them must know of something.'

She'd been teasing me, but now her tone changed. 'No, don't ask them. Of course you can stay here, for as long as you like. Although I'll never get any work done with you around.' She leaned across to kiss me. Then a second time, fiercely, intensely. I needed the reassurance that I was loved, that everything was going to be all right.

'Let's celebrate!' Joe exclaimed, jumping to her feet. 'Let's have a drink.' She went over to the cart to fix our current favourite tipple – gin with sweet vermouth and a curl of orange peel. 'To our newly found domestic bliss,' she grinned, as we clinked our glasses together.

I fell silent, unable to find quite the same levity in my

predicament. I was beyond grateful that Joe had been so generous, so understanding, but I was truly dependent on her now. My mother didn't want me, my aunt and uncle had thrown me out, I had no possessions except the clothes I was wearing. I felt vulnerable and frightened but hopeful for the future; white light refracting through a prism into a brilliant rainbow of colours.

'Joe...' I began hesitantly. 'If we're really going to do this – you and me, together – I need you to be honest with me.'

'Sure. What about?'

'Everything. Your background, your history, your whole life before me. You never talk about it and I don't know anything.'

Joe rose abruptly and walked over to the window. Outside, the garden was calm and peaceful, an oasis of greenery with a tangle of yellow roses and a yucca plant in rare full bloom. I could see the tension in the set of her back before she slowly turned around. 'All right. Why not?' She came back and sat down beside me. 'So I was born in Chicago, in 1890.'

'Chicago?'

'Yes. Are you going to interrupt the whole way through?'

It was meant as a joke, but I could tell she was on edge. She reached for a cigarette, visibly relaxing as she inhaled.

'Chicago, the "City Beautiful". My hometown. My mother was an Irish immigrant. Her name was Bridget, but everyone called her Birdie. She was beautiful. I'm not just saying that, she truly was. She had thick auburn hair – so much nicer than mine – and the most arresting eyes and the kindest heart. She would help out anyone in trouble.

'My father... Well, I never knew my father. My mother

barely did either. She told me he was a French lawyer, passing through the city on business, and that she gave me his surname, but... I don't know. My mother was a chorus girl at the Blue Saloon on West Argyle Street. The job didn't pay very well, but there were plenty of other ways for the girls to make money, and... let's just say my mother never went hungry.

'She said that when she fell pregnant, she knew right away that she wanted to keep me. We were lucky – Mother could have been thrown out onto the street, or forced to give me up to an orphanage, but Al Brooks, who owned the club, had a soft spot for her and let her work right until she started to show – no one wants to see a pregnant chorus girl, right? But in that time she saved a little money, paid her rent a few months in advance so she didn't have to worry about keeping a roof over her head. Mrs Piotrowska, our landlady, was sympathetic to her situation. Her own son had been killed in an accident – he worked downtown on a construction site and was crushed instantly when a steel beam fell from a crane. Understandably, she'd never really gotten over it.

'After I was born, my mother went back to work as soon as she could. Al was happy to give her her job back – she was still young, still terrific looking. She'd kept her slim hips and flat stomach, not a stretch mark on her skin. Some nights, Mrs Piotrowska would look after me while my mother was working, warming a little milk and giving me my bottle. As I got older, Mother took me with her. I used to sit in the corner of the dressing room, quiet as a mouse, my eyes wide as saucers.'

Joe laughed softly and lit another cigarette. 'I loved those times. The others treated me like I was a daughter to them all. I was cossetted and petted and I adored all of them in return. Oh, but you should have seen them, Maybelle. So glamorous! Some of my happiest memories are watching them get ready in front of that grimy mirror, pencilling their eyebrows and pinning their hair. And the costumes! Sometimes they'd dress me up in their hats and boas, put a little rouge on my cheeks or rag my hair. Of course, I wanted to be just like my mother. What little girl doesn't?'

I shifted awkwardly but made no comment, letting Joe tell her story. It seemed to be cathartic.

'My mother hated the idea of me ending up like her and insisted I get an education. On the whole, school didn't interest me, but good grades came easily and I was passionate about anything creative – writing, drawing, performing. By the time I was 15, I was desperate to try my luck in the big wide world, to find a job and support Mother financially. She didn't approve, but she didn't really have a choice in the matter. Of course, she'd long since stopped working at the Blue Saloon – Al kept her for as long as he could, but she was almost a decade older than the new recruits. She worked in a couple more downmarket shows for a few months, but after that she did whatever she could so that we could get by – factory work, domestic work. She managed a tavern for a while, then ran a boarding house.'

'She never married?' I couldn't resist asking.

Joe shook her head. 'She always said that she wasn't the marrying kind. I was glad, in a way. I loved it being just her and me – the two of us against the world. I wanted to look after her, to give her all the nice things she deserved but had never had.'

Joe got up to pour herself another drink, with a more-than-generous measure of gin. She was well on her way to getting drunk and when she went to refill my glass I almost declined – it was only early afternoon – then thought, what the heck, and accepted.

'I landed a secretarial post pretty much right away, at an insurance firm in one of the fancy new buildings on Jackson Boulevard. My mother was so proud of me.' Joe bit down hard on her lip, staring straight ahead. 'I guess I was kinda wrapped up in my new job because it took me a while to notice… Mother was suddenly exhausted the whole time. She lost a ton of weight. Then she started vomiting, lost her appetite, too weak to even get out of bed. Two months later, she was gone.'

'Oh, Joe. I'm sorry.' I'd never seen her looking so heartbroken, so vulnerable. I took her in my arms and held her, wanting to do more but knowing there was nothing that would take the pain away. I understood what it was like to lose a beloved parent, and felt guilty for asking her to speak about it when it was clearly still so raw. I was devastated for her, and sad for myself that I'd never had that kind of closeness with my own mother.

After a few moments, Joe disentangled herself and wiped her eyes. 'I didn't want to stay in Chicago after that. There were too many memories. I saw her on every street corner, thought I was losing my mind. So I moved to New York. I didn't want to be a secretary – that was what my mother wanted for me, and I'd done it for her. I wanted to be a performer – to follow in her footsteps and succeed where she hadn't. I had dreams of becoming an actress, a dancer – a star, at any rate. But New York is a tough city. It takes no prisoners, and life was hard at first. Really hard. Even the weather doesn't cut you any slack – an icebox in winter, a furnace in summer. I had some awful jobs, working in real dives. I was so green, I got taken advantage of more times than I can remember.'

'So what changed?'

'I met Alla.'

Joe looked directly at me and I stiffened. Since she'd first introduced me to Alla, it was the one question that had haunted me, the one thing I'd never dared to ask.

'We were in a show together – *A Doll's House*, at the Bijou on Broadway. She was playing Nora, the lead, of course, and I had a blink-and-you'll-miss-me role as the maid, Helene. Alla… took a shine to me, I guess. Took me under her wing. When I didn't have a place to stay she let me live with her for a while. I wasn't the greatest actress by any means, but she helped me with auditions, with my lines. I owe her a lot. Who am I kidding? I owe her everything. When she signed with Metro Pictures and moved out here, she was the one who suggested I come too. Paid for my ticket, gave me a place to stay, hooked me up with contacts at the studio which was how I got my first screenwriting credit. A hideous little movie called *The Kingdom of Horses* that nobody went to see.' She laughed ruefully, untucked her legs and stretched them. 'And I guess that just about brings us up to right here and now, and me sitting here with you.'

We were both silent, digesting the revelations along with the cocktails. Despite everything, I was fascinated by the life Joe had led, a world away from my own sheltered upbringing.

But I still had one question that needed answering. 'Were you and Alla ever…'

'…Lovers?' Joe made no attempt to avoid the subject. 'Yes. In those early, heady days in New York I was quite infatuated by her. We were running with a glamorous, bohemian crowd, and she had such energy, such magnetism. We were never exclusive – and it wasn't long before she moved on to the next pretty young thing.'

'And recently?'

Joe shook her head, half-smiled. 'No. That's all in the past. We're the best of friends, but that ship has sailed. Besides, I'm too old for her now.' She laughed once again.

I couldn't see the humour, couldn't stop asking questions. 'Was she your first?'

'My first lover? No. My first love…? Yes, I'd say so. I'd been intimate with women before, had brief affairs. But she was the first one that really meant anything.' Joe saw my expression and gripped my hands tightly. 'I'm telling you all this because I don't want us to have secrets. I want to be honest with you, no skeletons in the closet. It doesn't change anything – it's in the past, and I'm with you now. I love you.'

I stayed mute and Joe bristled; something shifted in the atmosphere and she said defensively, 'So what about you?'

'Me?'

'I've told you my life story, but you're still a mystery. What are you hiding, *ma belle* Maybelle?'

I felt caught in a trap of my own making. It was true that Joe had been frank and deserved the same in return but, aside from me, there was no one else who knew the entirety of what had happened back in Kentucky. Sure, certain people knew certain parts, and no doubt did their best to fill in the blanks, but I never wanted to think about that summer ever again.

I glanced at the clock. It was almost three, but we had all the time in the world and nowhere else to be. I was all out of excuses.

'All right,' I said. 'Fix me another drink and I'll tell you everything.'

Chapter Ten

ALLA

Moscow, Russia, 1896

My dearest Volodya,

Please forgive my brevity, but the nature of my request is rather urgent and so I will delay no longer in coming to the crux of the matter: my financial situation is somewhat precarious. To be blunt, I have no money. Could you send my share of Papa's inheritance as soon as you are in receipt of this letter? Winter is swiftly approaching, far colder here than in Yalta, and I am badly in need of a winter coat and new boots. I find myself in arrears with my rent and my landlady threatens to put me out onto the streets.

I hope my letter finds you well, and give my love to my sister. Please fulfil my request with the utmost haste.

All my love,
Alla

Alla addressed the envelope and waited for the ink to dry. She hoped Volodya would respond quickly, that he wouldn't dismiss her plea, thinking she was lying or exaggerating. Her situation was becoming desperate. She was a month behind on her rent, although the squalid room was barely worth the money she paid for it, Alla thought indignantly, looking around at the cracked ceiling, the dinner-plate sized patches of damp and the bloom of black mould in the corner. The curtains were so thin she could have strained cheese through them, and the stained mattress was revolting, offering a fluidic history of its previous occupants.

Alla folded the letter and sealed the envelope, pulling her summer coat over her flimsy dress, her clothes offering little protection from the fierce Moscow weather. The seasons were turning, and a bitter wind blew into the city from Siberia.

She walked down the unlit hallway with its peeling walls, out into the street where scraps of newspaper swirled round her feet, the stench of rotten vegetables carried on the air. She waved hello to the one-legged beggar who sat slumped in his usual spot by the carriage stop, dodging a rat that scurried across her path and disappeared down an alleyway. But oh, how she loved Moscow! The Nikitsky Gates may not have been the most salubrious area but it was cheap and convenient for everything she needed: the Philharmonic School, the theatres, and the very heart of the city where she loved to walk the wide, sweeping boulevards, past the embassies and the palatial houses, the fashionable restaurants and the modish boutiques, imagining how different her life would be when she was a celebrated actress, swathed in furs and fêted by the public.

More than that, Moscow represented how far she'd come – both literally and figuratively. It symbolised escape from Yalta, where her brother and sister still resided; Volodya now ran the pharmacy following Yakov's death, whilst Nina was involved in a tempestuous relationship with the son of Yalta's leading moneylender. Being here was proof that Alla had overcome her background, her turbulent childhood, her cruel father, and made it all the way to the Russian capital to pursue her dream of performing. She would have moved sooner, but she needed her brother's permission as her legal guardian and he refused to grant it until she turned seventeen.

Alla called at the post office to send the letter, hoping it would swiftly reach her brother. Volodya had given her money that was intended to last six months but she'd spent it all in three, although she wasn't sure how, and now she needed funds for new gloves and a winter hat, not to mention food and lodging, books for her studies and warm underwear…

A few doors down from the post office was a shop displaying postcards of prominent figures. Alla stopped to study them, admiring the beautiful monochrome prints of the great and the glamorous: Eleonora Duse; Sarah Bernhardt; Nellie Melba; Grand Duchess Maria Feodorovna. She searched through her bag, beneath the ticket stubs and the play bills, the packet of tobacco and her school notepad, unearthing a few kopeks that she spent on half a dozen cards. She would tack them up in her room, to cheer up the dreary space and provide inspiration. One day it would be her face on a postcard, she vowed, and the thought made her smile.

'Again.'

'It is your fault that I have made nothing of my life.'

'Again.'

'It is your fault that—'

'Again.'

'It is—'

'Again! Come on, Alla, I don't believe you. Find the truth. Dig deep inside yourself.'

'It is your fault—'

'Again. Don't try to act. Just say the words truthfully.'

'It is your fault that I have made nothing of my life.'

'Again.'

'It is your fault that I have made nothing of my life.'

'Better. Again.'

'It is your fault that I have made nothing of my life.'

'There! That was it! Did you feel it?' Nemirovich's expression was one of childlike discovery and Alla nodded excitedly. 'Did you see it? Did you all see it?' The other students, sitting in a semi-circle in the rehearsal room, murmured their agreement. 'But you must work on your voice, Alla. You need to get rid of that silly southern accent. Now, Dmitri, let's look at Torvald's response…'

Vladimir Nemirovich was approaching forty years of age, short and overweight, with a bushy black beard that dominated his face. He was Alla's acting tutor at the prestigious Philharmonic Society School of Drama, and she loved and loathed him in equal measure; his methods were intense, but his results were incredible, and he advocated a new style of naturalistic acting that didn't rely on pre-rehearsed gestures and artifice.

Three hours later, Nemirovich rose from his seat and walked out, his signal that the class was finished. Shoulders slumped, breaths were exhaled, as the exhausted students took a moment to gather their thoughts. Alla's classmate, Olga, leaned across with a smile, placing a hand on Alla's arm. She was dark-haired and dark-eyed, not dissimilar from Alla in appearance, and the two of them had grown close. 'We're all going to Nikolai's apartment, are you coming? His parents sent his allowance today so he's throwing a party.'

Alla smiled regretfully. 'I can't tonight. I have something I must do. Have fun, and I'll see you tomorrow.' The two women kissed, then Alla gathered up her bag, said her goodbyes and went out into the cold.

It was growing dark, the temperature dropping quickly, and Alla knew she had a long walk ahead of her. She passed through the theatre district and on to Lubyanka Square, crossing the city from west to east, keeping to the main avenues where the streetlights shone brightly and welcome blasts of warm air spilled out from the hotels and *kabaks*. It was almost three miles to Myasnitskaya Street. Alla found the number she was looking for, stopping just before she reached it to smooth her hair and straighten her clothes. She didn't need to pinch her cheeks to put the roses in them; the freezing air had already done that.

The house was imposing, and she tried not to be intimidated as she climbed the wide stone steps and rang the bell. It was opened by a man wearing a butler's uniform who looked her up and down and raised an unimpressed eyebrow.

'I'm here to see Mr Keller,' Alla announced. She knew she looked shabby, dressed inappropriately for the winter weather, but she drew herself up to her full five feet and three inches, imagining herself playing a character of high status. 'My name is Adelaida Leventon and I'm the daughter of Yakov Leventon.'

After a moment's consideration the manservant stood aside to let her in, his expression making it clear that he disapproved. 'Wait here, please.'

Alla rubbed her hands together, luxuriating in the warmth, as the butler disappeared into the depths of the house. The décor was as impressive as she'd anticipated; if she stole a pair of candlesticks, the money she'd get from pawning them would pay her rent for the next year.

It was now over a month since she'd written to Volodya and she hadn't heard a word. The only reply had come from her sister, Nina, who sent a terse letter telling Alla she would just have to manage. Alla had torn it up then thrown the pieces in the fire; if nothing else, her sister's harsh words would warm her frozen bones for a few moments. Lack of money consumed Alla's every thought, unable to concentrate even on her studies.

It was late one evening, when she was chronicling her plight in her diary, that she found the scrap of paper tucked inside the cover and remembered Volodya writing down Ivan Keller's name and address, telling her he was an old friend of their father and the family's only acquaintance in Moscow. It was her brother's way of trying to look after her, she supposed, letting her know that if she ever needed anything they were not entirely friendless in this strange new city. Neither Alla nor

Volodya knew anything about Ivan Keller except that he was extremely rich and, in her current circumstances, that was all that mattered.

'Do follow me, Miss Leventon.' The butler had returned, his manner now deferential. 'Mr Keller is about to have dinner, but he's asked if you'll join him.'

Alla was taken aback. 'I'd be delighted.'

She was shown into a wood-panelled dining room, with a long table set for sixteen: there were sixteen dinner plates and sixteen side plates, sixteen goblets, sixteen glasses, sixteen sets of cutlery and sixteen linen napkins. At the head of the table sat Ivan Keller. He was stout and bald, ruddy-cheeked and jowly, and he was dressed in a three-piece woollen suit, the waistcoat straining at the buttons.

'Oh, I'm so sorry,' Alla apologised. 'I didn't realise you were having a dinner party this evening.'

Keller frowned. 'I'm not. It's wonderful to have some company for a change. Do sit down.' He indicated the chair to the right of him.

Alla sat as two liveried servants entered the room. The first filled their glasses with wine and water. The second served blinis with caviar and dill sauce, and Alla's eyes widened. Even if Keller turned down her request for money, she would at least get a good meal from the expedition.

'So, what can I do for you?' asked Keller, as he slid a whole blini into his mouth and chewed with gusto. 'You're Leventon's youngest daughter, yes? I was sorry to hear of his passing. What was it?'

'A stroke. He'd suffered a number of them and spent his final years in a sanatorium.' Alla's tone was detached, and she realised once again that she needed to draw upon her acting skills. 'My brother and sister still live in Yalta, and I haven't seen my mother since I was a very young child. I'm all alone in the city, and I'm finding life very hard. My dream is to be an actress, and I'm studying at the Philharmonic School – a very prestigious institution, I'm sure you're aware. But my brother hasn't sent the money he promised me, and now winter is coming and I have no suitable clothes. I've fallen behind on my rent and I have no one to turn to, but I can't abandon my vocation. I wondered whether...' Here Alla paused, considering flirtation. She reached across to touch his hand, looking up at him from beneath her eyelashes. 'I wondered whether you might consider being a generous benefactor, and making a charitable contribution towards the art of this great nation...?'

'You're looking for money,' Keller said bluntly.

'Yes.' Alla was equally candid.

Keller sucked his teeth. 'Well, I'm certainly wealthy, as you can see. I made all my money importing mineral water – did your father tell you that? Bottles of the stuff from Europe. It's absurd that people will pay for it when it's just bubbling out of the ground there, flowing down French mountainsides and what have you. But pay for it they do, and handsomely.' He raised his water glass in a toast and Alla did the same. 'Did you know my wife left me? I gave her whatever she wanted – diamonds, rubies, dresses made from the finest silks, a stable full of horses, and servants to satisfy her every whim. Of course, I was never able to give her the one thing she really wanted, which was a child. I think that's why she left me. Ran off with some shipping magnate from

Vladivostok. It's been five years since she left. I've been terribly lonely.'

The room lapsed into an awkward silence, and Alla swallowed the last of her food. The servants returned to clear away their plates and to serve the next delicious course, followed by another, then another, as Keller droned on and Alla ate – borscht, chicken pie and creamed potatoes, venison with pickled cucumbers and black bread – trying not to scrape her plate.

She didn't dare to interrupt him; baffled as she was by his meandering anecdotes, she nodded attentively as he bemoaned his ex-wife, his servants, his gout and his melancholy.

'And, of course, I've barely had an appetite, not since developing this wretched stomach cancer. It seems such a shame – all this glorious food, anything I want in the world, and I can barely manage more than a few mouthfuls of each.'

They were finishing dessert, a delicious pastry and fruit concoction, when Keller unexpectedly came back to Alla's request.

'You seem like a fine young woman of talent, and I think I can do something to make your unfortunate predicament a little easier. Yes.' He stood up abruptly, throwing down his napkin. 'Come with me.'

Alla followed him out of the room, along a hallway lit by gold sconces. Keller turned left, then opened a door on his right, and Alla saw that she was in his private study. The walls were lined with leatherbound books, weighty tomes on economics and history and politics, and there was a large wing-backed armchair beside a polished mahogany writing desk. On the opposite wall hung a portrait of a handsome woman with dark blonde hair and creamy skin. She wore a royal blue gown, sapphires glittering at her ears and throat, and Alla walked over to admire the picture.

'That's my wife,' Keller explained softly.

Alla turned around and saw him turn the key in the keyhole, heard the click of the mechanism as it locked shut. She tried to keep the alarm from her voice. 'Mr Keller, why—'

'Now, my dear girl, if you could stand there, right where you are – exactly – and give me your best smile. There, that's it. Lovely. Keep smiling. That's right. Keep smiling...'

He backed away from her as he spoke, fiddling with the waistband of his trousers, growing increasingly red in the face. When he reached the desk, he let his trousers drop to the floor, followed by his undergarments, before sinking down onto the armchair. His bare bottom was splayed across the upholstery, his stubby penis erect and bulging.

Alla let out a cry of shock, and Keller hastened to reassure her.

'Don't worry, *malyshka*, just keep smiling. That's it. Very good.'

He gripped his member firmly and began to pump, his hand sliding up and down with increasing urgency, his fleshy stomach wobbling as his momentum grew. His hairy legs were surprisingly spindly, his trousers gathered in an undignified heap around his ankles. Alla didn't know whether to laugh or cry. All she could do was continue to stand in front of the painting of his wife and keep smiling as Keller's face contorted – whether in agony or ecstasy, she couldn't have said. He began muttering furiously, sometimes yelling out words that were unfit for a young lady's ears.

And still she smiled.

It was all over in less than two minutes. Keller ejaculated over himself with a climactic groan, his own fluid spurting over his naked thighs, landing wetly in the folds of his trousers. Alla noticed a dribble on the parquet floor and wondered about the unseen housemaid who would be expected to clean it.

Keller took a handkerchief from his waistcoat pocket and wiped himself before staggering to his feet and pulling up his trousers. He opened the top drawer of the desk and took out ten rubles. Alla's eyes widened; that would cover the rent she owed, with enough left over to buy new boots and perhaps even a pair of gloves.

Keller lumbered over to unlock the door before handing the money to Alla. 'Very good,' he said cheerily. 'Pass by again tomorrow – same time?'

Alla hardly knew how to reply. She smiled one final time, put the money in her purse and fled.

Chapter Eleven

MAYBELLE

Los Angeles, USA, 1920

One of the things I'd come to love most about California was the ocean. I'd never laid eyes on a body of water bigger than the Cumberland River before I moved west, and having the boundless blue of the Pacific just a short ride across the city was a joy. Sometimes Joe and I would drive out to Venice or Santa Monica, or along the coast to Malibu, and inhale the pure, piquant air as we watched the waves crest and break. We'd take a picnic of avocado salad and boiled eggs, gorging on fresh peaches as we emerged wet and sleek as dolphins from an invigorating dip, salt in our hair and sand on our skin.

Tonight's excursion to Venice Pier was markedly different from our relaxed weekend beach jaunts. Dressed to the nines and dining at Baron Long's Ship Café (an eccentric reproduction of a Spanish galleon, with dancing on the top deck, a restaurant and hotel rooms below), we were seated at the best table in the house alongside Alla and her husband Charles, and a dozen of their closest friends – who'd now become *my* closest friends by dint of association – including June Mathis, a female screenwriter who'd taken Hollywood by storm, and Chinese American actress Anna May Wong, who'd had a small role in Alla's last movie.

Snuggled up beside Alla, hands brushing beneath the table, feet touching playfully, was Dorothy Arzner, a script typist at Paramount with ambitions of one day becoming a film director. Her hair was cropped short like a man's, and tonight she was dressed in a suit and tie as she and Alla whispered in one another's ears and giggled at private jokes. I wondered what Charles made of it all, but he didn't appear to care, merely looking on benignly. I was intensely curious about their marriage, which was unlike any I'd ever witnessed, but I'd learned since coming to Los Angeles that relationships could be far more complicated than my sheltered upbringing had allowed me to imagine.

At that time, Alla was at the height of her powers, a global movie star who seemed to know everyone in the place and was treated with due reverence by the rabble who clustered around, hoping she might sprinkle a little stardust in their direction. I'd remember evenings like this in later years – albeit infused with a hazy, dreamlike quality, as though seen through a gauze of cigarette smoke and nostalgia – long after Alla had lost her crown and it had all come crashing down around our ears. But right now, the moment was magical.

'Have you ever tasted oysters?' Joe asked, as an enormous bowl, served on the half-shell over ice, was placed in front of us.

I pulled a face. 'They look disgusting.'

'They're an aphrodisiac. Look, like this.' She squeezed a wedge of lemon over the gelatinous mollusc, tipped back her head, chewed twice and then swallowed.

I followed her lead and was pleasantly surprised; there was something in the sweet, creamy flesh that reminded me of the Kentucky catfish I'd been raised on, and for a moment I felt a pang of homesickness so strong it made me catch my breath.

'Come on, let's dance,' Joe grinned, oblivious, as she pulled me to my feet and we went whirling onto the floor amidst the crush of revellers. We'd had a few drinks and were both pleasantly soused; despite the restrictions, Baron Long's served alcohol if you were willing to pay the right price, and the monied crowd that frequented the Ship had no qualms about dishing out the dollar. That was how we lived our lives in those days: a nonstop party, where the champagne bottles never ran dry and there was always a newer, better, bigger experience to be had.

Right now, we only had eyes for one another, uninhibited and carefree in our glorious, impenetrable bubble. Here, no one paid heed if two women – one wearing breeches and suspenders, complete with slicked back hair – danced a little too closely together, let their hands linger a moment too long on the other's waist. But outside in the real world we were forever on our guard: walking down the street I had to remember that I couldn't take Joe's hand, that I couldn't kiss her in the grocery store or even look at her in a way that might reveal too much. We could be arrested, charged with obscenity, thrown in jail. It seemed a bitterly unfair price to pay for being in love.

We danced until our feet were aching and when we paused for breath I found myself sitting next to Alla, as Dorothy excused herself to use the restroom. Alla was wearing a diaphanous gown of black and silver that looked as though it were a costume from one of her movies. Her hair was styled in waves, giving her a softer appearance than usual, and her eyes were thickly lined with her trademark kohl.

'It's wonderful to see her so happy.' She inclined her head towards Joe who'd squeezed herself in between sisters Constance and Norma Talmadge – the latter out tonight without her much older husband, the Russian-born film producer Joseph Schenck – and was laughing uproariously.

I smiled at the implicit compliment. 'Can you believe it's almost a year since we first met? When Joe invited me to your house and I snuck out at night, creeping across the city like a criminal. It feels like forever ago.'

'What's the phrase…? Time flies when you're having fun.' Alla enunciated the words carefully, as though she found the idiom peculiar.

'It sure does. My world turned upside down.'

'And you have no regrets?'

The question was meant without guile but it shook me, my mind a sudden tumult of uncertainty and hesitation and gin cocktails.

'Sometimes I… sometimes I feel like a spare part.' I hadn't planned to say the words until they were out of my mouth, and I wondered where they'd come from. *In vino veritas*, perhaps. 'Joe has her writing. She owns the bungalow, the motor car, she pays the bills. And in return I keep the place tidy and brew the coffee and wash her clothes and fix her a drink at the end of the day just the way she likes it and… I never wanted to be someone's *wife*. Some domestic drudge spending my days cooking and cleaning. If that had been my ambition, I could have stayed in Kentucky and married a farm boy. But it feels like that's what I've become.'

The band seemed too loud suddenly, the room too busy. I closed my eyes and pinched the brow of my nose, hoping to avert the headache beginning to pound at my temples. 'I'm being silly, forget I said anything.' If I could take back my words, I would have done it in a heartbeat. I still found Alla intimidating and suspected I always would, our every conversation distorted by my knowledge of her history with Joe. I was all too aware – despite Joe's denials – that I could never match up to her first love, the woman who'd rescued her from career failure in New York and brought her to Los Angeles, who'd gone on to become a movie star, the highest paid woman in Hollywood, an icon to millions around the world.

'What's your passion, Maybelle?' Alla leaned forwards, looking at me intently with those arresting eyes.

'My passion?'

'Yes. I don't mean Joe. I mean, something you feel compelled to do for you and you alone. Something that brings you happiness. What drives you? What makes you get out of bed in the morning?'

'I… I don't know.'

'Then you must find out!' Alla banged her fist on the table. 'For me, clearly it is my acting. For Joe, her writing. But what about Maybelle? This is what you must discover – your purpose, your passion, the ambition for which you're willing to fight, to endure any hardship. If you place all your energy into someone else, it's *their* dream you're pursuing, not yours.'

She sat back, triumphant, her point emphatically made. I knew that she was right – I'd been so dazzled by Joe, so grateful to her for rescuing me from my drab existence, that I'd put myself entirely at her disposal. And in doing so I'd lost myself.

'Come to the studio on Monday,' Alla suggested. 'I will arrange a tour, introduce you to people. Perhaps you will find something to ignite the spark. And Joe will learn to be without you for a day.'

'Speak of the devil…'

Joe had extricated herself from the Talmadge sisters and was heading over, frowning at our cosiness. 'What are you two plotting?' she asked suspiciously, sitting down and draping her arm around the back of my chair.

Alla didn't miss a beat. 'Maybelle's future,' she replied, lighting a cigarette and smiling at me.

'Miss Maybelle Crabtree for Alla Nazimova,' I announced to the guard on the gate at Metro Pictures, trying to sound undaunted though my heart was racing like a locomotive. He checked his clipboard, made a note and directed me round to the enormous parking lot. Joe had been teaching me to drive and, despite a heated altercation at the intersection of Santa Monica and Gower, there was something wonderfully liberating about driving myself the few blocks to North Cahuenga Boulevard in Joe's Chevy.

The backlot was a hive of activity even before I set foot inside any of the gigantic concrete hangars. I felt like Alice landing up in Wonderland, wide-eyed as I spotted an army of background artists dressed as Confederate soldiers, marching to a beat of hammering and sanding and sawing as sets were constructed and rigs were erected. Rounding a corner I was almost flattened by an enormous cine camera perched atop a dolly; the man wheeling it looked me over and let out a low whistle, and I couldn't help but wonder how he'd react if he knew the truth – that my lover was a woman, and in the dawn light I'd slipped out of sheets still warm from our coupling. I put my head down and hurried away, counterfeit confidence deserting me.

On the east side of the lot, a small bungalow had been constructed for "Madame Nazimova", so that the studio's most important asset could prepare for her scenes in peace and privacy. It was homelier than Hayvenhurst, modest and comfortable, and it was here that I found Alla, swathed in a black silk robe, as her hair and make-up were attended to by two sprightly assistants. A handful of industrious others scurried back and forth and to and fro.

"Maybelle is my guest of honour today,' Alla announced to the room with a wave of her hand. 'She's searching for her passion, so please do all you can to assist.'

I blushed at her teasing, embarrassed by the smirks and stares, turning my attention back to Alla in the hope that everyone else would follow suit. 'Thank you so much for inviting me, it's so exciting. There's so much happening, I'm sure I don't know where to look.'

'Well you must take it all in. Life is about experiences – throw yourself headfirst and see where you land.'

'I will. You look so beautiful today.' Her make-up was immaculate, her hair magnificent.

'Like a Russian princess?'

I laughed. 'Surely that's the role you were born to play.'

I knew from Joe that Alla's latest film was called *Billions*, a romantic comedy adapted from a French play by her husband. Charles was also playing the male lead – an American poet and the love interest of Alla's character, Princess Triloff, whom she dissuades from giving up his artistic endeavours when he inherits a fortune.

'And how was Joe this morning? Will she survive without you for one day?'

'Truthfully, I think she's looking forward to having the place to herself.'

'She must learn to miss you,' Alla nodded sagely. 'And she will. What is it they say? Absence makes the heart grow fonder…'

There was a knock on the open door and a woman strode in. She was tall and slender, fine-boned with Slavic features and startling violet eyes. She wore her dark hair in plaited knots on either side of her head and she held herself like a dancer.

'Good morning! I've spoken to Mr Smallwood and he agrees that we should open with your close-up – I've briefed the lighting director accordingly – and I've switched Charles' hat for the proposal – I thought the newsboy worked better. Your white poppy suit is with the seamstress for alterations, and I'm heading to the set now to do final checks for the Rabbit Dance.'

'Thank you, Natacha. Please make certain that the girls look absolutely identical – it must be impossible to spot a difference between them. Now, do you remember Maybelle? You've met before, I'm sure.'

Natacha Rambova noticed me and broke into a wide smile. I'd encountered her at Alla's parties – where else? – where she'd increasingly become a fixture in recent months, accompanied by a heavy-set, brutish-looking man. 'Of course. Nice to see you again, Maybelle.'

'We are trying to stoke the fire in her belly,' Alla asserted, as I felt my cheeks flame once again. 'Perhaps you could help her with that? Show her the set, the costumes and so forth. Is that all right, Maybelle?'

'Of course. And thank you again for today.'

'The pleasure is all mine.'

I followed Natacha out of the bungalow and across the lot, the sun warm on our faces as we wove between the buildings, falling into easy small talk.

'Have you known Alla for long?' I wondered.

'A couple of years now. My fiancé, Theo, is Russian, so they have mutual acquaintances, and they worked together on *Stronger than Death* – he's a choreographer and she hired him to give her dance lessons. Alla happened to see some sketches I'd drawn and loved them – turns out we have very similar tastes and ideas – so she asked me to design some clothes for her. This is the first time I'm art directing too, which means I have responsibility for set design, costumes, and the overall look of the movie.'

'Oh my!' I breathed, mightily impressed and decidedly overawed. Natacha was only a year or two older than me, yet she seemed so assured and accomplished. I was still floundering, trying to discover who I was and who I was going to be.

'What about you? How do you know Alla?'

'Through my… friend, Josephine Colbert.'

'Of course, I've seen the two of you together at Hayvenhurst,' Natacha said easily, and I felt relieved that I didn't have to explain myself, that nothing seemed awkward.

'Joe's a brilliant writer and Alla thinks I need to discover *my* vocation. My passion.'

'And she thinks it might be here?' Natacha grinned. 'Then let's go find it.'

She slipped through a side door into one of the colossal hangars and in the blink of an eye I found myself transported to a fantastical garden, giant flowers blooming high above me, spotted toadstools towering overhead. It was another Alice moment, as though I'd imbibed the Drink Me potion and shut up like a telescope, finding myself ten inches high in a whimsical land. My feet teetered on the edge of a fairy pond, a shimmering waterfall spilling over rocks behind, whilst the black backdrop was painted with art nouveau imagery of sunshine and clouds and sweeping calla lilies reaching to the sky. It was lavish, highly stylised, and like nothing I'd ever seen before.

'Found your inspiration yet?' Natacha asked, laughing at the way my mouth had fallen open.

'It's astonishing. Did you do all this?'

'Well I can't take credit for building the set but it's all my design. Alla's and my vision. It's for a dream sequence, hence why it's so outlandish. Come this way – I've lots more to show you.'

We passed crew members adjusting arc lights on tripods as a besuited man bellowed instructions, cine cameras re-angled and re-checked, cables snaking across the floor. There were actors in rabbit costumes with enormous whiskers, and a cluster of lithe young women in one-shouldered Grecian gowns with their backcombed hair painted silver.

'This is my office.' Natacha opened a nondescript wooden door and gestured for me to enter.

It had been a morning of wonders, and this was perhaps the most wondrous of all. The room was small but extraordinary; everywhere I looked something caught my eye, the walls plastered with postcards and cuttings, samples and swatches and curls of ribbon. A tailor's dummy stood in one corner, resplendent in a spectacular winged gown; beside it a rail of clothing, predominantly black and silver, all filmy and dramatic and ethereal. I longed to reach out and touch them, to let my fingers linger over their exquisite surface, but I was afraid to soil such precious works of art. I turned around. There were wigs on stands, mocked-up sets in miniature, books, journals, measuring tapes, dressmaking shears, beads and buttons. It even smelt intriguing – of perfume and pomanders, of must and mothballs and something unidentifiable yet exotic. It was beautiful chaos.

Against the far wall, Natacha's desk was half-buried beneath a heavily annotated script and piles of sketches, page after page of set designs and costume concepts, all skilfully drawn in ink and painted in watercolours.

'You're so talented,' I marvelled. 'May I look through?'

'Of course.' Natacha seemed flattered by my response, as I tentatively picked up a sheet of paper with as much care as if it were a newborn.

The drawings were miniature masterpieces. Natacha's flair was undeniable, her style innovative and distinctive. I could feel my pulse start to race, a sense of excitement flooding through me.

'I love this one. The colours are so vibrant, and it's so clever how the flowers at the hem echo the floral pattern of the fabric. Look how beautifully this—' here I snatched up a piece of gold mesh from her desk, '—would fit with the yellow train.' I spoke instinctively but immediately checked myself, worried she might see my comments as criticism. 'Oh, I didn't mean—'

'No, no,' Natacha waved away my concerns. She studied the design, picking up a pencil and scribbling a note on her pad. 'I think you might be right. You have a good eye.'

I glowed beneath her praise, but my joy was curtailed by a commotion outside on the soundstage. I glanced at Natacha who explained in a single word:

'Alla.'

The great Nazimova had indeed arrived, costumed and in character, looking every inch the imperious Russian princess. I sensed the abrupt change in atmosphere, now charged with anticipation, the idle chatter and barked instructions instantly stopping. Alla was a dazzling sun, everyone else mere satellites in her orbit.

I hung back, afraid to approach her. I didn't recognise *this* Alla; I'd never seen her pre-performance and didn't dare disturb her process. Natacha led me silently round the edge of the set to a spot where we could watch without disturbing.

'That's Ray Smallwood, the director,' she whispered, pointing out the slim, dark-haired man with whom Alla was now deep in conversation. They spoke intently, whilst the background artists I'd seen earlier – the troop of girls in Grecian dresses, the rabbits and the nymphs – were ushered in and swiftly took up their places.

Alla swept onto the set, positioning herself perfectly for the angles of the camera and the lights which had been set up to flatter those fascinating features. A voice called for quiet and a young boy with a clapperboard stepped up to mark the scene. A moment of suspension, like the deep silence before an explosion, then Ray Smallwood called 'Action!' and the spectacle began.

I'd never been to the theatre but I imagined this was what it must feel like: the thrill of live performance, the moment unfolding right in front of you as the actors did what they were born to do and magic was created before your very eyes. Alla was breathtaking; I couldn't tear my gaze away as she moved through the surreal space, every fibre of her being ablaze, every emotion transmitted through the lens to be captured on film and consumed by her adoring public.

I realised I was holding my breath, so absorbed in the scene that I'd forgotten to exhale. Over the past few months, I'd spent countless hours around folks from all aspects of the movie business – from producers and directors to grips and gaffers, attending parties and premieres and screenings – yet I'd had little idea of what actually went into the making of a motion picture. I saw now that it was like alchemy – myriad ingredients combined in just the right quantity in the hope of creating pure gold.

By the time Mr Smallwood called cut, I was spellbound. I didn't know how it would happen, what role I would play, but I knew I wanted to be part of this brave new world.

And then I realised: it had happened, just like Alla had predicted. I'd found my passion.

I turned, smiling, to Natacha, willing her to understand in the silence. She smiled back at me and her violet eyes were shining.

Chapter Twelve

ALLA

Moscow, Russia, 1897

The man whose name she didn't know pushed and grunted, climaxed and withdrew, turning over and rolling himself a cigarette. He didn't offer one to Alla, and she hastily dressed and prepared to leave. Once, she would have felt awkward asking for the money, but now it was a matter of necessity.

'Can I see your ticket?' the man asked.

Alla froze. 'I, er, must have forgotten it…' Working as a prostitute wasn't illegal, but you needed to be registered and she wasn't.

The man said nothing, sucking on his cigarette and staring at her expectantly. He was sitting on the edge of the grimy bed, belly hanging, hairy legs apart. Alla was in equal parts disgusted by and envious of his lack of self-consciousness.

'If I could just have my money…' She tried not to make it sound as though she were begging.

'If I could just see your ticket…'

Alla swore under her breath. She was living virtually hand to mouth, any money she earned spent immediately on essentials. Although the rubles from Ivan Keller had been relatively easy to acquire, Alla hadn't accepted the invitation to return to his house. Instead, a few days later, she'd sold her virginity to a softly-spoken man in her boarding house and from there it hadn't been a huge leap to make the move into prostitution proper. Over the past few months she'd seen scores of squalid rooms like this, unshaven, sweaty men heaving on top of her as she quite literally stared at the cracks in the ceiling. But she'd never gone official and she didn't have her yellow ticket.

Alla eyed the man resentfully, knowing there was nothing she could do.

'*Mudak*,' she spat, snatching the packet of tobacco in a pitiful attempt not to leave empty-handed. The man jumped to his feet, but she was quicker – and clothed – as she ran from his room and out into the street, worn shoe leather pounding the pavement.

Two hours later, after she'd rushed home and washed and changed her clothing – from the provocative dress of a tawdry prostitute to the provocative dress of a gadding young gal-about-town – Alla arrived at the building on Tverskaya Street. The concierge stood in respectful silence as they rode up in the caged elevator, discreetly looking into the middle distance whilst Alla rearranged her overcoat to hide the hole in her stockings.

'Come in, come in,' Tatyana sang as she opened the door, long blonde hair cascading like a willow over water, looking wildly glamorous in ermine-trimmed satin.

'Happy birthday!' Alla kissed her. 'You look sensational. And this apartment is incredible.' It was the first time Alla had visited her friend's home and the contrast with her own hovel was stark; it was impossible not to feel a stab of envy.

'I did well, didn't I?' Tatyana laughed. 'I'm almost ready, come with me.' She led Alla through to a dressing room, furnished all in white with fresh flowers on the chest of drawers and an embroidered silk kimono discarded over a marquise chair. A crystal decanter surrounded by four glasses stood on a low table. 'Help yourself to a drink. Alexei and Viktor will be here soon.'

'Alexei and Viktor?'

Tatyana was pinning up her hair, perusing her reflection: high cheekbones; full lips; doe eyes. Alla knew that Tatyana's beauty meant she struggled to be taken seriously as an actress, but she could think of worse problems to have.

'Alexei is my… guardian. He's the reason I have all of this,' Tatyana smiled, gesturing round the extravagant apartment. 'He looks after me very well.'

'And you look after him in return?' Alla raised an eyebrow suggestively as Tatyana giggled. 'And what about Viktor?'

'He's Alexei's friend. I've never met him, but Alexei says he's a good man. A good man trapped in a bad marriage. Did you know the apartment across the hall is vacant?' she continued airily, dabbing scent on her wrists and behind her ears. 'Play your cards right tonight and we could be neighbours...'

Alla opened her mouth and then closed it again, unsure how to reply. The doorbell filled the silence.

'That'll be them,' Tatyana trilled. She was the kind of girl who trilled and glided, whose laugh tinkled and whose eyes danced. Alla felt a rather different set of words might apply to her: scrappy, unpolished, unorthodox.

The gentleman callers were of a type – in their late thirties, expensively dressed and possessed of an unshakeable confidence bestowed by wealth and privilege, by the ability to survive unscathed from the hardships of life; bullion and breeding impregnable in the face of war or disaster or plague.

'This is Alexei,' Tatyana giggled, pushing her body promisingly against his as she tilted her head to kiss him. He was tall and dark and classically handsome, with smooth skin and chiselled features, wolfish eyes beneath thick brows. Alla disliked him immediately.

'Happy birthday, *moya lyubov*,' he grinned devilishly, reaching into his breast pocket and presenting Tatyana with a jewellery box. She gasped as she opened it, the substantial ruby earrings dazzling in the light; too garish for a wife, but perfect for a mistress.

'Oh! They're just divine!' Tatyana gushed, thanking him with another kiss before taking the diamonds from her ears and replacing them with her newest acquisition. 'But how rude of me, I haven't made the introductions. This is my friend, Alla. Alla, this is Alexei. And this is Viktor.

Alla smiled and offered her hand which Viktor kissed somewhat stiffly, his rough beard grazing her skin. 'Enchanté.'

There was something awkward in his manner which Alla found endearing. He was solidly built, his brown hair flecked with grey, and he wore knee-length leather boots with a rich woollen cape and a fox fur hat.

'Ladies...' Alexei gestured towards the door, helping Tatyana with her velvet cloak. 'Are we ready? Then let's celebrate.'

The Hermitage was one of the ritziest restaurants in Moscow. Housed in a grand building on Trubnaya Square, the interior was decorated in gold and green, famed for its fine French cuisine and its fashionable clientele. The maitre d', dressed in a traditional white shirt with a silk sash tied at the waist, greeted Alexei deferentially and ushered them into a private room, away from the prying eyes of ordinary diners. Tatyana looked perfectly at home in this rarefied world and Alla tried to emulate her nonchalance, her natural sense of entitlement.

The waiter pulled out her chair and Alla sat down, Tatyana on one side of her, Viktor on the other, then a bottle of champagne appeared and they all toasted the birthday girl. Beneath the table, Tatyana squeezed Alla's hand reassuringly then turned her attention to Alexei, flirtatious and adorable as she giggled her way through some anecdote.

Viktor cleared his throat. 'So you study with Tatyana?'

'Yes, at the Philharmonic. Acting is my passion. Escaping the real world into someone else's life – be it a duchess or a scullery maid or a star-crossed lover – is such a gift. Do you like the theatre?'

'No.'

'Perhaps you haven't seen the right plays,' Alla persevered. 'Or the right actors. My tutor, Vladimir Nemirovich, advocates a new kind of acting, based on emotional truth and inner justification – there are no artificial techniques, no unnecessary gestures. It's truly revolutionary. He's building a whole new movement and it's an honour to be a part of that.'

'And what…' Viktor paused, searching for the unfamiliar terms. 'What roles do you like to play?'

'Do you know Ibsen? He's a Norwegian playwright who writes wonderful parts for women. Take Nora in *A Doll's House* – she's a complex, spirited woman who walks out of her unhappy marriage to gain her independence. It's inspiring, challenging. Far more satisfying than playing a lovelorn noblewoman, or a consumptive courtesan.'

Viktor tilted his head, his eyes narrowed as he listened intently. 'Why don't we go to the theatre? One night next week. Anything you think I might enjoy.'

Alla was taken aback. Her eyes softened as she looked at him admiringly. 'All right. Why not?'

The waiter arrived with their first course: Salade Olivier, the restaurant's signature dish, presented on gold-rimmed plates. Alexei toasted Tatyana once again, and she smiled and tossed her head delightedly.

As the conversation resumed, Alla turned back to Viktor. 'So what is it that you do? Are you a lawyer, like Alexei?'

Viktor waved his hand dismissively. 'Something very dull that makes me a lot of money, and that's all you need to know. Let's talk about you instead. You're far more interesting than me, I'm sure. Oh, to be… how old are you?'

'Eighteen.'

'Oh, to be eighteen and living in Moscow. The world is truly your oyster. Were you born here?'

'No, I was born in Yalta, but spent most of my childhood in Switzerland...'

Alla was funny and charming as she regaled him with tales of holidays spent by the lake in Montreux, of practical jokes played on school friends and memories of a travelling circus with a wizened fortune-teller who'd examined her palm and predicted her future. The horrors of her youth were erased, every story light and bright and breezy; Alla knew that what she couldn't offer in conventional looks, she could make up for with wit and sparkling conversation.

As the evening wore on and the alcohol flowed, Alla wondered how she could ever have thought Viktor stiff and uptight. Undoubtedly, he was different to the men she usually encountered, and a world away from her current lover, a penniless drama student named Alexander Sanin. Alex was hot-headed, artistic, bohemian – the polar opposite of the man sitting in front of her – but, in spite of everything, Alla found that she liked Viktor. He was good company, and there was a caring, protective side to him that was evident in how he retrieved her napkin without fuss when it slid from her lap, or the way he solicitously refilled her water glass before the waiter could attend to it. He listened attentively, didn't look at her lasciviously.

Alla said as much to Tatyana when they visited the ladies' room together, as Tatyana pirouetted across the tiled floor, flushed and giddy at the attention from her lover.

'Alexei's promised to take me to the horse racing,' she

declared. 'And I'm to have a new outfit especially for the occasion. Can you imagine? Being on his arm at such a public event. And the people I'll meet!' Tatyana stopped spinning and stared in the rococo mirror, her hands flying to her face. 'Do I look older? There are wrinkles round my eyes that I'm sure weren't there yesterday...'

'You're nineteen,' Alla laughed. 'And I've never seen you look more beautiful than you do tonight. Alexei clearly adores you.'

Tatyana was temporarily placated, blowing Alla a kiss. 'And what do you think of Viktor? He likes you, I can tell. Alexei said he's rarely seen him in such good spirits. He said Viktor deserves to enjoy himself for putting up with his old harridan of a wife.'

The mention of Viktor's spouse gave Alla pause; she wondered whether she should feel guilty about her existence. But the woman was faceless, nameless, and Viktor was the one who was cheating, not Alla. Not that their behaviour thus far had violated any marriage vows. Alla thought of the various men she'd bedded in her new profession, those who made no attempt to hide their wedding rings, or who brazenly carried a photograph of their family in the wallet from which they paid for her services. She remembered the way her father had treated her mother – coldly, dismissively, violently. Were all men the same? It was a depressing conclusion to reach.

'He seems nice,' Alla admitted. 'He has kind eyes.'

'Kind eyes?' Tatyana roared with laughter. 'You're such an old romantic. Yes, yes, he has kind eyes, and a million rubles in the bank, and a summer home in Rublyovka.'

'That doesn't interest me,' Alla insisted.

'No, of course not, you're devoted to your art. But no one would judge you if you *did* take advantage of the opportunities Viktor could offer you. Life is to be enjoyed, Alla, not endured. Now, come on. It's still my birthday for the next two hours, and I intend to make the most of it!'

At the end of the evening the couples parted separately. Alexei disappeared into the night with a jubilant Tatyana and Viktor offered to accompany Alla back to her boarding house. They took a sleigh, bundled up beneath a pile of furs as they flew through the darkness, streetlamps blurring and snow falling softly on this freezing March night. Alla was relaxed and comfortable, her belly full of fine food – a welcome change from the usual bread and sausage bought from a street seller for a couple of kopeks. The conversation arced and flowed as they travelled westward across the city, and Alla watched Viktor's face change as they approached the insalubrious neighbourhood she called home.

'Is this where you live?'

'Yes,' Alla replied quietly, willing herself not to be ashamed.

Viktor said nothing, and Alla sensed he was calculating how quickly he could make his escape. She felt certain that, for all his promising talk of theatre trips and future engagements, she would never see him again.

The driver stopped outside her shabby building and she scrambled to get out, intent on saving herself further embarrassment, but Viktor stopped her.

'I've been thinking,' he began. His hand was resting lightly on her arm, and Alla realised that her heart was beating fast. 'I wondered whether you might like to move? I could get you a nice apartment, in a respectable area. It might take me a few days to organise. Take this, in the meantime.'

Viktor rifled in the depths of his cloak and pressed a wedge of notes into her hand. Alla tried not to stare, but a practiced glance told her there was almost two hundred rubles. Her initial instinct was to decline, to insist she couldn't possibly accept, but she stopped herself. 'Thank you,' was all that she said.

Viktor's large hands enveloped hers as he helped her down from the carriage. 'I'll be in touch.' He signalled to the driver and the sleigh pulled away.

Alla stared after him in shock. The snow began to fall more heavily around her, but right now she couldn't feel the cold. She'd expected Viktor to invite himself up to her room but he hadn't so much as hinted at it, hadn't even tried to kiss her. He was polite, chivalrous, and incredibly wealthy – and she was going to be his mistress. A kept woman! It was the answer to her prayers.

The sleigh was out of sight and Alla did a giddy little dance, letting out a whoop of joy, not caring about the way the dampness soaked through her boots or how the biting wind found her bare legs through the holes in her stockings. With shaking hands, she unlocked the front door then climbed the stairs to her ramshackle room, clutching the money tightly in her fist. She would give notice to her landlady in the morning.

Chapter Thirteen

MAYBELLE

Los Angeles, USA, 1921

I pulled up smartly on Fairfax Avenue. My driving was much improved, even if I did say so myself. Joe had begun to grumble that I was forever borrowing the motorcar, and I was thinking of buying one of my own – I had my eye on a smart Roamer Roadster in a beautiful golden yellow, like a sunflower.

It would match my new dress perfectly, I thought, as I climbed out of the Chevy and skipped along the sidewalk, feeling the light chiffon swirl around my legs. It was a vibrant shade of citrine, cut daringly close on the bodice with a three-tiered drop skirt, and it was rather outrageous – I couldn't imagine myself wearing anything like it a few months ago. My hair was pinned up, a length of matching ribbon wrapped around my forehead. It was terribly unfashionable to keep it so long, but Joe had pleaded with me not to cut it and for now I'd relented.

The bell clanged as I entered Rosa's, a popular neighbourhood bakery recommended by all the people whose opinions I respected. On the counter were luscious-looking displays of flavoured meringues piled high on pastel-coloured stands, coconut macaroons and snickerdoodles, sticky cinnamon rolls and apple tarts and a luscious-looking pecan pie.

'Oh, that looks beautiful, thank you so much,' I gushed, as the assistant presented the angel food cake I'd ordered, topped with whipped cream and fruit, with *Happy Birthday Natacha* piped on the top. 'Have a great day!'

I breezed out into the bright January day, balancing the cake box as I went. Life was good right now, I reflected. It was hard to believe that it was more than a year since that New Year's Eve where Joe and I had skipped Alla's party and surrendered, ecstatically, to our long-fought desires. My life was unrecognisable from that day. *I* was unrecognisable from the naïve, God-fearing farm girl I'd been back then.

Since my trip to Metro Studios and subsequent epiphany that I wanted to be involved – in whatever capacity – with motion pictures, Alla had offered me a role as her Girl Friday, an assistant who ran errands, replied to fan mail, helped to organise her legendary parties and whatever else was required. I sensed that Joe disapproved, that she thought it rather odd – incestuous almost – that Alla would hire her ex-lover's new paramour. But I didn't care one jot, and loved my newfound, gainful employment.

Every day was different. I was always busy, I met new people, I gained an insight into all the different departments and discovered skills I'd never imagined I possessed. I also harboured a sneaking suspicion that Joe was rather annoyed I was no longer kicking around the bungalow all day, available to wait on her hand and foot, and I rather enjoyed the way the balance of power had tilted a little in my favour.

Alla was currently in pre-production for *Aphrodite*, her most ambitious project to date. It was no exaggeration to say she was consumed by it, brimming with ideas to make it more dramatic, more daring, more controversial. The early script drafts were wildly scandalous with scenes of murder and torture, orgies and sapphism, and I found it incredibly exciting to be part of something so modern and free thinking.

Natacha Rambova had once again been engaged as art director and, when I wasn't needed by Alla, I spent my time shadowing her. She was exceptionally talented, and I felt honoured that she considered my opinions worthwhile. She encouraged me to submit my own ideas and experiment with my own designs, challenging me to be bolder, to think bigger and, in return, I kept trying to sneak a little colour into her preferred palate of black and silver.

We'd become good friends, and she'd introduced me to her fiancé, Theodore Koslov, a Russian ballet dancer and choreographer. I have to confess, I didn't like him. There was something brutish about him; he was tall and broad-shouldered, with a deep voice and a short temper, and he used his physical size to dominate.

Through gossip on the film set, I'd learned that he was fifteen years her senior, and that she'd been a seventeen-year-old student at his New York ballet school when they met. Natacha's mother, Winifred, had been furious when she discovered the relationship, and tried to have Theo deported for rape, but he and Natacha fled to England, only returning when Winifred agreed to drop the charges. Furthermore, when the two of them first encountered Alla, Theo had tried to pass off Natacha's designs as his own work.

In short, he was a liar and a charlatan, and I couldn't understand why Natacha stayed with him. She was a formidable force when it came to her career, yet couldn't muster the courage to send the objectionable Theodore packing. There'd been no mention of setting a date for the wedding, with both claiming to be too busy, and for that I was glad, but it pained me to see Natacha unhappy. In her more confessional moments, after a gin cocktail or three, Natacha admitted that she longed to leave him but was simply too fearful. Theodore Koslov was all she'd known for the past seven years, by her side as she evolved from schoolgirl to accomplished young woman, and she was afraid of his reaction if she—

Something up ahead caught my attention and I froze. I didn't know what it was about the young woman standing on the sidewalk, dressed in a simple white cotton dress, but suddenly I found it hard to breathe, my chest tight, my heart hammering. My instinct was to flee, except that she was standing between me and the motorcar.

A middle-aged gentleman walked by and she handed him a pamphlet which he accepted without comment. I caught a glimpse of it as he passed, words and phrases leaping out: 'The Lord is Your Saviour' and 'Southern Baptists of California'. My hands were clammy, and I almost dropped Natacha's cake.

As though my legs were acting independently from the rest of my body, I found myself walking – no, *marching* – towards the girl. I didn't recognise her; she was slim and pretty, with dark blonde hair in a loose bun at the nape of her neck.

'Find salvation in the Lord Jesus Christ,' she smiled, proffering a pamphlet.

My throat felt thick, my hand moving through the air as though it were quicksand as I reached out and took the printed paper, placing it on top of the cake box. The words swam before my eyes, but I recognised the familiar Bible verses (*'The Lord is my Light and my Salvation – Whom shall I Fear?' – Psalm 27:1; 'Stand Up and Bless the Lord Your God for Ever and Ever' – Nehemiah 9:5*).

And there, right at the bottom: *Service led by the Reverend Henry J. Walker*.

I couldn't move.

The girl mistook my inertia for interest. 'We're the first Southern Baptist Church in California and every day more and more people repent in the name of the Lord Jesus Christ, being born again through baptism and sharing in eternal joy...'

I recognised the words, phrases, arguments. I'd once used the very same, standing awkwardly on a street corner trying to entice new congregants. Did she believe what she was saying, I wondered? I watched this young woman as she ploughed on with her monologue, internally congratulating herself on the likelihood of a new convert. Was she merely going through the motions, hating every excruciating minute or, like Uncle Henry, did she revel in the oration, unshakeable faith behind every word she uttered?

'...All your sins can be forgiven, by the sacrifice the son of God made for you...'

I almost laughed out loud. Would Uncle Henry really think

that my sins could be forgiven, or were my crimes too heinous for even God Himself to absolve?

'Is there... is there a large congregation?' I found myself asking, wondering how successful my aunt and uncle had been in my absence.

'We're growing in number every day, and about to break ground on our own physical church. The Lord has truly blessed us.'

'And the Reverend...' I pointed to his name with a shaking finger. 'Is he...' I didn't know what I was attempting to ask, but the girl chimed in:

'The Reverend Henry J. Walker is the most God-fearing man you could ever hope to meet, and the most passionate preacher. He's one hundred per cent committed to doing the Lord's work, and if you commit to his teachings, I guarantee your soul will be saved. Do you want to perish for all eternity?' The question was rhetorical, I presumed. 'Why don't you come to the service on Sunday, find out what it's all about? We're up in Atwater, just off the red line...'

My hearing warped, her voice becoming muffled. The cake in my hands seemed awful heavy; I imagined the cream inside, curdling in the warm sun. Spoiled beyond redemption, just like me.

'Is he... is he well?' I interrupted. 'And his wife, are they both well?' Tears had sprung into my eyes, and the girl eyed me suspiciously.

'Do you know the Reverend and his good wife? Have you been to the service before? Why don't you come on Sunday – they'd be right pleased to see you, I'm sure.'

I could only stare dumbly. I wanted to ask if she'd heard of

me, if I was ever spoken of, if Marisol and Herb and Billy –
goddamn snitch Billy who'd probably done me a favour as it
turned out – were still at the farm. Whether I was remembered
fondly or if my name was mud, *persona non grata,* forbidden to
be mentioned.

But I said nothing. The girl returned to her pitch, to her
lines learned by rote and her second-hand beliefs, before it all
became too much and I choked back a sob, running to the
Chevy and hurling myself inside, dumping the cake carelessly
in the passenger seat, as the girl stared after me in confusion.

The short drive was erratic, the road seemingly awash as I
gave free rein to the tears that spilled down my cheeks, paying
no heed to the honking horns as I wove across the road and
turned without signalling.

I hadn't seen Aunt Ida or Uncle Henry since the day I'd fled
to Joe's. I'd left no forwarding address; I had no desire for
them to know where I was living, or who I was living *with.* I'd
left everything behind – my belongings were scant, but I
regretted leaving the book of poetry that Joe had given me, my
box of trinkets, and my childhood toy – hitherto my
unwavering comfort in times of tribulation.

Of course, I thought about Ida and Henry – regularly at
first, but lessening over time, the pain gradually losing its bite
when I recalled the merciless way I'd been treated. It wasn't
their fault, I reasoned. They had their unshakeable beliefs and
couldn't conceive of what I was. The gulf between Aunt Ida
and Alla would have been impossible to bridge. I mused,
sometimes, on what they might do were I to turn up at the

farm one day. Would I be welcomed back with open arms, the prodigal daughter returned to the bosom of the family? Or cast out into the wilderness, never again to darken their door?

I suspected the latter.

I wiped my eyes as I pulled up outside Hayvenhurst, leaving the cake with Alla's long-standing housekeeper, Carmela, who informed me that Madame Nazimova was working by the pool. I thanked her and headed through the house, stopping briefly in the nearest bathroom to splash cold water on my face. There was no sign of Charles, and for that I was glad. I'd never really got to know him – he seemed uninterested in me, and I got the impression he saw me as nothing more than one of his wife's many hangers-on. I rarely saw him at Hayvenhurst, unless his presence was expected for a party, and the two of them seemed to lead very separate lives.

Outside, Alla was seated at a table beneath the shade of a parasol. Her hair was tied up in a vibrant silk scarf, a script open in front of her, a pen between her teeth.

'Hello,' I called softly, so as not to startle her.

She looked up, took the pen from her mouth, and smiled, taking a moment to return from whatever world she'd been inhabiting before my interruption. 'Maybelle!'

'I've been to collect Natacha's cake. Is she here yet?'

'No. What time is it?'

'Almost noon.'

'Then she should be here any moment. I hope she's not...'

'Not what?'

'Never mind.' Alla stared at me for a moment, squinting in the sunlight. 'Is there something wrong?'

I opened my mouth, primed for denial, but fresh tears sprang to my eyes, hot and humiliating.

'Is it Joe?' Alla pressed.

I shook my head. 'A ghost from the past is all…'

'Would it help to talk about it?'

'Oh no.' I swiped at my wet cheeks then waved my hands dismissively. 'No…'

Alla closed the script and stood up. She was half a head smaller than me, but radiated authority. 'Maybelle, you know I think very highly of you, and if something is upsetting you then I want to try and make it better. Now, take a seat, and I will go fix us a drink. And then we'll talk.'

I sat down beside the chair Alla had just vacated, grateful for her insistence. My head was swimming, and I could feel the beginnings of a headache. Seeing that girl had brought up everything I'd been trying so hard not to confront, stirring emotions I'd suppressed for months. I let the tears flow unchecked, my hands shaking where they lay in my lap.

When I'd lived at the farm, I'd dutifully written to my mother once a week. Since leaving, I hadn't been in contact with her at all. I assumed Aunt Ida would have divulged the details of my downfall, and I was too… too ashamed? Too busy enjoying my hedonistic life with Joe that I'd put it off and pushed my family to the back of my mind? I'd drowned myself in alcohol and good times and doing whatever I damn well pleased, never thinking about the past because the pain was too raw.

Alla returned with two high tumblers of gin and tonic, so strong I almost grimaced. I longed for a glass of cold water, or an iced lemonade like the ones Emmett Fisher used to make, back home in Jonas Springs, but I didn't want to seem ungrateful. I took a sip and set it down.

'Thank you,' I said. 'And I'm mighty sorry to put you to so much trouble. You're busy. I'm being silly.'

'I doubt that very much.' Alla's gaze was scrutinising – rather terrifying, if truth be told – and I knew there was no escape. I closed my eyes and inhaled, breathing in the faint scent of magnolia from the blossoming trees. 'I don't know if Joe's ever told you about… about my life before I met her.'

Alla said nothing, taking a sip of her own drink and watching me closely.

'I lived with my aunt – my momma's sister – and my uncle. They're very religious. Very strict. They wouldn't approve of my life now, not at all.' I laughed hollowly. 'I haven't seen them, or had any contact with them, since I moved in with Joe. And then just now, when I came out of the bakery, I saw a girl on the street. I didn't know her, but she was doing what I used to do. Being a missionary, I guess.' The colour flamed in my cheeks at the mortifying memories. 'I had to stand in the streets, preaching to strangers, handing out pamphlets, encouraging people to join our church.

'Seeing that girl today… it was like seeing a ghost. Like seeing myself a year ago. It brought up a lot of memories – not especially good ones.'

I gulped down my drink, thankful now that Alla had made it so strong. 'My father passed, almost three years ago now. I was the apple of his eye. I've got two brothers, but everyone knew I was my daddy's favourite. I didn't get on well with my momma – part of the reason I was sent to California – but since I moved from Atwater, we've completely lost touch. We haven't been in contact for more than a year. I'm thinking I should write to her but I... What if she doesn't want to hear from me? What if she never replies?'

It was the fear I'd never voiced, the possibility that filled me with dread and haunted me in the small hours – the ultimate rejection by my own mother.

'I understand,' Alla said with feeling. 'I lost my mother when I was five.'

'I'm so sorry. How did she...?'

'She didn't die. She's still alive, as far as I know. My father divorced her. She left in the middle of the night without saying goodbye.'

I said nothing, unsure how to react. Alla had never shared anything so personal with me and, although Joe had often alluded to Alla's difficult childhood, I'd never known any of the details.

'My father was a horrible bully of a man. I'm not exaggerating when I say that I hated him. When he died, I felt nothing but relief, knowing he could never hurt me again. But my mother... I spent my whole childhood longing to be reunited with my *mamochka*. I moved a lot – my father was always sending me to different schools, different relatives. He hated me as much as I hated him. Every time he sent me away, I hoped against hope that this time he was sending me to Mama. That this was the place she was going to be, and we could finally be happy, together again. But it never was.'

Alla paused, the garden silent save for the sound of birdsong and the chattering of the cicadas. I realised how much pain she still carried inside of her – despite the house and the money and the career, those childhood wounds had never fully healed. I wondered if that was what made her such a good actress, able to draw on depths of emotion that she'd truly experienced.

'I had only a child's memories of my mother. In my mind, she was always kind and smiling. She was clean and fresh and smelt of rose water and face powder. She was… so beautiful, with dark hair and red lips. I can still feel the warmth of her when she held me in her arms.

'She left my father once, you know. Ran away with her lover and took me with her. Left my brother and sister behind, but took me, as though I was the only one she wanted. She loved *me* the most. I was so happy – that was all I ever wanted, just to be with her. But my father found us and brought us back and… well, I'm sure you can imagine. It wasn't pretty.'

Alla stared out across the pool, dark eyes unseeing, lost in her thoughts.

'Did you ever see her again?'

It took Alla a moment to reply, as though she'd forgotten I was there.

'Once. I was sixteen and she was living in Odessa. I'd spent my whole life waiting for that moment, desperate for us to be reunited. And when it happened it was… nothing but disappointment. I didn't know who this woman was, and she wasn't interested in me. We were total strangers to one other. She'd grown older, fatter. I suppose that was to be expected, but it was still a shock, to see how much she'd changed. She told me that she'd remarried, that she was happy. And although she didn't say it explicitly, I knew there was no place for me in her life.'

My heart was breaking as I listened to Alla tell her story.

There was such melancholy in those huge, expressive eyes; no camera had ever captured the sorrow she exuded right now.

'So you think I shouldn't go back?' I ventured tentatively. 'Leave the past in the past?'

Alla smiled wryly. 'No, my darling. I'm saying quite the opposite. If you have a chance to build the bridge then take it. I left it too late. You might not have done.'

Her answer took me by surprise. I'd been preparing to walk away, to sail into the future with Joe and harden my heart against memories of the past, keeping them locked up tightly in a little box where no one would ever find the key. But Alla's counsel had let a chink of light penetrate that dark space.

'Do you think you'll ever go back? To Russia, I mean?'

Alla exhaled slowly, tilting her head to one side as she considered the question. 'Not now, with all this fighting and upheaval and the Bolsheviks.'

I didn't know much about the situation over there – politics was far from my area of expertise – but I knew there'd been a revolution a few years ago, that the Tsar and his family were rumoured to have been imprisoned then killed, the country taken over by Vladimir Lenin and his Bolshevik Party. Since then, Russia had descended into civil war, plagued by famine and poverty, privation and lawlessness.

'Once again, I think I've left it too late. I wouldn't recognise the old country now.' Alla looked at me and raised an eyebrow. 'Perhaps I'll become an American, apply for citizenship.'

'We'd love to have you.'

Alla smiled, then her expression grew despondent once more. 'It is very sad, to think that you cannot ever go back. Take your chance if you can, Maybelle.'

We sat in silence, a light breeze blowing up through the valley, disturbing the trees the way Alla had stirred my thoughts.

So much had changed of late and my mind was in tumult as I tried to navigate my way through a world beyond my wildest imaginings. I'd run towards Joe at full pelt, desperate to escape the mundanity of the everyday, dazzled by the bright lights and glamour she offered. Now the first flush of excitement had faded, and I feared it wasn't enough. That Joe wasn't enough. I'd thought that meeting her had revealed who I was, but now I saw that my epiphany was merely the beginning of that journey, not the end.

I reached for the last of my drink and a distant noise caught my attention; a motorcar bumping up the track. It was approaching at speed, honking its horn furiously. Alla and I glanced at one another, instinct telling us something wasn't right, leaping to our feet and running round to the front of the house where Carmela was doing the same as a taxicab pulled to a halt and Natacha stumbled out, covered in blood.

'My God! What happened? Call a doctor, quickly!' Alla shouted at Carmela, who raced back to the house. I stood there, uselessly, overcome with shock; the cab driver looked as horrified as I did, and I paid him quickly, with an extra generous tip to buy his silence.

'Theo shot me,' Natacha gasped. There was a bloody wound on her calf, crudely bound with a piece of fabric that had turned crimson. 'The bastard shot me! I didn't know where else to go… I finally told him I was leaving him, but he got his rifle… He screamed at me to get back into the house and I refused… I ran to the cab and he shot me. He fucking shot me!'

'Lie down,' Alla instructed, seeing how pale Natacha had grown. 'Elevate your leg. We'll get help. The doctor's on his way.'

Natacha complied. Even from here, I could see lumps of buckshot lodged in the mangled mess just below her knee. Alla knelt down beside her, cradling Natacha's head in her hands.

'It's all right. You're safe now, I promise. I won't ever let that bastard touch you again.'

Chapter Fourteen

ALLA

Moscow, Russia, 1899

'*Bol'shoy spasibo*,' Alla murmured. She turned slowly, taking in the beautiful apartment for the final time. 'Thank you for everything.'

She'd lived there for almost two years now and wondered if she were an utter fool for giving it all up – the prestigious address on Stoleshnikov Lane, the furs, the jewels, the sense of security – to move over four hundred miles away to a small theatre in the provinces. It was far from the bright lights and glamour she'd envisaged.

'I'll miss you,' Viktor sighed, his forehead rumpled, the corners of his mouth turned grimly downward. He opened his arms and Alla hurled herself into them, pressing against his barrel chest, inhaling the musky scent of his cologne, the musty scent of his summer coat.

'I'll miss you too. You've been so good to me.'

And it was true. Viktor had been exceptionally generous

towards her. Despite the luxurious surroundings in which she was currently standing, Alla remained practically penniless, but to work in regional theatre she needed to provide her own costumes; Viktor had financed her latest career move, furnishing her with a whole new wardrobe, a selection of wigs, a stack of rubles and – an added gift – a portable rubber bathtub.

Throughout their liaison, he'd been kind, respectful and considerate, treating her almost as an equal, not a mistress. Viktor had never forced the physical side of their relationship even though, considering the nature of their arrangement, he had every right to demand her submission. And last summer, when Alla had abandoned him for six weeks to spend the holidays with Olga Zhdanova, her good friend from the Academy, he'd never once remonstrated with her decision, despite his obvious unhappiness. Yes, Viktor was undoubtedly a good man, and Alla knew that she'd been incredibly lucky to find him.

'It's time to go. Your train leaves in an hour,' he reminded her reluctantly.

Alla nodded and pulled away, determined not to look back at the bare apartment empty of her belongings, at the gilded wooden furniture covered in dust sheets. Her maid, Simka – another present from Viktor – was waiting by the door. She'd supervised the loading of the carriage, full to bursting with trunks containing Alla's new wardrobe, her expanding collection of novels and plays and, strapped proudly to the roof, the venerable rubber bathtub.

Viktor helped Alla into her seat, softly kissing the back of her hand just as he'd done the first time they'd met. Then he stepped back and nodded to the driver, watching stoically as the horses moved off and the party retreated into the distance. Alla waved and blew kisses, all too aware of how their positions had reversed since that first meeting where she'd stood in the snow outside her dilapidated boarding house and watched him drive away.

The carriage rounded the corner and rolled along Tverskaya Street towards Belorussky Station, Viktor slipping out of sight and out of mind as Alla drank in the sights of her beloved Moscow. How she adored the grand architecture, the bustle of the streets, the wide, green spaces of the parks, the churches, markets, flower sellers and hawkers. It was a city that was forever moving forwards yet mindful of its noble history, that was home to rich and poor – and Alla had experienced it as both. It had been a proud achievement for her to leave her childhood behind and start afresh in the Russian city, to follow her dream and study at the Philharmonic. And now she was leaving for the back of beyond, a deliberate leap into obscurity. Fear clutched at her chest and her throat tightened. Could she really abandon the life she'd made for herself? Was she making an irrational decision, one which she'd invariably come to regret?

'Stop the carriage!' Alla cried out, alarming both Simka and the driver who pulled sharply on the reins, coming to a halt outside the post office. Alla rifled through the bag on her lap and took out a letter, handing it to Simka. 'This needs to make the next post.'

Simka looked down at the name on the envelope – Alexander Sanin – and back up at Alla, her eyebrows raised. Alla stared back defiantly, and Simka knew better than to pass comment. Wordlessly, she stepped down from the carriage and did as she was bid.

Alexander Sanin was the real reason Alla was leaving Moscow for Babruysk. They'd been involved in a thrilling affair and she'd fallen madly, deeply, hopelessly in love. But then Alex had finished things between them, told her it was over, and Alla was devastated.

Her tutor at the Philharmonic, Vladimir Nemirovich, had found a kindred spirit in the actor and director Konstantin Stanislavsky, the two of them bonding over a shared belief in a new kind of acting – one that prized emotional truth and naturalism to reveal the inner life of the characters. The two men had formed the Moscow Art Theatre, and Alla had been invited to join as an apprentice extra. It was an exciting, heady time to be at the forefront of a pioneering new movement and Alla was giddy with expectation.

Alexander Akimovich Sanin – tall, dark, and with exceptional facial hair – was an actor in the company, as well as Stanislavsky's assistant. Ten years older than her, he was dashing, dynamic, and in a position of power when he took over rehearsals for the MAT's production of Tsar Fyodor. He'd studied history at Moscow University, and was intelligent and cultured, in addition to being a wonderful actor. Alla never tired of watching him work, and the two of them would stay up until the early hours after rehearsals, waxing lyrical about plays, literature, art and – Alex's passion – the opera. Alla was always eager to learn, to soak up new experiences, and Alexander undoubtedly provided those.

Their relationship was tempestuous, every day bringing fresh break-ups and make-ups. Alla would accuse him of not respecting her talent, whilst Alex was wildly jealous of Viktor, hurling accusations at Alla that she despised him for not being rich, for being a poor artist unable to keep her in the style to which she'd become accustomed. There was envy and pride on both sides, but their chemistry was undeniable, their fling brief yet intense.

Alla was distraught when it ended and, furious at losing roles to her rival Olga Knipper – Stanislavsky's regular choice of leading lady – she made the impulsive decision to leave the MAT. Her acting tutor, Nemirovich, duly recommended her to a company in Babruysk who were looking for a versatile actress for their summer season, though there was another reason why he didn't press her to stay; whilst Alla kept her religion a closely guarded secret, Nemirovich had long suspected she had Jewish ancestry. Anti-Jewish pogroms had swept across Russia for the last two decades, following the assassination of Tsar Alexander II, and the May Laws – a series of harsh restrictions on Jews – were enacted by the new tsar. If her secret were exposed, Alla would never be allowed on stage in Moscow. A smaller city, like Babruysk, would be much safer.

Simka returned from the post office, climbing back into the carriage and settling herself beside Alla.

'Is it done?'

Simka nodded. 'Yes, it's done. Now let's hurry, or we'll miss the train.'

Babruysk was nothing like Moscow. Alla had grown used to the hubbub of city life, the anonymity of a crowd, the contrast to be found in the grandiose buildings beside the poverty-ridden slums. Here, the pace of life felt much slower, the inhabitants homogenous, the neighbourhoods colourless. Every day she questioned whether she'd made the right choice.

Her fellow actors in the Babruysk Theatre Company were mostly pleasant and welcoming – some even moderately talented – but here no one was interested in the experimental techniques she'd learned at the Arts Theatre, or the inner truth she'd studied with Stanislavsky. Her Zaza was expected to be outrageous, her Camille larger than life, every character purged of subtlety and nuance. But Alla accepted her director's wishes, putting her shoulder to the wheel and getting on with her work.

One evening, she returned to her lodgings in a quiet street near St Nicholas' Cathedral. It was late and she was tired, her mind awhirl with lines and actions and motivations.

'Come, sit down,' smiled Simka, ushering Alla inside and taking her coat. 'I've made *pelmeni*.'

'Thank you, you're a treasure,' Alla sighed, squeezing her hands gratefully then sinking onto the plain, wooden chair, reaching for the fresh water Simka had placed on the table.

'A letter arrived for you today,' Simka remarked, passing it across on her way to serve the dumplings.

Alla took it and her heart leapt as she recognised Alexander Sanin's handwriting, all thoughts of work and weariness forgotten as she tore open the envelope, a million fantasies flying through her head: he loved her, he couldn't live without her, she must return to Moscow right now so he could make her his wife. And she would do it, Alla vowed, as she liberated the letter from its papery prison. She would leave on the next train if that was what he wanted!

The reality was rather different.

Alla skimmed over the cruel words, her heart breaking anew. Alex didn't care what she did. He was glad she'd left Moscow. He no longer loved her and she was not to contact him again.

Disappointment and shame burned through her, swiftly followed by bitterness, then rage. She leapt to her feet and paced the room as Simka looked on in concern.

'Bring me my writing things,' Alla demanded. Simka did as she was told, swiftly setting up the paper and fountain pen on the table beside the forgotten *pelmeni*.

Alla sat down and began to write, almost tearing through the paper in her haste. The words flowed out of her, her hand barely keeping pace with her thoughts. When she'd finally finished, the dumplings were cold. She addressed the envelope triumphantly and handed it to Simka.

'Please take this to the post office tomorrow morning, straight away.'

Simka nodded, glancing at the envelope as she tucked it in her pocket. To her surprise, the name on the front wasn't Alexander Sanin, as she had expected. Instead, it was addressed to Sergei Golovin.

Sergei Golovin was seated at his desk in the shabby boarding room in Moscow, learning lines when the post arrived. He was of medium height, passably handsome, with hooded eyes and full lips, nondescript hair and an upright posture. He was a drama student, and his path had crossed with Alla's at a party where actors mingled with poets, painters with would-be revolutionaries. Sergei had found her instantly fascinating – full of life and ideas, intense and charismatic. It was no exaggeration to say that he'd fallen in love with Alla, albeit of the unrequited kind; she responded gladly to his flirtations, but he'd never been able to definitively capture her heart.

Sergei thought of Alla as a beautiful bird of paradise, exotic and beguiling, but desperately unhappy when confined to a cage. He knew that she had other lovers, and that her lifestyle was unconventional, but that only added to her allure in his eyes.

Sergei was heartsick when she moved to Babruysk, seemingly on a whim. He considered following her, but his life and studies were in Moscow, and anyway, he didn't know if she would accept him. He stoically and patiently bore the loss and, as he read the letter he'd just received, it appeared that his forbearance had borne fruit. Alla's effusive words spoke of love and longing, of her desperation to be reunited with her darling Sergei, commanding him to come at once to Babruysk where she longed for his tender caresses and sweet kisses.

Sergei jumped to his feet, the script lying abandoned on the table and all thoughts of his upcoming tutorial forgotten. He reached for his leather travelling bag, threw in a change of clothes and the copy of *Anna Karenina* he was reading, and set off for the station to find out when the next train to Babruysk departed. He loved Alla and would make her see that he was the man for her. This was his opportunity and Sergei was going to grasp it with both hands.

The wedding dress was plain, white silk overlaid with long, lace sleeves. No embroidery or beading or embellishment. Her hair was tamed and pinned beneath a lace cap, from which hung a long train that surrounded her like a butterfly caught in a net.

Alla felt nauseous. And guilty. She'd squandered the last of the money Viktor had given her on this inappropriately white gown and was almost certain he hadn't intended for her to spend it on a dress in which to marry another man.

'Are you ready?' asked Simka.

Alla nodded. She daren't open her mouth to reply in case she vomited.

'You don't have to do this,' Simka cautioned, but the reminder fell on deaf ears as Alla turned and made her entrance into the small chapel.

The actors from the Babruysk Theatre Company were seated on both sides of the aisle and only added to the overwhelming sensation that this wasn't real, that she was merely an actress playing yet another role. But Alla had never suffered this badly from stage fright, never had nerves so intense that she thought she might faint if she took just one more step. If this was a play, then she was giving the worst performance of her life. But all anyone else saw was a sweetly nervous bride on her wedding day.

At the front of the church, beside all the relevant props – altar, candles, priest in robes – stood her fiancé, smiling adoringly. In a matter of minutes, he would be her husband.

As Alla reached him, Sergei took her hands, kissing her

fingertips softly before releasing them. They both turned to the bearded priest, a rather terrifying figure whom Alla was convinced could see right into the depths of her black heart and perceive her true feelings. He began to speak, Alla's lips automatically finding the required responses, though her mind was detached as though she were floating high above, an audience member in this badly written love story which had rapidly descended into farce.

Furious at Alexander's second rejection, Alla had penned the impulsive, impassioned missive to Sergei Golovin. She knew he'd fallen in love with her back in Moscow, and what could be better to soothe the ego than knowing that whilst one man had rejected her, another had been quite captivated by her charms and unequivocally fallen head over heels?

Somewhat pathetically, Sergei had done everything she asked, arriving from Moscow on the evening of the third day after the letter had been despatched. He'd appeared breathlessly at the boarding house, falling to one knee and proposing marriage, whereupon Alla, thrilled by the drama and the archetypal gesture, had immediately accepted. Who wouldn't want a whirlwind romance, and a white dress more lavish than any costume, and to be the centre of attention before a handpicked audience? She would write to Alexander immediately and tell him of all that he had lost.

And now here she was, once again dealing with the consequences of her impetuosity, every eye upon her as she recited her vows and pretended to gaze adoringly at Sergei. Alla had never spent a lot of time imagining her wedding day but, if she had, it probably wouldn't have looked like this – in a small funeral chapel in the cemetery, no family in attendance for either of them, no friends except the transient camaraderie of her theatre company.

The elderly priest pronounced them husband and wife, and Sergei kissed his new bride. Alla allowed herself to be lost in his moustache, smothered by his unfamiliar breath and, for the thousandth time since she'd moved to Babruysk, reflected on the wisdom of her decisions.

'A toast! To my beautiful wife. I love you. Here's to many happy years together.'

Sergei reached down, his hands either side of Alla's head as he pulled her towards him, kissing her passionately to the approval of the whooping guests who echoed their congratulations to *"Madame Golovin"*. No one seemed to notice Alla's expression as she pulled away, appalled by the way Sergei had manhandled her. She'd felt as though she were suffocating when his large hands clamped her cheeks, and she'd broken out in a sweat, her breathing restricted by the corseted gown. The room seemed to grow hotter even as the summer evening cooled, and Alla began to feel light-headed, certain she was going to pass out.

She touched Sergei lightly on the arm, muttered something about using the bathroom, and fled, pushing past the revellers in her voluminous dress, bursting through the door into the welcome fresh air where she stood for a moment, hands on hips, gulping like a fish pulled from the sea. The light was fading, the air faintly perfumed with the scent of chamomile flowers. A few passers-by regarded her curiously, this distressed bride in all her finery.

After the ceremony, the happy couple and their guests had decamped to an inn where Sergei had booked a private room for them to eat, drink and make merry. The food had been basic and the alcohol plentiful, the evening becoming inevitably more raucous with speeches and toasts, singing and cheering, all conducted at a volume expected of a troupe of actors being fed and watered at someone else's expense. Alla had picked at the cold meats on her plate before pushing it away, succumbing to several shots of vodka in an attempt to inure herself to her new reality.

'Are you all right?' Simka had followed her mistress outside and regarded her worriedly. Tall, broad and no-nonsense, she'd been a good and loyal friend to Alla in recent weeks, trying to dissuade her from marrying as she suspected – presciently – that Alla might well regret her impulsive action.

'Yes, yes, I'm fine.' Alla turned from side to side as though she didn't know which way to go, then threw her hands up in the air, clearly in a state of some agitation. Nearby, a train whistled as it approached the station, rails clanking and grey smoke billowing into the firmament. 'No. No, I'm not. Simka, please, go back inside and tell Sergei I've gone back to the boarding house. I don't want him to follow me. I don't want… there will be no wedding night. Please… make my excuses. Say I'm unwell. Tell Sergei I'll speak with him tomorrow.'

Simka hesitated, but knew better than to question Alla. She nodded her agreement and went back inside.

Alla began to walk, instinct urging her to get as far away as possible from the scene of the crime, to go back to the safety of her rooms. She felt numb, trying not to think about what she'd just done – marrying a man she didn't love to spite another – and she stumbled as she walked, seemingly impossible to place one foot in front of the other.

The train had pulled into the station and a crush of people streamed down the street towards her, barely bothering to conceal their curiosity at the sight of the unhinged-looking woman in the wedding dress, the hem filthy where it trailed along the dirty cobbled street. Alla put her head down and pushed on, until *something* – something inexplicable yet visceral – caused her gaze to alight on a figure in the crowd, intuition identifying a familiar curve of the shoulder, the broad brace of the back, the sweep of the thick, dark hair she'd dreamed of running her hands through. It took her a second to place him, his presence was so unexpected, and she stopped dead, as though struck by a thunderbolt, certain she must be dreaming.

'Alex!' she gasped. She began to run towards him, shock giving way to joy. 'You came. My God, I don't believe it, you came!'

Everything would be all right now. She would throw herself into Alexander's arms and he would rescue her, would take her far away from here, back to Moscow, and everything would be all right. She didn't register the horrified look on his face, but couldn't fail to miss the way he recoiled as she reached for him, how he stepped backwards, shaking his head in disbelief.

The crowd swarmed around them; some paused to watch, anticipating a scene.

'I got your letter.' His voice had that deep, arresting timbre, yet his throat sounded tight. 'You said you were to be married, but I never thought…' He gestured wordlessly at her.

Alla looked down at the billowing dress, realising it was impossible to deny the unspoken accusation.

'But you don't love him… I know you don't.'

'You're right. I love *you*. I only married him to make you jealous, and—'

'This is madness.' Alexander laughed mirthlessly. 'You're insane.'

'It's not madness,' Alla protested, though even to her own ears it sounded anything but rational. 'I love you, and you obviously love me or else you wouldn't have come all this way when—'

'You're wrong. I thought I did but I… I don't want any part of this lunacy. This circus. Are you acting, Alla? Are you playing a role right now? You're like some demented Dostoyevsky heroine—'

'Alex, my love—' Alla reached for him but he pushed her hand away, more forcefully than intended.

'I can't believe I came here. What was I thinking?'

Alla opened her mouth but she had no more arguments with which to convince him. She could sense him slipping away from her, that panicky, freefall feeling in the pit of her stomach that told her it was happening all over again. She'd come so close but now she was losing him a second time and this time she'd never get him back.

'Goodbye, Alla.'

Alexander turned and walked back into the station. Alla could only stand and watch, taking in every heart-rending detail – the small leather suitcase, the smart coat that she knew had been borrowed from the MAT costume cupboard, the way his hair had grown long and curled over his collar – before he disappeared inside. But she wouldn't follow him. She knew when she was beaten. Instead, she sank to the ground in her cursed white dress and sobbed as though the world was ending.

Chapter Fifteen

MAYBELLE

Los Angeles, USA, 1921

The inconsequential city of Vernon, barely five miles southeast of Los Angeles, did not seem the most likely location for one of the hottest nightclubs in the state. Confounding expectations, it was home to the Vernon Country Club, a haven for movie stars and fashionable Angelenos looking to flout the prohibition laws in favour of showgirls and illicit liquor, gambling and dancing and good times.

Right now the atmosphere was raucous, bordering on febrile. Alla, who usually stayed in control of her drinking, was undeniably intoxicated, calling for the waiter to bring shots of vodka, calling an ironic '*Na Zdorovie*' over the noise of the Paul Whiteman band. June Mathis and Patsy Ruth Miller, a young actress who'd had a small role in Alla's latest film, were there, along with Rose Dione and Eva Le Gallienne, an old friend of Alla's from her time on Broadway.

She'd gathered her closest friends and we'd all turned out

to support her. Metro Pictures – the studio which had brought her across the country from New York, made her into an international film star, and paid her $13,000 a week at the height of her fame – had terminated her contract. On reading early drafts of *Aphrodite*, they'd been appalled at the sex and violence it contained and abruptly cancelled the project. Alla's next film, *Camille*, managed mediocre ticket sales and split the critics; she was no longer the box office gold she had once been, yet her list of demands grew ever more extravagant. And, although I hated to acknowledge it, Alla was now in her forties, playing ingenues in their twenties, and the American public found it unpalatable. She still carried herself like a queen, but I knew the termination had hit her hard, and Joe and I had been rallying round.

Natacha had supported her too, as best she could during her recovery. After turning up at Hayvenhurst that terrible afternoon, Natacha had been rushed to hospital where they removed the lead shot from her leg, her bloodstained silk dress unsalvageable. Unbelievably, she returned to Theo during her convalescence, despite me begging her not to and Alla insisting she could stay with her. As Natacha physically healed, she became mentally stronger, summoning the courage to leave her abusive fiancé once again. This time, her departure was far less dramatic; Theo behaved rationally, realising he couldn't change Natacha's mind, and willingly let her go. The scar below her knee would never fully heal, but now she was thriving.

Alla staggered to her feet, tapping a knife against her glass to get our attention – as feeble against the nightclub noise as a lone piccolo against the might of a full orchestra. She had shunned her usual black for this evening and was wearing a silver satin number that Natacha had designed, clearly a statement that she didn't intend to fade into the background anytime soon.

'I have an announcement to make. No, *two* announcements,' Alla corrected herself. 'The first is that Marcus Loew—' her voice was dripping with disdain as she named the head of Metro Pictures, '—can go and fuck himself.' This elicited whoops and cheers and the raising of champagne coupes, as we all expressed our view, in the most impolite way possible, that Loew had never known his father and was likely illegitimate.

'The second is that my husband and I—' here she grasped Charles' hand and raised it skyward, '—are going to make a movie. It will be financed by Nazimova Productions, it will be independent, and I will be able to do whatever the fuck I choose without being dictated to by those ignorant, unimaginative, wet-the-bed-at-night assholes.' More shouts in solidarity and yells of approval.

'And all of *you*—' now she took time to gesture round the table at her assembled entourage, looking each of us unsteadily in the eye, '—are going to be a part of it. All of us, my friends. And it's going to be like nothing anyone has ever seen before, the pinnacle of art and creativity. It's going to be extraordinary. It's going to be a triumph. And Marcus *mudak* Loew is going to realise he made the worst decision of his life.'

The roars and whistles had reached fever pitch; even in the rowdy atmosphere of the Vernon Country Club we were beginning to attract attention.

'We're making a movie of *Salomé*. I will play the lead, of

course – a woman who dances with her bare feet in the blood of a man she has craved for and slain. And my handsome, talented husband will direct.'

She kissed the back of his hand and, even in my hazy state, I noted the incongruity of the gesture. I confess, I still found the relationship between Alla and Charles a curious one, and Joe was frustratingly evasive if I tried to question her about it. Physically they were opposites: Charles was blond and well-built, classically handsome and towering a whole twelve inches above his diminutive wife. Perhaps it was their immigrant status that provided a common bond, for Charles was an English gentleman who'd moved to the States when he was seventeen. They clearly got on well together, both personally and professionally, having co-founded a production company where Alla would play the lead and Charles would co-star or direct. And they were obviously fond of one another, despite Joe once letting slip that they slept in separate bedrooms, like brother and sister. Charles certainly didn't seem to mind the harem of young women that forever surrounded his wife. Even now, Eva was sitting beside Alla, gazing at her adoringly as she delivered her announcements.

'Joe, my wonderful, talented, beloved friend – you are going to write this movie.'

'I think Oscar Wilde got there before me, darling,' Joe quipped, to the amusement of the table. Despite her throwaway comment, I could tell she was thrilled at the prospect of adapting Wilde's translation. I looked across at her, properly seeing her for the first time in a long time. She'd grown out her blunt bangs, and favoured wearing her russet bob in Marcel waves, a style which I felt aged her. Faint lines appeared at the corners of her eyes when she smiled, and she rebuffed all my attempts to update her style, preferring baggy trousers and a man's shirt at home, plain skirts and sweaters if we were out in public.

Joe was a decade older than me and, though this had initially felt irrelevant, at times now it seemed insurmountable. I was still excited to be learning, discovering, having adventures. In contrast, Joe was... comfortable. Though still ambitious, she knew who she was, what she liked and disliked, what she would and wouldn't tolerate. But that dearth of curiosity made her intractable, and I found her lack of interest in new experiences a source of frustration. I was ready to go out and conquer the world and had found new friends to help me do that; I was no longer reliant on Joe, and it was hard to remember a time when we had been inseparable.

'Natacha – you, of course, will be the art director. How could I possibly have anyone else's vision but yours?'

A delighted Natacha blew Alla a kiss.

'Maybelle.' Alla turned to me and my surprise was evident. 'You look glorious tonight, as you always do.' I was sporting a vibrant pink dress that I'd made myself, with an oversized silk bow at the waist, the hem trimmed with marabou feathers. 'I thought you might like to second Natacha. Assistant art direction and costumes.'

'Me? Of course... th... thank you,' I stuttered. I was flattered by the trust she'd placed in me, emotional in a way that wasn't solely a result of the alcohol I'd imbibed. My first real role! I thought about how far I'd come, how my life had changed since I'd moved from Kentucky. Then I remembered the conversation I needed to have later with Joe, and my glow dimmed a little.

Alla moved on, naming other people around the table, handing out their hallowed roles. Her enthusiasm was infectious, and it really did sound as though *Salomé* would be an incredible production – dramatic, groundbreaking, sexual and heavily stylised. It would prioritise movement and dance, giving it the feel of a theatrical performance or even a ballet, a bold new interpretation of the story of King Herod's stepdaughter who requests the head of John the Baptist on a silver platter as a reward for performing the Dance of the Seven Veils. I knew this was something Alla had longed to do for many years, but the studio had always been too apprehensive. Now that she'd been released from her contract, she could do whatever she liked.

Across the table, Natacha mouthed her congratulations, and I moved to sit beside her, my mind already brimming with ideas. I admired her hugely, was in awe of her talent and ambition, and I couldn't wait to learn more from her.

For the past few months, since escaping the clutches of Theodore Koslov, she'd been stepping out with Rudolph Valentino, whom she'd met on the set of *Camille*, and who'd since become a huge star due to his role in *Four Horsemen of the Apocalypse*. Ironically, his first job after moving to California was at the very establishment we were in right now – the Vernon Country Club – as a tango dancer. And in another peculiar twist of fate, two years ago he'd married Jean Acker, the woman Alla had brought from New York and who'd made fun of me at the first Sunday pool party I attended, diving into the water and claiming to be born again. Jean had regretted the marriage immediately, refused to spend the wedding night with Rudy and fled to the house of her ex-lover Grace Darmond, with whom she'd lived ever since. Rudolph and Jean had been living in denial, trying to pretend the marriage had never happened, and only filed for divorce a few months ago. Although Rudy and Natacha were an unlikely match, it seemed to be going well.

'Alla's talked of making a movie of *Salomé* as long as I've known her.' Natacha grinned as I settled in beside her.

'I'm so excited,' I gushed. 'I can't thank her – and you – enough for trusting me to work on this.'

'You wouldn't have been given the job if she didn't think you could do it.' Natacha shrugged. Her voice dropped lower, and she leaned in towards me: 'I know Alla wants this production to be very sensual, very erotic – are you up for the challenge?'

I couldn't help but notice the way her red lips curved as she spoke, the way her dress bagged a little as she leaned forwards, displaying a hint of décolletage. Alcohol made me bold, and I held her gaze. 'As long as you're on hand to help me...' I breathed.

There was a moment where time seemed to stand still, then Natacha sat back, breaking the spell. 'What about the colour palette?' she wondered, sipping her drink. 'What do you think?'

'Let's do it all in black and white,' I suggested eagerly.

'Black and *silver*,' Natacha corrected – her preferred aesthetic.

'Of course,' I laughed. Across the table I caught Joe's eye;

she was speaking to Alla but watching us intently. I gave her a little wave. 'And the costumes need to be… minimal.'

'Even the men's!' Natacha squealed. 'We need big men – muscle men. And dwarves!'

'All in metallic silver loin cloths.'

'We'll get everything from Maison Lewis in Paris – it's the best! Are you familiar with Aubrey Beardsley's illustrations?'

'Yes! Joe has prints in her – *our* – bungalow.'

'Marvellous! Say, what are you doing tomorrow? Let's meet for coffee, compare ideas. Do you want to come to my place, around 11?'

'Perfect. I'm so excited, I can't wait for us to work together again.' I reached out to give her a spontaneous hug. She smelt wonderful – of amber and jasmine with a hint of something more intense, like patchouli – her cheek brushing against mine, my fingers on the bare skin at the nape of her neck. I held on for longer than I should have done.

In the car on the way home, Joe was in an odd mood. The road was dark as we drove too fast through unilluminated scrubland, and there was a definite atmosphere between us – and not in a good way. I remembered how it had been in the early days, how excited I was to sit beside her when she picked me up from the farm and whisked me away to a world of infinite possibilities. My leg resting alongside hers had filled me with lust, an undeniably erotic charge between us. Tonight, Joe held herself tightly, lips pursed, body far away from mine.

I chattered on, trying to lighten the mood.

'Alla and Charles are such a strange couple, don't you think? I've never understood their relationship.'

'Other people's relationships are usually a mystery from the outside. You don't have to understand them – it's none of your business.'

Joe's tone was sharp, and I was briefly chastened, but the alcohol in my bloodstream meant I didn't stay silent for long.

'I'm so happy for Alla that she's decided to produce *Salomé*. Natacha said she's wanted to do it for years, and it'll keep her busy now that Metro... I mean... it's such a bold decision. She's not scared of anything is she?' Silence met my outburst, and I pushed on. 'And you must be delighted – to script *Salomé*, to adapt Oscar Wilde!'

'Yes, well, Alla's always looked out for me.'

'And it's a big step up for me, too,' I replied, starting to get annoyed at Joe's terse responses, her lack of acknowledgement that this was a huge moment in my fledgling career. 'Won't it be fun for us to work together on the same project?'

'Mm hmm.'

We were back in suburbia now, rumbling through silent streets past rows of identical houses whose occupants were engaged in blissful slumber, unaware of the quarrel unfolding in the erratically-driven Chevrolet.

'I'm meeting Natacha tomorrow to go over our ideas. We could have waited I guess, but I wanted to do it before I go away and—'

'Before you go away? Where are you going?'

I hesitated, furious at myself for the drunken slip. I hadn't meant to tell Joe like this. 'I'm going home.'

'*What*? Are you being serious?'

'Eyes on the road, *please*!' I begged as she swerved onto the sidewalk, almost mowing down a skulking raccoon whose terrified eyes gleamed bright in the headlamps. 'Just for a few days. My brother Frank's getting married. I got the letter yesterday.'

'Were you going to tell me? Or were you going to leave a note and sneak out in the middle of the night? I guess that's more your style.'

'*Joe!*'

'What?'

'Of course I was going to tell you. Tonight didn't seem like the right time, that's all. Why are you reacting like this?'

Joe said nothing, merely huffing and sighing and making her displeasure clear. I could tell we were tumbling headlong into an almighty argument and I did nothing to avoid it.

'They're my family. I want to see them. What's so terrible about that?'

'I didn't even know you were still in touch with them. Do they have my address?'

'I wrote to my momma a few months ago. It came out of a conversation I had with Alla, actually. She told me what had happened with *her* mother and… I didn't want to regret anything.' We stopped at a red light, but Joe kept her tiger eyes firmly fixed on the road ahead. 'So I sent a letter. Nothing much, just telling her my address, that I was well and happy. I assumed she knew that I'd moved out from Aunt Ida's. I didn't hear anything for weeks. I didn't think she was going to reply, thought she'd probably burned my letter. Then I heard back. Frank is getting married in two weeks. About time too; he and

Betsy Rose have been sweethearts since practically the first day of school.'

We were almost home, the familiar sights of our neighbourhood passing by outside the window. Still Joe remained stony-faced.

'Why are you being so strange about this? They're still my family. I thought you of all people would understand.'

'Do you want me to go with you?' she asked quietly.

'Joe, I…' I was stunned, not knowing how to reply. 'Surely you can see… We can't.'

'Are you ashamed of me? I reckon you'd take Natacha in a heartbeat.'

It was late. We were drunk. This was absolutely the worst conversation to be having as we pulled up outside the bungalow.

'Are you jealous?' I didn't bother to keep my voice down. Already I could see blinds flickering, curtains twitching. Light was gathering in the eastern sky and soon it would be sunrise.

'I've seen the way she looks at you. The way *you* look at *her*.'

'Don't be ridiculous.' I slammed the car door as Joe walked down the path to the bungalow. 'Natacha's not… like that.'

'Isn't she? Maybe you should ask Alla the next time you're having a cosy chat.'

I frowned, taking off my hat and stole and throwing them down on the armchair. Was Joe implying that Alla and Natacha had had a relationship? I felt tired, and sick of arguing. 'I'm going to bed.'

'Why don't you ever want to talk about anything? Lately it feels like you're always avoiding me.'

'It's not that. I'm just… tired,' I finished, knowing how pathetic the excuse sounded.

Joe followed me into the bedroom, undressing as I removed my make-up. She stared hard at me, asking the question that must have been playing on her mind since I mentioned returning to Jonas Springs. 'Is Sarah Beth going to be there?'

The sound of her name, so unexpected yet so poignant, set my heart racing, and suddenly I understood why Joe was so angry. I remembered that afternoon when I'd turned up at Joe's bungalow, when I'd fled the farm in nothing but the clothes I was wearing, and we'd cried and made love and told one another everything.

She knew what had happened that summer with Sarah Beth, and right now it seemed as though Joe could read my thoughts – or perhaps I really was that transparent, my cheeks flushing even as I removed my rouge. I had to admit that Sarah Beth had been on my mind recently; faced with the prospect of returning home for the first time in two years, I'd been speculating on whether I would see her. Would she still look the same? How would she behave towards me? Anticipation mingled with fear and nerves. I knew I'd been distracted recently, my thoughts elsewhere, and I'd probably been distant with Joe.

I'd barely thought of Sarah Beth when Joe and I were first together, my head turned, everything fresh and exhilarating, but of late I'd found myself thinking what if… what if things had turned out differently between us? What if I'd stayed and fought? Life with Joe had made me realise there *could* have been a different future – though perhaps not in the close-minded community of Jonas Springs.

'I don't know,' I mumbled, finding I couldn't look Joe in the eye.

She came up behind me, slipping her arms around my waist, burying her head in my shoulder, her naked body pressed against me. 'Please don't go.'

I knew she wanted reassurance, kind words, for us to fall into bed together and for everything to be all right once again, but at that moment I found her physical presence stifling. I unwrapped her arms from my waist, quickly stripped down to my slip, then climbed into the far side of the bed, closing my eyes as I rolled over to face the wall.

Chapter Sixteen

ALLA

Kostroma, Russia, 1900

There was no sound in the world like the applause of an audience, Alla reflected, as she emerged for the curtain call and took her bows. It nourished the spirit and fed the ego. It reminded her why she'd chosen this path – why she poured her heart and soul out on stage every night for this faceless audience in the freezing provinces. And it reminded her that she was a damn fine actress, whatever her demons might whisper in the darkness of the small hours.

She slunk into the wings, deprived of the bright lights and adoration, her fellow cast mates congratulating one another on a successful performance, eager to open the vodka and release the adrenaline. As the lead, Alla was spared the indignities of a shared dressing room and had her own space, albeit barely more than a broom cupboard. She used a thick cream to remove the heavy stage make-up, her reflection transformed in the grimy mirror as her thoughts turned once again to her current circumstances.

Her marriage to Sergei was all but over. She'd been a fool to marry him in the first place and was astute enough to recognise that she'd only done it to hurt Alex Sanin; the impetuosity and recklessness that Sergei had loved about her had come back to bite him. Alla had left Babruysk, moving back to Moscow to follow Alex, but a puppy-eyed Sergei had gone with her, refusing to believe they were finished. Alexander had refused to see her, announcing his engagement to an actress named Lika Mizinova and, not knowing how else to react, Alla had done what she always did, throwing herself into her acting and moving far away – two hundred miles, in fact, to the city of Kostroma. This time, Sergei didn't follow her.

The new year had provided Alla with ample opportunity for resolutions and renewed ambition; she'd vowed to reinvigorate her career, to be diligent and disciplined, determined to focus on her art. And yet here she was, barely months into the futuristic-sounding twentieth century, resigned to playing unimportant theatres in insignificant cities, drifting through life like a ship with no anchor and—

There was a knock at the door.

'Come in,' Alla called.

Maxim Kovalenko, her director, entered, accompanied by a short, stocky man, roughly a decade older than her. He had dark curly hair and large, heavy-lidded eyes, whose redness hinted at a love of alcohol.

'This is Pavel Nickolaevich Orlenev,' Maxim introduced them. 'He will be joining the company as a guest star for a number of performances, and we're delighted to have him with us.'

Alla's eyes lit up. She'd heard of Pavel Orlenev; he had a reputation as a maverick, having starred in a controversial, anti-tsarist production in St Petersburg that was closed down by the censor. He'd declared his belief in "theatre for the people" and was known for his brilliance, his daring, his wild reputation. When he strode across the room to clasp her hands, kissing her on both cheeks and telling her how magnificent he'd found her performance, Alla found herself breathless.

'I'll leave you two to get acquainted,' Maxim murmured, discreetly leaving the room.

'Your performance was spellbinding,' Orlenev told her eagerly, his eyes never leaving hers.

'Your Tsar Fyodor is the stuff of legend.'

'You're wasted here.'

'If it comes from your lips then it must be true.'

'Come with me.'

'Where?'

'Anywhere. Everywhere. Follow me to the ends of the earth.'

'I will.'

'When my contract finishes here, I'm touring *The Brothers Karamazov*. Do you know it?'

'Dostoyevsky.'

'Yes. Will you be my Grushenka?'

'It would be an honour.'

'I'm a mess. I drink too much, smoke too much, spend too much. I need a good woman to take care of me.'

'I'll do it.'

'You must protect me from myself.'

'I'll be your maid, your nurse, your mother, your lover – whatever you want me to be.'

'Swear it.'

'I swear. God be my witness, I shall stay with you until you command me to leave you.'

'Amen,' finished Pavel, as he pulled Alla to him and kissed her passionately.

She succumbed willingly to the embrace, her head spinning and her heart singing. *This* was the grand passion she had sought for so long! The *coup de foudre* she had anticipated for a lifetime. The emotion she had only read about in books, heard sung about in songs, imagined in her performance. Here was a man she could love and adore, who understood her, and whom she would gladly follow to the ends of the earth. She had promised herself to him, and she intended to keep that promise.

'My love,' Alla murmured, winding her fingers distractedly through Pavel's thick, black hair. They lay naked on their narrow double bed, his head resting in the curve of her waist. If the counterpane were a clockface, their bodies would have marked the time at 11.35.

'Mmm?' Sunlight streamed through the sloped window of their rented attic room, rendering the air stuffy and soporific. An open playscript lay discarded at Pavel's side; they'd been running lines, but it was too hot to do anything productive.

'What's the plan?'

'The plan?'

'Yes. Once this tour is over, what are we going to do next?'

Pavel stretched languorously – less like a sleek cat, and more like a sturdy pug extending its comically short legs. They were currently in Yekaterinaburg, touring *Crime and Punishment*, and this last year had been the whirlwind – physically, emotionally, professionally – that Alla had always expected life with Pavel to be. They'd performed together in *The Brothers Karamazov*, in *Trilby*, in *Zaza*, touring from St Petersburg to Siberia, becoming inseparable to an unhealthy degree.

To obtain a passport, she'd had to contact Sergei in Moscow for his permission to travel out of the country. Alla realised that she had no lingering romantic feelings towards him, but she was fond of him, and grateful for his understanding.

Life with Pavel offered the drama that Alla had always craved. She believed in his genius as an actor and enjoyed the cachet that came with his star status but, like any deal made with the devil, there was a darker side: his alcoholism, his mood swings, his inability to manage money. As she'd vowed, with prescient accuracy, she had indeed become his maid, his nurse, his mother, and his lover. But she'd given herself over to him, mind and body, following wherever he led.

'I thought we might visit Anton.'

'Chekhov?'

'Yes. We could take a house near him for the summer.'

Alla had heard a lot about Anton Chekhov. Pavel's writer friend had enjoyed considerable success with his short stories and his recent plays *The Seagull* and *Uncle Vanya*. Stanislavsky was a great admirer of his, and Alla was intrigued to meet him.

'That sounds wonderful. Where does he live?'

'He used to be in Melikhovo, in the countryside south of Moscow, but he's suffered terribly with tuberculosis so the doctors advised him to move to Yalta. It has a wonderful climate apparently, and he's built himself an enormous house minutes from the seafront.'

Pavel didn't seem to notice the way Alla's shoulders stiffened, the way she inhaled sharply at the very mention of the Crimean city. She could almost swear her heart stopped beating for a moment.

The thought of returning to Yalta... She hadn't been back since she'd left at 17, almost four years ago now. It held a whole world of unhappy memories; she wouldn't care if she never saw the place again. Alla had never told Pavel the dark secrets of her childhood; he was only concerned with the present, and the future. He didn't look back and neither did she – until now.

'How does that sound?' Pavel rolled over onto his stomach, his chin resting on her bare hip bone.

Alla gazed down at him, at his dark brown eyes, his puppyish enthusiasm. She'd sworn to follow him to the ends of the earth, and she would.

'My love, it sounds heavenly,' Alla lied, offering a beaming smile that didn't reach her eyes.

She would write to Nina and tell her to expect a visit. With Pavel by her side, Alla felt she could face anything. Even her own family.

Anton Chekhov's garden was glorious, abundant with cedars, palms, acacias, almond and mulberry trees. One hundred rose bushes had been planted as a tribute to the poet, Pushkin, and two black and tan dachshunds lay panting in the heat in the shade of the table. The house – known as the White Dacha – was a masterpiece, a towering, three-storey structure with turrets and balconies and irregularly shaped windows, the asymmetry used to striking effect.

The man himself was tall and slender, round-shouldered and dark-haired, wearing a mariner's cap and pince-nez spectacles. He and Pavel were seated beneath the shade of a cherry tree, along with another friend – the writer and political activist Maxim Gorky – while Anton's new wife, Olga Knipper, played hostess.

'More tea?' Olga asked Alla politely as she drifted over to the samovar.

'No, thank you. I shan't be staying much longer. I'm going to visit my sister.'

'Oh, does she live nearby? What's her name?'

'Nina Hofschneider. She and her husband run the pharmacy on the seafront. It used to belong to my father,' Alla continued, her tone almost challenging. She was being uncharacteristically open with Olga – perhaps wanting to gauge Olga's reaction and discover whether her history and her family were known in the town.

'Well, have a lovely time,' Olga smiled enigmatically, as she turned her back to draw tea for the men.

Alla watched her. Olga was tall and slender, handsome and

elegant, and the two women were already well acquainted; they'd trained together at the Philharmonic School and the Moscow Arts Theatre, where Olga had been Stanislavsky's protégée and favoured lead actress, leaving Alla relegated to supporting roles. In fact, Olga had been part of the reason Alla had left the city for the suburbs – a decision which had ultimately turned out positively, now that she'd met Pavel, but Alla had undoubtedly struggled along the way. By contrast, Olga was married to Anton Chekhov, mistress of this magnificent house set in exquisite gardens, leading an idyllic life entertaining their guests in the sunshine. Olga was given the lead in Anton's wildly successful plays, and remained a favourite of Stanislavsky, with whom she still worked. Alla struggled to suppress her envy.

'My love, I'm leaving,' she said, kissing Pavel and nodding politely at Anton and Maxim, exuding a calmness she didn't feel. Her heart was racing as Pavel squeezed her fingers to reassure her, before turning back to the earnest discussion at hand: how theatre should reflect the experiences of the proletariat in order to engage them.

Alla let herself out of the gate and walked the short, well-trodden distance along the river to the promenade, crowded with people on this warm summer's day. With each step, Alla could feel herself regressing, her confidence dissolving, her shoulders hunching as though braced for blows. Sitting in the garden of the White Dacha, as the guest of a famous writer and lover of a celebrated actor, Alla could almost forget that this was the same town in which she'd spent her adolescence, in which her stepmother had ostracised her and her father had physically abused her. But as she neared the house that was so horribly familiar, Alla couldn't ignore the way her pulse quickened, her stomach lurched, her throat tightened. Even though the rational part of her knew that Yakov could no longer hurt her, the memories came rushing back and she shivered, her fear undeniable.

The house loomed large and the sun went behind a cloud. Alla rang the bell.

From inside she heard the shout of a young girl, and the sound of little feet running along the hall. For a moment, Alla had the bizarre sensation that it was herself as a child, that the door was about to open and she would come face to face with ten-year-old Adelaida Leventon. She could feel herself getting hotter, hear her breath growing shallower, gripping tightly to the white stone portico to stop herself from falling to the ground in a faint.

Then the door opened and the girl who stood there was blonde-haired and skinny-limbed, immaculately turned out and no more than four or five years old. Behind her stood Alla's sister, Nina. She was still purse-lipped and charmless, dressed puritanically in a drab, high-necked dress of indeterminate colour, and Alla noticed for the first time the similarities with their stepmother, Dasha.

'Hello,' Alla said awkwardly. She'd written in advance to let Nina know to expect her.

'Hello,' the child piped up.

'Ludmilla, this is your Aunt Adelaida.'

'You may call me Alla,' she smiled. She wasn't used to being around children, and it felt like a long time since she'd been one herself.

'You can call me Lucy,' the girl beamed in reply.

'Well,' said Nina, looking her over and raising a disapproving eyebrow. 'I suppose you'd better come in.'

Alla followed her sister along the corridor, feeling the same sense of unhappy déjà vu she'd experienced throughout her return to Yalta, a turn of the kaleidoscope leaving everything familiar yet subtly altered, like a bad dream that leaves you heavy headed and off-kilter for the rest of the day. Nina had removed some of the larger ornaments their father had installed – the Chinese vases, the anonymous busts – and had the walls repainted in a warmer tone. But the life-size painting of Yakov still remained, his disapproving glower watching over the entrance and judging anyone who dared to cross the threshold. Alla suspected she would be found wanting.

She paused for a moment, unable to help herself, staring up at her tormentor and examining her feelings. Even this, nothing more than oils on canvas, could reduce her to an attack of nerves, a sick feeling lodged in her stomach whose intensity she'd not experienced for many years. Yet he was gone. He held no power over her now, she reminded herself, holding his gaze defiantly.

'That's Grandpapa,' Lucy told her. 'He was a wonderful man, wasn't he, Mama?'

Alla snorted, and Nina shot her a sharp look.

'Go to your room, Ludmilla.'

'But—'

'Go.'

Showing as much defiance as she dared, with an exasperated sigh and a shrug of the shoulders, Lucy trudged reluctantly up the stairs as Alla followed her sister into the parlour at the back of the house. The shabby-looking chairs had been replaced, the old chaise-longue re-upholstered, the marquetry table polished and restored. The French doors were open, letting in the balmy air, and on the sideboard sat the old samovar. Nina poured tea for the two of them, hot and sweet.

'Where's your lover today?' Nina asked archly before Alla had even taken a sip.

'With his friends. We've spent much of our time here with Anton – Chekhov, that is. The writer. He owns the white—'

'Yes, yes, the fancy white house behind the big gates. Everyone knows Mr Chekhov and his *dacha* in this town. Rather boastful if you ask me,' Nina sniffed. 'Although it's good to see that's he's finally married that mistress of his. Too little too late, in my opinion – her reputation's already ruined. *And* she's one of your lot.'

Alla raised a questioning eyebrow.

'An *actress*.' Nina drew out the word to emphasise her distaste. 'I suppose she'll give all that up now. It's not a respectable trade for a married woman. Well, it's not a respectable trade for *any* woman, is it?'

Alla drank her tea silently and wondered why she'd come. What was she hoping for from her sister? Sibling conviviality? A warm welcome based on shared parentage?

'And what are your plans when you leave Yalta?'

'We're going to Kherson, to tour. Pavel needs to raise the funds and then—'

'Why are you living like this? In sin, with a man who can't even afford to keep you? If he really loved you, then he'd marry you. If he respected you at all, and cared for your reputation, then he'd make an honest woman of you. Don't you *want* to marry him?'

A fresh breeze blew into the room, bringing with it the well-remembered scent of sea salt and clematis. Alla hid her smile; it was almost worth telling the truth to see the look on her sister's face – to admit that she was already married, now estranged from her husband, and her relationship with Pavel effectively made her an adulterer. 'No,' was all that she said.

Nina threw up her hands in despair. 'Well, I'm glad you didn't bring him here today. He wouldn't be permitted to enter my house.' She sat back, satisfied with the opportunity to emphasise her virtue.

Alla couldn't help snapping in response, 'Yes, much better to marry the son of a moneylender. A far more honourable trade.'

Nina's lips clamped harder than ever as white lines of tension ringed her mouth. 'Max is hardly responsible for his father's occupation,' she spat, as Alla nodded sagely, knowing it would infuriate her sister.

'And where is my dear brother-in-law today? Such a shame he wasn't able to be part of our family reunion.'

'He's working. We're not all accustomed to a life of idleness, dressing up and playing pretend and calling it a profession. You can go and see him if you like – he's in the pharmacy.'

'Yes, of course. So convenient that he was able to take over our father's business like that. In fact, you've done rather well out of the whole arrangement, haven't you? The house, the pharmacy…'

'It was all left to me in Papa's will. If you hadn't had such a bad relationship with him, you might have done better.'

'Nina, he beat me,' Alla whispered, her voice breaking. She

stared at her sister, realising how much she looked like Yakov – the same narrow face, disapproving stare, cold eyes. She wondered whether she and Nina looked alike at all, if it were possible for a stranger to recognise that they were sisters. There was so little of their mother in Nina – no roundness, no softness, no kindness. 'With his fists, his belt, whatever he could lay his hands on. You know how badly he treated me. How could I love a man like that?'

'It's not true.' Nina shook her head. 'You behaved so badly. Papa had no choice. If you'd given him a chance, he could be so loving and caring. But you were just like Mama – demanding and self-absorbed and attention-seeking.'

'Don't you ever say that about Mama!' Alla was shocked to find herself on the verge of tears.

But Nina hadn't finished: 'What is it they say? The apple doesn't fall far from the tree…'

'How dare you! If you even knew how I've had to live all these years… completely alone, taking care of myself. You never returned my letters, just cut me off, penniless. Where was *my* share of Papa's inheritance? Perhaps I should ask your husband about that!' Alla's eyes were blazing as she voiced her long-held suspicion – that the money that was rightfully hers had been sequestered and split between her siblings. Volodya was now living in Berlin, pursuing his dream of studying journalism, and the move would have taken a great deal of capital. Nina was clearly living in some style and had somehow managed to end up with the bulk of the money, as well as the pharmacy once Volodya had vacated it.

'I married an honourable man.' Nina rose to her feet as her voice grew louder. 'A successful man, who can afford to keep me. You're clearly jealous because you're a whore – just like our mother.'

Alla's hand itched to slap her sister, heat flooding her body as the anger bubbled up. But she restrained herself, standing up and striding to the door. 'A pleasure to see you as always, sister.' Her tone was withering. 'I'll see myself out.'

Chapter Seventeen

MAYBELLE

Jonas Springs, USA, 1921

The First Baptist Church on Main Street looked beautiful inside. A posy of wildflowers hung from the end of every pew, whilst the altar was decorated with white candles and yet more flowers. I stared round, taking in every familiar detail. I'd spent so many hours of my life here whilst growing up – attending on Sundays, on holidays, for weddings and funerals, feast days and Harvest Festival. God had been largely exorcised from my new life and I felt I was doing just fine without Him, but I certainly felt conflicted coming back here.

I'd arrived late last night. Two of my trains had been delayed, so by the time my brother, Walter, collected me from the station it was almost midnight and Momma had long since gone to bed – a veritable blessing in disguise. I slept in my childhood room, the memories making for a troubled slumber, and woke early to a house in disarray as Frank, dressed in his Sunday best, paced the kitchen in a state of high anxiety. I picked a handful of Christmas roses from the garden and pinned them to his lapel.

'Thank you for coming,' he said gruffly, and the sudden tenderness made me want to cry, my emotions heightened by nerves and apprehension. We weren't an affectionate family, but I impulsively hugged him, his tall, broad-shouldered frame reassuringly steadfast, and the opposite of Walter who was small and slender. Frank and I shared the same blond curls, like our daddy, whereas Walter had inherited the dark looks of our momma.

The four of us were the first to arrive at the church, ostensibly to make final preparations, but in truth I was glad to take my place in the front pew before anyone else arrived. To not have to walk the length of the aisle past the curious eyes and judging minds of every gossiping harridan in Jonas Springs was a great relief to me.

I stood tall, back erect and head held high, beside my momma; she seemed to have shrunk since I'd last seen her, smaller and greyer than I remembered, that disapproving expression now etched into her skin like a permanent fixture. Today of all days, I hoped to see her smile.

It wasn't long before I heard voices and footsteps, the church filling up behind me. I didn't turn, kept my gaze fixed firmly ahead, but I could *feel* the inquisitive stares that made my breath quicken and my adrenaline flow. I knew that I stood out, and not just for the obvious reason – my return to the small town causing quite a stir given the scandalous nature of my departure. But I was wearing a dress I'd designed myself, made from pale blue silk, and I knew it was ten times chicer than anything the other women would be wearing, my

Californian style far more elegant and striking than anything to be found in Kentucky.

In front of the altar, Frank looked increasingly nervous as the guests arrived and the volume of chatter grew ever louder, mopping his pale brow on his handkerchief, nervous energy making it impossible to remain on the spot as he paced back and forth, exchanging a few words with Pastor Abbott. Then the organ struck up and the congregation fell silent, turning en masse to where Betsy Rose processed up the aisle on her father's arm. She looked tiny and birdlike, her dark hair swept into a simple bun at the nape of her neck, her gown plain and simple, and she carried a posy of wildflowers that matched the church decorations. I was somewhat acquainted with Betsy; I knew that she was sweet and obliging and loved my brother dearly, and I felt sure they'd get the happily ever after that they deserved.

But whilst all eyes were on the blushing bride, mine were scanning the crowd, impossible to restrain myself any longer. My gaze swept over the elderly Misses McCleary, identical unmarried twins who lived in the big house on the outskirts of town, past Sawyer Franklin, who hadn't uttered a word since he returned from the war, alighting briefly on Betsy's eccentric Great Aunt Adeline until, finally, I found her. It was as though she'd been waiting for this moment, as her dancing eyes met mine, and for a second I forgot to breathe.

Sarah Beth.

She held a toddler in her arms – a boy – and I could see the sweep of her belly beneath her coat, full with another child. Her husband, Clarence, was standing beside her, his arm protectively around her thick waist. Instinctively I turned away, my heart racing, clutching my hymn book as though it were a life buoy.

Betsy had reached my brother, the two of them gazing at one another with such simple wonderment that it would have made even the hardest, most bruised heart believe in true love.

Then Pastor Abbott began to speak but I heard none of what followed, witnessed none of the vows spoken or the rings exchanged. My mind was far away, flashing back to that fateful summer more than two years ago.

I'd known Sarah Beth since I was a child. We'd all grown up together – Birdie, Vivian, Clarence, Tucker, Bobby, Cash – all the kids from the town itself and the neighbouring farms. We'd sat in rows in the school room, roamed the fields during the long vacations when we could sneak off from our chores, climbed trees and had first kisses and got up to all kinds of (largely innocent) mischief.

Sarah Beth and I grew closer in our teenage years, finding a natural compatibility, an easy friendship. We'd talk about the handsome men we were going to marry, and how many children we would have, and what their names would be. Occasionally, we speculated on a world outside of Jonas Springs – what it might be like to visit New Orleans or New York, or even travel overseas to London or Paris. We'd imagine other futures for ourselves: running away to join the circus; becoming pioneering inventors or explorers; or as great ladies who'd married into fashionable society and spent our days nibbling on delicacies from Europe. Lives that didn't involve working on a farm and replicating what our parents before us had done, and their parents before them. In short, we understood one another, and our bond only grew tighter as the months and years progressed.

The year my father passed, she was there for me – my shoulder to cry on, my confidante, my constant companion while I raged at the injustice of the world – and of God, for taking him too soon. In my grief I grew wild and rebellious, neglecting my duties, taking no notice of my mother or my brothers, despite their threats of a whipping.

The following spring, the heat came early to Kentucky. In late March, you could feel the first burnings of it, the sweltering days and uncomfortable nights, skin roasted to the colour of a ripe tomato if you didn't cover up on a short walk to the store. By April, it was like an inferno, impossible to keep the milk fresh or stop the butter from melting. Not even the sunset caused the temperature to dip, and I longed to sleep naked on top of my sheets but propriety obliged me to wear a nightdress.

Us neighbourhood kids were now on the cusp of adulthood, and we took to sneaking out when darkness fell. Every night, anything up to a dozen of us could be found hanging out by the creek, cooling our feet, teasing one another and feeling like this time in our lives would never end. Once, Sarah Beth stole a bottle of her daddy's moonshine and we all got drunk, staggering home sick as dogs. I caused such a commotion that it woke Frank; I expected a beating, but he let me go on up to bed and sleep it off, telling Momma I was sick with a bug. I never did quite understand why, but I was grateful to him nonetheless.

On one of those hot, hot nights in 1919, as spring slipped stickily into summer, I waited until it fell dark and all grew quiet before sneaking silently out of the house and racing down to the water's edge. It was the perfect temperature, a delicious coolness tempering the heat of the air, a three-quarter moon playing hide and seek behind the clouds. I was the first to arrive at our usual spot, and I tugged off my boots to soak my feet in the dark water, lying back in the long grass and listening to the nocturnal noises. I wasn't afraid; it didn't occur to me that anything bad could possibly happen within the safe confines of Jonas Springs.

There was a rustle of corn leaves, a crack of dry twigs underfoot, and a grinning Sarah Beth appeared. She had straight, copper hair that fell to her lower back, and a slender, boyish figure – long legs, slim hips, small breasts.

She sat down close beside me, thighs stretched alongside mine, and dangled her bare feet in the creek, our calves colliding as we let our ankles drift with the current.

'Sometimes I wish we could stay like this forever,' she sighed, resting her head on my shoulder.

'But what about Paris?' I teased. 'And London? And all our grand plans?'

'You know what I mean.' There was a long silence, and I sensed that she had something else to say, something I wasn't going to like. 'Clarence proposed. I said yes – well, my parents wanted me to say yes, so I did, even though I don't know if *I* wanted to. But now it's done and I've gotta make the best of it.'

I blew out the breath I didn't realise I'd been holding. 'Oh. *Clarence?*'

'I know, I know.'

'I didn't realise that he… Well, that you and him were…'

'We weren't,' Sarah Beth clarified. 'We *aren't*. I didn't expect it at all. But he's a nice boy, with a good future ahead of him and…'

'Sarah Beth Montgomery,' I murmured, trying out her married name. 'I guess that's your future all tied up then. A wedding. Babies. Grandbabies.'

'You don't have to make it sound so predictable,' Sarah Beth winced. 'It might not be so bad.'

'I'm sorry,' I apologised. 'It's just … unexpected is all. And so quick. I s'pose I should congratulate you.' The sense of melancholy was overwhelming. I knew that I was unhappy, and had been for some time now, but this announcement merely compounded my misery. My day-to-day life on the farm was dull, with no prospect of change on the horizon, and I was forever fighting with my momma and brothers. I wasn't interested in a future here, but equally couldn't contemplate moving away from Jonas Springs. Where would I go? I had no links to anywhere else.

'Don't leave me,' Sarah Beth pleaded, as though she'd read my thoughts. 'You're my best friend. Nothing has to change, we can still see each other all the time, every day.' She looked me dead in the eye, so earnest and sincere, her face so close to mine that I could see every freckle and mark and curve and indent.

The night seemed to grow hotter all of a sudden, and I could feel my cheeks burning. 'This heat just won't let up.'

'Let's swim,' Sarah Beth suggested, her expression unreadable. 'No one else is here, we can strip to our underwear.'

I hesitated. As children, we'd often taken our bathing suits and bathed in the creek during the scorching summer months. But tonight didn't feel like one of those nostalgic hazy days; tonight was just the two of us, alone in the darkness. There was a sense of anticipation, a unique intimacy created by the circumstances. Despite the warmth, I felt goosebumps peppering my arms.

Sarah Beth rose to her feet. I could trace the outline of her white dress as she pulled it over her head, standing before me in her chemise and bloomers. 'Come on,' she dared me.

We'd undressed in front of one another plenty of times before, but this time I felt wildly self-conscious. I caught a glimpse of her pale flesh, her white underwear, as the moon slid out to expose her before disappearing behind a cloud. I heard a gentle splash and, when my eyes adjusted to the darkness, I saw she was swimming in the black water.

'It's glorious, come on!' she called, rolling over and floating on her back, her distinctive hair splaying out around her.

I followed suit before I could think about what I was doing, tugging off my dress, a yielding press of mud between my toes as I stepped forwards, reeds brushing my bare calves. The water was deliciously cool and I gasped, then giggled, as I stepped further out. Sarah Beth began to laugh too, our joy infectious, both of us giddy at our own daring.

'Have you ever wondered what it'd be like to swim naked?' Sarah Beth mused, her voice both teasing and confident, the question holding a clear challenge.

I gasped once again as her undergarments sailed past me, catching on an overhanging tree. The moon peeped out and I glimpsed small, high breasts with the palest pink nipples, before Sarah Beth sunk beneath the surface. Now I no longer felt the chill of the water; my whole being was ablaze, my body warmed by a deep, intense heat burning within.

'It's just like taking a bath,' Sarah Beth sighed luxuriously, and once again her voice spurred me on to imitate her, shedding my saturated underwear and discarding it on the bank. She was right; I felt... extraordinary. Free and wild and reckless and—

I shrieked in shock, then delight, as Sarah Beth soaked me, my hair hanging heavy, my body light and buoyant. Seeking revenge, I dove down beneath the water, aiming to surface beside her and give her a fright. But I misjudged the distance in the darkness, my hand brushing against her hip. *I* was the one to be startled and I surfaced immediately, pushing my hair back from my face, wiping my eyes to find we were inches from one another. I could barely see her, could only hear her breathing – a little quicker than normal, it seemed to me. The air felt charged with an intensity that thrilled me, as though the heat could break at any moment, giving way to an almighty thunderstorm.

I could sense her, so close, an undeniable charge pulsing between us, and I don't know who moved first but the next moment our mouths had found one another, so soft and gentle, as though we were mutually asking permission. Consent granted, our tongues explored, bodies moving closer until we were pressed against each other, hot and wet and naked. I'd kissed a couple of the local boys before, but it had never felt like this – not this overwhelming desire, this wish to surrender to sensation and longing for the moment to never ever stop.

My cheeks burned with shame even as I let my hands

explore, the shape of her body so familiar to me, but so excitingly different to my own. I knew that what we were doing was wrong, so terribly wrong; it had never been referred to explicitly, but I felt sure we were breaking all kinds of unwritten rules. Pastor Abbott would never have approved.

I pulled away, panting, and there was a moment's pause. It could have stopped there. We could have swum back to the bank and put on our clothes and gone home without thinking of this moment ever again.

But it didn't stop there.

Beneath the cover of the creek we discovered every inch of one another. Nothing was off limits and the pleasure was endless and all-consuming. There was no breeze to carry our cries across the fields, our moans and sighs drifting up to the starless heavens like an offering.

Some time later, in silent agreement, we climbed out to lie side by side on the grassy bank. The night air felt cool after the warmth of the water, but I was burning up, heat flooding every part of me. Our exploration continued – neither of us wanted to stop – and Sarah Beth did things to my body that I hadn't even done to myself in the privacy of my own room.

I didn't want to think about what all of this might mean, didn't want to think about anything except the exquisite sensation of our bodies together, the mutual pleasure, and how I never wanted this to end.

Dazed and sated, we fell eventually into a kind of satisfied stupor, our legs intertwined, our breathing slowing, as our hands brushed lazily over one another's bare skin. Neither of us spoke, unwilling to break the spell.

A sudden breeze, cool and unexpected, made me shiver, as

the moon appeared with dazzling brilliance, bathing us in white light. And then we heard it – the kick of a stone barely yards away; the unmistakeable sound of another human within striking distance of where we lay.

I sat bolt upright, grabbing my clothes and clutching them to me.

'Who's there?'

There was no reply. I stared hard into the shadows, my heart pounding with fear and shame. A silhouetted figure broke cover from the tall rows of corn, dry grass crunching beneath their feet as they fled, then the clouds rolled in and everything went dark.

I was paralysed with fear, my mouth dry, pulse racing, unable to move. I almost jumped in terror as fingers brushed my naked skin, then realised it was Sarah Beth, her hand snaking around my waist. I responded instantly and we clung together, hot breaths and wet lips, urgency in our kisses, desperation in our touches, as though we knew this would be the final time. Everything would change after tonight, and we would deal with the consequences in the morning.

We fell to the ground, the corn scratching at our backs, red lines on white flesh. Then we took our leave of one another, a long, slow goodbye, committing every inch of each other to memory.

As the earliest light pierced the sky, we dressed quickly, silently – there was no need for words. Sarah Beth held out her hand and I took it, palms sliding together, before the two of us ran swiftly across the fields, home before the dawn broke and real life intruded.

I didn't go back to the creek after that. I barely left the house unless I was asked to run an errand, convinced that everyone I passed would be the one who'd been there that night, or that word would have spread and I'd be shamed and catcalled as I walked down Main Street.

A few days after the incident, Momma sent me to the general store to buy flour and sugar. I kept my head down, slinking along pathways and taking a circuitous route to avoid the busier roads. I purchased the items without issue, but on my way home I ran into Sarah Beth. I was terrified that she might ignore me, but she smiled warmly and the relief was immense. We spoke quickly, not wanting to be seen for too long in one another's company.

'I'm to marry Clarence next week,' she said, and I felt my heart lurch. 'I hoped you'd hear it from me.'

I searched her eyes, looking for the truth.

'I wish things could be different,' she whispered. 'I wish everything could stay the same.' She stood next to me, angling her body towards mine, murmuring low so that we wouldn't be overheard. She was close enough that I could smell the fresh soapy scent of her skin, the sweetness of her breath. I fancied I could even feel the heat from her body, and I flashed back to that night, a memory so visceral it almost made me gasp.

And then I knew.

I knew that I was different. I knew that I didn't feel anything for the local boys, and never would. And I knew that Sarah Beth had no option but to yield to the future that was planned for her and make the best of the situation. And I didn't blame her for that.

'But it can't,' I said sadly, drinking in every inch of her before I turned and set off for home.

I was deep in thought, taking a deserted track through the hayfield on Jefferson's farm, when my musings were interrupted as Cash Wheeler fell into step beside me. He was a year or so younger than me, with messy brown curls and dark eyes framed by thick brows.

'How's tricks, Maybelle?' he asked cheerily. 'Haven't seen you around much.'

'No, I've been... I've been a little sick, but everything's fine now.'

'And your momma? And your brothers?'

'They're all fine too, thanks Cash.' I smiled at his solicitousness.

'And Sarah Beth?'

My cheeks flamed and I stared at him with wide, petrified eyes, instantly betraying my guilt. He grinned – a sly, hideous leer – and I felt as though I might vomit, knowing that whatever came next couldn't possibly be good.

'I saw you. I saw everything,' he added unnecessarily. 'I know what you are. What you did.'

'Please don't tell anyone.' My instinct was to beg. 'Please, Cash. Don't tell my momma.'

'What you did was wrong. It was against God. And you need to be taught a lesson.'

He stopped walking, his breathing coming heavily, his pupils dilated. My intuition hollered at me to get away. There was no one else around. The fields were empty. Even the birds seemed to have fallen silent. I wanted to run but found myself rooted to the spot.

Cash lunged for my arm, and as I tried to scream he clamped the other hand over my mouth. I fought harder as I saw where he was taking me: into the old barn, with its missing roof panels and abandoned, rusting farm equipment. He was only seventeen but almost a man, his arms brawny and his body powerfully built from farm work. Despite my anger and adrenaline, I was no match for his sheer brute strength.

Pushing me roughly against the wall, he pinned me there and tried to kiss me, forcing his tongue inside my mouth. When I turned my head he spat in my face, hissing that I was sick, that a proper woman would enjoy this, that he would show me the natural order of things.

Then he pulled me inside and closed the door, blocking out all traces of sunlight.

It was my mother who guessed first, around six weeks later when my blood hadn't come and my face and breasts had developed an unexpected fullness.

'Whose is it?' she demanded. 'Tell me!'

I refused, protesting that it wasn't what she thought, shrinking from the blows and the wicked names she called me.

'What will people *say*? What will they *think*? Your daddy would be so ashamed of you,' she hissed, her face contorted in an ugly fury. 'I've done everything I could for you – Lord knows it hasn't been easy – and *this* is how you repay me?'

'Momma, it's not—'

'You gotta tell me who he is, Maybelle.' She gripped my shoulders so tightly it hurt. 'Your brothers will *make* him marry you.'

'I don't want to get married! I don't want anything from you. Just leave me alone.' I pulled myself free and ran upstairs, flinging myself down on my bed and sobbing inconsolably. What did it matter what people said, or thought, or whether I was married or not? I already knew that I wasn't like everyone else. That my future wouldn't – couldn't – follow the conventional path expected of me. I didn't want to marry one of the local boys, didn't want to bear their children and cook their meals and grow old and bitter and unsatisfied like my momma.

For the next few weeks I stayed within the confines of the farm, but soon everyone in Jonas Springs seemed to know of my condition, and the rumours grew increasingly outrageous: that I was a seductress with my sights set on both men and women; that the baby in my belly was conceived by unnatural means and would be born demonic and disfigured; that I'd been seen by the creek at midnight dancing naked with the devil. A kind of fervour gripped the town – if I dared to venture out in public I was stared at, jeered, degraded, as though it were Salem in the 1600s, not modern America on the cusp of the 1920s.

When I was no more than three or four months along – my belly softly rounded, my thirst unquenchable, my sickness subsiding – I lost the baby. I knew it was coming; the bleeding, the agony like nothing I'd ever experienced that lasted for hours that felt like decades. Exhausted and empty, I saw the infant briefly before my momma took it away. It was tiny, no bigger than the palm of my hand, impossible to tell whether it was a boy or a girl in that split second.

I don't know what happened to it, and I never asked. Whether its body lay buried on our land, or something worse; I tortured myself wondering if it had been added to the pile of trash Walter burned the following day. But from that moment on, Momma wanted nothing more to do with me. I was no longer her beloved daughter – I was a liability, an inconvenience, a source of shame to be forgotten and disposed of just like my baby had been.

She wrote her sister in California, and it was agreed that I needed the guiding light of God in my life. To be set upon a fresh path by a steady hand in a new place where I could be anonymous. And so I was sent to Atwater to live with Aunt Ida and Uncle Henry, passed along like an unwanted gift.

Chapter Eighteen

ALLA

St Petersburg, Russia, 1903

The clock in the corner struck five and Alla stirred, her limbs stiff and an uncomfortable crick in her neck. She'd fallen asleep in the armchair, but now the first slivers of daylight were creeping through a crack in the curtains, the sun rising over the Karpovka River three stories below.

Alla shifted, the blanket covering her knees dropping to the floor as she stretched out her legs and listened carefully. Only the monotonous ticking of the clock and the dawn chorus outside her window could be heard. Pavel still wasn't home.

She stood and threw open the drapes, letting the morning light flood the room. Outside the city was waking up, fishing boats and barges slicing through the water, the newspaper stand and flower seller setting out their wares on Silin Bridge, a handful of pedestrians making their way along the embankment. Alla and Pavel had spent much of the past two years touring and travelling – Vilnius, Venice, Vienna, amongst others – before landing up in St Petersburg, where Pavel was engaged to star in Ibsen's *Ghosts*. It was undoubtedly a glorious city, the cultural and actual capital of Russia, but Alla didn't love it the way she loved Moscow.

She moved away from the window as she heard a noise that grew louder – a crashing and stumbling and swearing and slurring – the unmistakeable sound of her lover finally making his way home. She heard him fumble with the key, then drop it, followed by another round of flamboyant cursing. Alla didn't move to help him. She remained where she was, arms folded across her chest, her fury mounting, as the opening door took Pavel by surprise and he literally fell into the room.

He took a moment to notice her, another moment to focus. 'You're awake!' he exclaimed delightedly before his face crumpled into confusion. 'What time is it?'

His clothing was as creased as his expression, his shirt half undone, his trousers unbuttoned. His chin was bristly, he stank of alcohol and women's perfume, and there was a rakish glint in his eye. Alla fought to contain her temper and lost.

'It's after five. Again! What is wrong with you? Night after night I sit here waiting for you, and I'm sick of it! I can't live like this!'

'Well why didn't you go to bed?' Pavel rose to his feet, swaying, infuriating her with his logic.

Alla let out a scream of frustration. 'Don't you dare try and tell me what to do! Do you have any idea how dull my life has become? Waiting up for you night after night whilst you run around the city with your harlots and your whores, spending *our* money on jewellery and champagne for any passing strumpet who so much as smiles in your direction—'

Pavel was paying little attention as he half-heartedly began his ablutions, Alla following him from room to room, continuing to berate him as he splashed his face with water then pissed in the chamber pot, both hands against the wall to steady himself.

'Look at the state of you! If only your adoring public could see you now. Who was it tonight, hmm? Countess Obolensky? Baroness von Lieven? Or some pretty young actress willing to lift her skirts for a role in your next play?'

'Alla, my darling, you really must try not to be so jealous. It's a very unbecoming trait in a woman.'

There was a loud crack as Alla slapped him.

'How dare you! If it wasn't for *me*, you'd be lying in the gutter covered in your own shit. *I'm* the one who waits and worries every single night. *I'm* the one who sobers you up and gets you to the theatre on time every single day. And this is the thanks I get?'

'I *deserve* this!' Pavel roared, and Alla thought briefly of their neighbours, knowing they'd been woken up by this exact same argument a dozen times in the past fortnight. 'Do you know how hard I've worked? The sacrifices I've made? This is my moment of glory and I'm damn well going to enjoy it.'

'What about the sacrifices *I've* made? You promised me Regina. You promised me Rebecca. Then you threw me aside the moment you tasted success. And now I'm stuck here, all day every day, while you're out cavorting 'til the early hours and I'm saddled with a drunken layabout who cares nothing for me.'

'I'm going to bed,' Pavel yawned, clearly tired of the conversation.

But Alla was too angry to let the matter drop. 'You disgust me,' she spat. 'What happened to the man I fell in love with? When I met you, you were ambitious, rebellious, revolutionary. Now you're a product of the establishment you claim to despise, falling over yourself to kiss the feet of the very people you once fought against. You're a hypocrite, a charlatan, a pathetic—'

Her tirade ended in a scream as the glass from the bedside table whistled past her ear and smashed against the wall, falling to the floor in a hundred pieces.

'Would you stop that godawful racket! I'm *trying* to get some sleep.' Pavel glared at her, his mouth set in a mutinous line. Without even undressing, he landed heavily on the bed and rolled over into a troubled slumber.

Alla didn't sleep. Instead, she paced the apartment in frustration before pulling on her boots and winter coat and heading out for a walk, slamming the door on her way.

The spring day was fresh and cold, the bright dawn light having given way to the clear blue skies it had promised. It was a time of day that Alla rarely saw; theatre life was not conducive to early rising.

She made her way south, keeping to the quieter side streets that ran parallel to Kamenoostrovsky Avenue. St Petersburg was arguably more beautiful than its eastern counterpart, its people more refined, its culture more celebrated, but Moscow was in her blood and under her skin. It was the city to which she'd escaped, in which she'd studied, in which she'd first tasted success, and it would forever have her heart.

She was living in St Petersburg because she'd followed Pavel, as she'd sworn to do, but recently she'd been wondering if that impulsive, rash decision had been the correct one. It was months since she'd appeared on stage and, once again, Alla felt as though her career had stymied, that she'd become little more than a nursemaid to Pavel, there to nurture him, indulge his whims, sober him up when he was drunk. Their arguments were daily, her frustrations hourly. Should she leave him? She'd been penniless before, destitute before, friendless before, and Alla knew she didn't want to go back to those days. She still loved him, she realised, as the bitter wind chilled her cheeks and she sank down lower into her coat. And there was no doubt that it added to her status, being the common-law spouse of a star – and a star was what Pavel had become.

He'd appeared in Ibsen's *Ghosts* (a play Alla herself had brought to his attention) and promised her Rebecca, the female lead, in his next show *Rosmersholm*. But Pavel had cancelled that production when *Ghosts* proved wildly popular and propelled him to prominence. If only she had a chance to prove herself too! If only she could soar to those same dizzy heights as her lover, they'd be the toast of St Petersburg together.

She was still in touch with Sergei, and they wrote each other occasional letters. When they first separated, he'd asked for a divorce, but Alla had begged him to give her time, terrified that if she were free she might make yet another foolish decision. As long as she was wedded to Sergei, Alla was prevented from impulsively marrying someone else, as she feared she might. She knew very little about his life now, but he clearly hadn't met anyone else he wanted to make his bride. Perhaps he still loved her, Alla mused, and held out hope that one day she might return to him. Alla knew that she no longer loved Sergei – if, indeed, she ever had – but would be forever grateful for the kindness he'd shown her.

She reached the end of the street, the breathtaking expanse of the River Neva laid out in front of her. A small army of workers were finishing the construction of Trinity Bridge – an exquisitely designed metal structure with cast-iron railings and ornate streetlamps, a triumph of engineering over half a kilometre long. It was due to open at the end of the month to celebrate two hundred years since the city was founded by Peter the Great, and Alla watched as the men scurried like a swarm of ants to ensure no final detail was overlooked.

Suddenly overcome with hunger, Alla bought a *vatrushka*, a sweet pastry, from a street seller, warming her hands and her stomach as she strolled further along the embankment. The river was vast, passing through St Petersburg on its journey from Lake Ladoga in the east to the Gulf of Finland. It was humbling to think that the Neva had followed the same route for hundreds of years, that it had witnessed the birth of a city and would continue to flow long after Alla had ceased to exist, past the grand palaces in shades of pastel and gold erected by tsars and nobles as a monument to their achievements. The realisation made Alla feel insignificant, memories of cowed little Adelaida Leventon never far from the surface, taunted by her failure to become the great actress she aspired to be. But she'd made it from the misery of Yalta to the glories of St Petersburg – why not further?

Alla brushed the pastry crumbs from her gloves and

stopped walking. When she'd left the apartment, she'd been determined to teach Pavel a lesson – to let him oversleep and be late for his performance, then everyone would see his true colours. The wardrobe mistress and his fellow actors already knew of his deficiencies, his anger and his alcoholism, but the audience remained blind, mistaking his tremors for quivers of emotion, interpreting his forgotten lines as masterful pauses. But Alla's conscience pricked and she knew that, despite everything, Pavel relied on her to manage and minister to him, to gently wake and feed him and ensure he arrived at the theatre in time for his call.

Reluctantly, Alla turned her back on the magnificent skyline and set off towards their apartment. ***

She was surprised to find Pavel awake and seated at the desk when she returned. He was dressed in long underwear and last night's shirt, his eyes swollen and his dark, curly hair unkempt, but he looked remarkably spritely considering the state he'd been in barely hours earlier. It amazed Alla how Pavel's constitution could withstand such heavy drinking, leaving him largely unscathed the following day.

As he heard the door open, Pavel jumped to his feet, bounding across the floor towards Alla, taking her face in his hands and kissing her hard. 'You're a genius!' He smelt of stale alcohol and sweat.

'I am?'

'Yes! I was thinking about what you said—'

Alla winced, remembering how she'd berated him, the names she'd called him. 'I'm surprised you remember.'

'—and I realised you're right.'

'Of course. About what?'

'I'm wasting my life. I've been lured in – seduced by wealth and high society and all the beautiful, aristocratic women.'

Alla pulled a face. It wasn't quite the apology she'd been expecting.

'I used to be feared. I courted controversy, laughed in the face of infamy. *I* played Tsar Fyodor and the Tsar's censor himself shut down the very theatre where I went about my work. And now I roll over like a fat cat to have my belly tickled by the bourgeoisie. No—' here he paced across the apartment, back to the desk, picking up a sheaf of paper, '—No more. Things are going to change. *This* is to be my next production. And you, my dearest love, are going to perform at my side.'

Alla burst out laughing as he sat down and pulled her onto his knee, all wrongs forgiven by his sheer exuberance, his rediscovered fervour. 'What is it?'

Pavel cleared his throat, his voice booming out: '*The Chosen People* by Evgeny Chirikov. It was recommended to me by my great friend Maxim Gorky. He told me it was offered to your old tutor, Vladimir Nemirovich, but he turned it down because he was afraid. *I* am not afraid!' Pavel roared. 'Let no one say Pavel Nickolaevich Orlenev is a scared man. This play is controversial, it is challenging, it will cause outrage amongst all who see it. Tell me, my love, are you with me? You promised to follow me to the ends of the earth – will you take on the world at my side?'

Alla turned to look at him; his skin was pale and clammy, his face puffy from the alcohol but suffused with the passion that had first attracted her. She threw her arms around him and kissed him impulsively. 'Of course, my darling. To the ends of the earth and beyond.'

Backstage, Alla breathed in through her nose, out through her mouth, trying to slow her racing heart. Her ribs were constricted due to the corset she wore beneath her blouse, pushing down on her lungs, exacerbating the sensation of being trapped with no escape. Yet she knew that these nerves were a blessing, the adrenaline giving her the surge she would need to deliver a masterful opening night performance.

The theatre itself was small and insalubrious, located just off Ligovskaya Street near Nikolaevsky railway station. Alla had left the claustrophobic confines of her dressing room to pace in the wings, and from here she could hear the audience as they filed in and took their seats. It sounded as though the auditorium was full, the crowd noisy and far less refined than the patrons who'd turned out to watch Pavel's celebrated turn in *Ghosts* at the Nemetti Theatre.

As though her thoughts had summoned him, Pavel emerged from the shadows and Alla jumped as he appeared beside her. He looked confident and carefree, handsome in a frock coat and well-cut trousers that Alla had painstakingly tailored, his unruly hair oiled into a side parting.

'Nervous, *moya zhidovka*?'

'No,' Alla lied.

Pavel laughed and kissed her on the nose, retreating back into the darkness.

Their brief encounter had unsettled Alla, disturbing her concentration at a time when focus was crucial. She was irritated too; she despised that nickname, *moya zhidovka*. My Yid. On occasion, Pavel called her that in public and she hated him for it, unable to prevent herself glancing fearfully over her shoulder to see who might have heard. It felt too reckless, too dangerous right now.

Since the late 1700s, almost a hundred years before Alla's birth, the Jewish people had been subject to strict limitations on where they could live, banished to an area of western Russia known as the Pale of Settlement. Her father had grown up there, her grandfather an illiterate miller. But Yakov's university education allowed him to move out of the area to Berdichev, where he met Sonya, and his sandy hair and light blue eyes lent ambiguity to his origins.

The assassination of Tsar Alexander II in 1881 triggered a wave of anti-Jewish riots and bloody pogroms, and "audacious conduct" – a wide-ranging, non-specific offence which included something as trivial as a Jew's failure to raise his hat when passing a policeman in the street – was now a crime for which Jews could be sent back to the Pale of Settlement.

For the past two years, *The Swindlers* – a violently anti-Semitic, government-sponsored production – had been playing to sell-out audiences in Moscow. *The Chosen People* was Evgeny Chirikov's response to that, a *Romeo and Juliet* story about a Christian boy falling in love with a Jewish girl. Alla and Pavel were playing the star-crossed lovers. It would be hugely controversial, she knew, bringing her to the attention of the authorities and putting her at great risk. The apprehension she felt tonight was more than simply opening night butterflies. But Alla had chosen to follow her instincts, and to follow her lover, and now there was no backing down.

'Beginners.' Yuri, the stage manager, passed by with Alla's five-minute call. She nodded in return, not trusting herself to speak without vomiting, before making her way onto the set and taking up her opening position.

She took a few moments to breathe, to gather her thoughts and put herself into the mindset of a youthful, vivacious Jewish girl, then the curtains opened, the glare of the spotlights rendering the audience invisible.

The first scene was set in a busy marketplace, requiring almost the entire cast on stage. Alla, as Lia, strolled amongst the stalls, inspecting their wares. Pavel, full of boyish exuberance as Nachman, spotted her amongst the crowd and instantly fell in love, performing a rhapsodising soliloquy to her beauty. But he'd barely begun his speech when Alla became aware of a commotion at the back of the auditorium, angry shouts and frightened screams. Pavel faltered, then attempted to continue, before breaking character as Alla followed suit, shading her eyes and straining to see what was happening.

Moments later, all hell broke loose: cries, yelling, a gunshot, and then people were pouring out of the theatre in terror. Someone switched on the electric lights and Alla absorbed the scene in an instant – the audience fighting to reach the exit whilst a dozen men wearing the distinctive blue uniform of the Cossacks ran up the aisles and leapt on stage.

Alla tried to scream, to warn Pavel as two officers rushed up behind him, one twisting his arm violently behind his back as he cried out in pain, the other bringing a knee to his stomach whereupon he collapsed to the floor.

She moved towards him, but her way was barred by two more Cossacks, and Alla experienced a flash of fear more intense than she'd ever felt, even at the hands of her father. It was the manifestation of her darkest nightmares, the terrifying possibilities flashing before her: capture, imprisonment, exile, worse—

A sharp blow to the back of her head ended any further speculation, as Alla crumpled to the ground like a discarded rag, her vision fading to black.

Chapter Nineteen

MAYBELLE

Los Angeles, USA, 1922

S *alomé* was a dream to work on – for me, at least. I'd never imagined that life could be so fulfilling, or that working for a living could be so gratifying. The days were long – sometimes we finished in the early hours then returned to the studio before the sun was up, and in these winter months the sets were freezing, with enormous fan heaters brought in to warm the half-naked cast – but it was a non-stop whirlwind of creativity and joy.

Alla's extravagance knew no bounds. Everything had to be the best, from the costumes to the props to the latest innovations in cine cameras, and there appeared to be an unlimited budget. I'd heard rumours that the cost to her, personally, was already in excess of $100,000, and could quadruple by the time the movie was ready for release. But we all believed in what we were creating – so much more than a motion picture; a groundbreaking, artistic, cinematic experience – and felt confident that Alla would more than recoup her costs at the box office.

Joe and I were like ships in the night. Despite being engaged on the same production, we were both incredibly busy, wrapped up in our own worlds. Sometimes, at home, I'd share the sketches I was working on, or Joe would read out loud a re-drafted scene to canvass my opinion, but mostly we existed in separate spheres. We were seldom intimate these days, and I suspected we were using our conflicting schedules as an excuse to avoid one another. On the rare occasions we found ourselves alone together, a tension we couldn't quite shake hung over us like a thundercloud and, given that everything else in our lives seemed to be going rather well, we gave in to the temptation to ignore the festering problems rather than address them.

In the six months since I'd returned from my brother's wedding, I'd sensed a restlessness within me that I'd done my best to hide, but Joe wasn't a fool. We'd been going through the motions, buying one another expensive yet impersonal gifts at Christmas, for example. Now we could afford luxuries, but nothing would come close to the sweet sentimentality of the book of Sappho's poetry and the embroidered handkerchiefs we'd exchanged that first year. Back then there'd been a purity to those choices; they were given with love and open-heartedness and it made me both nostalgic and sad to reflect on those times. I remembered how Joe had monopolised my every thought, both waking and sleeping, but now others dominated my fantasies: sometimes Natacha, sometimes Sarah Beth.

I hadn't spoken to Sarah Beth after Walter's wedding – I'd

deemed it prudent not to – but across the churchyard, and across the barn where the party had taken place after the ceremony, I couldn't take my eyes off her, watching her every movement. Did she look happy? Did she still think of me? I longed for her to give me a sign. When Clarence placed an arm tenderly on her shoulder and she reached up to lace her fingers through his, was that genuine affection? If it weren't for *Salomé* keeping me occupied on my return to Los Angeles, I feared I might have lost my mind to speculation and regret.

'Shall we grab a coffee?' Natacha asked one morning. She and I had been at work since dawn, and we were beginning to flag.

'Sure.' I headed for the cafeteria, but Natacha steered me towards the parking lot.

'Let's have a change of scenery.'

She owned a cornflower blue Liberty Touring motorcar, and we sped along the few blocks to North Fairfax, to a little café Natacha frequented, seating ourselves at an outdoor table. The February air still held a chill, but it felt wonderful to inhale the fresh air beneath the clear cerulean sky after so many hours spent in the dingy hangar.

'Did you know Charles has moved out?' Natacha sat back in her chair, inhaling a cigarette through a black holder. 'He's taken rooms at the Athletic Club.'

'No! Why?' I'd barely seen Charles on set the past few days. Although he was nominally the director, everyone knew that *Salomé* was Alla's baby, and that she called the shots.

'Oh, Maybelle, you're so naïve. It's one of the things I love about you. Have you not seen the way Alla's been carrying on with Paul?'

'Ivano? The cameraman?'

'The very same. Don't get me wrong, Alla and Charles have always had a rather relaxed attitude to marriage. Charles has turned a blind eye to Alla's previous encounters – and she to his. But this one is… different.'

Even though I'd long presumed they must have some mutually beneficial arrangement, it was still a shock to hear those suspicions confirmed. I'd never been aware of Alla carrying on with another man before – though perhaps that was what made this tryst so unpalatable to Charles, and so different to Alla's previous paramours.

'He's leaving for New York as soon as we've wrapped – Charles, that is. Alla won't be going with him.'

'Are they getting a divorce?' I was wide-eyed.

Natacha shrugged. 'I don't know. Their relationship is… a complicated one.'

I drained my coffee and digested the revelations. However strange I'd found their marriage, it had been a constant since I first met Alla over two years ago, and I couldn't help but feel that the sands were shifting beneath me, that everything which had seemed so certain and immovable when I first met Joe was, in fact, changeable and pervious.

I glanced across at Natacha, struck by her handsome profile, her confidence and poise. Her violet eyes were luminous, her fingers long and slender as she extinguished the cigarette in the ashtray. She turned to me and I quickly looked away, fiddling with my empty cup.

'And how's everything with you and Rudy?' I asked

hastily. I felt odd every time I broached the subject of Natacha's relationship, and I wasn't sure why; it would have looked stranger to avoid it.

'Can I tell you a secret? We're getting married!'

'Oh!' I tried to stop my voice from faltering. 'Congratulations. When? Where? Tell me all the details.' I smiled disingenuously.

'Whenever we both get a break. Rudy's about to start work on *Blood and Sand* so it might not be until late spring, or early summer. We're going to stay with my friend in Palm Springs then slip over the border to Mexicali for the ceremony. You should come! And Joe too, of course.'

'Oh, I'd love to,' I lied. 'I'll speak to Joe about it.'

We lapsed into silence once more, Natacha presumably wrapped up in excitement about her forthcoming nuptials, whilst I tried not to reflect too closely on the cold, sick feeling in the pit of my stomach.

'Is Rudy allowed to get married again? Legally, I mean. I thought he had to wait a year after the divorce.'

Natacha shrugged, not looking overly concerned. 'Technically, he does, but who's counting? Anyway, that's why we're going to Mexico. Do you know Dagmar Godowsky? She married Frank Mayo in Tijuana, and his divorce only came through three months earlier, but when they got back here the marriage was recognised. So why not the same for us? Besides, Rudy's a huge star now. Who's going to put Rudolph Valentino in jail?'

~

In May, we drove in convoy down to Palm Springs – Natacha and Rudy in the first car, followed by Alla and Paul Ivano, then me and Joe. It was my first time in the desert and, despite the soaring heat, the journey was a riot: drinking champagne en route; belting out jazz songs at the top of our lungs; screaming at imagined rattlesnakes when we stopped for a bathroom break behind a giant cactus.

We stayed overnight with Natacha's friend, Dr Fioretta White, who owned a sprawling ranch that was easily large enough to accommodate us all, before driving on to Mexicali bright and early the next morning. It was the first time I'd ever been out of the United States, and I was giddy with excitement as we passed through the Coachella Valley, the others laughing at my naivety.

'What does Mexico look like?' I wondered, wide-eyed.

'California!' quipped Paul. He was a tall, dark-haired Frenchman, who'd worked as a photographer for the American Red Cross after the war, before moving to the US permanently where he'd found his calling as a cinematographer.

'What do they eat? What do they wear? Will they speak English?' I asked, the questions pouring forth until the rest of the party grew tired of answering and begged me to be quiet.

When we reached the town of Mexicali, almost five hours later, I was charmed by the brightly coloured buildings and the narrow streets, the squares lush with greenery and the distinctive churches whose bells rang out as we passed by. We rented rooms in a hotel called the Casa Blanca; we weren't intending to stay overnight, and planned to drive back to Palm

Springs straight after the ceremony, but it would give us somewhere to freshen up and change.

I was acutely aware that Joe and I were now alone together in this adorable little room with its white walls and dark furniture and its twin beds for propriety's sake. The windows were open, thin white drapes shifting in the welcome breeze. After the group camaraderie, the atmosphere felt distinctly flat, and we washed and changed awkwardly.

'I love that dress,' Joe smiled softly, watching me as I pinned up my hair. She came over, resting one hand on my waist, softly kissing my neck.

'Thank you,' I replied, sounding inexplicably prim.

'I like it better when you're not wearing anything,' she murmured, and I couldn't help but shift uncomfortably beneath her touch.

'Later,' I protested. Less of a promise, more a way of buying myself a little time.

'*Now,*' Joe whispered, her hand stroking the bare skin of my arm, her body pressing insistently against mine.

I wriggled out of her grasp. 'The wedding's in less than an hour. We don't want to be late.'

'Natacha would understand.'

'I don't think she would,' I snapped, my tone harsher than intended.

Joe got the message and backed off, sitting down on one of the beds, lighting a cigarette and regarding me coolly. Natacha had asked that we didn't draw any more attention to ourselves than necessary, so Joe had foregone her preferred tuxedo and opted for a rather drab lavender day dress.

'You know, you're a lot less fun than you used to be,' she pronounced finally.

The blow stung, but I refused to let her see it. 'I don't think so.' In truth, I went out more than ever these days – I had a group of girlfriends I'd met through Natacha, and it was nice to feel less dependent on Joe. Some nights I'd go out dancing straight after work then head right to the studio the next morning; I was still young enough to be able to do that whilst, ten years older than me, Joe now needed her sleep in order to function effectively. 'What you actually mean is, I'm less fun when I'm with *you*.'

'Oh yeah, I bet Natacha thinks you're a riot. Saving the fun times for her, right? I'm sure you're devastated she's marrying Rudy. What are you going to do, object and stop the wedding?'

'Screw you,' I hissed, my eyes blazing, as Joe laughed infuriatingly.

We finished getting ready in stony silence, my make-up applied with angry strokes of the brush. As we were about to leave, Joe placed her hand on my arm.

'I'm sorry. I don't want us to fight, not today.'

I hesitated, then relented. 'I'm sorry too.' Deep down, I knew that I should be grateful to Joe. If it weren't for her, I wouldn't have my new career, wouldn't have met these amazing people, wouldn't even be in Mexico right now. Despite my newly discovered independence, I still relied heavily on Joe: my anchor, my security, my North Star. I kissed her and she pulled me closer, one hand on the back of my head, fingertips digging into my hair. 'Joe, be careful!' I exclaimed, pulling away and patting my elaborate style to see if it was still pinned in place.

Tendrils had come loose, falling around my face. I felt a stab of irritation, a flash of annoyance with Joe, but then something shifted inside me, a frisson permeating the air between us. I glanced up at her and we locked eyes. She was staring at me, her gaze challenging, and I could see her breath rising and falling in the hollow at the base of her throat. We moved towards each other, so synchronised that it was impossible to tell who made the first move, and our kiss was almost aggressive.

It had been a few weeks since we'd last been intimate. We'd both been busy with work, and I'd been having regular nights out with friends from the *Salomé* set. Even last night, after the meal at Fioretta's, I'd claimed to be tired from travelling, given Joe a peck on the lips, and fallen asleep. In truth, I knew I was making excuses. Now, all the pent-up frustration came spilling out, the tension between us finally finding a release.

We were due downstairs at any moment and knew we had to be quick. The knowledge added an extra sense of urgency, driven on by the forbidden nature of what we were doing; it was one thing to make love in a private home in liberal Hollywood, quite another in this rented hotel room in a Roman Catholic country where neither of us were familiar with the laws.

Joe pushed me backwards and I fell against the wall and gasped. Hurried, hasty hands searched beneath skirts, pushing dresses up to waists, navigating garter belts and stockings and bloomers. We found each other at same time, wet and wanting, both working for mutual pleasure. Despite our recent differences, there was something comforting in the familiarity of her body, her scent, the feel of her against me and inside me.

Our knowledge of one another was of the most intimate kind, and we both knew exactly what to do to bring the other to dizzying heights of pleasure in the shortest possible time.

Beside the open window, Joe clamped a hand over my mouth to hide my moans, whilst the other worked expertly, my breathing ragged as she brought me to a quick, intense climax. I buried my head in her shoulder to muffle the sound, my body juddering against hers, my stomach spasming as Joe found her own release, cupped in my palm.

My cheeks were flushed, my hair a mess. We held each other close as we exhaled shakily, heart rate slowing, luxuriating in the closeness of the moment, as though we'd called a temporary truce.

I kept my eyes closed, savouring the moment, as Joe let her fingers trail over my stomach, my hip, covering my face in soft, butterfly kisses.

'Do you ever wish it was us?' she asked quietly.

'What?'

'Getting married.'

I opened my eyes to look at her. 'Is this a proposal?' I teased.

'Oh, I know it's foolish, but is there some part of you that thinks about it? That wants the normality? Being able to show everyone that we're together and in love and don't give a damn what the rest of the world thinks?'

I pulled away from her, rearranging my skirts, moving across to the mirror to fix my hair. 'Of course,' I said, not meeting her gaze. 'I don't want to hide, I wish we could be open. But we can't. Come on, time to go. Let's not dwell on the impossible.'

I thought of Joe's words as we watched Natacha and Rudolph exchange their vows in a beautiful, traditional building with whitewashed walls and tall wooden doors. They seemed so happy together, Natacha and the man she loved, hardly able to take their eyes from one another. When they kissed, Joe let her hand graze mine, ever so slightly. I knew she longed to take my palm in hers, to let our fingers intertwine, for us to declare our love as publicly as our friends had declared theirs. But for now, we could only brush skin with the most inconsequential of touches, and for now, that would have to be enough.

We drove back to Palm Springs immediately afterwards, arriving at Fioretta's house in the early evening. Although we were exhausted from all the travelling and the excitement of the day, Fioretta – a raven-haired, free-spirited, Italian American in her mid-thirties – had laid out a stunning meal of avocado soufflé, followed by rib steak with a vegetable salad. It was accompanied by yet more champagne and we ate by the pool in her backyard, candles scattered around to both ward off the mosquitoes and give the grounds a festive atmosphere as the dusky twilight slipped into darkness.

Everyone cheered as Fioretta presented Rudy and Natacha with an incredible cake, iced in white and decorated with black feathers and jewels. By now, we were all a little loose, operating at our usual raucous volume as the performers around the table did their best to one-up one another. Alla was sitting in Paul's lap, kicking her legs and switching positions with the ease of a gymnast; Joe's hands kept straying beneath the table to find my thighs, her fingers steadily working their way beneath the folds of my dress; whilst the newlyweds put on a sufficiently besotted display and Fioretta watched over the proceedings with amusement.

'Do you have a release date for *Salomé* yet?' Rudy asked Alla, as he fed a forkful of wedding cake to a giggling Natacha.

It was an innocent enough question, but Alla's face darkened. 'Those bastards are refusing to set one.'

I slapped Joe's hand away from where it was exploring the lacy edge of my bloomers and glanced at her anxiously. We both knew the pressure Alla had been under; she'd invested $300,000 – almost all of her money – in *Salomé*, and taken out a loan of a further $100,000. Allied, part of United Artists, had agreed to distribute the movie, but were now getting cold feet, with rumours and speculation beginning to circulate in the press about the reasons for this.

'They're assholes,' Natacha interjected loyally. 'It's an incredible movie. A piece of art.'

'Why don't you put on a screening for the critics?' Rudy suggested. 'Then when they love it, Allied will have no choice but to set a date and distribute it.'

Alla sipped her champagne thoughtfully. 'That's a very good idea.'

'He's not just a pretty face, are you, my love?' Natacha cooed, squeezing his cheeks as everyone laughed. I found Rudy fascinating to be around; undeniably exquisite to look at, radiating sexuality, I'd known him for a couple of years now and seen the adjustment from aspiring actor to bone fide movie star. He'd coped well with the transitions in his life, with becoming the object of slavish female devotion and the target of unjust male hostility, and there was no doubt that the Great Lover was, in fact, desperately in love with Natacha.

'Do excuse me,' Fioretta apologised as the telephone rang and she made her way into the house.

'Anyway, let's not talk shop.' Alla waved her hands dismissively. 'I find it very depressing, and this is a happy occasion. So tell us, Rudy, Natacha, what are your plans for the future? There is a magnificent house for sale on Doheny, perfect for raising children.'

Natacha raised her eyebrows. 'Then that's not the right house for us. Children get in the way of a career, I've observed.'

There was a slight edge to her voice, and the rest of us stayed quiet, but Paul – two gin cocktails and the best part of a bottle of champagne inside him – showed no such reserve. 'And what does your husband think about that, huh?'

'Rudy understands. Don't you, darling.'

There was a telling pause, before Rudolph threw his napkin on the table and exhaled heavily. 'Natacha is still young.' He shrugged. 'I had the most wonderful mother, who kept a beautiful house and cooked delicious meals – if I think about her *tiella* it makes me want to cry, I miss home so much. And, of course, she was French, so incredibly chic. In the future, Natacha may think differently. Every woman longs to be a wife and a mother sooner or later,' he smiled, addressing Natacha and stroking her arm.

'If you wanted a housewife, you've picked the wrong

spouse I'm afraid,' she returned, unable to keep the arch tone from her voice.

Distracted by the brewing argument, we barely noticed Fioretta as she ran from the house, her face ashen. 'Rudy, there's a Jack Lloyd from Paramount on the line. He wants to speak with you urgently.'

'Jack Lloyd?' Rudy frowned. 'I don't think I know that name. Did he say what he wanted?'

Fioretta hesitated, and I felt my stomach turn over, my instincts warning that something was wrong.

'He said he's from the legal department. He said… word of your marriage has leaked and you have to return to Los Angeles immediately. You're to be charged with bigamy and anyone with you—' she looked around the table, her eyes wide and terrified, '—will be tried as co-conspirators.'

'Fuck. Fuck!' Rudolph jumped to his feet, sprinting across the lawn and into the house, the rest of us staring dumbly at one another.

Chapter Twenty

ALLA

New York City, USA, 1905

New York City in the early years of the new century was crowded, frenetic, exhilarating, exhausting. Alla hated it.

'All this smoke and noise and people,' she complained to Pavel as they trudged along Broadway, almost losing her hat as she jumped out of the way of an oncoming streetcar. It was February, it was freezing, and Alla was unimpressed by the tall buildings that blocked out the daylight, the incessant rumble from the trains thundering overhead.

'This is the future,' Pavel told her, beaming. '*Our* future. Our fortune.'

Alla remained unconvinced. She pulled her coat more tightly around her, viewing her surroundings with dark-eyed suspicion.

After their violent arrest on the opening night of *The Chosen People*, they'd been unexpectedly released without charge. Alla revelled in their good fortune, but Maxim Gorky (under house arrest in Nizhny Novgorod) had written to Pavel with a warning: if the company had not been thrown in jail, it was because the authorities had instead decided to keep them under surveillance. They heeded his advice and lay low for some months, performing dull, inoffensive, uncontroversial plays to get a little money in the pot, before applying for permits to travel abroad. The permission had taken an age, lost in a tangle of bureaucracy, but then – miracle of miracles! – the visas were granted and the St Petersburg Players travelled to Berlin to perform *The Chosen People* with the aim of stirring up protest against the Tsarist regime.

Following a two-week run in Germany, the actors moved on to London, where a crowd of mostly Russian exiles gave Alla a standing ovation. The play quickly found a supportive audience, with a benefit matinee given at the Haymarket Theatre to raise funds for the company's forthcoming venture; Pavel had decided that New York should be their next destination, and received a letter of introduction from the writer Jerome K. Jerome to Broadway producer Charles Frohman.

Which was why, only one day after arriving in the country, and with Alla barely over her seasickness, they were walking more than thirty blocks from their hovel of a hotel on 8th street to Frohman's offices on 40th.

'May I help you?' asked Frohman's secretary as they entered the bureau above the Empire Theatre. She was brisk and efficient, slim-faced and older than the pair of them, and she regarded them coolly over pince-nez spectacles.

Alla and Pavel had only a few words of English between them.

'Hello,' Pavel said brightly, handing over the letter, brazening it out as his showmanship came to the fore. 'Thank you!'

They waited anxiously, not daring to sit down on the chairs, speaking to one another in low tones, despite being certain that no one in the vicinity could speak Russian. A few minutes later, the woman returned.

'Mr Frohman will see you now,' she said, smiling more warmly. 'His office is just through there.'

Alla and Pavel exchanged glances. Neither of them understood what the woman had said, but her friendly manner and the open door beyond indicated they'd overcome the first hurdle.

'Thank you!' Pavel repeated, beaming, as he bowled in confidently and Alla followed.

The man seated in the chair was round and bald, in his mid-forties and Jewish, wearing a dark suit and a wide collared shirt. Even without speaking he projected an air of power and success, and he stood up with an outstretched hand.

'Good to meet you, I'm Charles Frohman.'

'Pavel Orlenev.' Pavel's grip was firm, his shake enthusiastic. He turned to Alla, who smiled. 'This, Alla Nazimova.'

'Have a seat, have a seat,' Frohman gestured, as the two actors did as they were bid. 'So, this is quite the letter of recommendation. I've never met him, but I've heard good things about Jerome K. Jerome. He's quite the writer.'

'Jerome,' interjected Pavel, picking up on a word he recognised. 'Very good man.'

'Sure. It seems like your performance impressed him. And this play – *The Chosen People*, right? – it sounds pretty interesting. There's a lot of immigrants arriving here right now, a lot of Jews, from Germany, Hungary, all over Eastern Europe. I think you might be onto something.'

'*The Chosen People*, yes,' nodded Pavel, once again parroting the words that he knew. 'Your theatre, one afternoon, for free. Yes?'

Frohman roared with laughter. 'You're pretty upfront, aren't you? But I like that. Hell, you've travelled all the way from Russia. What kind of guy would I be if I didn't give you a chance? All right, we have a deal. You can have the Herald Square Theatre for one afternoon in two weeks' time, okay? Come back tomorrow morning. Ten o'clock. I'll find an interpreter.'

'Tomorrow?' Pavel narrowed his eyes, unsure whether he'd understood.

'Yes, tomorrow. Here. Ten o'clock.' Frohman held up all ten digits. 'Understand?'

'Thank you,' was all Pavel could say, reaching across the desk to pump his hand once more. 'Thank you.'

Alla gathered up a handful of newspapers and impulsively added two postcards of Broadway actresses – Maude Adams and Fanny Rice. The act reminded her of when she'd first arrived in Moscow, drawn to the images of celebrated, inspirational women staring seductively into the camera, and she had reason to believe that she herself was drawing ever closer to achieving her dreams, closer to seeing her own face rendered in monochrome 6x4 as a renowned, illustrious performer.

'Thank you,' Alla smiled at the newspaper seller, as she dropped the now familiar coins into his hand and began to walk back home, admiring the view across the East River to the ever-rising skyline of Manhattan.

She and Pavel had moved out of their squalid hotel and were living with her Uncle Osip in Brooklyn. Alla had always known that her mother's brother had settled in the city, but his address remained a mystery until she became acquainted with a Russian doctor who knew Osip Horowitz. On reuniting and explaining her circumstances, Osip – who was, by profession, a dentist – had suggested his niece and her companion move into his apartment, alongside his wife and son. Pavel, always keen to make a saving, had readily agreed to the prospect of rent-free living, and the two of them soon found themselves part of a welcoming Russian exile community, where there was always someone looking to reminisce about the old country over tea from the samovar and a packet of Russian cigarettes.

'I have the newspapers,' Alla declared as she burst into the kitchen where her uncle and his family were seated around the table. Pavel was nowhere to be seen; she'd left him sleeping in their bed. 'Please, Uncle, can you translate them for me?'

Osip Horowitz had the same full, round face that was familiar to Alla from photographs of her mother, though his was partially obscured by a neat beard and whiskers. He had the dark hair and sharp blue eyes that Alla associated with

Sonya, and she couldn't help but feel a pang of loss whenever those eyes were trained on her.

'Of course,' he agreed, almost as excited as his niece.

Plates and cups were hastily shuffled to one side and the *New York American* was duly spread out over the kitchen table, eggs and rye bread quite forgotten as the four of them pored over the newspaper. Alla's heart was thumping as her uncle skimmed over the words, taking a moment to translate them into his native tongue.

'Oh, Alla, it is wonderful! They mention you by name – here, see – *Alla Nazimova*.'

'But what do they *say*?' Alla thought she might burst with anticipation.

'"*We could not understand the language of the play, but the language of Alla Nazimova is universal. It is the language of the soul. Her name will be a household word... She wept beautifully. American actresses are afraid to ruin their make-up and weep from their temples and foreheads... Nazimova shed tears from her eyes, mopped them with a handkerchief, and at the end of her grief, she actually had a red nose*".'

'He talked about my red nose?' Alla frowned.

'Forget that, he said you're going to be a household name. My niece!' Osip threw his arms around her. 'And this one, *The New York Times*, the reviewer says: "*Nazimova is an actress of wonderful temperamental and technical quality.*" *The New York Times*, Alla! Can you believe it?'

Alla's face was radiant. 'I must go and wake Pavel. He'll be delighted.'

The curtains were still closed in the attic room she shared with Pavel; he'd had a rather heavy night celebrating the offer of a two-matinee-per-week run for *The Chosen People* at the Grand Street Theatre, and the air was thick with stale sweat and fetid breath.

Alla climbed onto the bed beside him, gently shaking his shoulder to rouse him.

'My love,' she murmured. 'I have the papers, the reviews.'

Pavel grunted and rolled over, bleary-eyed as Alla came into focus. 'What?'

'I have the reviews from the two critics who attended – *New York American* and *The New York Times*. Look!'

Pavel sat up and wrenched the papers from her, his gaze scanning greedily over the lines of incomprehensible words. 'Well? What do they say?'

Alla repeated the lavish praise she'd received, the effusive words imprinted on her brain, her heart soaring with pride to hear them again.

'Yes, yes,' Pavel snapped dismissively. 'But what did they say about *me*?'

Alla paused, taken aback. 'Um… they said that you put in a strong performance as Nachman, that we made a thoroughly believable couple and our styles complemented one another…'

Pavel was staring at her through narrowed eyes, his jaw set firm. 'But no *"language of the soul"* for me? No *"household word"* for me?'

'I can ask Uncle Osip to translate again, I may have forgotten something—'

'I don't want your *pity*,' Pavel roared, causing Alla to shrink backwards in fright. 'This is the thanks I get? *This*?' he repeated, snatching up the newspapers and pushing them into her face. 'For standing by your side all these years and bringing you to America, hanging off my coat tails?'

'But this is good for both of us,' Alla protested. 'For the play, for the company—'

'*I'm* the star,' Pavel cut her off. '*I* will be a household name. These American reviewers? Know-nothing sons of bitches, producing their *garbage*. They wouldn't know talent if it spat in their vodka,' he yelled, tearing into the papers, ripping the words to shreds so the pieces fell to the floor like ashes from a fire. 'Get out! Just get out, you traitorous bitch!'

Alla was horrified by his reaction, but knew better than to try and reason with Pavel when he was in a temper. She closed the door and retreated back down the stairs, wincing as she heard a great crash; Uncle Osip's porcelain vase being thrown against the wall, she would wager. She would wait an hour then bring him tea and blinis to ease the effects of the drinking, and he would forgive her and all would be well again.

'Ah, Madame Nazimova. I'm delighted to meet you. I've been following your career for some time now and eagerly awaiting your arrival in Chicago.' The woman who was speaking was elegant and earnest, expensively dressed with diamonds at her ears and three strands of freshwater pearls at her throat. 'My name is Mrs Hobart Chatfield-Taylor – but you can call me Rose. I adore the theatre, and your performance tonight was superlative.'

Whilst Alla didn't follow everything her new friend had said over the buzzing noise of the crowd, she'd picked up sufficient English to feel confident that Mrs Hobart Chatfield-Taylor – Rose – was praising her effusively.

'Thank you,' Alla smiled. 'You are very kind.'

'Not at all. I only give praise where praise is due – and well deserved in your case.'

Alla smiled once again, unsure how to reply. She and Pavel had arrived in Chicago two days ago, and tonight had been the opening performance of a two-week run of *Ghosts* by Ibsen. The past few months had been a veritable rollercoaster as *The Chosen People* moved from theatre to theatre in New York, with varying degrees of success, before Charles Frohman decided to send the St Petersburg Players on tour. Now this party had been thrown for them in the gilded ballroom of the Palmer House Hotel, attended by theatrical types, writers and artists, and the very cream of Chicago society. Alla and Pavel were the guests of honour – a heady, and at times overwhelming, distinction.

'Tell me, Alla – if I may – what are your plans for the future?'

Alla shrugged. 'When our luck runs out, we will go back to Russia.'

'Oh no, you mustn't! That would be too great a loss. You know, my dear, you're wasted in these small productions. Your talents deserve to be seen by a wider audience. Tell me, have you ever considered a career on Broadway?'

'Oh no, I couldn't. My English...' Alla trailed off, proving her point.

'Then you must learn! Listen, why don't you take my card? I'm regularly in New York. My husband is a writer and I have some excellent contacts. I'd love to help you.'

'But why?'

'We women must stick together and assist one another in whatever way we can,' Rose enthused. 'It's a new century, and the world is changing. Mark my words, the future is female. But you must recognise your own talent and your own power. You, my dear, can make your own career without having to rely on anyone else.'

Alla looked up to see Pavel watching her; he was in conversation with the financier John Pierpoint Morgan and Edward Fitzsimmons Dunne, the city mayor, but his eyes turned accusingly in her direction. Alla cast her gaze downwards, feeling oddly guilty, made her excuses to Mrs Hobart Chatfield-Taylor, and swiftly moved on.

During the fall of 1905, Alla and Pavel moved from Uncle Osip's to a one-room walk-up in a rat-infested tenement on East 4th Street. Pavel had opened his own theatre – the Lyceum, on East 3rd – which he'd managed to finance by charming Emma Goldman, a wealthy Russian Jewish immigrant who'd fallen in love with both the theatre and with Pavel. But despite this newly found source of funding, audiences were thin on the ground, and by the end of the year the dilapidated Lyceum had been declared a public hazard and closed down by the New York Fire Department.

In March 1906, Pavel was arrested for grand larceny, having allegedly purloined $1,500 from the profits of a fundraiser. Emma Goldman was on hand to pay his bail, but it was this incident that led to Pavel's decision to take the St Petersburg

Players back to Russia, and this decision that saw him – hungover and running late – rushing around the dishevelled apartment, attempting to throw his worldly belongings into a trunk before the ship left without him.

'Come on, Alla,' he chided, rolling up the dusty rug and throwing it into the open case. 'We don't have much time, and you haven't even started.'

Alla sat quietly on the bed, staring blankly ahead.

'What's the matter with you? Are you ill?'

She mumbled something unintelligible, her voice barely audible.

'What? Speak up woman, they can't hear you in the back row.'

'I said I'm not going.' Alla's face was drawn and tense as she finally met Pavel's enquiring stare. He stopped what he was doing, turning his whole body slowly towards her, forehead creased in confusion.

'What do you mean, you're not going?'

'I'm staying here. In New York.'

'Don't be ridiculous,' Pavel scoffed. 'What will you do?'

Alla hesitated, chewing her bottom lip. 'I've signed a contract with Lee Schubert. Five years. He thinks I can be a Broadway actress.'

Pavel made an alarming noise, somewhere between a snort and explosion. 'You don't even speak English! What role are you going to play? Ugly Russian whore?'

Alla ignored the spiteful comment. 'He's going to get me a tutor.'

'You're not clever enough to learn. You're... He's... This is preposterous!'

'Pavel—'

'No!' Pavel roared, crossing the floor, pressing his face to hers. 'How dare you betray me like this? All I've ever done is my best for us – for *you* – and you've been sneaking around signing deals behind my back? If it wasn't for me, you'd still be in Russia playing provincial theatres in backwater towns nobody's ever heard of. You disgust me.' He spat on the floor at her feet, and Alla was overcome by guilt and despair and fear.

'What would you have done?' she asked. 'If the shoe were on the other foot? It makes my head spin to think how fast you'd have signed that contract and left me in the dirt. Can't you see what an opportunity this is for me? How could I turn it down?'

'You should have told him what we agreed – that we're together, that we come as a package. You could have refused to sign unless he signed me too. But no, you're a selfish, cold-hearted bitch who's only concerned with looking after herself. Did you fuck Schubert to get yourself a contract? Is that what happened? Because that's the only explanation I can see. You're not an actress – you're a slut, a whore, a—' Pavel let forth a string of expletives, and Alla leapt to her feet as he reached for the wash pitcher. Seconds later, it was in pieces on the floor, swiftly followed by the basin. With the sweep of an arm, their small collection of crockery was liberated from the shelf above the table and lay smashed on the ground, whilst Pavel stood panting with exertion.

Alla said nothing, unmoved by his dramatic display. She'd seen it too many times before, been on the receiving end of his rage and quite literally picked up the pieces afterwards.

Seeing her reaction, Pavel changed tack, falling to his knees and beginning to weep. 'Don't leave me, Alla. Please don't leave me. What will I do? You know I can't look after myself – I'm a mess without you. You promised, you said you'd follow me anywhere. What about your vow?'

'Pavel—'

'Come with me, my darling!' His eyes were bright and shining wet with tears as he looked up at her. 'We'll go back to Russia – to Moscow, St Petersburg, wherever you want – and we'll be the toast of the town. Don't you want that? You and me, our own theatre, fêted by society, wealth and fame beyond our wildest dreams. What do you say?' Alla wavered, and Pavel pressed on, 'Do you really think you can have that here? In this foreign country with its ungraspable language and its strange customs? We'll always be outsiders in America – immigrants, second class citizens, we'll never be accepted. Your home is in Russia, by my side. You and me, together, the way we always agreed.'

His passionate words had moved Alla to tears, but she vowed to stay strong. She knew better than anyone what a gifted actor Pavel was, with the power to tug at the heartstrings and manipulate his audience's emotions – and today he was giving everything to an audience of one. She had to stand firm. She didn't know what this opportunity – America! Broadway! – would bring, but she believed she would regret it for the rest of her life if she didn't pursue it.

Alla shook her head, tears streaming down her face as she crudely wiped her nose with the back of her hand. 'I'm sorry,' she whispered. 'I can't.'

'Bitch!' Pavel screamed, jumping to his feet, his mood

changing in an instant. 'Fucking ungrateful *bitch*!' He slammed the lid down on the trunk, locking it shut. 'Don't come crawling back to me when this town discovers you have no talent and you're all washed up. You're an ugly, aging fraud who'll never be a success. I hope you rot in hell.'

With that, Pavel walked out and slammed the door, dragging the trunk behind him. Alla heard the tramp of his boots along the corridor and down the stairs. She moved to the window, which offered a partial view of the street below, and saw him emerge from their building, marching furiously to the streetcar stop. Within minutes, one arrived, and she watched him board and leave.

So he was gone. Truly gone. And Alla was alone in a foreign country where she barely spoke the language and was friendless save for her uncle and his family. Pavel's criticisms had tapped into her darkest fears – that she was unattractive, stupid, talentless; that she'd betrayed him and without him she was nothing – and the temptation to catch the next streetcar and follow him to the dock to beg his forgiveness was overwhelming.

Instead, she threw herself down on the bed they'd shared, onto the messy, crumpled sheets that still smelt of him, and cried out like a wounded animal, sobbing as though her heart were broken.

Chapter Twenty-One

MAYBELLE

Los Angeles, USA, 1923

'Good morning!' I called out brightly as I climbed the stairs to Alla's office, precariously balancing a pile of newspapers, magazines, letters, and a cup of coffee. I tapped lightly on the door.

'Come in.' Alla sounded exhausted, and I was shocked when I saw her; she was slumped at her desk, hair wild and face bare of make-up. The blinds were half closed, and she was wearing black silk pyjamas.

'Here's your coffee,' I smiled, placing it down in front of her. 'And the papers... and some mail.' I left them on the desk and scooted round to open the blinds. Alla winced as the mid-morning light flooded in.

She picked up the letters, her expression bittersweet, her voice listless. 'Do you know, Maybelle, five years ago they brought my fan mail by the sack-load. I had to employ a full-time secretary to keep up with the replies. Sometimes I spent two, three hours a day autographing copies of my photograph. And now...' She let the envelopes fall back and forth. 'A dozen? Fifteen, perhaps?'

I didn't know what to say. Alla was astute enough to see straight through any platitudes I might offer and so I stayed silent, the atmosphere stilted and awkward. My hours had been reduced over recent months to a day or two per week; Alla's life seemed to have grown much smaller and there was no longer the same volume of work. It was rather sad really. The house was quiet, and Madame Nazimova rarely received visitors. It was nothing like the buzzing, bacchanalian, hotbed of hedonism I'd first visited just a few years ago.

When I wasn't needed by Alla, I assisted Natacha. After the incident in Mexico, Rudy had pleaded guilty and been thrown in jail for 48 hours, garnering a fabulous blaze of publicity for both him and Paramount. The rest of us *had* been called as witnesses – a terrifying experience – and we confirmed that the marriage had never been consummated, therefore, the marriage could not be said to exist, so no laws had been broken and Rudy was acquitted. He and Natacha had quietly remarried earlier this year in Indiana; Joe and I hadn't attended, and neither had Alla.

Natacha's own talent, plus the status of being – officially this time – Mrs Rudolph Valentino, had seen her own career soar, and she'd been engaged on a production of *Monsieur Beaucaire* which was to be Rudy's comeback film. She was designing the costume and sets, had final approval on the story, and even over the choice of actors. It was due to start filming in New York next year, but I was assisting her in LA with pre-production, costumes and set design.

'Could you quickly look through the post, make sure there's nothing important,' Alla requested, the strong, black coffee working its magic.

'Of course. And look, it's been a while since your last movie. I'm sure the fan mail will start flooding in again once *Salomé* is released.' I smiled, resorting to triteness after all.

I pushed the newspapers towards her, hoping to pique her curiosity. Alla reached for the *Los Angeles Examiner*, and I detected a crackle of excitement, of anticipation. It had taken all my willpower not to peek at the reviews, but I felt Alla should be the first to see them. I hoped they were positive. We'd all worked so hard on *Salomé* and longed for it to be a success.

I began sorting through the fan letters, handwritten envelopes postmarked from all over the country, all over the world in fact: Kansas City, Seattle, Tallahassee, Providence; Canada, Mexico, France, Italy. Near the bottom one packet stood out – brown paper, stamped with words I didn't understand, an alphabet I couldn't read. I'd occasionally seen Alla's old books lying around the house, written in Cyrillic, and some instinct told me that this came from Russia. It had been sent to 8080 Sunset Boulevard, but was addressed to a Madame Golovin. I frowned, about to bring it to Alla's attention, when she cried out as though in pain.

'It's over!'

'What?' I was alarmed. 'What's over?'

'Everything – my career, my future. I've lost all my money. Allied will never agree to release *Salomé* now.'

Open in front of her was a copy of *The New Republic* magazine. I spun it around, reading the damning words for myself: *"Degrading and unintelligent. Nazimova has attempted a part for which she has no qualifications… Try as she will, she cannot be seductive… The deadly lure of sex, which haunts the Wilde drama like a subtle poison, is dispelled the instant one beholds her puerile form."*

'Alla, that's just one review,' I tried desperately. 'What does this guy – Thomas Cranen – know anyway? What do the others say?'

She pushed *Screenland* across the desk towards me: *"It is worth something to watch Nazimova balance her Christmas tree headdress."*

'Is that it? Almost half a million dollars, and they're laughing at my costume? I'll be a joke once this gets out. Everything I've worked for, Maybelle, all these years. I'm going to lose everything. My beautiful house. Half of my friends have already deserted me. Charles has gone to New York and doesn't plan on coming back, and now those assholes in the press have begun to comment on it, like a pack of lions circling a wounded animal.'

I reached across the table to grasp her hand.

'I'm *old*,' she wailed.

'You're not,' I insisted.

'I was foolish, delusional, to believe I could play a 14-year-old. I'm almost forty-four. Any sex appeal I might once have had has long since departed. I knew this day would come, but I closed my eyes and ears to it, hoping I might delay it. And now I look foolish in front of the whole world. I might as well return to the stage and prepare to take on Marina or Anfisa.'

I didn't understand what she was talking about, but I

desperately wanted to comfort her. She looked broken, as if a light inside her had been extinguished.

'Is there anything I can get you? Anything I can do for you?'

It took Alla a moment to respond, as though her thoughts were a long way away from the present moment.

'You're a very sweet girl, Maybelle. I know that Joe loves you very much, even though it might not always seem that way.'

I squirmed with discomfort, wondering how we'd gone from talking about Alla's career to my relationship.

'Is there anything I can get you?' I repeated. 'Anyone you'd like me to call?'

Alla slowly shook her head. 'No. I think the best thing for me right now is to be left alone. I have a lot of thinking to do. Take the rest of the day off, Maybelle. Is Joe working? Go and do something fun with her. Enjoy your life, whilst you're still young and free and beautiful. It passes so quickly.'

'Are you sure?'

'Yes. There's nothing to do here anyway. I'm like the final passenger aboard a ghost ship. Having you here is sheer vanity on my part.'

I squeezed her hands and stood up to leave. 'You'll always be an icon to me. Always. You changed my life and… I'll always be grateful. Please don't ever forget that.'

Alla blew me a melancholy kiss and I walked away, a sinking sensation in the pit of my stomach. It felt as though the way of life I'd known since I'd met Joe was changing; I'd finally had a glimpse behind the curtain, and the future I'd thought seemed so certain was revealed to be little more than an illusion.

~

'Poor Alla. Should we go see her?'

'She said she wanted to be left alone for a while.' I shrugged, spearing a forkful of chicken salad. Joe and I were eating at one of our favourite restaurants, Lowry's in Beverly Hills. I'd arrived home early and offered to take her for lunch. I thought it would be good to do something together, to take Alla's advice and seize the opportunity to put a little romance back into our relationship.

'I'm devastated about the reviews. Were any of them good?'

'Some of them were – some were quite positive. But she only focused on the bad ones. Honestly, I've never seen her like that. She's usually so upbeat and full of life. It was like, this time, she was beaten and she didn't want to fight.'

Joe stretched in her seat, looking concerned. 'I'd better go see her later. She has a lot going on right now.'

'You mean with the *Salomé* reviews? And Charles being gone?'

Joe noticeably hesitated before replying. 'Yeah…'

I scrutinised that face I'd come to know so well, understanding every glance and grimace and nuance of expression. She avoided my gaze. 'Joe, what's going on?'

'What do you mean?'

'I'm not stupid. Alla's not just upset over a few bad reviews. There's more to it than that. Is it anything to do with the letter that arrived from Russia today? Addressed to Madame Golovin?'

Joe's eyebrows shot up in alarm and she instantly shushed me, looking around the restaurant to ensure we hadn't been overheard.

'Well, that touched a nerve,' I commented archly. 'Look, whatever it is, you know you can tell me. I'm worried about Alla. I want to help, in any way I can.'

Joe chewed thoughtfully, as though considering something. She pushed the half-eaten plate of baked eggs with rice away from her and leaned back. 'I'm not hungry anymore.'

'Joe…' Not only was I worried about Alla, I felt affronted that Joe hadn't been able to confide in me, that she'd kept Alla's confidence even when it meant having secrets between us.

'Alla's in serious trouble – financially,' Joe began quietly. I already knew that Alla had ploughed most of her savings into *Salomé*, and that if the studio failed to release it, she'd have no way of recouping the money. I stayed silent, anticipating that Joe would say more. 'She thinks she might have to sell the house – and you know how much she loves Hayvenhurst. There's no way she can repay the loan she took out from Allied.'

'What about Charles?'

'What about him?'

'Can't he help? I thought he was working in New York, he must have some money coming in.'

Joe's expression was sceptical. 'Charles isn't as in demand as he likes people to think he is. He… As long as I've known him, Charles has always used Alla, like a commodity. *She's* been the one with the wealth and the fame. He just went along for the ride while Alla paid for everything – the house, the cars, the clothes…'

'And that's why he's left her now? Because she's lost all her money? What a bastard!'

'Not exactly… A few weeks ago, he made Alla sign a document saying she'll always be responsible for paying his taxes, whatever happens between them. He's nervous that the IRS will audit his returns and demand back payment.'

'But why would she agree to sign? That's crazy.'

Again, Joe hesitated. 'He's blackmailing her.'

'What?' I burst out. 'With what?'

'Maybelle, you know as I well as I do that Alla lives a very… unconventional lifestyle. If details of that were made public, she'd never work again. He threatened to give the press details of all her relationships – male *and* female – if she didn't sign.'

'But that's… that's not fair!' I exclaimed, outraged. I thought of the Charles I'd met many times over the years; he'd seemed like the perfect English gentleman, quiet and polite, supportive of Alla. Perhaps he hadn't been as happy playing second fiddle as he'd appeared to be and was now relishing the way the balance of power had swung. '*He* hasn't been faithful either. Why can't Alla threaten him in return?'

'It wouldn't work.' Joe shook her head. 'He's not a star the way she is. Who, really, would be interested? Plus, there's the double standard – Alla would look like a slut, he'd look like a lothario. It might even bolster his image. Plus, all his affairs have been with women.'

I immediately understood what Joe was implying. The

reality of Alla's situation only highlighted the unfairness of the hundreds and thousands of people just like us who didn't fit into the prescribed mould that society demanded. Most days I could push the threat to the back of my mind, and carry on seemingly as normal, but at times like this I realised what was at stake were Joe and I ever to be found out, and it frightened me.

'Can't she divorce him?' I wondered.

'It's... complicated.'

'Why?'

Joe paused, clearly reluctant to say too much. Again, I felt that burst of anger that she didn't consider me trustworthy, that she would still choose Alla over me. And then I remembered. 'What was that letter from Russia? Do you know? And who's Madame Golovin?'

Joe drained her soda and signalled the waiter for another. She leaned across the table towards me, keeping her voice as low as possible. 'Madame Golovin is Alla.'

'I don't understand. Is Nazimova a stage name?'

'Yes, actually, but Golovin is... it's her married name.'

I gasped, although I didn't fully understand what Joe was telling me.

'She was married, many years ago, in Russia. She regretted it immediately – she did it to spurn a former lover – and I don't believe it was ever consummated. Neither, however, was it ever dissolved.'

'So she's a bigamist?' I whispered, my eyes wide as saucers.

Joe shook her head. 'She and Charles aren't married.'

'What?' I hadn't touched my food since Joe started

speaking. As the waiter brought her drink, I gestured for him to take my plate away.

'You mustn't breathe a word of this to anyone, Maybelle. Do you swear?'

'I swear,' I promised, growing increasingly frustrated at her lack of faith in me. 'So they were never together? It was all a sham?'

'They *were* in a relationship. They were definitely attracted to one another, and they got along very well… They talked of marriage, and as time went on, people just assumed they *were* married. They referred to one another as husband and wife. I believe Alla did intend to divorce Sergei – her husband – but it proved too difficult to get the papers, so when people started assuming she and Charles were married… well, it worked for both of them.'

'And the letter from Russia?'

'Now that it looks like everything's over between Alla and Charles, she wants to make sure he's out of her life for good. If she can obtain a divorce from Sergei, she'll travel to Europe, announce to the press that she's "divorced" Charles, and when she re-enters the States, she'll legally be single. Come on, let's get the check.'

My head was reeling. I sat in stunned silence, trying to process everything as Joe paid the check and went to the bathroom. I felt horrible for Alla, and what a tangle she'd been caught up in. But I couldn't believe that Joe had known about this – *all* of it – the entire time we'd been together, and never once felt able to confide in me.

I felt like a fool. A trusting, gullible fool. All those times when I'd commented on Alla and Charles' peculiar marriage, when I'd taken what I was told at face value, and Joe had known everything all along yet let me carry on looking like a simpleton.

I stood up to leave as Joe returned. She could see I was upset and placed her hand gently on my arm, but I shook it off.

'What's wrong?' she asked.

'I just... I can't believe you never told me.'

'Maybelle, I didn't tell *anyone*. I don't believe anyone else knows apart from me. I don't even think Alla told Charles about Sergei, about the real reason they never got married.'

'But *you're* always there for her, aren't you? Alla's knight in shining armour, whenever she needs you. She says "jump", you say "how high?"' I couldn't hide my bitterness as we walked out of the restaurant and into the parking lot, our voices growing louder.

'I can't believe you're making this all about yourself! Surely you can see that if this had gotten out, Alla would have been destroyed in an instant. I *had* to keep it a secret. For her sake.'

'I don't know what to believe, Joe. I think you treat me like a child – that you've always seen me that way. I think you liked it better when I was ignorant little Maybelle, fresh off the farm, in awe of you and your world and not asking awkward questions.'

Joe's lips were tightly pursed and she looked furious. 'Get in the car, Maybelle.'

'Don't you dare tell me what to do! That's what you've always done, isn't it? Clicked your fingers and I've fallen in line. Well now I have a life of my own, and opinions of my own, and you clearly don't like it.'

Joe had climbed into the Chevy and opened the passenger door. 'Are you coming?'

'No. I'll make my own way home,' I retorted petulantly. I walked out of the parking lot and down the street, hearing Joe call after me as the engine started. Right now I didn't care.

The revelations about Alla had shocked me. Joe's behaviour had shocked me. And more than anything, I needed time to think.

Chapter Twenty-Two

ALLA

New York City, USA, 1906

I t was a bitter December day, and Alla was warmly ensconced in a bustling diner just off Union Square, nursing an enormous cup of coffee and picking at a slice of French toast. On the table in front of her was a terrible dime store novel entitled *The Cowboy and the Murderer*, but her attention had long since wavered from the unfamiliar English words and threadbare plot. She was absorbed in the sights and sounds around her, listening to the buzz of chatter – a furious argument between a serviceman and his sweetheart; a frazzled mother whose child was demanding dessert – and mouthing words which were new to her, repeating them under her breath to ensure the correct pronunciation.

Lee Schubert had been as good as his word and engaged a tutor – Carolyn Harris – who worked with Alla daily. Carolyn was full of vim and vigour, her teaching style unconventional; she threw grammar out of the window, advocating learning via conversation and reading, and she was always accompanied by her young son who brought his pet rats to their lessons. Alla adored her. Following Carolyn's rules, she had banned herself from conversing or corresponding in Russian. The only time she allowed herself was when writing in her diary; she needed that outlet to keep a link with the past, to ensure she never lost touch with who she'd once been.

The door opened, bringing with it a blast of cold air, and a woman walked in. It was her clothing that first caught Alla's attention; she wore a full-length overcoat in rich, crimson wool, a mink fur stole draped around her shoulders, its head lolling lazily on her ample bosom. On her head was the most extravagant hat Alla had ever seen – wider than her shoulders, with what appeared to be an entire florist's stall nestled on top.

Alla watched as the woman ordered from the girl behind the counter, saying something unintelligible in low, throaty tones that made the waitress smile.

On reflection, perhaps it wasn't merely the clothes that had sparked Alla's interest. The woman, in her fifties, walked with two canes, but her confidence was such that you barely noticed them, and Alla could only hope to emulate such innate self-assurance. The woman looked around and caught Alla staring; cheeks flaming, Alla dropped her gaze. But there'd been something in the woman's expression, a flash of recognition perhaps, that made Alla consider whether—

'Would you mind if I sat here?'

There was a certain inevitability to the question.

'Not at all. Please…' Alla said carefully, delighted to try out her language skills on a native.

The woman settled her bulk slowly into the chair opposite,

assisted by the canes, arranging herself until she was comfortable. Sipping her drink, she scrutinised Alla, who pretended to be engrossed in her book.

'Madame Nazimova, isn't it?'

Alla was startled, wondering how this stranger knew her name. She groped for the right phrase, but the woman interjected, holding out her hand for Alla to shake.

'I'm Elisabeth Marbury, but you can call me Bessie. I'm a literary agent. I work with Charles Frohman. I saw you in *The Seagull*, and you were quite outstanding. Lee Schubert was absolutely right to sign you.'

Alla didn't follow all of the words, but understood the sentiment. 'Thank you. Please, call me Alla.'

'How are you finding New York, Alla?'

She hesitated, taking a moment to find the words to express her thoughts. 'At first, I hated New York. Now, I like it better…'

'Good. You should get used to it. You have a great career ahead of you.' Bessie's style was direct and no-nonsense. 'Do you have friends here? I understand the rest of your company went back to Russia.'

Alla nodded. 'I do not know many people but… I hope I shall, very soon.'

'I'm having a small festive gathering this evening at my place. Old friends, new friends, interesting people. I think you'd fit right in. Would you like to come?'

'Thank you. Yes.' Alla nodded enthusiastically, eager and shy all at the same time.

'I live in Irving House, between Park Avenue and Third. Do you know it?' Alla's blank expression gave her the answer she needed. 'It's only a couple of blocks east of here. Let me show you.' She took a notebook from her purse and scribbled an address, drawing a rudimentary map in stark, black ink, before tearing out the page and passing it across the table.

'Can you read my messy writing? Come for drinks at seven o'clock. I'll serve supper after eight.'

Alla took the paper, tucking it inside *The Cowboy and the Murderer*. 'Thank you. I look forward to it,' she smiled, and Bessie seemed satisfied.

As she gathered her belongings and took her leave of Bessie Marbury, Alla was still reeling, unsure of what exactly had just happened. But as she clutched the book tightly to her chest to ensure its precious contents remained in place, she realised that things were starting to happen for her in New York City.

Irving House was a grand, three-storied building on the southwest corner of East 17th and Irving Place. Its red-brick exterior was painted white, with smart white canopies above the first-floor windows, and an intricate cast-iron porch at the side entrance.

Alla's teeth were chattering as she climbed the stone steps to the door; she couldn't have said whether it was nerves or the cold, but both were in plentiful supply right now. It felt as though she were about to step on stage, taking a leap of faith into the unknown, hoping that adrenaline and chutzpah would see her through the next few hours. For despite the butterflies dancing in her stomach, Alla was undeniably excited. She'd sensed from Bessie Marbury's demeanour that she was *someone* – her clothing luxurious, her scent Parisian, her style incomparable – and Alla was curious to find out more about her. She took a deep breath and pulled the doorbell.

A liveried butler answered. Alla gave her name, and the next moment she was being escorted through the house, a glass of eggnog thrust into her hand, her senses overloaded by the French-style décor, the gilded antiques, the bouquets of fresh flowers. As they approached the drawing room she could hear the buzz of conversation, the clink of glasses, and for a moment she thought her anxiety might overwhelm her. But then the doors were opening, and the butler was announcing her, and Bessie Marbury was there in front of her, kissing her cheeks and exclaiming delightedly over her.

'Darling, you look quite, quite beautiful,' Bessie declared, and Alla was pleased she'd made an effort. She had no suitable clothing, and was unsure of the dress code, so in the end she'd adapted a ballgown from her costume trunk.

'And you,' Alla replied truthfully. Bessie was wearing an incredible ruby-coloured creation of silk and fur, revealing acres of décolletage which, far from making her look matronly, only added to her statuesque appearance.

'Alla, this is Henry Clay Frick, a great businessman who's passionate about the arts,' explained Bessie, turning to the gentleman nearest to her. He was a similar age to Bessie, bearded and imposing. 'Henry, this is Alla Nazimova, the most marvellous actress, all the way from Russia. When I first saw her she didn't speak a word of English and performed entirely in Russian, but I felt as though I understood everything she said. She was quite, quite brilliant and conveyed every emotion so thoroughly that one hardly noticed she was speaking in a different language.'

'It must be true if Bessie says so,' smiled Henry. 'She has a unique eye for spotting talent, and I've never known her to be wrong. I hope to see you perform one day. Tell me, what would be your ideal role?'

'Oh, I love Ibsen,' Alla gushed, pleased to have found a like-minded ally.

'Ibsen, eh?' Henry stroked his beard thoughtfully. 'I saw Minnie Maddern Fiske play *Hedda Gabler* at the Manhattan Theatre, but I have to confess, her performance left me quite cold. I think, perhaps, *you* might be able to make a better job of it, huh?'

'I'll speak with your agent, see what I can arrange,' Bessie winked.

Alla was about to reply with her thanks when she heard a shriek, and a familiar figure came bustling over.

'Alla!'

'Rose!'

The two women hugged delightedly, thrilled to see one another. Rose Chatfield-Taylor, whom Alla had first met in Chicago, and who'd encouraged her to pursue a career in the United States, had become a close friend over the past few months. Rose had been as good as her word, squiring Alla to galleries and matinees across New York whenever she happened to be in town. She was also Alla's self-appointed sponsor; indeed, the fact that Alla was currently living in the splendid surroundings of the Judson Hotel on Washington Square was only made possible by the fact that Mrs Hobart Chatfield-Taylor was picking up the check.

'I didn't know you two were acquainted,' marvelled Bessie.

'Rose is very kind to me,' Alla beamed. 'Very generous.'

'Well, we do what we can, don't we?' Rose said rhetorically, as Bessie and Henry nodded in agreement.

'Rose, you can have Alla back in a moment, but first I simply must introduce her to Elsie. You don't mind, do you?'

'Not at all. We'll speak later, Alla,' Rose promised, before turning to Henry and striking up a conversation about the exhibition she'd attended that afternoon.

Alla was swept across the room, through the press of people, whereupon Bessie stopped by the towering Christmas tree, criss-crossed with beads and illuminated with slender candles. 'Elsie,' Bessie addressed an immaculately dressed woman standing beside it, 'This is Alla – the girl I was telling you about.'

Alla felt a shiver of pleasure to learn that Bessie had spoken of her.

Elsie examined her, and Alla did the same in return; she was slim and stylish, a few years younger than Bessie, with a winsome expression and an elegant bearing.

'How lovely to meet you. I've heard so much about you,' Elsie greeted her, her expression open and genuine.

'Elsie used to be an actress,' Bessie explained. 'But fortunately for all who had the misfortune to see her, she gave up the stage some time ago.'

Elsie pretended to be outraged, then burst out laughing; it was clearly a piece of repartee that the women had performed several times before.

'She's now dedicated herself to interior decorating, at which she's far more skilled,' Bessie continued before she found herself pulled away by another guest, and Alla was left alone with Elsie.

'Do you live close by?' Alla asked, attempting small talk with one of the phrases she'd learned.

Elsie broke into a smile, as though Alla had said something amusing. 'Yes, very close by. I live *here*.'

'Oh.' Alla frowned, her voice faltering. 'I thought this was Bessie's house?'

'It is. We live together,' Elsie explained easily, no shame or hesitation.

It took a moment for it all to fall into place. Alla remembered the tender way Bessie had placed her hand on Elsie's arm, noticing the way Elsie seemed equally at ease in the palatial house. It was a Boston marriage, she realised. A mansion with two mistresses.

Alla wasn't shocked; within the theatre world she'd encountered many homosexual men, but it was rarer to meet two queer women, particularly ones who were as open as Bessie and Elsie.

'It's a beautiful house,' she managed, realising she ought to say something.

'Thank you. I designed it.'

'Yes? It's very French.'

'How perceptive of you. That's certainly the style I was aiming for – clean lines and light colours, none of that heavy Victorian décor, no dark wood or depressing, dusty potted plants. I adore France – the culture, the language, the people. We have a place in Paris too, near Versailles. We usually spend six months of the year there, in spring and summer. Do you know, Bessie once calculated that she'd made forty-two transatlantic crossings in her lifetime. Isn't that astonishing?'

'Astonishing,' Alla repeated, relishing the new vocabulary.

'From the second floor here you can see right to the East River, see the ships sailing in and out, if that's your kind of thing. Tell me, have you ever been to France?'

'I once spent a summer in Paris.'

'Oh, how delightful. For work?'

'For love.' Alla smiled, remembering the passionate affair she'd had with the modernist painter, Maurice Sterne. 'One day we visited Versailles – the Palace.'

'It's magnificent, isn't it? Like nowhere else on earth. And the affair didn't work out?'

Alla shook her head. 'It was a summer romance.'

'Oh, the best kind. I remember being young – the joy of meeting new people, of falling in love, experiencing *le grand amour* around every corner. Enjoy yourself, my darling. You have plenty of time ahead of you.'

Alla smiled. She liked Elsie's forthright way of speaking, the ease with which she discussed subjects that others might shy away from.

'Now come on, you shouldn't be spending time with an old lady like me,' Elsie teased. Let me introduce you to some young folk…'

Back in her hotel room, her head fuzzy from the alcohol, her mind whirling from the night's events, Alla felt like a debutante after her cotillion ball. She'd drank and danced and met some fascinating people, delighted to find herself seated beside Rose Chatfield-Taylor at the dinner table, who'd promised to get them tickets for the Broadway production of *Jeanne D'Arc* opening in the new year.

Alla had realised that evening just how influential her new friends were: Bessie knew the Morgans and the Vanderbilts, the Astors and the Rockefellers; professionally, she represented George Bernard Shaw, Jerome K. Jerome and a whole host of renowned French writers. She'd even been Oscar Wilde's American agent, and a starstruck Alla had to restrain herself from questioning Bessie non-stop about the great man over their starter of turtle soup.

Bessie's partner, Elsie de Wolfe, was a social tour de force, acquainted with bankers and businessmen, actors and artists, doctors and politicians. She was warm and welcoming towards Alla, quick-witted and intelligent and entirely at ease with herself.

For perhaps the first time in her 27 years, Alla felt truly optimistic about her future, confident that staying in America without Pavel had been the right decision. Tonight had seemed like the beginning of a new life – one where she was respected and successful on her own terms – and as she turned off the light and slipped between the freshly laundered bedsheets, she was impatient to see what the next day would bring.

Chapter Twenty-Three

MAYBELLE

Paris, France, 1925

'It's incredible,' I breathed, shielding my eyes as I stared up at the extraordinary façade of Notre-Dame cathedral. Scores of sightseers milled around, each one awed in their turn, but I had the oddly selfish sensation that it was *my* discovery and mine alone. 'When did you say it was built?'

'They started in the twelfth century, but it wasn't completed until thirteen forty-five,' Joe informed me, consulting her guide book. She was dressed in long shorts and a white shirt, a sunhat on her head and a camera case around her neck.

'Thirteen forty-five? That's almost six hundred years ago. That's—'

'Older than America. Crazy, huh?'

I marvelled at the twin towers and the rose window, the Gothic architecture and outlandish gargoyles, the limestone walls so steadfast and unyielding it seemed as though they could survive anything, could go on standing for another six hundred years or more. I thought of all the changes the cathedral had seen in more than half a millennium: the monarchs and the revolutionaries, the battles and sieges, poverty and riches. It was almost too much to comprehend.

'Do you want to look inside?'

I hesitated. I hadn't been inside a church since my brother's wedding. Besides, Notre-Dame was Roman Catholic, and there was part of me that would always be Southern Baptist, no matter how much my life had changed. 'Not today.'

'Scared you'll burst into flames?'

'Something like that. Let's walk along the river instead. It's so pretty.' I linked my arm through Joe's as we strolled. I felt comfortable doing that here, as though we were merely two female companions enjoying the afternoon. Whether it was the glorious weather or the liberal, European influence, but I felt freer, lighter than I had done in a long while.

Alla had decided to travel to France to finalise her "divorce" from Charles, enabling her to announce their separation and return to the States a free woman. The situation was complicated, but Joe explained that Alla had been required to declare her marital status when first arriving in the US at Ellis Island – indeed, she'd entered under the name "Alla Golovina Nazimova". Sergei had eventually agreed to a divorce, and the final papers had arrived at Hayvenhurst in 1923 – in the package I'd seen addressed to Madame Golovin. Now, in order to be rid of Charles, Alla planned to leave America, tell the world's press that she'd divorced him, and when she re-entered she could legally write "single" on the necessary documents.

In addition to the practical aspect of the trip, Alla wanted to have fun. She'd had a tough time of late – although, ironically, she'd received some of the best notices of her career for her latest film, *My Son* – and now she wanted to blow off a little steam. Where better than Paris?

She'd invited Joe and me to accompany her and we jumped at the chance. *Gay Paree! Vive la France!* I'd pored over photographs and read endless articles in magazines, but hardly dared to imagine that one day I might actually go there. Perhaps inevitably, my thoughts turned to those grand plans I'd made with Sarah Beth, our nebulous childhood dreams conceived in a more innocent time finally becoming a reality for me.

I remembered long hours whiled away by the creek, the sun high in the sky, the sweet, nutty scent of corn being harvested in late summer. We'd talked of going overseas, imagining the freedom and acceptance we might find in a more liberal Europe. The fact that I'd made it all the way to the French capital proved it was possible, and I would forever wonder if Sarah Beth and I could have travelled this road together, if we'd been braver and made different decisions.

Sarah Beth had chosen to remain in Jonas Springs, to marry Clarence and bear his children and live the life we'd said we'd shun. I couldn't judge her for it; I knew the strength it took to break free of that world – for me, it had taken Joe to show me the escape route – but it saddened me that Sarah Beth had never tried. Lord only knew what we could have achieved together.

Joe was just as excited as I was to visit Paris. Surprisingly, despite chaperoning Alla all over the United States, she'd never visited Europe before, and I suspect we both hoped that a romantic break would reignite the spark between us, as it had to an extent in Mexico. So far, the city was working its magic.

We travelled out on the RMS Aquitania and were staying in an apartment on the bohemian Left Bank, spending our days seeing the sights and our nights escorting our hostess to glamorous parties. I'd fallen head over heels for Paris. It was like nowhere I'd ever been before, though I was acutely aware I was by no means well-travelled. The perfectly designed capital was like something from a fairytale, its winding cobbled streets and stately boulevards so far from the tiny town of Jonas Springs, and the low concrete sprawl of Los Angeles, that it might as well have been on the moon. I'd even learned a few words of French, though I'm sure they sounded ridiculous with my enduring southern drawl.

'What time is it?' I wondered, as we browsed the stalls selling books and paintings, enjoying the smell of the food drifting out from the cafés, so deliciously different that my mouth watered at the mere thought of boeuf bourguignon accompanied by a glass of rich red wine.

Joe checked her wristwatch, opening her mouth to reply, and we both burst out laughing as the bells of Notre-Dame rang out across the city, just as they had done for centuries. 'Four o'clock,' Joe grinned, counting the chimes, the shadows cast by her sunhat falling across her face.

'We should head back,' I said reluctantly. I wanted to ensure we could have a leisurely return to the apartment, leaving plenty of time to dress for the evening. 'Where are we going tonight?'

'I'm not sure. But before we leave...' Joe unbuckled the

camera case and pulled out her Kodak Brownie. It had been her constant companion on this trip, and she adored her new hobby, experimenting with light and angles, working her way through endless rolls of film.

I'd served as her muse and obligingly struck a pose on the charming little bridge we were crossing, the mighty Seine flowing beneath us, behind us the rooftops and spires stretching as far as the eye could see.

Joe pressed the button and the camera clicked, the moment captured forever, frozen in time.

The three of us were squeezed into the back seat of a taxicab, rattling through the city at speed. Paris was even more beautiful after nightfall, lights blazing out in the darkness, the Eiffel Tower illuminated with the word "Citroen" like the world's biggest advertising board. Joe and I were desperate to visit. Alla said it was overrated, but we were fascinated by the striking structure that had become an instantly recognisable symbol of the French capital.

'What exactly is this place we're going to?' I wondered.

'A kind of club, I think,' Alla replied. 'Called "The House of All Nations". I'm told Edward VII used to frequent it – before he became King of England and had to stop going to nightclubs – as did Toulouse-Lautrec.'

'And it was recommended by the couple you met today?'

'Yes, Henry and Clara Denby. They're American, and they recognised me, and struck up conversation. They're unbelievably rich – he's made millions buying Chinese hair to make hairnets, would you believe – and they've taken a suite each at the Crillon!'

I still had to pinch myself that this was my life now. I often felt out of my depth, as though I were an imposter in this rarefied world, and everyone could see that I was really just Li'l Ole Maybelle Crabtree from Kentucky. Alla was a social whirlwind and generous with her invitations; thanks to her, Joe and I had spent our evenings at the theatre, at music halls, at suppers and soirées and galas. She knew le tout-Paris, forever catching up with old friends like Mercedes de Acosta and Eva Le Gallienne, with a handy knack for making new ones too. She'd been thrilled to encounter Dolly Wilde – niece of Oscar, with a penchant for dressing like her uncle – and the two of them had gotten along like a house on fire. Dolly certainly seemed to be helping Alla forget her ongoing problems with Charles, and the fact that her relationship with Paul Ivano had all but fizzled out.

The cab pulled up outside a tall, narrow building on rue Chabanais in the second arrondissement, a smart neighbourhood with classic Parisian architecture. There was no sign on the door, but as we climbed out a discreet doorman stood aside and invited us to enter. We swept through to the entrance, a cave-like space with bare stone walls, where Clara and Henry Denby were waiting for us. They looked delighted to be reacquainted with Alla, and there were kisses and introductions all round.

'You came!' exclaimed Clara. She was in her forties and dressed as one would expect for a woman married to a millionaire, her dark hair cut in a sharp bob, her make-up immaculate.

'Of course. Why wouldn't we?' Alla smiled, returning Clara's affectionate greeting.

Clara linked arms with Alla, and Henry – short and stout, with ruddy cheeks and a balding pate – gestured for Joe and I to follow as he brought up the rear. We were each handed a glass of champagne by a uniformed waiter, and as we ascended the stairs I stared round at the paintings on the walls, surprisingly sensual images depicting powerfully built men wrestling one another, reclining women with come-hither eyes, bodies barely concealed by the fabric draped across them.

Clara and Henry had clearly visited the venue before; they bypassed various doors, each one guarded by its own uniformed attendant, before coming to a stop in front of a lavishly decorated entrance surrounded by mirrors. I caught a glimpse of my reflection, my complexion flushed from the stairs and the heat and the champagne.

'We've reserved a table,' Henry informed us. 'I do hope you ladies will enjoy yourselves. I think you'll find it's to your tastes.'

He smiled at all of us as the door opened and I heard music – a classical, operatic piece, playing low in the background – and we stepped inside.

It took a moment for my eyes to adjust to the darkness; the room was lit only by candles – scores of them, in sconces and candelabras – causing human shadows to leap and writhe across the walls. I was watching my step, following Alla, when Joe grasped my arm. There was something about the urgency of her touch that made me look up and as I took in the room in more detail, I saw half a dozen tables arranged on the periphery at a discreet distance from one another, the chairs upholstered in red velvet. Thick curtains hung at the windows; dozens of mirrors lined the walls. And in the middle of the room, on a raised bed like a stage, were men and women in various states of undress, some wearing eye masks to conceal their identity, performing all manner of sexual acts on one another.

I gasped and stopped still, unable to move with shock.

'Here we are,' I heard Clara announce, as she came to a halt beside an empty table. 'Isn't it wonderful? They'll do anything you ask, for the right price. Now, you can simply watch or, if you like, you can participate.' She shed her coat to display a revealing lace dress, its V-shaped neckline plunging well below her breasts, the material close-fitting like a second skin. I doubted she was wearing undergarments.

I found myself unable to stop looking at the scene before me, the room pulsing with a tangle of limbs and tongues and genitalia. The faces were ghoulish and distorted in the candlelight, and my cheeks burned with shame and embarrassment and a hitherto unsuspected puritanical mindset. But I was also curious and, I'll admit, a little aroused. I'd never witnessed anything like the scene before me. Alla had held some outrageous parties over the years, but nothing as downright debauched as this. I glanced at Joe, who seemed to be experiencing the same tumult of emotions, and drained the remainder of my champagne in one.

A hostess slunk over to our table. Her long, black hair was loose, her eyes heavily lined with kohl. She was naked apart from an intricate series of leather straps criss-crossing her body, like a horse in harness. I wanted to look away but couldn't, my gaze roaming unrestrained over her bound breasts, the curve of her waist, the triangle of dark fuzz between her legs. She held out her hand in an invitation. Alla turned away in disgust.

'Come join us,' Clara purred, taking a seat as her husband sat down beside her. 'We can just watch for a while if you'd like – Henry and I prefer that. Or there are other rooms, if this isn't to your taste. They cater to all proclivities here.'

Alla was incandescent, visibly shaking. 'How dare you bring me here! What is the meaning of this?'

'Madame Nazimova, your reputation proceeds you.' Henry smirked. 'My wife and I thought this would be exactly the sort of evening you – and your female companions – would enjoy. There's no need to be concerned – the club is extremely discreet, as are we. Your secret is safe with us.'

Alla drew herself up to her full five feet and three inches. 'I'm sorry, but you have the wrong impression. Your invitation was very kind, but I'm afraid you've misunderstood. Please, do not try to contact me again.'

She swept out of the room, leaving the bemused Denbys in her wake, Joe and I trailing behind.

Outside, Alla set off at a furious pace, as though she were tainted merely by her proximity to the licentious happenings in the brothel. Joe and I raced to keep up. The new shoes I'd bought earlier that week were pinching my toes, and just as I was about to yank them off and march through the streets in my stockinged feet, Alla hailed a cab and barked out the address of our apartment.

'Are you sure you wouldn't like to go for dinner instead?' Joe wondered tentatively when we were all seated. 'Salvage the night and forget all of this?'

'I'm sorry,' Alla apologised. 'You and Maybelle should go out if you want – please, don't cut short your night on my behalf – but I would simply like to go home.'

'Of course,' Joe nodded. 'We'll come with you.'

We drove in silence for a short time, then Alla unleashed her anger. 'I'm so upset. *So* upset! And furious, and… saddened. I'm not offended – in other circumstances, it would have been amusing – I'm just… disillusioned. I thought these people were *nice*. I thought they were interested in *me* – not Nazimova the actress, or Nazimova the star, but *me*. It was a serious error of judgement on my part, to trust them so quickly. Is that what people think of me? I'm almost forty-six, I'm too old to be gallivanting around the city like a twenty-year-old. Of course, I'm so grateful to the two of you, I know I can trust you. I would trust you with my life. But I came to Paris to have fun and… suddenly I'm not having fun anymore.'

She looked so disheartened, those enormous eyes liquid beneath the glow of the streetlamps, her thoughts far away. We crossed the river, traversing the Pont Royal, the shadowy city exquisite at this late hour. I felt both grateful that we were here with Alla, and dismayed that she was clearly so unhappy. I leaned over and squeezed her hand.

'We're here for you. Whenever you need us. Always.'

'Yes,' Joe agreed heartily. 'Exactly what Maybelle said.'

Her words raised a small smile, as Alla nodded appreciatively, seeming to understand what I wasn't able to articulate.

The three of us held hands the whole way back to the apartment.

We returned to Los Angeles in late August. Alla formally announced that she and Charles had divorced, then retreated to the sanctuary of Hayvenhurst, refusing to answer questions or grant interviews on the subject.

Her statement, however, was soon eclipsed by what the press and public considered an even bigger scandal; Natacha declared that she was "taking a vacation" from Rudolph Valentino, and the women of America decided collectively that she must be insane. I knew that Natacha and Rudy had been having problems before I left for Europe, but I'd obviously missed out on recent developments. Naturally, we hadn't been as close since she'd been living in New York for *Monsieur Beaucaire* – which, unfortunately, hadn't performed well at the box office – but I was looking forward to seeing her again now that we were both back in California.

Three months later, in November, I was sitting in the garden catching the winter sun, flicking through a fashion magazine. Everything was rather quiet for me professionally – Natacha was taking a break from work so didn't need my assistance, and Alla had gone to New York – so I was enjoying being a lady of leisure with few demands on my time, trying not to go out of my mind with boredom or mope about dwelling on the stagnation of my relationship with Joe.

As though my thoughts had summoned her, I heard the front door bang and Joe called my name, sounding flustered.

'I'm out here!'

Joe ran into the garden, a newspaper in her hand, panic etched on her face. 'I need to call Alla.'

'Why? What's happened?'

Joe thrust the *Los Angeles Times* towards me and I skimmed over the page until I saw the headline that had caused the disturbance: *Charles Bryant Marries Marjorie Gilhooley.*

I frowned, quickly reading the article. It said that the union had first been announced in the *New Milford Gazette*, a provincial Connecticut paper – the bride's home state – and that Charles, 43, had married local girl Marjorie, 23, on November 16th at the First Congregational Church.

I got up and went inside to where Joe was on the phone, asking to be put through to the Buckingham Hotel. Alla had gone to New York in the hope of resurrecting her stage career now that the movie offers were becoming increasingly rare, and Noel Coward was keen to meet with her about a new play he'd written.

'Do you think Alla will really care that Charles has remarried?' I wondered aloud. 'She barely spoke about him when we were in Paris, other than to discuss the divorce.'

'It's not the marriage – it's the declaration,' Joe hissed, as she waited to be connected.

I looked back at the newspaper, unsure what she meant.

'Charles stated that he was single when he applied for the licence. But he's supposed to have been married to Alla for the last fourteen years! That was their agreement. He promised Alla he'd never reveal their secret. But now the papers are asking if they *were* ever married – and if not, then why did they pretend to be? Alla will be terrified right now, humiliated. She's always been petrified of being deported, and if her documents aren't right, or her tax declarations then – Hello? Yes, my name is Josephine Colbert, could you please put me through to Alla Nazimova, she's a guest of yours. Yes, I'll hold.'

Joe waited on the line, ashen-faced, as the consequences of Charles' betrayal began to sink in. Alla had been on a veritable rollercoaster over the past months, struggling with the downturn of her career, the failure of *Salomé*, and the associated financial problems. If the public felt she'd deceived them, if the studios felt she was tarnished, if the government discovered financial malpractice…

'Dammit,' Joe swore, hanging up. 'She's refusing all calls. I imagine she's being besieged right now. Perhaps I could send her a telegram, tell her to call me.' Joe turned and saw me watching her, the distress on her face reflected in mine. 'Do you understand now?'

I nodded slowly. 'Yes, I understand. I… Poor Alla.'

Chapter Twenty-Four

ALLA

New York City, USA, 1906

*'Well, I shall have one thing at least to kill time with in the
meanwhile.'*
'Oh thank heaven for that! What is it, Hedda. Eh?'
'My pistols, George.'
'Your pistols!'
'General Gabler's pistols.'
*'No, for heaven's sake, Hedda darling – don't touch those
dangerous things! For my sake, Hedda. Eh?'*

'Very good. Very good indeed.' Henry Miller nodded
thoughtfully. 'Right everyone, let's take a fifteen minute break,
then we'll move on with Act Two.'

The actors duly exited the stage, laying down their scripts
and heading for the coffee pot, breaking off into small groups
to chat or run lines.

'Alla, could I have a word?'

'Of course.' Alla smiled amenably and strode over to the director who'd summoned her. Henry Miller was an English-born actor, also managed by Charles Frohman, who'd enjoyed considerable success on Broadway. In recent years he'd developed an interest in directing and producing, and had now given Alla her first big break in the title role of *Hedda Gabler*.

'Is everything all right?' Alla asked demurely. She liked and trusted Henry, but it was still early days in their professional relationship, and she was acutely aware that she was working in her non-native language.

'Yes, yes, absolutely. More than all right, in fact.' Henry nodded once more. He was a solidly built man in his forties, with an intelligent face and dark hair slicked down with oil. 'Your interpretation of Hedda...' he paused again, trying to find the right words. 'It's quite extraordinary. I've never seen anything like it. Hedda is usually a victim, rather powerless – a mere housewife trapped by society's expectations. But that is not how you play her.'

'Oh, I have never seen her like that,' Alla agreed vehemently. 'For me Hedda is angry, aggressive and... what's the word...? Subversive. She is not a tiny mouse of a character. To me, she is so large that Ibsen had to make her smaller just to fit her on the stage. Do you understand?'

Henry was still nodding, fascinated by Alla's insights. Somewhat unusually, in the male-dominated world of theatre directing, he wasn't threatened by Alla's ideas and proposals – he was more interested in what she could offer, both to the performance as a whole and to the other actors.

'You have some of the strongest instincts of anyone I've ever worked with,' he told her with genuine admiration. 'And your methods are quite unique. Tell me, where did you learn them?'

'My training in Russia. I worked with Stanislavsky and Nemirovich. They taught me that there is no such thing as a small part, only small actors. Every role is equally important, because all of the roles are interrelated. So the actors should play to one another, not to the audience. And their movements and voice should be simple and natural and truthful – not forced or exaggerated.'

'Astonishing,' Henry muttered. He'd pulled out his notebook and was scribbling away.

'In fact, there is something I wished to talk with you about.'

Henry looked up from his notes and stared at her, ready to listen.

'For the opening of Act Four, I was thinking if I were to play the scene upstage, facing the wall, speaking to Miss Tesman over my shoulder.'

Henry frowned. 'You mean, with your back to the audience? Oh no, Alla, that's just not—'

'If I were to stand on a footstool it would elevate my position, but I would wear a long, black cloak so it would not be visible,' Alla rushed on. Her suggestion was reminiscent of an effect used by Orlenev in one of his previous productions; Alla was like a sponge, remembering what worked and what didn't, an intuitive understanding of how to make a better production.

'I can't see how... I mean...' Henry broke off, staring into the middle distance.

'Just let me try it,' Alla begged. 'Just once, in rehearsal. If it doesn't work, I'll never mention it again, I promise.'

Henry hesitated.

'Go on, take a risk! Imagine how dramatic the visual image will be. How controversial to break a cardinal rule of the theatre.'

'Very well, we will try it,' Henry agreed. 'But if I say it doesn't work, my word is final.'

Alla was glowing, eyes dancing, eager to get back to work. 'All right, but I am very sure it will. Trust me. You will not regret it.'

'And are you ambitious?'

Alla sat back in her chair and considered the question. The woman opposite her was slim and well-groomed, her pencil poised above her notebook to record Alla's answer.

'Of course, yes. Doesn't everyone want to be the best they can be in their profession? I am sure you hope to be editor one day. But I do not want to be a star,' Alla added hastily. 'No, that is the fatal thing, to be a star.'

'Why?'

'It limits you in the roles you are able to play. It confuses the audience's expectations – they don't see the character you are inhabiting, only the actress they have read about. And it's hard, as an individual, to remain humble and open as you need to be to find the truthfulness in a role.'

'I see. So if you don't want to be a star, then what *are* your ambitions?' Lilian Gilbert, fledgling journalist for *Theater* magazine, wondered.

The two women were backstage at the Princess Theatre, which Alla now considered to be her second home. Her fellow cast and crew felt like the family she'd never had, and her Hedda Gabler was going down a storm, with sold out performances and standing ovations. Almost across the board (there were always one or two exceptions) the critics were united in their praise, with the *New York Times* writing: *'One of the most illuminating and varied performances which our stage has seen in years'*.

'I want to create truth and art and beauty,' Alla replied. 'Of course, I want to entertain – if the audience are not enjoying themselves, or are not moved in some way, then it doesn't matter how truthful or how artistic the performance is. The connection with the audience is perhaps the most important connection of all. And I hope to continue playing strong women in New York theatre. The city has been so welcoming to me, so accepting of my strange accent and limited English.'

'Oh, but your English is so good,' Lilian praised her. 'And you're so talented. Everyone at the magazine is raving about your performance.'

'Thank you.'

'I think your accent only adds to your allure.' Lilian smiled as she uncrossed her legs, re-crossing them in the other direction, offering Alla a glimpse of shapely ankle as her long skirt rode up an inch or two, the elegant arch of her foot emphasised by the low heels she was wearing. 'What exactly *is* your background, Madame Nazimova? You're Russian, is that correct?'

Alla's focus quickly returned to the interview. She was immediately on her guard when people questioned her history, frightened of revealing too much. 'Yes, that's correct,' she replied, experience having taught her that it was easiest to keep it simple and close to the truth. 'I trained in Moscow, at the Philharmonic School, and at the Moscow Arts Theatre under Konstantin Stanislavsky.'

'And how on earth did you find yourself in New York?' Lilian sat forward now, her voice breathy with anticipation.

'I was with a touring group,' Alla explained succinctly. 'We left Russia to perform in Berlin, then London, then travelled to America. I was lucky enough that Lee Schubert liked me enough to take a chance on me.'

'And do you have a husband, or a significant other?' Lilian pressed. 'Our readers like to gain that extra insight in our interviews, and it's always good to open up a little.'

Alla smiled tightly. 'No. For me, I am devoted to my profession. I have no time for a personal life. In fact, it is after four o'clock and I have a meeting with my agent shortly. Thank you so much for coming, Mrs Gilbert.'

'It's *Miss* Gilbert. Although, please, feel free to call me Lilian.' She closed her notebook, putting it back in her purse. 'Thank you so much for speaking with me, I've enjoyed it immensely. Here's my card, with my office number.' Lilian flipped it over and scribbled something on the back. 'And this is the number for my floor at the Martha Washington. Please don't hesitate to contact me, day *or* night, if you think of anything else *Theater* readers might like to know. Or if you need to get a hold of me for any other reason…'

She let the moment hang, smiling at Alla without breaking eye contact.

'Thank you, Lilian. I've enjoyed meeting you too,' Alla returned the smile, as the two women shook hands.

~

'And how was the interview?' asked Lee Schubert, rolling a pen between his forefingers and regarding Alla. He was still in the same small office, with the same efficient secretary, but it was clear that his wealth was only increasing – as evidenced by the artwork on the walls and the cut of his suit.

'It went well, I think...' Alla replied cautiously. She and Lee had always had a good working relationship; she had the highest respect for him and would forever be grateful for the way he'd signed her based on little more than gut instinct. But being called in for this meeting reminded Alla of her days at the Catholic boarding school, being summoned to see the headmistress for some misdemeanour or another. 'Am I in trouble?' she asked, deciding that a forthright approach was the best.

'What? No!' Lee Schubert roared with laughter and Alla instantly relaxed. 'Quite the opposite, in fact. I'm extremely pleased with your progress. Extremely pleased. Your reviews are stellar, and – most importantly for me – you're selling out the theatre, which is how we make the money. I hear nothing but good reports from everyone you've worked with, so I've been thinking...'

Alla watched him carefully, pleased that he was pleased, wondering what was coming next.

'I'd like you to add a second performance of a different play. Your choice – although I have to agree to it.'

'*A Doll's House*,' Alla replied instantly, not needing even a moment's thought.

Lee mulled it over. 'Two Ibsen plays? That could work. It would be like performing in rep. And you've already proved that Ibsen suits your style of working, and that there's an audience for it. All right then, *A Doll's House*. Why not?'

Alla was fizzing with excitement. She already knew exactly how she would play Nora – which was to say, in complete contrast to Hedda. Where Hedda was fierce and dark and held herself tightly, Nora would be girlish and light, in ruffled clothing and with soft hair.

'Now,' Lee continued. 'I'd like to give you a later time but, as you know, *The School for Scandal* is already playing at the Princess in the evenings. So I'm proposing to move you to the Bijou – it's a little smaller, but you'll have the evening slot, and you can alternate *Hedda* and *A Doll's House*. Does that sound okay?'

'Yes. Yes, of course,' Alla agreed, clearly thrilled at the prospect. She decided to take a gamble, declaring boldly, 'I want Henry Miller to direct.' Alla enjoyed working with Henry, finding him very open to her methods and suggestions. In truth, it appeared sometimes as though *she* were the director, and he merely a kindly overseer, indulgently allowing her free rein to pursue her ideas.

'Sure,' Lee shrugged, equally unwilling to break up what had proved itself to be a successful collaboration. 'Why kill the goose that laid the golden egg? I'd like the two of you to take the lead on the casting – although I'll retain a final veto.'

Alla was nodding so hard she felt her neck would ache later, hardly able to believe the change in her fortunes. After so many years of playing second fiddle to Pavel, of being emotionally and physically broken by him, she was emerging like a butterfly from a chrysalis. Her career was on the rise, her agent believed in her, and she was – for the first time in a very long time – in a position of power, with control over her own life.

'Make sure you have a relaxing night. Maybe pour yourself a drink, or buy yourself something nice to celebrate,' Lee suggested. 'Because after that, it's time to get to work.'

The red velvet seats were undeniably uncomfortable, Alla reflected, momentarily pitying the audience that usually sat on them. After three interminable hours of auditions, with actors ranging from the dire to the promisingly talented, Alla's backside was definitely feeling the pressure.

'Thank you,' she called out, cutting off a rambling Shakespearean monologue. The woman nodded, looking disappointed, and left the stage. Alla glanced across at Henry and saw him put a line through the woman's name; she agreed wholeheartedly. 'Next!'

They were holding auditions in the Princess Theatre in the mornings before their matinee of *Hedda Gabler*, so Alla was familiar with the theatre, with its layout and quirks and the feeling of the space. Now a suited man strode onto the stage and Alla weighed him up for the role of Torvald, Nora's husband. He was a little old, a little tall, perhaps. His voice had a pleasant timbre, but she wasn't sure it would reach to the back rows, and she found herself tuning out as the speech continued, reflecting instead on how excited she was to be in this position, and how she was longing to give some undiscovered actor their first major opportunity. She was almost begging the auditionees to come and impress her, to step onto the stage and blow her away with their talent, but instead she'd witnessed average performance after average performance.

'I'll go get us some coffee,' Henry whispered, creeping away as Alla shot him a grateful look. She badly needed it to stop her falling asleep.

'Thank you,' she called out, as the man on stage finished his piece and walked off. 'Next!'

Moments later, a woman stepped into the bright lights, squinting a little as she looked out into the darkness of the auditorium. It took Alla a moment to acknowledge her presence.

'Hello?' the woman called out. She seemed nervous. 'I'm… I'm Josephine Colbert.'

She had beautiful red hair worn in a rather dishevelled Gibson Girl style, and she was dressed in a plain, well-worn outfit of a heavy wool skirt and ruffled blouse. The dowdy clothes couldn't fail to disguise the youthful, slender figure, or the determination in those startling amber eyes. Alla sat up a little straighter.

'I'm going to perform Isabella, from *Women Beware Women* by Thomas Middleton.'

'All right,' Alla said expectantly. 'In your own time…'

Josephine stared down at the floor for a moment, closing

her eyes and exhaling, as she found her character. Then she raised her head, a confident, playful look stealing across her features as she began to speak.

Alla watched her intently, barely noticing when Henry returned and set two cups of coffee on the floor between them. The choice of audition speech was an interesting and brave one, from a rarely performed play whose plot included incest, adultery and murder.

'Oh, the heart-breakings; Of miserable maids, where love's enforc'd!'

It spoke of Isabella's upcoming marriage to a man she considers to be an idiot, ruminating on the sadness of women who are obliged to marry against their will. Alla couldn't take her eyes off Josephine; there was something about the way she moved, something in her looks, that Alla found compelling. She was clearly inexperienced – not yet ready for the role of Mrs Linde, but perhaps something small... Helene, the maid?

'O but this marriage!'

The piece came to an end and Josephine broke out of character, suddenly the nervous young girl again.

'Thank you,' Alla said softly. 'It was very nice to meet you today, Josephine.'

Josephine blushed adorably, hearing the sincerity in Alla's voice.

'We'll be in touch.' Alla nodded, not feeling the need to confer with Henry. 'Very soon.'

Chapter Twenty-Five

MAYBELLE

Los Angeles, USA, 1926

I t was a perfect summer's night in early July. Hot and still, the sky was an inky black and a lambent moon – almost full – presided over proceedings.

As Joe and I climbed out of the old Chevy I could hear the sounds of revelry – laughter, music, the explosion of champagne corks – and it was impossible not to reflect on that first time I'd visited the Garden of Alla. How naïve I'd been back then, how unsophisticated and terrified and impossibly brave. And how much had happened since that night, a gamut of experiences from the wondrous to the scandalous and the heart-breaking.

Seven years ago, I'd tentatively entered Hayvenhurst full of naivety and awe, the atmosphere within both magical and overwhelming. Tonight, I felt a deep sadness, all too aware of the malignant presence hiding in the shadows to bring down the curtain on the end of an era.

Perhaps these dark thoughts explained my behaviour later that night. Explained it, yes, but didn't excuse it…

Joe placed her hand on my waist, the heaviness of her rings solid against my hip bone. 'Are you ready?'

I nodded, stepping away from her touch, as we made our way – likely for the final time – into Alla's home.

Stepping over the threshold we made a beeline for our hostess, finding her outside by the swimming pool. She was resplendent in a gold sheath dress with layers of silver jewellery and a complementary beaded turban, surrounded by courtiers as befitted a queen overseeing the final days of her reign.

'I'm so sorry,' I whispered, as I kissed her on both cheeks. 'You look spectacular, by the way.'

Alla shrugged off both the compliment and the sympathy. 'Such is life. One must move on. It's only a building after all, only bricks and mortar.' Her skin was luminous, her eyes alive; a phoenix blazing brighter than ever before inevitably crumbling into ashes. She took a long, slow sip of her drink, gazing at the revellers as she observed the bacchanalian scene. 'You know, in a way, I'm grateful to leave. When I'm alone and I look around, I don't see the parties and the friends and the many good times. I see this as the house where my career died, where my relationship with Charles fell apart, where I have been so unhappy. I see it as a symbol of my greatest failures.'

'Oh, don't say that! You've achieved so much. You've

inspired *me* so much. And I'm sure the best is yet to come for you.'

'Oh darling, that's sweet, but I don't believe it to be true. For tonight, however, I shall drink and make merry. I shall be… the consummate actress, as ever.' She turned from me as Joe struck up conversation, and the two of them slipped into their own little world.

An outsider looking in at the black-market champagne and the ostentatious jewels and the carefree, wealthy, fashionable crowd might not have suspected it, but the truth was that Alla – the movie star earning $13,000 a week less than ten years ago – had run out of money. *Salomé*, of course, had heavily drained her reserves, and she no longer had the lucrative film roles or the high-paying theatre shows to sustain her level of spending.

Recently she'd become acquainted with a woman named Jean Adams, who had inveigled her way into Alla's confidences and somehow become a trusted business advisor with access to Alla's financial affairs. Joe didn't like Jean at all, certain she was both a fraudster and a bad influence, but the upshot was that Jean persuaded Alla to sell Hayvenhurst to a development company. They planned to turn it into a hotel, for which Alla would receive an annual sum of $14,500, plus a percentage of profits when it finally opened. I knew that Alla was deeply embarrassed by the decision she'd had to make – she felt that she was prostituting her home – but had few other options. The contract stated that she had to vacate the property by the first of August, so tonight was to be her final hurrah before the boxes were packed and the bulldozers moved in.

Alla and Joe were still gassing. They'd been joined by the usual crowd – June Mathis, Rose Dione, Norma Talmadge and her husband Joseph Schenck – and I deemed myself superfluous. With a cursory wave in Joe's direction, I slunk away to discover who else might be in attendance – in short, to go in search of more fun than Joe could offer.

I breezed through the grounds and back into the house. It was decked out beautifully, with hundreds of fairy lights and extravagant displays of fresh flowers – Alla was certainly going out in style, I'd give her that – and I called hello to a few acquaintances, exchanging small talk but never stopping for long. Although I hadn't admitted it to myself, there was a person I was searching for. I drained the glass of champagne I'd picked up on arrival and helped myself to a Tom Collins.

'Maybelle!'

I heard Natacha's voice above the rabble and turned to see her looking glorious in a dramatic black gown with jewelled spaghetti straps, acres of milky white flesh exposed across the hollow of her throat, the curve of her shoulders, her long, slender arms.

'Oh my! Divorce suits you,' I quipped as Natacha rolled her eyes.

'Don't even *allude* to that man.'

'Come on, let's go find somewhere to catch up,' I suggested, grabbing her hand and weaving through the tightly knit crowd. The strangest thought popped into my head as I realised how the decline in Alla's fortunes had mirrored the decline in mine and Joe's relationship; back in those early, heady, lovestruck days, I wouldn't have dreamed of leaving Joe's side at a party, as though an invisible rope bound us together. I ached to spend as much time with her as possible, to luxuriate in her presence, to tempt and tease and flirt and make the most of every stolen moment together. Now that we'd been living in one another's pockets for over half a decade, occasions like this were my opportunity to escape, to mingle, to encounter old friends and make new ones, to hear stories I'd never heard before and have my own oft-repeated tales told afresh to new ears. I still longed to tempt and tease and flirt – but Joe was rarely the recipient of my attentions these days.

Tucked away in a shallow alcove on a quiet corridor was a purple velvet loveseat; Natacha and I flopped down gratefully upon it.

'So tell me, what's going on with you? I barely see you these days.'

Natacha grinned, a flash of pearly white teeth bordered by carmine lips. 'Not a lot, to be entirely honest with you. I'm just taking time to breathe. To be myself. To remember who I am after that man tried to erase my identity and turn me into some robotic wife and mother. He *knew* who I was before he married me, so why try to change me?'

Natacha looked agitated and lit a cigarette. I spotted a waiter at the end of the corridor and flagged him down, taking two gin cocktails from his tray.

'And now, because his career is bombing, his agent and his producers are trying to blame *me* for that. Did you know that by the end of our marriage he'd banned me from his movie sets? It was written into his contract that if I turned up at the studios I was to be removed immediately. Asshole.'

I said nothing, drinking and listening and reflecting that if *I* were Rudy, I would never have let Natacha go so easily. He was handsome, but a fool.

'What are your plans for the future?' I wondered, hoping there might be something in there that would allow us to stay close. In truth, we were all somewhat in limbo at the moment – Alla, Joe, Natacha and myself. The industry seemed to be changing around us, a new generation rising up, our skills and knowledge overlooked in the studios' quest for the Next Big Thing. The kaleidoscope had been shaken and the pieces were in flux; all we could do was wait and see where they landed.

Natacha shrugged, extinguishing her cigarette and immediately lighting another. 'I don't know yet. I'm enjoying not being tied down, experimenting with new art forms. I'm too old to go back to dancing. I'm thinking about writing a book. I designed a doll, did you know that? The patent came through a few weeks ago. And the film I made last year is about to be released, so I'm busy as a bumblebee. Maybe I'll open a shop – high end, couture, you know the kind of thing. And I'd like to study too. I'm fascinated by ancient civilisations – the Greeks, the Romans, the Egyptians.'

Anyone else might have seen this jumble of thoughts and ideas as an inability to focus or a lack of commitment, but I took it as further proof of how talented Natacha was, how diverse and extensive her interests and abilities. 'You're incredible,' I murmured, and her frown of confusion made me realise that I'd slurred my words, my remark incomprehensible. Embarrassed, I waved away the sentiment, dragging my eyes from Natacha's face and looking around to see that the house was filling up and our quiet corridor was almost overrun. The advantage of this was that the waiters were passing by more frequently, and I swapped my two empty glasses for two full ones.

'Oh my, who's that over there?' I instinctively grasped Natacha's arm to get her attention, only becoming aware of the action after I'd done it. My foggy brain took a moment to register her bare skin, soft and warm beneath my palm.

Natacha didn't react; she followed my gaze to the willowy, blonde, glamorous woman surrounded by admirers. Even from afar you could tell that she had presence, a coolness and poise that betrayed no sign of nerves. Her bone structure was incredible, her melancholy eyes hinting at a thousand other lives, and she stood out amongst a sea of gowns and tuxedos by wearing a stunning white silk trouser suit.

'That's Greta Garbo,' Natacha explained. 'She's MGM's latest protégée, fresh off the boat from Sweden. I think it's terribly sweet of Alla to invite her – a passing on of the baton, so to speak.'

'She's stunning. I'd love to design for her, wouldn't you? I can just visualise how perfectly clothes would hang on that figure…'

My eyes followed her as she moved through the crowd, followed by a cluster of hangers-on. She looked *young*, I realised. Fresh-faced and unique and already imbued with that elusive star quality. I'd become older without realising it, jaded and exhausted and no longer the novelty I'd once been. Innocence lost, just another cynic disillusioned by Hollywood.

'Let's go mingle,' Natacha suggested, standing up, my hand sliding off her arm. 'I need to find my next husband.'

It was meant as a joke, but the comment inexplicably vexed me. It took me a moment to get to my feet, holding onto the arm of the chair, and I realised I was much drunker than I thought. My head was spinning and I stopped for a moment. It felt good to be out of control, to not be fully accountable for my actions. I felt reckless, standing on quicksand, sensing that *something* was going to happen tonight.

'Come this way. I know a shortcut.'

I set off down the corridor, away from the crowd. Natacha frowned – she knew the house as well as I did – but gamely followed me. I opened one of the heavy wooden doors that led to the library and slipped inside. Light spilled through the windows from the festivities outside, and I briefly registered that much of the room had already been packed up, shelves empty, cardboard boxes piled high. In the darkness, I stumbled against a writing desk and Natacha caught me, helping me upright.

'What are you doing?' she giggled.

My head felt heavy, events unfolding at a speed I couldn't quite gauge. Dimly, I heard the sound of conversation and laughter somewhere in the distance. Alcohol absolving me of responsibility, I acted impulsively, groping for the curve of Natacha's waist and pulling her towards me. Then I kissed her, my lips pressed fiercely on hers, my hands running all over her body, sheer lust overwhelming me. I hadn't experienced desire like this in a long time as I tasted her, smelt her, touched her, giddy with the excitement of someone new.

And then she pulled away. I tried to hold onto her, but I was unsteady on my feet and she was easily able to step backwards out of my grasp.

'No, Maybelle,' she said softly. 'I'm sorry, it's not going to happen. I'm not… I love you very much, as a friend. You're so very dear to me. But not this. I'll see you later, all right? Go and find Joe.'

She walked out of the library, leaving me alone in the blackness.

'Fuck you,' I yelled at the closing door, embarrassed and angry and intoxicated. I kicked the box in front of me, blaming it for what it had just witnessed. It was heavy and full of books and it hurt. My toe would be bruised tomorrow, along with my ego.

I couldn't think straight, didn't know what to do. I didn't want to be here, I realised. I *would* go and find Joe, as Natacha had suggested, and tell her that I was leaving. If she wanted to stay then I'd damn well drive myself.

I pulled open the door. Natacha was nowhere to be seen. Neither were Joe or Alla. I launched myself into the revellers, head down, pushing past people, not caring if I was rude. Everything was fuzzy, images blurred around the edges. Misguidedly, I picked up a champagne coupe and drained it; unsure what to do with the empty glass, I simply opened my hand and let it fall, hearing it shatter on the tiled floor. Around me there were gasps and shrieks as guests moved back, staring at me accusingly as a waiter rushed in to clear the mess. I turned around and kept moving.

Outside, the night air hit me like a restorative, and I took a moment to steady myself, leaning gratefully against a stone pillar, unfocused eyes searching for Joe. Why was I looking for her again...? Leaving, yes, to tell her I wanted to leave. What had she been wearing? Her gown was green, wasn't it? Or perhaps blue. Or had she worn a man's suit? I couldn't recall.

I turned round and caught a glimpse of long, copper hair and smooth, alabaster skin disappearing into the melee. Sarah Beth! How on earth had she found her way here? She must be looking for me. *I'm here*, I tried to shout, but, like in a bad dream, no words escaped my lips, just an inarticulate noise that made the people beside me gape. Where had she gone? I'd lost Sarah Beth. I staggered towards the spot where I'd seen her but somehow misjudged where I was and the next moment I'd tripped over the low concrete barrier, the ground disappearing beneath me to send me falling through the black night, grasping at nothingness, landing with a great splash before everything went quiet as the swimming pool swallowed me up, water rushing into my ears, up my nose, forcing its way between my tightly closed eyelids.

I flailed in the silence, instinctively holding my breath, my beaded dress weighing me down, before I finally surfaced. And as I took in vast, grateful lungfuls of air, I was dimly aware of the crush of people gathered all around the edge of the pool, their expressions variously concerned, pitying, amused, condescending. They were staring, pointing, laughing, as I thrashed like a landed fish, trapped in some kind of hellish nightmare.

And then I saw her. At first I thought I must be imagining it, but as she reached out for me there was no mistaking her face – it was Gloria, my guardian angel, who'd swooped to my aid the very first time I came to Hayvenhurst by finding Joe when I was searching like a lost soul. She'd subsequently rescued me from the unfriendly girls and their belligerent stares at the Sunday pool party, and tonight completed the trilogy.

Gloria held out her hand and I swam towards her, like a dying woman moving towards the light. I grasped her palm, sobbing at my salvation and, with assistance, she pulled me out onto the poolside whereupon towels arrived and the mob dispersed a little. I was shivering, sobbing, and then my stomach heaved and I vomited – all over myself and the flagstones and into the pool. I felt wretched, assaulted by the cruel comments and the exclamations of disgust, sensing the stares and the judgement. It felt as though everyone at the party was gawking at me right now, but as I scanned their hostile faces, I still couldn't see Joe or Alla amongst them.

'I want to go home,' I begged Gloria. 'Please, take me home.'

'Of course I will,' she said kindly. She helped me to my feet, wrapping a fresh towel around my shoulders, and guided me towards her car.

Chapter Twenty-Six

ALLA

New York City, USA, 1916

I t was surreal, Alla thought, as she looked around at the small crowd that had gathered, at the photographers taking her picture and the fans shouting her name. Wonderful, exhilarating – but ultimately surreal.

Of course, the premiere of *War Brides* had to be modest and understated; everything was subdued whilst the war in Europe raged on, the Battle of the Somme finally reaching its bloody conclusion. The United States appeared to be on the brink of entering the fray; there'd been a change of rhetoric from President Wilson in recent weeks, and public opinion was moving away from neutrality and towards the Allies. Alla herself had been personally affected by the conflict: Charles Frohman, her early champion when she first came to America, had lost his life the year before when travelling from New York to Liverpool on the RMS Lusitania. The ship was sunk by a

German U-boat off the coast of Ireland, killing almost 1,200 people and causing outrage in the US.

But despite the muted celebrations, the glamour of the occasion was inescapable, and Alla was determined to enjoy her first film premiere, her first starring role. She was dressed in an exquisite pale gold evening gown, made from silk velvet and overlaid with embroidered lace, decorated with seed pearls and bugle beads. Over the top, to keep out the November chill, she wore a full-length mink fur. And on her arm, the ultimate accessory; her current paramour, Charles Bryant, dashing in white tie with tails and a smart woollen overcoat, blond hair slicked down and his jaw resolutely set.

He turned to her, his arm resting on her elbow as he gently steered her to a better angle for the cameras. 'Everything all right, Allikins?' he murmured under his breath, in that well-to-do British accent.

'Never better, Chumps,' she smiled back, the pet names a shortcut to the easy affection between them.

The pair had met four years ago, performing in a show called *Bella Donna* which had a short run at the Empire Theatre. The attraction between them was instant – the level of intimacy more opaque – and before long there was talk of marriage as Charles moved into Who-Torok, Alla's newly-purchased country house in upstate New York.

'Alla,' came a shout from the small pool of journalists, and she looked up to see her old friend, Lilian Gilbert, who'd first interviewed her following her success in *Hedda Gabler*. The two women had met professionally many times over the past decade, and Lilian was now a section editor on the *New York*

Times. Alla waved and walked over to where Lilian was poised with her notepad.

'Madame Nazimova, what are your thoughts on the women's suffrage movement? Do they have your support?'

'Of course.' Alla nodded earnestly. 'Those women who don't believe in suffrage, they're not awake, that's all. The woman is counting for more and more every day. She has real work to do, and she has found it out, and is not going to give it up.'

'Thank you,' Lilian smiled, pleased with the quote, as Alla drifted back to an amused-looking Charles.

'Who would have thought it?' he teased. 'My little Allikins, the darling of the suffragists.'

Alla rolled her eyes at him as everyone began to move inside, past the enormous bouquets of fresh flowers and the publicity posters, taking their seats for the premiere. Charles was on one side of her, Herbert Brenon, her director, on the other, and they exchanged friendly greetings, delighted to see one another again. He'd been wonderful – helpful, kind, understanding – throughout the making of her first motion picture, recognising that it was an entirely different art form to acting for the stage. One of the major changes was constant direction as she played a scene; due to the soundtrack being added afterwards, Herbert was able to talk Alla through the picture on a moment-by-moment basis, guiding her emotions, heightening her reactions. He believed that acting should be even larger on screen than in the theatre, defining his method as 'stage technique emphasised and enlarged'.

There was a palpable sense of excitement in the auditorium as the lights went down and the first reel was loaded up. Then came the music, the opening titles, and... Alla! Her face in close-up, five metres high, every feature on display, impossible to hide from scrutiny. Watching the film begin, Alla felt her stomach churn. It was excruciating yet fascinating. She tried to view the piece dispassionately, to take in her performance on a purely objective basis, but the elation of seeing herself on the big screen was overwhelming. Beside her, Charles squeezed her hand and she squeezed back, immensely grateful for him in this moment, as his face appeared next to hers on screen and the scene played out, Alla and Charles as husband and wife.

Alla had first appeared in the stage production of *War Brides* almost two years earlier. It had begun life as a short play on the bill of a vaudeville show at the Palace, but unexpectedly became a huge hit, driven in no small part by Alla's stellar performance.

War Brides was a piece of anti-war propaganda, highlighting the consequences of conflict for women – the loss of fathers, husbands, brothers, sons – and it found support amongst feminist organisations. The New York Association of Suffragists called it "the Magna Carta of Woman", and Alla was temporarily transformed into a champion of women's rights as the play embarked on a six-month tour of the US.

Then came the call that little Adelaida Leventon, with her yearning for freedom and her dreams of success, would scarcely have been able to believe: Lewis J. Selznick Enterprises offered $30,000 for Alla to star in a movie of *War Brides*. The move to motion pictures marked the beginning of a new stage in her career, and one which – though she didn't yet know it – would change her life beyond recognition.

War Brides came to its tragic conclusion and the credits

rolled in flickering black and white. As the house lights went up there were cheers and applause, the cast and critics rising to their feet in a standing ovation. Alla, disbelieving, responded with thanks and kisses, as Charles leaned across and whispered in her ear, 'Congratulations, my darling. A star is born.'

It was a glorious summer's day in Westchester County, and Josephine Colbert was sipping a gin fizz, engrossed as Alla held court in the grounds of Who-Torok, her country estate. The two women had been enmeshed in an intense relationship after Josephine had been cast in *A Doll's House* but, before long, Alla's interest had waned and instead they became fast friends.

Seated on the picnic rug to Josephine's right was the striking Mercedes de Acosta, another of Alla's ex-lovers, this time thirteen years her junior. Tall and boyish, with dark hair and pale skin, Mercedes had first seen Alla on stage at Madison Square Garden and engineered an introduction. As with Josephine, Alla and Merecedes had remained friends even after their liaison had ended.

The final woman completing the intimate quartet was the cosmopolitan Eva Le Gallienne, just eighteen years old and an aspiring actress who'd already made her stage debut in London. Like Mercedes, she'd first laid eyes on Alla on stage, and been enraptured by her passionate, mesmerising performance, afterwards requesting a backstage introduction. Josephine had heard rumours that Eva was Alla's current lover but, if that was the case, then the two women were remaining discreet.

As Josephine glanced around, she couldn't help but feel that she was part of a harem. Young women seemed to be drawn to Alla like bees around a honeypot, fascinated by her star status, her exoticism, the sheer sex appeal she exuded both on and off the stage.

Alla noticed her staring and raised a questioning eyebrow.

'The gardens look beautiful,' Josephine commented quickly. 'It's changed so much since you bought the place.'

'Well, that's Charles' department,' Alla said languidly, lighting a cigarette. 'He's the one with all the good ideas.'

And you're the one with all the money, Josephine thought darkly, but kept her mouth shut. If truth be told, she didn't really understand the connection between Alla and Charles. Alla claimed – somewhat disingenuously, Josephine thought – that having him around improved her English, insisting that he was good at managing her business affairs which left her free to focus on her art. Alla and Charles undoubtedly adored one another, but Josephine knew they slept in separate bedrooms, and that Charles didn't object to all the young ladies that were regularly invited to the house as Alla's guests.

In fact, Josephine struggled to work out how Charles benefitted from the arrangement, concluding that it was both professionally – as Alla always chose to cast him in whatever production she was starring in – and, in no small part, financially. Their home in Rye, which had begun life as a small house in six acres of rugged parkland, had rapidly undergone various upgrades, with an extension to the main property and the construction of several neighbouring cottages, all with lavishly decorated interiors. The unkempt grounds had been transformed into manicured gardens, until the estate resembled a sprawling country manor rather than a rustic "little farm" – the English translation of "Who-Torok".

'And Charles is talking about putting in a swimming pool,' Alla continued, smoke curling into the ether. 'Won't that be heavenly? Can you imagine the frolics we'd have? I could invite all of my girlfriends over at the weekend and throw some outrageous parties.'

'Mmm, everyone in the sunshine in their bathing costumes.' Mercedes grinned. 'All that nubile young flesh on display.'

'I'll leave that to you ladies,' Alla smiled. 'I'm neither nubile nor young.'

'Oh Alla!' Eva rebuffed her comment. 'Of course you—'

But she was interrupted as Charles came running out of the house, clearly on a matter of some urgency. He bent down and planted a kiss on the top of Alla's head as she reached up to grasp his hand.

'My darling, I have news.'

Josephine gasped, the tension rising immediately. Everyone feared it would be some terrible announcement related to the war, knowing that Alla was awfully concerned about her brother in Germany who'd been interned as an enemy alien, and terrified that Charles himself would be called up for service.

'What is it?' Alla turned anxiously, but relaxed when she saw Charles' jovial expression.

'I've just got off a call with Maxwell Karger, the head of Metro Pictures East Coast.'

Alla stiffened once again, but this time with anticipation, not apprehension. 'And?'

'Metro would like to offer you a five-year contract.'

Alla exhaled slowly, shaking her head in disbelief. She'd been offered film contracts before, but Charles believed the terms were less than she deserved and had always advised her to turn them down. 'And are the numbers right?' she wondered breathlessly.

Watching the exchange, Josephine didn't think she'd ever seen Charles look quite so hubristic, or sound quite so smug. She couldn't pinpoint what exactly it was about him, as he knelt there in his linen suit and straw boater, but she didn't like him, and she didn't trust him.

'Oh, I'd say so,' he smirked. 'How does $13,000 a week sound?'

Alla looked as though she were about to faint; Mercedes almost dropped her glass in shock.

'But that's...'

'Four thousand dollars per week more than Mary Pickford? Yes, you're quite right. Which will make you, my clever little thing, the highest paid actress in Hollywood.'

Alla's mouth fell open. She tried to remain unaffected, to nonchalantly take in the enormity of what she was being told, but it was impossible not to squeal with excitement, not to kick her heels and almost burst into tears. It was quite something, Josephine realised, to witness someone's dreams coming to fruition. The women all hugged and congratulated Alla, emotions running high, toasting her with what was left of their cocktails.

'They're sending the contract by post,' Charles explained.

'I'll have our lawyers look over it. I also managed to negotiate your right to approval over the script, the director and—' here he looked more self-satisfied than ever, his blue eyes twinkling, '—your choice of leading man. So pack your bags, Allikins. We're moving to California.'

Chapter Twenty-Seven

MAYBELLE

Los Angeles, USA, 1926

'I see… Right… Thank you for letting me know… Yes, I will… Okay… Okay… I understand… Thank you… Goodbye.'

Joe's face was tense and drawn as she put down the telephone receiver. I was at her side instantly, seeing from her expression that something was terribly wrong.

'What is it?'

'Rudy. He's…'

Joe choked back a sob and I gasped, my hand flying to my mouth in shock. A little over a week ago, Rudolph Valentino had collapsed in Manhattan and been taken to the New York Polyclinic Hospital. Diagnosed with appendicitis and ruptured gastric ulcers, he was operated on immediately and, despite developing peritonitis, the doctors were initially optimistic about his progress. Scores of hysterical fans had kept vigil outside the hospital; unbeknown to them, he'd taken a turn for the worse a few days ago, and now…

'Apparently he rallied this morning. He was conscious, lucid, spoke with the doctors about his recovery. And then a few hours later…' Joe tailed off, too upset to say the words out loud, to make them a reality.

I understood her reluctance. It was impossible to comprehend that Rudolph Valentino – the handsome, vibrant, beloved movie star, whose smouldering sexuality on screen seduced an entire generation of women – was no longer with us. At thirty-one years old, he was only five years older than me; the first time I'd been confronted with my own mortality in such a stark manner. His demise was tragic, and cruel, and I said as much to Joe.

'It's unbelievable. It will shock the world.' She was already moving towards the drinks trolley, fixing herself a stiff brandy. 'Apparently mourners are flocking to the hospital, even though the news hasn't officially been released – I guess someone, somewhere, couldn't keep their mouth shut. It'll be in the evening editions of the papers. He's to lie in state for three days, to give fans a chance to say goodbye. Then the funeral will be held in a week's time at the Actor's Chapel on Broadway, before his remains are brought to LA for burial. I just can't… It doesn't make sense…'

'I know,' I agreed, filling in the words that Joe couldn't find. 'And poor Natacha.'

'What?' Joe turned sharply, and I instantly regretted the ill-thought-out comment.

'I only meant—'

'They've been separated for years. By the time the divorce

was finalised they hated each other. Alla told me he wrote her out of his will. I doubt she'll even bother with the funeral.'

My cheeks flushed, my gaze downcast beneath Joe's anger. I still didn't know whether she knew the full extent of what had happened last month at Alla's party. I doubted she did – I trusted that Natacha would have attributed my behaviour to a drunken mistake, and there was no reason to imagine she'd told anyone – but I inevitably felt guilty about my actions that night, and since then my relationship with Joe had become more strained than ever.

'All I was saying,' I pushed on, trying to recover my dignity, 'Is that when you've loved someone, there's a part of you that will always love them, surely, regardless of whatever else happens.'

Joe raised a sceptical eyebrow, and I couldn't resist goading her.

'You of all people must know that.'

Joe looked furious, and I knew I'd gone too far. She downed the remaining brandy in one gulp, slamming the dirty glass down on the side table.

'I'm going to see Alla,' she announced, snatching up her hat and purse. 'I need to check in on her, and she'll be devastated when she hears the news.'

Alla had left Hayvenhurst on the first of August, as per her contract, and moved in with her friend, the French actress Rose Dione. But the stresses and strains of the past few months had taken their toll and she'd been diagnosed with mumps. Joe had been visiting her regularly during her convalescence.

'Give her my best,' I said softly. But the front door slammed, and Joe had already gone. ***

Over the next few days, Rudy's death dominated the news; Joe and I followed the latest reports in the papers and on the radio and were kept up to date by mutual friends. The telephone hardly stopped ringing.

It seemed as though the whole world had collectively lost their minds. Wild rumours were circulating – that fans were committing suicide in droves; that the body that lay in state wasn't Valentino but a decoy, or a wax dummy; that Mussolini had sent a Fascist Blackshirt guard of honour from Italy. It was impossible to know what was fact and what was fiction. Both showgirl Marion Benda and actress Pola Negri claimed to have been in a relationship with him when he died; Pola even declared herself to be his fiancée and fainted over his coffin. The truth was irrelevant, it seemed; the press would report whatever made the best story. And, as Joe had predicted, neither Natacha nor Jean Acker – Rudy's first wife – attended the funeral.

For those of us left behind, it truly felt like the end of an era. The fledgling Hollywood we'd all been a part of, that had made our names and our fortunes, had been superseded by something bigger, hungrier, more demanding, that no longer had any use for us. We were the guests that had outstayed our welcome after the party had moved on; last night's trash awaiting disposal.

Alla, Joe and I attended the funeral ceremony in Beverly Hills at the Church of the Good Shepherd. As Rudy had no burial arrangements in place – he was primed for immortality, not death at thirty-one – he was laid to rest in the crypt belonging to June Mathis at the Hollywood Memorial Park Cemetery. I expected black skies and thunder and lightning, some acknowledgement by the gods of the severity of the occasion, but the day dawned bright and sunny as ever, the perennial Californian utopia.

Joe barely spoke to me that day, and Alla was unusually distant. I put it down to the wretchedness of the occasion – they'd both known Rudy for longer than I had – and to Alla still convalescing after her illness.

The following morning, I woke to find that Joe wasn't in our bed. I pulled on my robe and went through to the living room; she was curled up in a chair, a cup of coffee in her hands, staring blankly ahead.

'Everything okay?' I asked tentatively.

She turned to look at me, the light dimmed in those once radiant tiger eyes. Everything about her seemed so different to the stylish, sophisticated woman I'd met almost seven years ago. She'd been about to turn thirty, at the peak of her self-confidence and sexuality, and I'd been just nineteen. We'd been together during my formative years; for Joe, the same period had seen the transition from youth to middle age.

'Maybelle, we need to talk,' she said gently.

'All right.' I tried to sound casual but my heart was hammering in my chest. Instinctively, I sensed that this wouldn't be good, the culmination of the squabbles and silences and resentments of the past months and years. 'Can I get myself a coffee first?'

'Sure. There's some in the pot. It'll still be fresh.'

I fled to the kitchen, trying to slow my breathing, my mind racing through a million different scenarios but always coming back to the same conclusion. Was this the end? Were Joe and I about to break up? And, if so, how did I feel about it? Would I be devastated or relieved or—

'So,' I began with faux brightness, taking my cup and deliberately choosing the seat across from her. 'What did you want to talk about?'

Joe sighed, hesitating, clearly putting off what she wanted to say, although I didn't doubt that she'd already run through a dozen opening lines and every possible permutation of the conversation in her own head.

'Alla's decided to move to New York for a while. Obviously she's been thinking a lot about her future – she can't live with Rose forever. She wants a change of scene and thinks she'll have more luck finding work there, in theatre or maybe vaudeville.'

'Well… that sounds sensible,' I agreed, not seeing where this exchange was heading.

'She's leaving next week. And… I'm going with her.'

'Right.' I took a long, slow sip of my coffee, then set it down on the table beside me. 'And how long will you be there for?'

Joe's expression was sheepish, the shrug of her shoulders barely perceptible. 'I don't know. Weeks? Months? Years? However long Alla wants to stay…'

I was suddenly overwhelmed by panic, my stomach in freefall, my brain an incoherent jumble of words and emotions. I wanted Joe to spell it out, to stop talking in allusions and riddles. 'What are you saying?'

'I'm saying… it's over between us.'

'You're leaving me? For Alla?' An involuntary noise, somewhere between a scoff and a wail, escaped me.

'No, not exactly. I'm not… We're not *together*. Not in that sense. But she needs me, Maybelle. You don't. You haven't needed me for a long time. I don't even know if you've *loved* me for quite some time now.'

I opened my mouth to protest, then closed it again, knowing the truth of what she said. I noticed how pale she looked in the early morning light, the fine lines at the corners of her eyes and mouth a permanent feature. She looked heartsick and exhausted, and I wondered whether it was Rudy's death or my behaviour that was responsible. I longed to go over and throw my arms around her, but I stayed rigidly in my seat, opting for aggression over conciliation.

'What about *me*?' I burst out, unable to stop myself despite knowing how selfish it sounded. 'You're always so considerate of Alla's needs and feelings, but mine can just be discarded? Seven years together and suddenly I don't matter anymore?'

'What *about* you?' Joe shot back. 'Christ, can you even hear how childish you sound? Now you're free to do whatever you want. Isn't that what you've secretly longed for all these months? Free to do what you want, see who you want, flirt with who you want?'

I said nothing, appalled at how close she was to the truth, how bad I'd been at hiding my true feelings and how poorly I'd treated her.

'Let's face it, things haven't been right between us for a long time, have they?' Joe continued, her précis of the situation devastating but accurate. 'We've both been trying to pretend that everything's okay, but now we don't have to.'

I couldn't fault her logic, but I felt hurt and wrong-footed, aggrieved somehow that Joe had been the one to finally end things and I had no say in the matter. And I was scared on a purely practical level too – since I'd left the farm, Joe had always looked after me. The bungalow was hers, the car was hers, she paid the bills. I'd had the luxury of no responsibilities, spending the money I earned on frivolous trifles like clothes and adornments and cocktails in nightclubs. I barely had any savings.

'You can stay here for as long as you like,' Joe offered, as though she'd read my thoughts.

'No thank you. I don't need your guilty offers.'

'Maybelle,' Joe spoke as though to a difficult child, 'I still love you. I'll always love you. But you and I both know this isn't right. It's not working anymore – we're not making each other happy. But, oh, didn't we have some marvellous times? All the parties and premieres, Palm Springs and Paris! Aren't you glad that you had those experiences, that you're not still stuck on that parochial farm, married off to some hayseed and being forced to pray ten times a day?'

Once again, I knew she was right, but the stubborn part of me refused to acknowledge it, paralysed by fear and uncertainty and outrage. But then Joe opened her arms and my defences crumbled, as I let out a cry and raced across the room to be enveloped by her embrace.

For a long time we were silent, savouring the warmth and the feel and the scent of one another, acknowledging the familiarity and companionship, the lack of passion or desire. Joe kissed the top of my head in a way that seemed almost maternal, and I closed my eyes to commit the sensation of her to memory.

'I remember the first time I saw you,' she murmured softly. 'I thought you were the most adorable creature; you utterly charmed me, in your pure white dress and that tumble of blonde curls. I was such a mess that day, I couldn't imagine you'd ever be interested in me.'

'You were a mess? I thought you were the most sophisticated woman I'd ever met,' I replied honestly. 'I was so intimidated by you, but fascinated too. Did you think I'd actually come to Alla's party?'

Joe shrugged lightly. 'I don't know. I hoped so. And then when I saw you there... in your walking boots, a green ribbon in your hair... I knew I was lost. You looked as though you'd stepped right off the train from Kentucky, but the fact you were there at all told me you had nerves of steel.'

I shook my head. 'I barely recognise that girl now. I only wish I had her confidence. But the truth is, I'm terrified. I've never been alone before. I don't know what to do, how to live...'

'You won't be alone,' Joe assured me. 'You have dozens of friends who adore you. You're young and beautiful. The world is your oyster – it's up to you to find your pearl.'

Tears sprang to my eyes in the wake of her kind words, as I faced the reality and uncertainty of my future. I owed her so much it was impossible to acknowledge it all. Instead, I tentatively raised my head and let my lips find hers. I wondered if she might push me away, but she acquiesced, our embrace tender and affectionate and comfortable as I tasted her for the final time.

Afterwards, we held one another as untold hours ticked by, and later that day she packed her bags and left. It was the last time I ever saw her.

Chapter Twenty-Eight

ALLA

New York City, USA, 1926

Hanging low over the skyscrapers, the heavens turned a uniform grey. Fat drops of rain began to fall and people ran for cover, disappearing into shops and diners, scuttling beneath awnings or clambering into taxis, newspapers held uselessly above their heads.

Alla and Joe merely opened their umbrellas and continued to stroll, not seeming to notice the puddles that pooled around them, heedless of the cars that raced by and showered them with spray. Both were bundled up against the changeable fall weather in raincoats and cloche hats and sensible shoes.

'My God, can you believe we've known one another for almost twenty years?' Alla marvelled, as they ambled through the theatre district, reliving old memories and reacquainting themselves with old haunts. They were staying at the Hotel Buckingham, Alla's preferred address in New York, just along the street from Carnegie Hall. After three days of rest and recovery and relaxation, she'd declared herself ready to face the world again, and the two women had immediately headed for Broadway.

'Time flies,' Joe agreed, taking in the billboards and the store fronts, blurry from the sudden downpour like an Impressionist painting. She was thirty-six years old now, Alla eleven years her senior, their friendship unbroken and unshakeable. 'Everything's so familiar, yet so different. Nothing stays the same, does it?'

'No – however much you might want it to,' Alla smiled ruefully.

The lights from the theatres reflected in the saturated sidewalks. All around them – on illuminated marquees, on hoardings and posters – were the latest productions, the leading actors, the newest and most popular names emblazoned on the very fabric of the city. It made Alla feel old, past her prime. She'd once been the latest Broadway sensation, the apparent overnight success that everyone wanted to see and be seen with. A decade ago, she'd left New York in triumph; now she returned mired in failure, hoping to recapture a little of her former glory.

'We were mere children the last time we lived here,' Alla reflected. 'Both of us running away from our old lives, running towards our dreams.'

'And what about the future?' Joe asked hesitantly. 'What's the plan?' She'd been more than willing to allow Alla the time she needed to gather herself, mentally and physically, but knew that her friend needed to keep busy to avoid falling into a slump.

'Well, my diary is filling up with meetings. I've spoken to

Noel Coward four or five times now. He's such a darling. We'd love to work together but need to find the right project – I'm not sure this new play he's proposed is a good fit for me. And I'm having lunch tomorrow with Jenie Jacobs – you know, the vaudeville agent. She's been making encouraging noises about a tour – they'd pay me $2,500 a week. That's my priority right now,' Alla sighed. 'Gone are the days of producing pictures like *Salomé*, crafted with artistry and passion. Now it's all about the cold, hard cash.'

'It doesn't have to be quite so mercenary. Try and find something diverting, a role you'll enjoy. In a few months, your fortunes might have completely changed. It wouldn't be the first time…'

'I admire your optimism, but even a cat only has nine lives,' Alla noted wryly. 'I may have used up my share of luck. Anyway, in a few weeks I must go to Chicago, then back to LA in the new year for a premiere. There's talk of London later next year… And what about you, my darling, constant, Josephine? Will you come with me? Stay by my side?'

'Of course. For as long as you want me. I'll follow you to the ends of the earth,' Joe teased, only half-joking.

Alla smiled sadly, her gaze far away as though lost in a memory.

They walked on, coming to a halt in Times Square where it was impossible not to pause and take in the enormity of the street, the very vastness of humanity, as cars honked and people scurried by and the buildings soared ever upwards, surrounded on all sides by advertisements and illuminations, an unstoppable flow of manmade creation.

'Do you know, I hated New York when I first moved here,'

Alla recalled. 'I didn't speak the language, and it was so busy and dirty. I didn't see the beauty in the city at all, the way I did with Moscow and St Petersburg.'

'I wasn't so keen on it myself. I was longing to make a fresh start, but when I arrived I was the most unhappy I'd ever been. I discovered that however far you run, you can't leave your problems behind you.'

'I learned that lesson myself. We were two lost souls, and we found one another. And I will forever be grateful for that.'

'A friendship that's outlasted all our relationships.' Joe nodded. Like so many of their observations that day, it was bittersweet.

A nearby couple sheltering beneath an umbrella were eyeing Alla curiously, speaking in low tones between themselves. Joe noticed what was happening and gently took Alla's arm, steering her along the sidewalk away from their stares.

'It's fine.' Alla smiled at Joe's protectiveness. 'It's quite rare to be recognised these days. Perhaps I should start to enjoy it a little more, before I'm just a nameless old lady lost in the crowd.'

'As though you could ever be anonymous,' Joe scoffed. 'The most famous actress in Hollywood.'

'Once upon a time, perhaps,' Alla conceded. 'But no longer.'

They passed through Times Square and on into Midtown, lamenting the disappearance of a once-favoured bagel shop, or recollecting a long-demolished hotel in whose bar they'd danced the night away. Construction seemed to be taking place on every avenue, every street, with plans afoot to build taller, bigger, faster than ever before.

'Men and their phallic obsession,' Alla tutted, rolling her eyes as Joe laughed. 'And what about *your* plans for the future? You need to pursue your vocation too – you must not give up your dreams for mine.'

'Well, I've been thinking of writing a novel...' Joe confessed. 'I've begun drafting ideas in my notebook, toying with characters and plots. It's a very different beast to a script, but one I'd like to attempt.'

'What a brilliant idea! And what will be the subject of this novel?'

'I haven't quite decided yet. It will be about life and about love, in its many different shades. That's all I know so far.'

'It sounds marvellous. In fact, I should introduce you to Bessie Marbury. Lord, she must be seventy years old by now. It would be wonderful to catch up with her – she's a real character, and knows absolutely everyone, from HG Wells to Somerset Maugham to George Bernard Shaw. Her connections are impeccable, so you'd be in excellent company.'

'Thank you,' Joe replied quietly, wondering whether she was right to have confided in Alla about her writing ambitions. Sometimes, it seemed as though her whole career had been built on the scraps of Alla's success. But she knew it came from good intentions, that Alla was generous with her introductions and wanted to help her friends however she could.

'And have you heard from Maybelle?' Alla asked gently.

Joe visibly stiffened at the name, shaking her head. 'No, but I wouldn't expect to. She sent a note when she moved out of the bungalow, but I don't know where she's living now. She didn't leave a forwarding address. It's for the best, I'm sure.'

Alla squeezed her arm reassuringly and the two women walked on. For a few blocks they didn't speak, lost in their own thoughts, until Alla stopped unexpectedly in front of a nondescript office building. 'Here we are!'

Joe frowned, not seeing anything familiar or interesting in the high-rise concrete structure. 'Where?'

'Oh, how quickly we forget,' Alla teased, explaining, 'It's the site of the original Bijou Theatre. They sadly demolished it in 1915. Then a couple of years later, they put up this monstrosity.'

'What a tragedy. What a *waste*.' Joe felt touched that Alla had brought her here, but undoubtedly her feelings were mixed. It was yet another example of how the past had been erased from existence, demolished forever with the swing of a crane. 'This building was once so full of life – think of all the drama and joy and creation that went on in there. The lights and the glamour and the greasepaint. And now it's full of dull men in suits and women clacking away at typewriters.'

'I'm sorry. I wouldn't have brought you here if I'd known it would make you unhappy. I thought it might be nice to remember... to reminisce.'

'No, you're right,' Joe agreed, feeling foolish. And it was true; after the initial shock, the memories came rushing back – the nerves, the exhilaration, the applause. She recalled the sensation of being on stage, how it felt to be thoroughly exposed before an audience, even though her character had barely any lines. She'd adored the rehearsal process, watching Alla at work, a true mistress of her craft and, indeed, learning from the whole cast. She revelled in the camaraderie of the theatre troupe, the close-knit relationships reminding her of the chorus girls at the Blue Saloon when she'd been little more than a babe in arms. Over those few short months, tight bonds were formed, the actors working together, eating together and, in many cases, sleeping together. Of course, once the show was over most went their separate ways; she and Alla might not have lasted as a couple, but they'd discovered a friendship that had lasted a lifetime.

'Look, there's a café over there,' Joe noted, reluctantly pulling back from her reminiscing. 'Let's go sit down awhile – my feet are aching.'

'We'll get a cab back,' Alla promised.

They crossed the road, shaking off their umbrellas as they entered, placing their order and taking a window seat.

'Was I really that bad an actress?' Joe wondered, sipping her hot chocolate as she watched the traffic pass by.

'Of course not. I wouldn't have hired you if you were bad.' Alla sounded indignant.

'Ah, but was that the only reason you hired me?' Joe teased, and Alla had the good grace to blush.

'Remember, darling, there are no small parts, only small actors,' she quoted, a smile playing on her lips. 'And, if you forced me to confess, I think you're a far more talented writer than you were an actor.'

'Thank you for your honesty,' Joe laughed. 'In fact, thank you for everything. It's been one hell of a ride, and I wouldn't have missed it for the world.'

'You're most welcome. There's no one I'd have rather had by my side,' Alla insisted, hastily gulping her drink before Joe noticed the tears that had unexpectedly appeared, threatening to spill down her cheeks.

Outside, the rain had stopped and the sun was valiantly attempting to part the clouds. Amidst the dirt and the grime, a rainbow had appeared, reflected a million times over in the puddles and the raindrops that raced down the windowpane, filling the city with dazzling colour.

As they drank their chocolate and stared out at the city, neither woman could predict what their future would hold; but they felt certain that, whatever might happen, they would face it together.

Epilogue

MAYBELLE

Vermont, USA, 1945

I was sitting at the kitchen table, a freshly brewed cup of coffee in front of me, looking out through the window at the glorious vista beyond. It offered mile after mile of farmland and woodland and meadow, not another building in sight as the view stretched away to the distant mountains, abundant with pines and firs and spruces and red oaks.

It was shaping up to be a beautiful day, the morning sunlight chasing away the last of the dawn haze. Doris Day was crooning on the radio, and I was leafing through the newspaper; the war in Europe had finally ended, with a major conference set to begin in Potsdam in the next few days, and President Truman seemed hopeful that Japan would soon surrender. Not a moment too soon in my opinion – this damned war had dragged on for far too long and claimed a sickening number of innocent lives. I was old enough to remember the Great War – how it had taken so many fine young men from Jonas Springs, and how my brothers had, fortunately, been too young to be drafted – but this time the bloodshed had hit particularly close to home…

Turning the page, I contemplated the crossword then decided to save it for later, moving on to the next section where it took a moment for the image to register: Alla's face was staring back at me. It was a publicity still from when she was much younger, likely taken for the film *Camille* if my memory served correctly. I must admit the portrait startled me, an unexpected intrusion to my largely uneventful routine. It was a long time since I'd seen a picture of Alla, although I'd thought about her often – less frequently as the years passed. I studied the photograph, remembering those haunting, dark eyes, the prominent nose and full lips and wild hair. Even in her youth, she hadn't been beautiful in the conventional sense, but her presence was impossible to ignore.

And then I realised: it was Alla's obituary. A tear fell onto the newspaper, smudging the print, before I'd even properly digested the news.

The article said she'd died at the Good Samaritan Hospital in Los Angeles, from coronary thrombosis, just weeks after her 66th birthday. It seemed ironic, given how much she'd loved and been loved, that a series of heart attacks should be what ended her life.

The piece skimmed over her early years, and I could only presume that little was known about them still. It noted her Russian origins, her move to the United States in 1905, and her theatrical triumphs before finding success in Hollywood during the silent film era.

I was more interested in later events, in what had happened

after Alla had left Los Angeles for New York. I'd followed her career somewhat, but without any real dedication. She'd performed in a number of well-received plays on Broadway – including *The Cherry Orchard* by Chekhov, and Ibsen's *Ghosts* – but never quite recaptured the success of her youth. In the late 1930s she returned to Hollywood, where she underwent something of a revival, cast in supporting roles that captured her greatness in both sound and Technicolor. And she made her home in Villa 24 at the re-christened Garden of Allah Hotel – built on the land where her infamous mansion had stood – where she remained until her death.

There was no reference to her marriage, no acknowledgment of Sergei Golovin, just a brief sentence on her relationship with Charles Bryant. *Salomé* was omitted from her list of achievements, her lovers and companions likewise excluded. Joe didn't merit a mention. Undoubtedly, Alla was portrayed as a trailblazer – but the obituary painted a sanitised version.

Inevitably, the terrible news brought back all kinds of memories for me – of the parties and nightclubs and the wild carousing, the trips to Mexico and France and cross-country for premieres and appearances. Of being by her side during the glory days when she was at the height of her stardom, her wealth vast, her appetite for living insatiable. I thought of how Alla's story was so much bigger and more colourful than the short black and white article suggested. That she'd been a pioneer, who deserved for everyone to know her name and her accomplishments, yet even before her funeral had been held, I sensed her slipping into obscurity.

Alla had lived her life fearlessly, to the fullest, accepting who she was and encouraging others to do the same. Encouraging *me*. Inspiring me to follow my heart and my passions.

My coffee had long since gone cold. I was still sitting motionless, staring into space, when the door clicked open.

'Maybelle? What's happened?'

I spun the newspaper round so it was facing Sarah Beth, letting her see the headline. She didn't say a word, simply sitting down beside me and holding me in her arms, her love and understanding and compassion everything I needed.

Later, when the heat of the sun had cooled and we'd eaten a tasty supper of devilled chicken and vegetable salad, Sarah Beth and I set out on a walk. She'd largely left me alone throughout the day, allowing me to wallow in grief and recollections, to wrestle with the ghosts Alla's death had unearthed. But I knew she would be by my side in an instant if I needed her, her calm, constant presence a salve to my wounds.

'How are you feeling?' she asked gently, as we crossed the field at the back of our house, heading into the countryside beyond.

'I'm not sure. It's strange, obviously. The definitive close of a chapter, I guess.'

I'd told Sarah Beth all about my years in Los Angeles – how I'd left the farm, my relationship with Joe, the people I'd encountered – Natacha Rambova, Rudolph Valentino, Greta Garbo. She was by turns shocked, awed, impressed, disbelieving, and I couldn't blame her for those reactions. But I felt it was important for her to know everything about my past if we were to have a future together.

After Joe moved to New York with Alla, I'd stayed on in LA. It had been my home for seven years, and I truly didn't know where else to go. I left the bungalow a few days after Joe had vacated it; my meagre savings allowed me to rent an apartment in a stylish new building in Santa Monica, where I adored living by the ocean, beginning and ending most days with a long walk on the beach.

I overcame my embarrassment and contacted Natacha; true to her word, she'd opened a clothing store in Manhattan, and she commissioned me to design and manufacture a handful of pieces. A few years later she moved to Europe to marry a Spanish Count and, in a plot twist more unlikely than in any movie, became a respected scholar of Egyptology. We didn't stay in touch.

Swallowing my pride, I made some calls with tentative enquiries about whether any costumier positions might be available for me – I was surprised by the sheer volume of people I'd come to know through Alla and Joe, and how many were keen to stay in touch despite me no longer being part of Alla's retinue – and, little by little, the work began to roll in. I was pleased to discover I'd built a strong reputation in the industry through my collaborations with Natacha, and I undertook the role of Head Costume Designer on a number of high-profile movies, dressing Joan Crawford, Jean Harlow, and Katharine Hepburn, amongst others – though I never did get to design for Garbo. I lived comfortably, counting my blessings that I was largely unaffected when the Great Depression hit.

I discovered that I didn't feel angry or resentful when I thought of Joe and Alla; they'd taken me along on their incredible journey, but now that journey was over. My time with them felt increasingly unreal as the months passed, a distant memory that one looks on with fondness but has no real bearing on day-to-day life. And as for relationships – I simply wasn't interested. I kept myself to myself, filling my days with work, my evenings with books and research for whatever project I was working on. I no longer went to parties – I'd had my fill of them. I rarely drank, even once Prohibition was lifted.

When my momma died in 1936, I returned to Jonas Springs for the funeral. My brothers were married and settled, Frank having taken over the running of the farm whilst Walter had opened his own garage, repairing motor cars and pumping gas. The Depression had undoubtedly hit them hard, but they were surviving, faring better than many of our poor neighbours.

I stayed for a couple of weeks initially; conscious that I was another mouth to feed, I contributed over-generously to the household grocery bills. But as time passed, I realised I didn't want to go 'home'. Los Angeles no longer felt welcoming, but instead like a strange, alien world where everything moved too fast and people's priorities were all wrong. It was only when I came back to Jonas Springs that I realised how exhausted I was, how tiring it had been trying to keep up with people's expectations for so long. I paid my apartment lease until the end of the term and arranged for my belongings to be boxed up and shipped to Kentucky; it turned out there was very little of it I needed in my new life.

A few days after my return to Jonas Springs, I learned that Clarence Montgomery, Sarah Beth's husband, had died three years prior of tuberculosis. She was raising her son, Clarence Jr., by herself, and had lost her second child, a girl named Scarlett Elizabeth – with whom she'd been pregnant at Frank's wedding – in infancy. My childhood friend, it seemed, had not been spared her share of tragedy.

She didn't attend Momma's funeral and, a few days later, unable to restrain myself or my curiosity any longer, I paid her a visit. Her husband had been from a good family, and he'd worked as an attorney; when he passed, his parents did right by Sarah Beth, and in addition, she received a small widow's pension from the government, which allowed her to keep the family home.

But from the first moment I saw her again, my feelings were as strong as ever. She was guarded at first, stoical about her losses, and the years since I'd last seen her had taken their toll. She was no longer the fresh-faced young girl I remembered – but then again, neither was I. Her once lustrous copper hair was streaked with grey, her hips widened from age and childbearing, her freckled face now softly lined and pigmented. We talked extensively, any awkwardness soon passing, but she played her cards close to her chest and I had no sense of what her feelings were, or whether she would act on them if she did acknowledge the chemistry between us.

I had no desire to push her into anything; above all I wanted to be around her, to admire her and spend time with her, even if that was as far as it went. But one evening in the depths of winter, when I stopped by her house and stayed later than I should have done, Clarence Jr asleep in bed and the bitter wind whipping outside, threatening snow flurries, it happened. We were sat in front of the fire, curling into one another for warmth, and then we kissed. It seemed so natural, so unquestionably right, and I knew that Sarah Beth felt the same.

Of course, we had to be discreet; the world had essentially changed very little in the twenty years or so since that summer's night by the creek. Sometimes we went days, even weeks, without enjoying one another's company. And oh! How I lived for those stolen moments! The passionate kisses, the ardent clinches, those snatched afternoons when Clarence Jr. was at school and we gave ourselves over to our desire, feverish bodies sliding perfectly together to reach such dizzy heights of euphoria that I vowed never to be without her again.

To fill the endless hours between our trysts, I needed something to keep myself occupied. Sarah Beth worked in the town library, and suggested I open a small dressmaking business. It took me some time to agree; I had plenty of savings and lived frugally, so an income wasn't a necessity, and I had no interest in making myself available to be judged by every gossip in town. But as the months went by and my restlessness grew, I began offering my services to a select few acquaintances. I kept my rates cheap, as I knew times were hard, and of course my designs were far less outrageous than anything I'd conceived in my Hollywood days. But I knew how to create a unique piece and flatter a figure, how to talk a shy young girl or an elderly matron into a brighter colour or bolder print than they might otherwise have chosen. Unexpectedly, I came to enjoy the work and the sociable aspect, becoming a legitimate part of the community that had once rejected me.

The situation might have continued indefinitely were it not for the war. Clarence Jr. joined up at the beginning of 1942 when he was 21, and was posted to an army base in Colorado. Just as we were daring to hope he might last the whole war without seeing conflict, we received word in late spring of 1944 that he was being sent to Europe. It was only when we began hearing news reports of the battles on the beaches of Normandy that we realised what danger he was in. Clarence Jr. was killed at Omaha within minutes of landing; his body was never recovered, likely swept out to sea.

Sarah Beth, of course, was utterly bereft. That was the best word I could find to describe her emotional state, but it barely came close to the sense of devastation, the veritable quagmire of despair she experienced. She'd lost her parents, her husband, and her two children, which seemed more than one woman should have to endure. After weeks of mourning, where at times I was afraid that she might fade so completely as to disappear herself, she suggested a solution: to leave Jonas Springs and move somewhere new, where no one would know us and we could make a fresh start. She'd seen a photo of the fall colours in Vermont and been inexplicably drawn there. I only wanted to make her happy, and would gladly have followed her to the ends of the earth. We packed our belongings, and I said goodbye to my brothers, whilst Sarah Beth made a heart-wrenching final visit to the graves of her husband and daughter. Then we drove north-east for two days straight. It was the beginning of September and the scenery was beyond divine. We found a charming little cottage in the middle of nowhere, and I paid for it outright.

Life, since then, had been idyllic; just the two of us, ensconced in our own world, making up for the lost years. Yes, we expected there might be some talk about us in the local village, the widow and the spinster who lived together in the secluded backcountry, but we genuinely didn't care. One of the few joys of aging was that our reputations were of little concern to us. Besides, we'd both experienced our fair share of heartache; our priority now was happiness, in whatever form it happened to arrive, and the opinions of others no longer mattered.

I couldn't help but reflect on how different our lives might have been if we'd accepted our fate – and been accepted by others – all those years ago. But I always reached the same conclusion: that it would have been impossible for us to live this life thirty years ago. The war, as it so often did, had changed everything. Millions of women were now working, gainfully employed in factories, on the land, driving ambulances and fire engines and tanks. I was forty-five years old, and it was almost incomprehensible how much had changed in my lifetime. I'd witnessed the birth of Hollywood and the era of silent movies, where alcohol was forbidden and it was the height of rebellion for a woman to wear trousers. I'd been at the epicentre of a world that no longer existed.

Sarah Beth and I were out of breath, panting lightly, as we made it to the top of the hill, scanning the horizon as our racing hearts slowed. We'd planted a sapling up here when we first moved, in tribute to Clarence Jr. Sarah Beth liked to tend to it, to see its progress, to imagine her son living on, healthy and strong and enduring. Sometimes she talked of visiting France, to see those beaches where so many had perished. If she wanted to go, then I would go with her. I would do whatever it took to fulfil her every wish. Always.

We sat down on the grass, watching as the fiery sun dropped low in the sky. I knew that we'd have to head back soon, as the light faded and the darkness stole in, but I could sense that we both wanted to take a few moments, to reflect on the past and on everything that had brought us to this moment right here and now. I reached across and took Sarah Beth's hand, our fingers lacing together. She sighed contentedly and laid her head on my shoulder. Neither of us spoke. Words weren't needed. I knew implicitly that she understood me, accepted me, cared for me unconditionally. If my life had taught me anything, it was that love, in its myriad colours and forms and variations, was, in the end, all that really mattered.

Acknowledgments

First of all my thanks must go to my wonderful agent, Emily Glenister, for falling in love with this book and offering to represent me. It's such a precious thing to be able to make dreams come true, and I'm so very thankful to her for taking me on, with such passion and enthusiasm.

And to my fabulous editor, Jennie Rothwell, who blew me away with her support for *Well Behaved Women*. I'm enormously grateful for her sure but light touch in steering the book to its finished article.

The whole team at One More Chapter for being so welcoming, and for producing such an incredible pitch document that had me longing to join them.

To my family and friends, for providing welcome distraction when needed, and childcare which is always needed. Most especially to Ross, for everything.

Author's Note

I first came across the Garden of Allah Hotel whilst researching a different project, and it immediately captured my imagination.

In the 1930s and 40s, through to its closure in 1959, it was *the* place to be seen, offering decadence, discretion, and a guaranteed good time. You might have found F Scott Fitzgerald scribbling away in his bungalow, Clara Bow diving into the pool in full evening gown, Cole Porter composing at the piano. Tallulah Bankhead, Marlene Dietrich, Frank Sinatra, Ava Gardner, Marilyn Monroe and Humphrey Bogart all visited the notorious venue during Hollywood's Golden Age.

It was the origins of the hotel that really piqued my curiosity. It had been founded by a woman I'd never heard of before – an actress, called Alla Nazimova, who'd lived in villa 24 of the hotel until her death. The property on the site had previously been her home, until she fell upon hard times and was forced to sell to developers who razed her mansion and built the Garden of Allah Hotel in its place.

The more I learned, the more I couldn't believe I'd never heard of Alla Nazimova. She was a huge star of the silent movie era, earning an astonishing $13,000 a week in 1917. She was also an LGBTQ+ icon, unashamedly bisexual, which saw her dubbed "the founding mother of Sapphic Hollywood". Her backstory was equally as fascinating: a horrific upbringing in Crimea, acting training in Moscow, then escaping provincial theatre in Russia to star on Broadway, despite speaking no English when she arrived in the US. She was incredible. I was hooked!

Yet, even before her death, Alla had slipped into obscurity. I wondered why, and how, this had happened. I also felt strongly that she deserved to be known again, that her incredible life and achievements needed to be brought to a wider audience.

I let her story sit with me for some time, unsure of how to approach it, not knowing the best way to tell it. Then I hit on the idea of Maybelle – an outsider in Alla's world, who was fascinated by her lifestyle just as you or I might be.

I was very conscious that I was dealing with a real life which, though a fictionalised account, does bring with it some constraints. Conversations were obviously invented, as were some events, and occasionally historical facts were shifted a little to fit the dual narrative timeline. But my intention was to convey the full magnitude and sheer magnificence of Alla Nazimova's life. I hope that I succeeded.

I'm indebted to Gavin Lambert's comprehensive work, *Nazimova: A Biography*, which served as my bible whilst writing *Well Behaved Women*. It's an excellent place to start if you want to find out more about this extraordinary woman, as is Martin Turnbull's website and social media – both offer a wealth of information about Alla Nazimova and Hollywood's history.